New Yor

Kerre

"An absolute deligh

—Lynsay Sands, *USA Today* bestselling author

"Full of vulnerability and tenderness . . . rich romance."
—*Publishers Weekly*

"Mixed paranormal romance with humor . . . Sparks clearly has a style all her own, one that readers love."
—*USA Today*'s Happily Ever After blog

"Infuse[d] with deliciously sharp wit . . . wickedly fun."
—*Booklist*

"Stellar . . . excellent storytelling."   —*RT Book Reviews*

Also by
Kerrelyn Sparks

HOW TO TAME A BEAST IN SEVEN DAYS

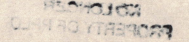

So I Married A Sorcerer

Kerrelyn Sparks

St. Martin's Paperbacks

This is a work of fiction. All of the characters, organizations, and events portrayed in this novel are either products of the author's imagination or are used fictitiously.

SO I MARRIED A SORCERER

Copyright © 2017 by Kerrelyn Sparks.

Excerpt from *Eight Simple Rules for Dating a Dragon* copyright © 2017 by Kerrelyn Sparks.
Excerpt from *How to Tame a Beast in Seven Days* copyright © 2017 by Kerrelyn Sparks.

For information address St. Martin's Press, 175 Fifth Avenue, New York, NY 10010.

ISBN: 978-1-250-10823-4

Our books may be purchased in bulk for promotional, educational, or business use. Please contact your local bookseller or the Macmillan Corporate and Premium Sales Department at 1-800-221-7945, ext. 5442, or by e-mail at MacmillanSpecialMarkets@macmillan.com.

Printed in the United States of America

St. Martin's Paperbacks edition / September 2017

St. Martin's Paperbacks are published by St. Martin's Press, 175 Fifth Avenue, New York, NY 10010.

10 9 8 7 6 5 4 3 2 1

For any of my readers
who have ever felt they were a member of
The Losers Club.
In my book,
you are all winners!

Acknowledgments

❧

Just like my heroes and heroines, who rely on some excellent friends in order to survive and accomplish their goals, I also have a merry band of friends and associates who are looking out for me and making sure each book is worthy of my fabulous readers.

So first, let me thank all the great people at St. Martin's Press. One last thank you and fond farewell goes to Rose Hilliard, and another big thank you to Monique Patterson and Alex Sehulster for graciously taking me on. My thanks also to Marissa, Brittani, Brant, Jordan, the team at Heroes & Heartbreakers, the art department, and everyone else who lent their time and support.

Like Luciana and Brigitta, I have a few women in my life who are like adopted sisters. A big thank you goes to my agent/buddy, Michelle Grajkowski of Three Seas, who has been my number-one cheerleader for over twelve years now. And quite frankly, I don't know how I would survive without my best buds/critique partners—M.J. Selle, Sandy Weider, and Vicky Yelton. Love you all!

I am also blessed to have a wonderfully supportive husband/best friend/tax man/road manager/personal superhero. Love you, Don!! Now if only you would stop posing for the covers of my books! <snort> My thanks, also, to our wonderful kids for putting up with their crazy parents.

And last, but certainly not least, I need to thank all my lovely readers who continue to read my books and share the laughs with me. May your lives be filled with love and magic!

So I Married
A Sorcerer

AERTHLAN

Rupert's
Island

Great Western Ocean

Isle of Mist

Isle of Moon

Convent of the
Two Moons

Danport

Ronsmouth

N

Prologue

In another time on another world called Aerthlan, there are five kingdoms. Four of the kingdoms extend across a vast continent. They have been constantly ravaged by war.

The fifth kingdom consists of two islands in the Great Western Ocean. These are the Isles of Moon and Mist. On the Isle of Moon, people worship the two moons in the night sky. On the Isle of Mist, there is only one inhabitant—the Seer.

Twice a year, the two moons eclipse. Any child born on the night the moons embrace will be gifted with a supernatural power. These children are called the Embraced. The kings on the mainland hunt and kill the young Embraced, and any who seek to protect them. Some of the Embraced infants are sent secretly to the Isle of Moon, where they will be safe.

For as long as anyone can remember, the Seer has predicted more war and destruction. But recently a new king and queen have ascended to power in the mainland kingdom of Eberon. King Leofric and Queen Luciana are both Embraced, so they have declared Eberon a safe haven for those who are born on the night the moons eclipse.

Because of the new king and queen, a new prophecy

has emerged from the Isle of Mist. The Seer has predicted a wave of change that will sweep across Aerthlan and eventually bring peace to a world that has suffered too long.

And so our story continues with Queen Luciana's four adopted sisters, who grew up in secret on the Isle of Moon. They know nothing of their families. Nothing of their past. They only know they are Embraced.

Chapter One

❧

"I cannot play," Brigitta told her sisters as she cast a wary look at the linen bag filled with Telling Stones. Quickly she shifted on the window seat to gaze at the Great Western Ocean. The rolling waves went on for as far as she could see, but her mind was elsewhere. *Calm yerself. The prediction will ne'er happen.*

At dawn they had boarded this ship, accompanied by Mother Ginessa and Sister Fallyn, who were now resting in the cabin next door. This was the smallest vessel in the Eberoni Royal Navy, the captain had explained, sturdy enough to cross the ocean, but small enough to travel up the Ebe River to the palace at Ebton. There, they would see their oldest sister, who was now the queen of Eberon.

According to the captain, Queen Luciana had intended to send more than one ship to safeguard their journey, but at the last minute the other naval ships had been diverted south to fight the Tourinian pirates who were raiding villages along the Eberoni shore. But not to worry, the captain had assured Brigitta and her companions. Since the royal navy was keeping the pirates occupied to the south, their crossing would be perfectly safe.

Indeed, after a few hours, it seemed perfectly boring.

"If we don't play, how will we pass the time?" Gwennore asked from her seat at the round table. "'Twill be close to sunset afore we reach Ebton."

"I wish we could wander about on deck," Maeve grumbled from her chair next to Gwennore. "'Tis a lovely spring day, and we're stuck down here."

Sorcha huffed in annoyance as she paced about the cabin. "Mother Ginessa insisted we remain here. I swear she acts as if she's afraid to let anyone see us."

"Perhaps she fears for our safety because we are Embraced," Gwennore said.

Sorcha shook her head. "We're safe now in Eberon."

But only in Eberon, Brigitta thought as she studied the deep-blue waves. Being Embraced was a death sentence anywhere else on the mainland. The other kings abhorred the fact that each of the Embraced possessed some sort of magical power that the kings, themselves, could never have.

When Brigitta and her adopted sisters were born, the only safe haven had been the Isle of Moon. They'd grown up there in the Convent of the Two Moons, believing they were orphans. But almost a year ago, they'd discovered a shocking truth. Luciana had never been an orphan.

Since then, Brigitta had wondered if she had family somewhere, too. Had they hidden her away or, worse, abandoned her? She feared it was the latter. For in all her nineteen years of life, no one from the mainland had ever bothered to contact her.

You are loved, she reminded herself. She'd grown up in a loving home at the convent. Her sisters loved her, and she loved them. That was enough.

It had to be enough. Didn't it?

Sorcha lowered her voice. "I still believe Mother Ginessa knows things about us that she won't tell."

Brigitta silently agreed. She knew from her special gift that almost everyone was hiding something.

"Let's play the game and let the stones tell us," Maeve said. "I need to do something. This cabin is feeling smaller by the minute."

Brigitta sighed. Sadly enough, this was the largest cabin on board. Captain Shaw had lent them his quarters, which had a large window overlooking the back of the vessel.

The ship creaked as it rolled to the side, and Sorcha grabbed the sideboard to steady herself.

"Have a seat afore ye fall," Gwennore warned her.

"Fine." Sorcha emptied the oranges from a brass bowl on the sideboard, then plunked the bowl onto the table as she took a seat. "Let's play."

Brigitta's sisters gave her a questioning look, but she shook her head and turned to gaze out the window once again. It had been twelve years ago, when she was seven, that Luciana had invented the game where they could each pretend to be the Seer from the Isle of Mist. They'd gathered up forty pebbles from the nearby beach, then painted them with colors and numbers. After the stones were deposited in a bowl and covered with a cloth, each sister would grab a small handful of pebbles and whatever colors or numbers she'd chosen would indicate her future.

"We'll just have to play without her," Sorcha grumbled. A clattering noise filled the cabin as the bag of Telling Stones was emptied into the brass bowl, a noise not quite loud enough to cover Sorcha's hushed voice. "Ye know why she won't play. She's spooked."

Brigitta winced. That was too close to the truth.

She could no longer see the Isle of Moon on the horizon. As the island had faded from sight, a wave of apprehension had washed over her, slowly growing until it had sucked her down into an undertow of fear and dread. For deep in her heart, she believed that leaving the safety of the convent would trigger the set of events that Luciana had predicted.

But how could she have refused this voyage? Luciana would be giving birth soon, and she wanted her sisters with her. She also needed Mother Ginessa, who was an excellent midwife.

"I'm going first," Sorcha declared, and the stones rattled about the bowl as she mixed them up.

"O Great Seer," Maeve said, repeating the line they spoke before each prediction. "Reveal to us the secrets of the Telling Stones."

"What the hell?" Sorcha muttered, and Maeve gasped.

"Ye mustn't let Mother Ginessa hear ye curse like that," Gwennore warned her.

"These stones are ridiculous!" Sorcha slammed them on the table, and out of curiosity Brigitta turned to see what her sister had selected.

Nine, pink, and lavender.

Gwennore tilted her head as she studied the stones. "In nine years ye will meet a tall and handsome—"

"Nine *years*?" Sorcha grimaced. "I would be so old!"

"Twenty-seven." Gwennore's mouth twitched. "Practically ancient."

"Exactly!" Sorcha huffed. "I'll wait nine *months* for my tall and handsome stranger, and not a minute more." She glared at the colored stones. "I hate pink. It looks terrible with my freckles and red hair."

Maeve's eyes sparkled with mischief. "Who said ye would be wearing it? I think yer true love will look very pretty in pink."

"He's not wearing pink," Sorcha growled.

"Aye, a lovely pink gown with a lavender sash," Gwennore added with a grin.

"Nay, Gwennie." Maeve shook her head. "The lavender means he'll have lavender-blue eyes like you."

"Ah." Gwennore tucked a tendril of her white-blond hair behind a pointed ear. "Could be."

"Are ye kidding me?" Sorcha gave them an incredulous look. "How on Aerthlan would I ever meet an elf?"

"Ye met me," Gwennore said. "And apparently, in nine months, ye'll meet a tall and handsome elf in a pink gown." She and Maeve laughed, and Sorcha reluctantly grinned.

Brigitta turned to peer out the window once again. Over the years, the Telling Stones had proven to be an entertaining game. But then, a year ago, something strange had happened. Luciana's prediction for her own future had actually come to pass. She'd met and fallen in love with the tall and handsome stranger she'd foretold in specific detail, using the Telling Stones. And if that hadn't been amazing enough, she'd become the queen of Eberon.

Eager to experience something equally romantic, Brigitta had begged her oldest sister to predict a similar future for her.

A mistake. Brigitta frowned at the churning ocean.

Blue, gold, seven, and eight. Those had been the stones Luciana had selected. Blue and gold, she'd explained, signified the royal colors of the kingdom of Tourin. Seven meant there would be seven suitors to compete for her hand. And eight . . . in eight months, Brigitta would meet a tall and handsome stranger.

The eight months had now passed.

She pressed a hand against her roiling stomach.

When they'd boarded this morning, she'd quickly assessed the captain and his crew. None of them had struck her as particularly tall or handsome. Captain Shaw was portly, bald, and old enough to be her father.

As for the seven suitors vying for her hand, she had initially been thrilled, considering the idea wildly exciting. But when her sisters had likened it to her being a prize in a tourney, she'd had second thoughts.

Why would seven men compete for her? She had nothing special to offer. Even the gift she possessed for being Embraced was hardly special. And did this contest mean she would have no choice but to marry whichever man won her? The more she'd thought about this competition, the more it had made her cringe.

So, five months ago, she'd played the game again, hoping to achieve different results. But to her shock, there had been four stones in her hand.

Blue, gold, seven, and five.

Had some sort of mysterious countdown gone into effect? Reluctant to believe that, she'd attempted the game again a month later. Blue, gold, seven, and *four*. Alarmed, she'd sworn never to play again.

But one month ago, Sorcha had dared her to play, taunting her for being *overly dramatic*. Those words never failed to irk Brigitta, so she'd accepted the dare. With a silent prayer to the moon goddesses, she'd reached into the bowl, swished the pebbles around, and grabbed a handful. And there, in her palm, four stones had stared up at her.

Blue, gold, seven, and one. A fate was shoving itself down her throat whether she liked it or not.

And she did not.

Brigitta had been raised on the Isle of Moon, where women were free to determine their own futures and everyone worshipped the moon goddesses, Luna and Lessa.

It was different on the mainland. Men were in charge there, and everyone worshipped a male god, the Light.

Luciana had been fortunate to find a good man who respected her independent nature. As king and queen, they had declared it safe to worship the moon goddesses in Eberon.

But it was not that way elsewhere. In the other mainland kingdoms, Brigitta would be executed for making the sign of the moons as she prayed. Executed for being Embraced. So why did she keep picking the blue and gold colors of Tourin?

And why would seven suitors compete for *her*? She glanced at her sisters. Sorcha had always seemed the strongest, with a fiery temperament that matched her fiery red hair. Gwennore had always been the smartest. Maeve, the youngest, had always been the sweetest. And Luciana—now married—had been their brave leader. Brigitta had never been quite sure where she fit in.

Gwennore, with her superior intellect, had always been the best at translating books into different languages. Maeve had excelled in penmanship, and Sorcha in artwork. Luciana had been good at everything.

But Brigitta . . . the nuns had despaired with her. When transcribing a book, she could never stay true to the text. A little embellishment here, a tweak there, and eventually she would take a story so off course, it was no longer recognizable. This, of course, upset the nuns, for their male customers on the mainland were paying for an exact copy of an old tale, not the romantic fantasies of an *overly dramatic* young woman.

Whenever the nuns had fussed at her, her sisters had come to her defense, insisting that her story was much better than the original. And each time the nuns tried to use Brigitta's *overly dramatic* mistakes for kindling, her sisters always managed to rescue the pages and give them to her. They'd even begged her to finish her stories about dashing young heroes, so that they could read them.

Brigitta adored them for that. She'd do anything for her sisters, including this voyage to Eberon that she was so afraid would activate the events she'd been dreading.

She shifted her gaze back to the rolling motion of the ocean, and her stomach churned. Did a person's destiny have to be set in stone, in this case the Telling Stones? This was *her* story, so why couldn't it be one of her making? Surely she didn't have to stick to a text that had already been written without her consent. Couldn't she be the author of her own destiny?

"Ye should watch the horizon, not the waves," Maeve said as she sat next to Brigitta on the window seat. "'Tis a sure way to make yerself ill."

"Oh." Brigitta turned to her youngest sister. "I didn't realize . . ." Her stomach twisted with a sharp pain, and she winced.

Gwennore gave her a worried look. "Ye look pale. Would ye like some bread or wine?" She motioned toward the sideboard and the food that had been left for them.

Brigitta shook her head. Perhaps if she sat perfectly still for a few moments, the nausea would pass. "Did ye finish playing the Game of Stones?"

"Aye," Maeve answered. "Didn't ye hear us giggling?"

Brigitta groaned inwardly, not wanting to admit she'd been too engrossed in her own worries to pay her sisters any mind.

"My prediction was the best," Maeve continued. "In four years, I'll meet a tall and handsome stranger with green teeth, purple hair, and three feet."

Brigitta wrinkled her nose. "Ye call that handsome? How can he have three feet? Does he have a third leg?"

Maeve waved a dismissive hand. "We didn't bother to figure that part out. But he is taller than most."

"Aye." Sorcha snorted. "By a foot."

Maeve grinned. "As ye can see, the game is nonsense. Besides, I have no desire to meet any man, no matter how tall or handsome. I plan to live the rest of my life with all of you at the convent."

"Aye," Sorcha agreed. "I'm not leaving my sisters for an elf in a pink gown. 'Tis naught but a silly game."

"Exactly." Gwennore gave Brigitta a pointed look. "So ye shouldn't believe anything the stones say."

They were doing their best to relieve her fear, Brigitta realized, and as her heart warmed, the ache in her stomach eased. "Thank you. What would I do without ye all?"

The ship lurched suddenly to the right, causing Brigitta and Maeve to fall against the padded wall of the window seat. The oranges rolled off the sideboard and plummeted to the wooden floor. Empty goblets fell onto the floor with a series of loud clunks.

Sorcha grabbed on to the table. "What was that?"

Loud shouts and the pounding of feet sounded on the deck overhead.

"Something is amiss," Gwennore said as she gazed up at the ceiling. "They're running about."

Maeve peered out the window. "I believe we made a sudden turn to the south."

"That would put us off course," Gwennore murmured.

The door slammed open, and they jumped in their seats.

Mother Ginessa gave them a stern look, while behind her Sister Fallyn pressed the tips of her fingers against her thumbs, forming two small circles to represent the twin moons.

"May the goddesses protect us," Sister Fallyn whispered.

"Stay here," Mother Ginessa ordered, then shut the door.

"What the hell was that?" Sorcha muttered.

A pounding sound reverberated throughout the entire ship. *Thump . . . thump . . . thump.*

"Drums." Gwennore rose to her feet. "The sailors beat them to set the pace. They must be using the oars."

"Why?" Sorcha asked. "Is something wrong with the sails?"

Gwennore shrugged. "I suppose we need to go faster. Perhaps we're trying to outrun another ship, but there's no way to know unless we go up on deck."

Sorcha slapped the tabletop with her hand. "Why do we have to stay here? I hate being in the dark."

Brigitta clenched her fists, gathering handfuls of her skirt in her hands. The prediction was coming true, she knew it. Her stomach roiled again, and her heart thudded loud in her ears, keeping time with the drums.

Thump. Thump. Thump.

The drums pounded faster.

Beads of sweat dotted her brow, and she rubbed her aching stomach as she rose shakily to her feet. "The fate of the Telling Stones has begun."

"Don't say that." Gwennore shook her head. "Ye cannot be sure."

"I *am* sure!" Brigitta cried. She'd had eight months to consider this fate. Eight months to prepare herself. " 'Tis happening now. And I will not remain hidden in this room, meekly accepting a future I do not want. I'm going on deck to face this me self."

Sorcha jumped to her feet. "That's the spirit!"

"Aye." Maeve ran to the bed where they'd left their cloaks. "And we will go with you!"

They quickly slipped their brown cloaks over their cream-colored woolen gowns.

Gwennore rested a hand on Brigitta's shoulder. "Ye don't look well. Are ye sure ye're up to this?"

Nay. Brigitta drew a deep breath. "I have to be . . ."

"Aye." Gwennore gave her a squeeze. "Ye'll do fine."

"Come on!" Sorcha opened the door, and they filed into the narrow passageway, then climbed the steep wooden stairs to the deck. When they pushed open the door, it bumped into a dog that had been sitting in front of it.

"Julia!" Maeve cried out when she spotted the shaggy black-and-white dog. "It is you, aye?"

With a low growl, the dog backed away.

"How many times do we have to tell you?" Sorcha grumbled. "That dog is a he."

Brigitta narrowed her eyes. The last time she'd seen this dog, he'd been guarding Luciana at the royal palace in Ebton.

"If I remember correctly, his name is Brody." Gwennore squatted and extended a hand to the dog. "Is that right?"

With a soft woof, the dog placed his paw in her hand.

She grinned. "Good boy."

"Nay, she's too pretty to be a boy!" Maeve wrapped her arms around the dog, and he whimpered with a forlorn look.

"Why is Luciana's dog here?" Sorcha asked.

Gwennore straightened. "I suppose she sent him to guard us."

Brigitta studied the dog closely. "I'm more curious about the first time we met him. How did he end up on the Isle of Moon?" A strong breeze whipped some of her hair loose from her braid, and by the time she pushed it away from her eyes, the dog had slipped away.

At least, the cool spring breeze was making her stomach

feel better. With a quick glance up, she noted the sails were full. They were mostly white, but two stripes crossed each sail diagonally in the colors of red and black, the royal colors of Eberon.

"What are ye doing here?" Mother Ginessa grabbed her and quickly pulled the hood of her cloak over her hair. "Ye mustn't let anyone see you."

Brigitta's breath hitched as a tingling sensation crept along her nerves and blurred her vision for a few seconds. The older woman's touch had triggered her special gift, and Brigitta was reminded once again that Mother Ginessa was hiding a great number of secrets.

A loud whistle sounded, and the drums abruptly stopped. The oarsmen were belowdecks, so Brigitta couldn't see them, but she felt the ship slowing down. After another whistle, crewmen began lowering the sails.

"Goddesses, protect us!" Sister Fallyn cried as she made the sign of the moons. "We'll be dead in the water!"

"Nay!" Mother Ginessa scrambled up the stairs to the quarterdeck where Captain Shaw was standing with the first mate and helmsman. "We cannot slow down! We must evade them!"

Them? Brigitta turned toward the bow of the ship, and her heart lurched. With the sails furled, she now had a clearer view. Three large ships were fanned out before them, blocking their passage to Eberon, and each ship had sails bordered with blue and gold.

"The royal colors of Tourin," Sorcha breathed.

Holy goddesses. Here was clear proof that the fate of the Telling Stones had begun. A sharp twinge shot through Brigitta's stomach, but she ignored the pain and stumbled up the stairs onto the quarterdeck.

"We tried evasion," Captain Shaw was explaining to Mother Ginessa. "But with three ships, they can continue to block our every move." He crossed his arms as he studied the ships. "They haven't gone to battle stations, so I believe they mean us no harm. I can only conclude that they want something."

"Please, Captain." Mother Ginessa latched on to his sleeve. "Ye cannot let them catch us!"

The captain gave her a curious look. "Do you know why the Tourinian Royal Navy has stopped us?"

Mother Ginessa quickly released him. "Of course not. But if we cannot move forward, then we must go back." She glanced at Brigitta. "We should go back to the convent. We'll be safe there."

"Not necessarily." Captain Shaw frowned. "If we return to the Isle of Moon, they could simply follow us."

"We have cannons." Sister Fallyn clambered up onto the quarterdeck. "Why don't we shoot at them?"

Captain Shaw gave her an incredulous look. "That would be suicidal. They have us outnumbered and outgunned."

"Holy goddesses!" Sister Fallyn made the sign of the moons. "We're doomed!"

"Calm yerself, Sister!" Mother Ginessa fussed.

"There is no need for you to worry," Captain Shaw assured them. "If they meant to attack, they would have already done so. And I seriously doubt the Tourinian king wants to start a war with Eberon. King Gunther's hands are full right now. Norveshka has been attacking him from the east, and on the west along his coastline, he's constantly plagued with pirates."

"Sir." The first mate handed him a spyglass. "The middle ship is waving a flag."

Captain Shaw peered through the spyglass. "Ah. White flag with a sun. I was expecting that."

"What does it mean?" Brigitta asked.

The captain lowered the spyglass. "Even though the mainland kingdoms are often at war, we have one thing in common—the worship of the sun god. That flag means they come in peace and merely wish to parley."

"Peace?" Sister Fallyn scoffed. "Tourinians don't know the meaning of peace. They are violent, vicious, and cruel! A bunch of murderers and thieves! Nothing good has ever come from Tourin!"

Brigitta gave the nun a surprised look. "I thought ye came from Tourin."

Sister Fallyn huffed. "Well, aye, but I escaped as soon as I could."

Brigitta wondered what had happened to the nun, but the ship suddenly tilted to the left, causing her to stumble toward the side railing. One look at the churning water below made her stomach lurch. Quickly she looked away, but even the sound of the ocean slapping against the sides of the ship nauseated her.

Mother Ginessa grabbed her by the shoulders. "Ye must go below. We cannot let the Tourinians see you."

Brigitta swallowed hard at the bile rising up her throat. "Why me?"

"Aye, why her?" Sorcha demanded as she and the other sisters scurried up the steps to the quarterdeck.

Captain Shaw winced. "Begging your pardon, ladies, but you're not supposed to be on my deck without my permiss—"

"Look!" Gwennore pointed at the middle Tourinian ship. "They've launched a dinghy."

The captain groaned as it became clear that his quarterdeck would remain overcrowded. "They're sending an envoy over to talk to us." He gave Mother Ginessa a pointed look. "I will ask you once again, madam. Do you know why they are so interested in us?"

"Aye!" Sorcha aimed a frustrated look at her. "What do ye know that ye're not telling us?"

Mother Ginessa heaved a resigned sigh. "Very well. I'll tell Brigitta after she comes belowdecks with me. We cannot risk the Tourinians seeing her."

"This is *my* ship," Captain Shaw growled. "I need to know what's going on."

A whistle sounded from the crow's nest above them. "Incoming from the south!" the sailor yelled.

Captain Shaw lifted his spyglass to study a new group of ships coming straight toward them. "Damn," he whispered.

Brigitta swallowed hard. There were nine ships on the horizon, the middle one leading the pack. The sails seemed mostly white with some sort of black markings, but they were too far away for her to see clearly.

"Are they Tourinians?" Mother Ginessa asked.

"Aye. But not the royal navy." The captain turned toward the first mate. "Sound the alarm."

As a horn blasted, Brigitta's stomach twisted with a sharp pain. "What's wrong, Captain? Who are they?"

"Pirates."

Brigitta gasped. A strong wind knocked her back a step and blew the hood off her head.

"We're doomed!" Sister Fallyn cried. "Doomed!"

"The wind is behind them, so they're coming in fast." Captain Shaw gave Mother Ginessa a stern look. "And the dinghy from the Tourinian navy will arrive in a few minutes. You need to talk now. What do we have that is so valuable?" He glanced at Brigitta. "Or is it whom?"

A wave of light-headedness struck Brigitta, and she grabbed on to the back railing to steady herself.

Mother Ginessa's eyes glistened with tears as she turned to Brigitta. "I am so sorry, child. I have tried to protect you all these years, but I fear I have failed."

"Nay, ye've always been good to me," Brigitta whispered. "Please tell me what I need to know."

"Very well." Mother Ginessa pulled Brigitta's hood up to cover her hair. "Ye're the princess of Tourin."

Brigitta's thoughts swirled. "Nay, I—" Her stomach heaved. She leaned over the railing as she lost her battle with nausea.

Chapter Two

Rupert stood in the crow's nest of the lead pirate ship, using his spyglass to study the vessels in the distance. His own design, the spyglass was better than any other he'd seen on Aerthlan. Not only did it give him a strategic advantage, but it provided some entertainment as well. For he could actually see people's reactions when they realized a fleet of pirate ships was headed their way.

Some captains and crew scrambled frantically about like a bunch of ants that had just had their ant bed kicked in. Those were usually the Tourinian naval ships, loaded with so much gold they became overly heavy and cumbersome.

King Gunther was too paranoid to have anyone but the royal navy transport his precious gold from the mountainous region of northern Tourin to his capital of Lourdon in the south. He'd equipped each of his naval ships with a dozen or more cannons, figuring that would keep anyone from attempting to steal his gold.

Rupert had been proving him wrong for seven years.

Now, as he watched the three Tourinian naval ships, he noted how easily they maneuvered around the lone Eberoni vessel. Obviously, they were not burdened with gold. No, they were on a different sort of transport mission—abscond with the Tourinian princess and deliver her to her older brother, Gunther. Already, they had launched a dinghy that was headed for the Eberoni ship.

Fortunately for Rupert, he had a spy who worked with the carrier pigeons at the Tourinian royal court. Whenever Gunther had a message sent, Rupert received a copy of it.

Unfortunately for Rupert, he and his fleet had been farther south, so it had taken longer for the message to reach him. But with a strong wind at their backs, Rupert's fleet had managed to arrive just in time.

Why? he wondered once again. Why was Gunther reclaiming a sister who had been declared dead years ago?

Was she truly alive? Rupert had read the message at least ten times before daring to believe it. She must have spent the last nineteen years in hiding. Just like him. The prospect that she'd also survived was more exciting than he cared to admit. He'd immediately headed north to see if she was, indeed, alive. And to capture her for himself.

For the ransom, he thought, correcting himself. She was nothing more than a tool that would allow him to torment her bastard brother and steal more of his gold.

"Have you spotted her yet?" Stefan yelled from below. "Will you even recognize her?"

Rupert winced inwardly. "I will." *Somehow.*

Stefan's dubious snort was his only answer.

With a groan, Rupert shifted his gaze back to the Eberoni naval vessel. How would he recognize a woman he hadn't seen since she was a babe? Hopefully, she'd be the only female on board. That would make it easy.

Holy crap. There were five—no, six females crowded on the quarterdeck with the Eberoni captain and two of his crew. Even worse, the women were all dressed exactly alike. Cream-colored woolen gowns topped with plain brown cloaks, the sort of clothes worn by nuns. Had the so-called princess been hiding in a convent all these years? If so, she'd brought half the damned convent with her. "Shit."

"What's wrong?" Stefan asked.

"Nothing." Rupert quickly studied the lineup. The women wore their hair plaited in a single braid down their backs. The first one had black hair speckled with gray. Another one had the white-blond hair and pointed ears of an elf. The next one looked like a Norveshki with her wild red hair slipping free from her braid. Three down.

The fourth woman was making the sign of the moons and appeared ready to faint at any moment. She looked Tourinian with her blond hair and pale skin, but she seemed a bit too old to be nineteen. The girl next to her looked a little too young. Black hair.

Dammit, what color hair did the so-called princess have? The last time he'd seen her, she'd been bald. And about two feet tall.

"Well?" Stefan called. "Do you see her?"

"I'm working on it." The sixth woman stood by the railing with her hood pulled up over her head. Suddenly everyone on the quarterdeck turned toward Rupert's fleet, and the captain lifted his spyglass.

"They've spotted us," Rupert warned his old friend.

"Is the princess there or not?" Stefan asked.

Indeed, that was the question. For if she wasn't, Rupert would turn his fleet back south. He focused once more on the woman by the railing. She had to be the one.

He tapped into his power. It swirled inside him, gathering energy as he inhaled deeply. Then he released his breath slowly, aimed straight at the sixth woman. As the air traveled, it became a wind, growing stronger and stronger till it buffeted against her, knocking her back a step and whisking the hood off her head.

Holy Light. It was her. *Brigitta*.

"Well?" Stefan asked.

"She's there." She'd grown up well. Extremely well. "Holy crap."

"Why the foul language?" Stefan chuckled. "Is she still bald?"

Rupert forgot to answer as he studied her through the spyglass. He forgot to think. Or even breathe. A few tendrils had escaped her long blond braid to curl about her heart-shaped face. Pale, creamy skin, high cheekbones, rosy cheeks and lips. Her eyes, they were as beautiful as he remembered.

With a quick intake of breath, he closed his eyes. *Dammit*. He didn't want to remember anything from that horrific day. It was the stuff of nightmares that had haunted him for the past nineteen years. Even so, for the few seconds that he had gazed upon the baby girl, life had seemed . . . perfect.

At the age of three months, she'd lain in a fancy white crib, festooned with ribbons and lace, and when she'd peered up at him, he'd been surprised by her eyes. Not only big, but a brilliant shade of turquoise. Were they the same color now? He opened his eyes and readjusted his spyglass.

"Why aren't you answering?" Stefan called, then lowered his voice. "Is she that ugly?"

She was more beautiful than ever. "She's . . . tolerable."

Brigitta. Rupert had been almost seven years old when he'd first met her, but he'd thought she was the most angelic baby he'd ever seen. A sense of peace had enveloped him, an odd but certain feeling that he'd found the one who would share his destiny. So he'd leaned over the crib to give her a smile.

Unfortunately, she'd reacted by spitting up milk all

over herself. He'd been surprised that a baby's stomach could hold that much milk. It had kept coming and coming.

Back on the ship, the oldest nun said something to Brigitta as she raised the hood back over her blond hair.

"What is she doing?" Stefan asked.

Rupert winced as the princess of Tourin leaned over the bulwark and lost her last meal. "The usual." *Don't feel sorry for her. She's the enemy.*

The other women fussed over her. The oldest one led her to a trunk where she could sit, while two others rushed off and quickly returned with a bowl of water, a towel, and something to drink. *They care about her.* And if she cared equally for them, it might be something he could use against her.

He tucked the spyglass under his belt, then positioned his black mask over his eyes. His forehead and most of his hair were already covered with a dark-red scarf tied in a knot over his right ear. He plopped a large hat on his head and adjusted the black, shoulder-length, horsehair plaits that were glued to its inside brim. With this hat on, everyone assumed he had black hair.

With this hat on, he became the most infamous pirate that the world had ever known. And after nineteen years, he would finally have his revenge.

"Are ye feeling better, child?" Mother Ginessa asked.

"A little." Brigitta passed the goblet of wine back to Gwennore, then rubbed her still-aching stomach. "How can I be a . . . a princess?" She certainly didn't feel like one.

Mother Ginessa sat beside her. "Yer father was King Garold. He sent ye to the convent when ye were barely four months old."

"Why?" Brigitta asked.

"I suppose he meant to keep ye safe." Mother Ginessa glanced away with a guilty look.

She's still hiding something. Brigitta's mind raced as she tried to recall everything she'd learned about Tourin from her studies at the convent. Civil war had plagued the kingdom for centuries. A long line of dukes from the south had rebelled against the northern kings from the House of Trepurin. Nineteen years ago, Duke Garold from the House of Grian had finally defeated the northern king and taken over the country.

I was a baby then, Brigitta thought. Had the Tourinian Royal Navy come here because of her? Did her father want her back? But no, King Garold had died five years ago in a battle against the Norveshki.

A pang of grief struck her, not just because her father was dead, but because she had no memories of him to mourn. He'd never sent for her. Were her fears correct and he'd rejected her? What about the rest of her family? "Is my mother still alive?"

Mother Ginessa shook her head. "I'm sorry, child."

Brigitta's shoulders slumped. She would never know either of her parents.

"Then the current king, Gunther, is her older brother?" Captain Shaw asked.

Mother Ginessa grimaced. "Half brother. He was born from King Garold's first mistress. I think he's about twelve years older than Brigitta."

The captain glanced over the portside railing, then ordered his first mate to oversee the arrival of their guests. "They're tying the dinghy off now. If King Gunther has sent for his sister, we can hardly refuse—"

"But we must!" Mother Ginessa jumped to her feet. "Do ye not know how Gunther became king? He killed the legitimate heir, Brigitta's younger brother."

Brigitta gasped. She'd had a younger brother? And

her older brother had killed him? Her stomach twisted again.

Captain Shaw frowned. "Surely he wouldn't send for her just to harm her."

Mother Ginessa shook her head. "We dare not take that risk. 'Tis not safe—"

"I don't want to go." Brigitta eased shakily to her feet. "Can I not refuse?"

"Aye!" Sorcha moved to stand beside her. "She belongs with us!"

"The Tourinian officer is asking permission to come aboard," the first mate called from the main deck.

"I'll deal with this," Captain Shaw said quietly, then shouted as he proceeded to the main deck. "Permission granted!"

Brigitta's heart pounded. The fate of the Telling Stones was unfurling around her. Would she be taken to Tourin against her will? How could she even face Gunther, knowing that he'd killed her younger brother? And what if she never saw her sisters again?

"Goddesses, help us!" Sister Fallyn made the sign of the moons.

Brigitta pressed a hand to her racing heart. It felt like she'd suddenly been flung into one of her *overly dramatic* stories. If so, wouldn't this be the perfect time for the dashing young hero to make his appearance? After all, the blue-and-gold part of Luciana's prophecy was coming true, so shouldn't the part about a tall and handsome stranger also come true?

She turned toward the newcomer who was climbing a rope ladder to the main deck. A striking blue hat with gold trim came into view, but then Captain Shaw stepped in front of the newcomer and blocked her view.

"Welcome aboard. I'm Captain Shaw."

"Thank you. I'm Lieutenant Helgar," the Tourinian

officer responded in the Eberoni language. He stepped onto the deck and removed his hat.

Good goddesses! Brigitta gasped in unison with her sisters, then quickly squelched the expression of horror that must have flitted across her face. The lieutenant's face was scarred with burns. He had a patch over one eye, and half of his mouth was twisted in a permanent sneer. Instead of an upstanding naval officer, he looked more like a notorious pirate.

She glanced over her shoulder at the pirate fleet that was rapidly approaching. Holy goddesses, they could look even worse.

"Your Highness," the lieutenant said, and it took her a moment to realize he was talking to her. She turned back to him as he bowed. "I bring greetings from your esteemed brother, King Gunther."

Captain Shaw motioned to the three ships. "You've gone to quite a bit of trouble just to extend greetings. May I know the purpose of your visit?"

"Of course." The lieutenant's smile looked strained, as if it pained him to move the muscles of his damaged face. "The king regrets being separated from his dear sister all these years. He invites her to join him at the royal court in Lourdon."

Brigitta winced. This lieutenant intended to take her against her will. She should have known dashing young heroes only existed in the stories she made up. There would be no one coming to her rescue. This was real life, and she would have to protect herself.

She squared her shoulders and attempted to look regal. "How kind of my brother to offer such a lovely invitation. But I fear I must respectfully decline."

The lieutenant's smile faded as his expression grew harsh. "Perhaps Your Highness doesn't understand. No one refuses King Gunther."

Captain Shaw cleared his throat. "My good man, this young woman didn't even know she had a brother until a few minutes ago. She has only now learned her true identity. Since I have orders from King Leofric to deliver her to the royal court in Ebton, I propose we let her continue the journey while she adjusts to her new—"

"No," Lieutenant Helgar interrupted. "She's coming with us."

As the tension mounted, Brigitta fought a growing sense of panic. When the dog, Brody, stalked toward the lieutenant and growled, Captain Shaw lifted a hand to calm him.

She should at least be as brave as the dog, Brigitta thought. She steeled her nerves and descended the steps to the main deck. "My sister, Queen Luciana, is expecting me to arrive this evening. I will gladly visit my brother at a later time. Surely he would not want the king and queen of Eberon upset with him."

The lieutenant gritted his teeth. "King Gunther will not allow foreign rulers to hold his sister hostage."

Was this situation going to endanger Luciana? Brigitta hesitated, but when Brody positioned himself in front of her, she felt encouraged. "Queen Luciana is a sister who is dear to my heart. I would be her guest."

"She is not of your blood. Your only family is King Gunther, and you must do as he commands." The lieutenant raised a hand, and a thundering noise emanated from the three Tourinian naval ships as cannons were wheeled into open gunports.

Brigitta gasped.

Captain Shaw stiffened. "I suggest you reconsider, Lieutenant. Your actions are tantamount to declaring war on Eberon."

"There will be no need for war if you return our princess," Lieutenant Helgar growled. "Need I remind you,

Captain, that you are outmanned and outgunned? If you wish to keep your other guests alive, you will do as I say."

A chill ran down Brigitta's back. She couldn't allow any harm to come to her sisters. Or the captain and his crew. She would have to go with this awful lieutenant.

Good goddesses, but the fate of the Telling Stones had seized her in a firm grip. Was there no escape?

"Heavenly goddesses," Sister Fallyn cried. "We must pray for a miracle!"

Suddenly the sky grew dark as large gray clouds covered up the sun.

As a shadow fell over the ship, the crew huddled together, whispering. Her heart thudding, Brigitta glanced up at the sky. The clouds raced by them on either side of their vessel, yet directly overhead a dark cloud hovered, eerily still. A strong wind whistled past their ship, headed straight for the Tourinian navy.

The ships floundered as the gale-force wind struck them hard, tossing them about. Shouts and screams echoed across the water as the Tourinian sailors fought to control the cannons that reeled back and forth. Several broke free from their chains and crashed through the sides of the ships to plummet into the sea.

"Dammit, no!" The lieutenant watched from the port-side railing.

The powerful wind continued to slam into the damaged Tourinian ships, eventually turning them until the wind filled their sails. With a great whooshing noise, the wind swept all three ships north.

"*No!*" the lieutenant shouted.

"Sir!" His two crewmen who had remained in the dinghy scrambled up the rope ladder to join him on deck.

"What's happening?" his first crewman cried in the Tourinian language.

"Holy Light, save us!" the second crewman yelled.

Brigitta ran to the opposite side of the ship to peer over the railing. The water surrounding them was strangely smooth, while in the distance huge waves and screeching winds were carrying the Tourinian navy far away.

As the ships faded from view, Lieutenant Helgar continued to pound his fists on the railing and bellow with rage.

Sister Fallyn fell to her knees. "The goddesses have answered my prayers!"

"Don't be a fool!" Lieutenant Helgar hissed at her. "Your silly female gods could never—"

"Don't ye dare insult our beliefs!" Mother Ginessa yelled.

Captain Shaw gave the lieutenant a stern look. "You will treat my guests with respect, sir. You and your men are now my guests, too."

The lieutenant stiffened. "You're taking us prisoner?"

Captain Shaw snorted. "Our countries are not at war. You will be treated well. But for now, we have another concern." He motioned toward the fleet of pirate ships. "They will be surrounding us soon."

Brigitta followed Captain Shaw back onto the quarterdeck. The pirate ships were steadily approaching. Somehow, the wind behind them was much milder than the one that had pushed the Tourinian navy away. "Why is the wind behaving so strangely?"

"Why, indeed?" The captain narrowed his eyes as he studied the pirate flagship in the lead. "I've heard rumors about him over the years, but I always assumed it was nonsense."

"It is true," the lieutenant grumbled as he joined them on the quarterdeck. "He's a bloody monster who can control the wind."

"What?" Brigitta blinked. How could anyone control the wind? As the nine ships closed in, she could see the black crossbones on their sails. A shiver ran down her spine. Had they escaped one dilemma to only land in a worse one?

"Who is this pirate?" Mother Ginessa asked.

Lieutenant Helgar's mouth twisted. "Rupert."

Brigitta and her companions gasped. Even on the Isle of Moon, they had heard of the notorious pirate Rupert.

"He's Embraced, so he has the evil powers of a sorcerer," Lieutenant Helgar spat out. "He should have been murdered as a child."

Brigitta exchanged a wary look with her sisters.

"So he can actually harness the wind," Captain Shaw murmured. "I never would have believed it if I hadn't seen it with my own eyes."

"Let the monster try to board this ship," Lieutenant Helgar growled. "I'll rip him to shreds."

Captain Shaw looked askance at the Tourinian. "This is my ship, Lieutenant. I'll make the deci—"

"He did this to me!" Lieutenant Helgar lifted his hands, curling them into fists.

"He set yer face on fire?" Sorcha asked.

The lieutenant turned, aiming a fist at her, but when Brody growled at him, he lowered his hand and took a deep breath. "It was five years ago. The bloody sorcerer had only four ships then, and we went after him with a fleet of twelve. Sneaked up on him in the fog, but when he noticed us, he blew the fog away. Just as we were preparing to fire our cannons, the bastard turned our ships on each other. Our entire fleet, blasted with our own guns! The ship I was on burst into flames. I survived . . ." He heaved a sigh. "Like this."

Brigitta winced. The lieutenant's story was definitely tragic, but she had a hard time feeling very sympathetic when he'd almost hit her sister. She glanced back at the pirate ships. They were spreading out as if they planned to surround the Eberoni ship. What on Aerthlan did they want?

An arrow whizzed over their heads and struck the mainsail mast with a *thunk*.

"There's a message attached." Captain Shaw motioned to one of his crewmen to retrieve the message.

"How did they manage to shoot an arrow so far?" Gwennore asked.

"Rupert must have done it," Lieutenant Helgar grumbled. "He put a strong wind behind it."

The crewman dashed onto the quarterdeck to hand the message to Captain Shaw.

He unfolded the paper. "It says, '*You will deliver Princess Brigitta to our flagship or suffer the consequences.*'"

Brigitta's heart lurched in her chest.

Mother Ginessa grabbed her arm. "How do they know she's the princess? I never told anyone."

"The Wind Sorcerer must have discovered it by using his evil powers," the lieutenant muttered.

"Rupert?" Brigitta asked. "Why would he want me?"

"No doubt he means to force King Gunther into paying a ransom," Lieutenant Helgar replied as he glared at the lead pirate ship. "The bloody monster."

"We cannot let her go." Mother Ginessa held on to Brigitta. "She couldn't possibly be safe there!"

Captain Shaw gave the pirate flagship a wary look. "If they seek a ransom, they would have to keep her safe."

Mother Ginessa gasped. "Ye mean to hand her over?"

"I don't believe we have any choice." With a grimace, Captain Shaw crumbled the message in his fist. "They have nine ships. We cannot evade them or outrun them, especially with this Rupert fellow controlling the wind."

With a sinking heart, Brigitta watched as the nine ships formed a circle around them. "What are the consequences if I don't go?"

A horn blasted from the pirate flagship, then crewmen on each pirate ship lined up with arrows aimed at the Eberoni vessel. One by one, the arrows were quickly lit.

"Damn," the lieutenant muttered.

Brigitta spun about. *Good goddesses!* They were completely surrounded by flaming arrows. One word from the horrid Rupert, and the arrows would set their ship on fire. Her sisters would either burn to death or drown.

Tears stung her eyes. "I have to go."

"Nay!" Maeve grabbed her.

"I have to go *now*!" Brigitta pulled away from Maeve and Mother Ginessa and ran down the steps to the main deck. In a panic, she turned toward the captain, who had followed her. "How? How do I leave?"

"The dinghy is still tied off to port." Captain Shaw motioned for two crewmen to come forward. "My men will row you to the flagship."

"Thank you, Captain."

He gave her a sympathetic look. "No, thank you. Your bravery is saving everyone on board this vessel. But please be assured that Rupert will not dare harm you, not when you can earn him a hefty ransom. As soon as we reach Ebton, I will inform King Leofric so we can mount a rescue."

Brigitta nodded. "Thank you."

While the two crewmen climbed down to the dinghy, Brigitta's sisters rushed forward to hug her.

"Fear not, child." Mother Ginessa touched her cheek. "I will come with you."

Brigitta shook her head. "Nay, ye mustn't. Luciana needs ye more than I. Ye're the best midwife around."

Mother Ginessa frowned. "I dare not send ye to those ruffians without a chaperone."

"I'll go with herself," Sorcha declared.

"And I," Gwennore added.

"Nay!" Brigitta cried. Here she was trying to keep her sisters safe, and they wanted to endanger themselves?

Mother Ginessa scoffed at the two girls. "Absolutely not! How can ye chaperone yer sister when ye're a year younger than she is?"

"Oh, heavenly goddesses," Sister Fallyn wailed. "What will become of our poor Brigitta?"

Mother Ginessa turned toward the other nun with a speculative look. "You."

"Aye." Sister Fallyn nodded as she made the sign of the moons. "I will pray for another miracle."

"Nay," Mother Ginessa replied. "Ye'll go with Brigitta."

"*What?*" Sister Fallyn squeaked.

Mother Ginessa grabbed the nun by the shoulders. "Ye must keep Brigitta safe. I'm counting on you."

"Holy goddesses!" Sister Fallyn turned pale.

Brigitta winced. How could she ask anyone to share this ordeal? "Perhaps we shouldn't—"

"Nay, she will go with you." Mother Ginessa gave the nun a stern look. "Ye can do this, Sister. Ye must be strong for Brigitta's sake."

Sister Fallyn nodded, her eyes filling with tears. "Aye, I will not disappoint you." She hurried to Brigitta's side and latched on to her arm. "Fear not, child. I will not let any harm come to yerself."

Brigitta smiled through her own tears, for she could tell the nun was as terrified as she was. "Don't worry," she told her sisters, who all had tears streaming down their cheeks. "I'll see ye again. I promise."

The captain helped her over the side, and slowly Brigitta made her way down the rope ladder to the dinghy. The two crewmen helped her settle on a wooden bench. As she waited for Sister Fallyn, she glanced at the pirate ships. One by one, the flaming arrows were being extinguished.

Ye made the right choice, she assured herself. Her

sisters would be safe. Surely the pirates would not harm her. She was a princess, after all.

But no matter how much she reassured herself, her heart still pounded with fear. And with a small but steadily growing spark of anger. For even though she'd chosen to leave her sisters, what choice had she really had? The pirate Rupert had orchestrated these events so she would be forced to submit to this fate. How dare he!

And what had happened to the fate of the Telling Stones? Was it still going to come to pass? Would she still go to Tourin and meet the tall and handsome stranger?

A sudden movement caught her eye and she blinked, not wanting to believe what she'd seen. But the splash in the water was undeniable. The dog, Brody, had jumped overboard!

Sister Fallyn settled on the bench beside her and whispered a prayer to the goddesses, Luna and Lessa.

"Wait," Brigitta told the crewmen as they untied the ropes and pushed off. Desperately, she scanned the surface of the water, but she couldn't see Brody anywhere. The sea was calm, eerily still like a sheet of glass, and she wondered if the pirate Rupert was causing it.

"What is it, my lady?" a crewman asked as they slowly floated away from the Eberoni ship.

"Never mind." She continued to search the water as the two crewmen rowed toward the pirate flagship. Where was Brody? Hadn't she seen him jump into the sea? It had happened so fast, perhaps she had imagined it.

She glanced at the Eberoni ship and her sisters. They were waving and giving her encouraging smiles, but she could see the pain in their faces and sense the fear in their hearts. Goddesses help her, she was feeling it, too.

Would she ever see them again? What would happen to her and Sister Fallyn? As a tear rolled down her cheek, she angrily brushed it away.

How dare the horrid pirate Rupert separate her from her sisters and force a fate on her she didn't want! Just so he could increase his coffers of gold? The man was worse than a sorcerer. He was a criminal, driven by greed.

He would regret kidnapping her, she'd make sure of that. For he would soon discover that she was not a willing captive.

Chapter Three

So two women were coming. They hadn't dared send the princess alone. From his position high in the crow's nest, Rupert watched the two women through his spyglass. The older blonde was making the sign of the moons while she prayed. She was probably a nun.

The younger one was scanning the water as if she was searching for something. Had she taken the vows of a nun, too? If she had, she wouldn't be allowed to keep them for long. Most probably, Gunther was planning to marry her off in order to gain a powerful ally. Whatever Gunther's reason was for suddenly wanting his sister back, one thing was clear: The bastard would use her to his advantage.

You could protect her. Rupert pushed aside that thought. He wasn't absconding with the girl to help her. His purpose, the sole purpose for everything he did, was revenge.

Using the power of wind, he eased his ship closer to the Eberoni vessel, so the dinghy would not have far to travel. As the rowboat came along the starboard side, his crewmen tossed over two long ropes so the rowers could tie the dinghy off at bow and stern.

While his crewmen lowered a rope ladder, Stefan

leaned over the railing and greeted the women in the Eberoni language. "Welcome aboard the *Golden Star*. I am Captain Landers."

A lie, but then most pirates avoided using their real names. Rupert included. He tucked his spyglass under his belt and waited for Brigitta to come into view.

And waited.

The longer he waited, the more tense he became. For one emotion after another was bombarding his senses. Nervousness? No, stronger than that. *Dread*. Part of him dreaded seeing her again. After all, the first time they'd met had proven to be the worst day of his life, a day that had condemned him to nineteen years of grief, heartache, rage, and an endless supply of nightmares.

At the same time, he was also eager, eager for the revenge that was now one step closer. His failure to kill Garold still rubbed at him. A Norveshki dragon had beaten him to the task. He'd also failed to kill Garold's legitimate heir, for the bastard, Gunther, had conveniently done away with his younger half brother. But Gunther was still left, and Rupert was determined to kill him. The House of Grian would be utterly and completely destroyed for all time.

The fact that Brigitta was also a member of the House of Grian was . . . unfortunate. It made another part of him, a tiny part, feel guilty. For he fully realized he was using her as a pawn. Just like Gunther would do. *Dammit*. How could he sink as low as that bastard?

Frustration buzzed around him like an annoying insect, but he swatted it away. He'd come too far, suffered too much to back off now.

As he chased away the guilt and frustration, another emotion bubbled up to fill the vacuum. *Curiosity*. What would she be like? If she'd been raised in a convent, would she be nothing like the wretched men in her family? What if she was totally innocent, as beautiful on the inside as she was on the outside?

His heart thumped, quickening its pace and pissing him off. What the hell did it matter if she was beautiful? She was the enemy, spawn of the rat Garold who had stolen the throne of Tourin through deception and murder. She would be his prisoner, dammit, and her brother would have to pay handsomely if he wanted her back.

Where the hell was she? Were the women refusing to board? *Shit.* By now the Tourinian naval ships might be trying to tack their way back.

Rupert slipped on his leather gloves, vaulted over the railing of the crow's nest, then slid down a rope to the main deck. As he approached the starboard railing, he asked Stefan in Tourinian, "What's taking so long?"

With a sigh, Stefan turned toward him. "Apparently it's difficult to climb a ladder in a long skirt. Not to mention the poor woman is trembling with fright."

Brigitta was afraid? Guilt pricked at Rupert once again as he glanced over the bulwark.

It was the older woman who was trembling as she ascended the ladder. Brigitta was standing on the rowboat, clinging to the rope ladder with one hand while she used the other to keep her companion's skirt from getting caught underfoot.

The older woman slowly climbed, pausing on each narrow wooden slat as if she needed a moment to rally her courage. She wasn't that old, Rupert realized. Perhaps four or five years older than himself. But she was definitely frightened. The princess smiled at her as she murmured encouraging words.

She's brave, Rupert thought. *And caring.* No doubt the older woman had come along to watch over the younger one, but it was Brigitta who was doing the comforting.

A barking sound broke Brigitta's concentration, and she whipped her head toward the sea.

A seal? Rupert was surprised to see a large black seal swimming next to the dinghy. Seals normally stayed much closer to shore where it was easier to catch fish.

Brigitta's shoulders slumped as if she was disappointed; then she turned back to help her companion. By now the older woman was halfway up, and soon she would be out of the princess's reach.

"Let's get on with this." Rupert motioned to two of his most muscular crewmen. "Pull the ladder up."

"Hang on, madam," Stefan yelled over the bulwark.

The older woman yelped as the two men hauled her up the side of the ship.

"We have you," Stefan said while the two muscular crewmen hefted her over the railing.

The woman took one look at the bare-chested, tattooed seamen who had manhandled her and shrieked, pulling away from them with enough force that she barreled into Stefan and nearly knocked him over.

Stefan regained his balance as he steadied her. "Don't worry, madam. You're—" His speech halted when she gazed up at his face.

For a moment they froze, then the woman apparently realized she was clinging to his coat.

"Oh! I beg yer pardon." She released him and jumped back, her cheeks blushing.

Stefan continued to stare at her in a daze.

Rupert snorted. But his amusement quickly soured into a pang of regret. For it was his fault that Stefan had taken on a life of deception and thievery. At the age of thirty-eight, Stefan should have been long married with half a dozen children by now.

"Your name, madam?" Rupert asked softly in Eberoni. The woman spun around and gasped, her eyes widening at the sight of a masked man. "Goddesses protect—" She stopped herself with a gulp and clenched her hands to keep from making the sign of the moons.

"You may worship as you please while on board, madam," Rupert told her. "As seamen, we are indebted to the moons and stars for navigation."

"Oh, thank you." She eyed him warily. "And ye are—?"

"Rupert."

With a look of horror, she stumbled back. Stefan caught her, and she jerked away from him. "I'm quite fine, thank you." She wrapped her cloak tightly around herself as her gaze flitted nervously about the deck. "I am Sister Fallyn from the Convent of the Two Moons."

Stefan winced. "Dammit to hell."

The nun shot a disapproving look his way. "I would appreciate it if ye refrain from using such foul language in front of my charge—oh, Brigitta!" She ran to the railing and looked over. "Are ye all right?"

The ladder had fallen back down the side of the ship.

Rupert peered over the bulwark. The princess had taken hold of the ladder to begin her ascent, but she was looking back at her companions on the Eberoni ship. After one last wave, she turned back to the ladder and glanced up.

Rupert stepped back out of view. *Holy crap.* There had been tears on her cheeks. *Don't feel sorry for her.* Her family was guilty of heinous crimes. But what if she was as innocent as she looked?

Dammit. Rupert scrubbed a gloved hand over the two-day-old whiskers along his jaw. Why should he feel guilty? He was doing her a favor by keeping her away from her evil brother.

"Be careful!" Sister Fallyn yelled to Brigitta.

Rupert glanced over the bulwark once again. The princess was holding a wooden rung with one hand while using the other hand to lift her skirt out of the way. Slowly but steadily, she worked her way up. Too slowly.

He opened his mouth to give the order to have her hauled up, but hesitated. The rope tied to the stern of the dinghy was right next to the ladder, so he could easily help her himself. *She's the enemy. Stay the hell away from her.*

But the image of her tear-streaked face needled him. Hadn't he made a pledge to that innocent baby girl in her lacy white crib? "Shit."

Sister Fallyn eased away with an appalled look.

Rupert swung over the railing and slid silently down the rope. He stopped with the toes of his boots resting on a large knot. Next to him, Brigitta was focused on her skirt and apparently oblivious to his arrival.

"Need any help?" he asked in Eberoni.

"I'm quite fine, thank—" She gasped as she finally noticed him. "Ack!" She jerked away so fast, her feet slipped off the rung, leaving her dangling from her hands.

"Careful." He looped an arm around her and pulled her close.

Another gasp. Her head lolled back, then her eyes glazed over and flickered shut.

What the hell? Had she fainted at the mere sight of him? She was still breathing, for he could feel the gentle pressure of her breasts moving against him. A lavender scent wafted toward him, tempting him to bury his nose in the beautiful curve of her neck. As he searched her face, he noted a few golden freckles amid the rosy pink of her cheeks. She looked so young, yet the body pressed against him was definitely mature. Well curved. Soft.

Don't react, he warned himself. *Remember who she is. The enemy.*

"Brigitta," he whispered, and her dark eyelashes

fluttered before opening to reveal her large turquoise eyes. *Damn.*

"What . . . ? Release me!" She frantically pulled away and scrambled to place her feet back on a wooden slat.

"Allow me." He lifted her skirt a few inches. The enemy had nice ankles.

"Stop that!" She swatted at his arm.

"I'm only trying to help."

She scoffed. "If ye truly wanted to help, ye would tell that horrid Rupert that he has no right to kidnap me or threaten the lives of my sisters."

"*Horrid* Rupert?"

"Aye. And he shouldn't have sent you here to startle me with that ridiculous mask ye're wearing."

"Ridiculous?"

"Aye, for it makes no sense for ye to wear it. It hardly conceals the fact that ye're a pirate. It rather confirms it, I would think."

His mouth twitched. Brigitta was more feisty than he had expected. "Shall I carry you on board?"

She blinked in surprise. "Don't be silly."

That was a first. He'd been called a bastard, thief, sorcerer, and monster, but never silly. He slowly smiled.

Her eyes widened, then she ducked her head to focus on her skirt as she went up another step on the ladder. "'Tis silly to think ye can carry someone and climb at the same time. Ye have only two arms like everyone else."

"Ah. That is true." He lifted himself up a bit higher on the rope to keep her at eye level. As his arms took on all his weight, his shirtsleeves pulled tight against his biceps.

Her gaze shifted to his arms, then back to the ladder. With her cheeks blushing, she carefully maneuvered up another step. "Ye would definitely need to keep yer hands free."

"True. A man should always be free with his hands around a beautiful woman."

She scoffed. "That is not at all what I meant and ye know it." Her cheeks bloomed a brighter pink. "Now please, leave me be. I can manage perfectly well without you."

"Aye, no doubt you can. But at this rate, the sun will have set by the time you reach the top."

She shot him an annoyed look. "Are ye in a hurry to set sail? Why? Do ye have a number of villages to plunder afore nightfall?"

He gritted his teeth. *Very well, let her think the worst of me.* If she hated him, he wouldn't feel so damned guilty about using her. "There's always another village for me to pillage."

"A poetic pirate," she muttered, then grabbed on to the next rung. "And have ye no remorse for the suffering caused by yer criminal behavior? No regret for forcing me to come here or threatening the lives of people I care about?"

His grip on the rope tightened. He had enough regret in his life to fill the ocean. "I would need a conscience for that, and it was ripped from me many years ago."

She blinked, then her gaze grew soft as she looked him over like he was some sort of lost puppy. "I'm sorry."

Holy crap. He wanted her anger, not her pity. If she abhorred the sight of him, she would avoid him while on board, and he wouldn't be constantly riddled with guilt. Or reminded that she was beautiful. More than beautiful. Brave and feisty. Intelligent. Compassionate. Everything he'd ever wanted—he crushed that thought with a mental fist. "This is taking too long. I'll carry you up."

"Nay." She adjusted her skirt and ascended another rung. "We've already established that it isn't possible."

"Oh, but it is." He leaned toward her. "All you have to do is climb onto my back and put your arms around my neck." When her eyes widened, those beautiful eyes, he lowered his voice to a whisper. "Then you wrap your legs around me and squeeze me tight."

"Enough! Leave me be." She quickly stumbled up another step, her cheeks flushed. With anger, no doubt. For he'd proven himself to be a complete ass.

Mission accomplished. His heart twisted with regret as he slowly hauled himself up the rope.

Rip.

"Oh, no," she groaned.

He glanced down. In her haste she'd managed to rip a section of her skirt away from the waistline of her gown. "Do you need—"

"Go away!" she yelled at him.

"As you wish." He hefted himself over the railing and ignored the disapproving glare of the nun. Even Stefan was glowering at him. "What?"

"We'll talk later," Stefan muttered.

With a snort, Rupert motioned toward the ladder. "Haul her up." Then he strode across the deck and climbed up to the crow's nest.

Distance. That was what he needed. So he couldn't smell the lavender scent of her skin and clothes. Or be tempted to touch her golden hair or pretty face. Or hear the lovely lilt of her island accent.

Dammit. He glared at her as his crewmen pulled her over the railing. Even if he kept her at a distance, there was no way to keep her out of his head.

As soon as Brigitta's feet landed on deck, Sister Fallyn snatched her away from the crewmen who had hauled her aboard. Only the slightest of tingles brushed against Brigitta's special gift as one of the Embraced. Apparently, the two sailors and Sister Fallyn harbored only a few secrets. Unlike the masked man.

Brigitta cast a nervous glance around the deck. Crewmen bustled about here and there, and a man in a fancy hat was giving orders, but *he* was nowhere in sight. All these years she'd thought Mother Ginessa was hiding a great deal, but the older nun's secrets were minuscule compared with the masked man. One touch from him and Brigitta's special gift had erupted like the fiery blast from a cannon. After the initial shock, the massive weight of his hidden burden had dragged her under, causing her to black out for a few seconds.

Don't let him touch you again. She'd tried her best to shoo him away, for she hadn't wanted to risk another touch. *Wrap yer legs around him and squeeze him tight? Ha!* That much contact might render her unconscious for a week.

Or it might be exciting. She banished that thought. Only a scoundrel would talk the way he did. And only a ruffian would wear a mask. Indeed, it was a great relief she couldn't spot him anywhere. Even though she was incredibly curious about his secrets. What was he hiding that was so huge? And how on Aerthlan did he survive with such a heavy burden?

"Brigitta!" Sister Fallyn shook her. "Are ye all right?"

"Aye."

"Oh, thank the goddesses. Ye seemed to be in a daze for a moment." Sister Fallyn lowered her voice to a whisper. "I completely understand. Ye poor child. It must have terrified you to be hauled over the railing by those burly, half-naked seamen."

"What burly, half-nak—" Brigitta stopped when Sister Fallyn placed a finger over her mouth.

"A young innocent like you shouldn't even repeat such words." Sister Fallyn shuddered. "Goddesses help us, ye can see their muscles. *And tattoos.*"

Brigitta glanced around the deck once more. Goodness, there were a number of muscular men without their shirts. And some rather interesting designs inked on their arms and chests. Why had she not realized that before? *Because ye were looking only for the masked man.*

With a small gasp, she pressed a hand to her chest. Why did she keep thinking about that scoundrel?

"Shocking, I know." Sister Fallyn grabbed her by the shoulders and turned her away. "Don't look at them. It might give you lurid thoughts. Thank the goddesses I am immune to such things." She waved a hand to fan her face. "Why, I hardly even notice it."

"Are ye all right?" Brigitta asked. "Ye seem a bit flushed."

"'Tis a trifle warm, that's all." Sister Fallyn turned her attention to the tear in the waistline of Brigitta's gown. "Don't worry about this. We can sew it back. We'll just need a needle and some thread." She turned toward the man with the fancy hat, and her cheeks blushed a brighter pink. "Captain—?"

"Landers." The man removed his hat as he made a bow. "Your Highness, welcome aboard the *Golden Star*."

Brigitta frowned at him. "It was an invitation we dared not refuse. If anything happens to my—" She glanced at the Eberoni ship.

"Your travel companions will not be harmed," Captain Landers assured her. "And neither will you. You will both be safe here."

"Safe?" Sister Fallyn gave him an incredulous look. "We're surrounded by burly, half-naked men!"

With a hint of a smile, the captain plopped his hat back on his head. "I'll make sure they're fully dressed from now on."

"Please do. Also, we will require needle and thread," Sister Fallyn said, and while the nun and captain continued to talk, Brigitta turned to the railing and waved at her sisters in the distance.

They waved back.

"I miss you already," Brigitta whispered.

A barking sound drew her attention to the sea. The seal was still there. It lifted a flipper and slapped the surface of the water as if trying to tell her something.

Below her, the dinghy had untied the mooring ropes and pushed off from the pirate ship. The rowers set a steady pace back to the Eberoni naval ship. The rest of the pirate fleet moved slowly away, leaving an open space to the east, so the Eberoni ship would be able to sail away. And leave her and Sister Fallyn behind.

She gripped the railing hard as her heart sank. What would happen to her now? The Telling Stones had always shown blue and gold, the colors of Tourin. So why was she on a pirate ship? And where was the tall and handsome stranger she was supposed to meet?

A tingling sensation crept down her spine, as if someone was staring at her. She glanced over her shoulder, but the crewmen were all busy hoisting sails and tying off ropes.

A sudden wind swept past her. She turned with it just in time to see the dinghy take off. The rowers yelped in alarm as their boat skipped like a stone across the water's surface all the way back to the Eberoni ship.

Brigitta blinked. It had happened so fast. It must have been caused by the Wind Sorcerer, Rupert. She glanced over her shoulder again, but none of the crewmen seemed to be paying any attention to the dinghy.

By the time she looked back at the Eberoni vessel, the rowers had already tied off the dinghy and were scrambling up the ropes like frightened mice.

The second the rowers landed on deck, another wind, an even stronger one, shoved Brigitta up against the rail.

It shot past her and blasted into the Eberoni ship, filling its sails and pushing it away.

"Nay," Brigitta breathed. That horrid Rupert was whisking her sisters away. She waved frantically at them, and they scurried to the back of the vessel to wave at her.

Tears burned her eyes as their ship raced away and became a smaller and smaller speck on the horizon.

"Goddesses protect us," Sister Fallyn whispered as she made the sign of the moons.

Brigitta wrapped an arm around the nun and gave her a tremulous smile. "Thank you for coming with me self."

Sister Fallyn blinked away tears. "I will try my best to protect you."

"I know ye will." Brigitta gave her a squeeze.

"Aye, well." Sister Fallyn sniffed. "We must be strong enough to confront the future without fear."

"Aye, Sister." Brigitta nodded.

"And we must always remember our training. Shoulders back. Chin up. No matter what, we will remain calm and dignified. Serene in the face of danger."

"Ladies?"

"Ack!" Sister Fallyn jumped when Captain Landers approached them.

He smiled. "I'd like to introduce Jeffrey." He motioned to a boy who looked about ten years old. "He'll be taking care of you."

"My ladies." The boy sketched an awkward bow, then gave them a lopsided grin.

Brigitta exchanged a look with Sister Fallyn. What on Aerthlan was a young boy doing on a pirate ship?

Sister Fallyn aimed a disapproving glare at the captain. "Why isn't this boy at home with his family? Don't tell me ye stole him!"

"I ain't stolen," the boy muttered.

Captain Landers's eyes narrowed as he returned the nun's glare. "We don't steal people. Only gold."

"Oh!" Sister Fallyn scoffed. "How magnanimous of you."

The captain stepped toward her. "We know what we are, Mistress Fallyn. We don't pretend otherwise."

Her chin went up. "It's *Sister* Fallyn."

He arched a brow, then turned to Jeffrey. "Escort them to the guest rooms, please."

"Aye, Captain!" Jeffrey saluted.

"Ladies." Captain Landers bowed, then strode toward the rear of the ship and climbed the steps to the quarterdeck.

"Infuriating man," Sister Fallyn muttered. The ship suddenly lurched, causing her and Brigitta to stumble. They grabbed on to each other to retain their balance.

Jeffrey grinned at them. "Don't worry. You'll soon have your sea legs."

"The ship is turning around." Brigitta looked over the railing. The other pirate ships in the fleet had fanned out in formation behind them. Was the horrid Rupert moving all the ships with his wind power? "Where are we going?"

"South, probably." Jeffrey shrugged. "We go wherever Rupert wants us to go. Come on!" He scampered toward the door that led below the quarterdeck.

As Brigitta followed the boy to the back of the ship, she scanned the quarterdeck, searching for someone who looked like he might be controlling the wind. But only the captain and a helmsman were there.

The tingling sensation inched up her spine once more, and she glanced back. Why did it feel like someone was staring at her? And where had the masked man gone? Why did he wear a mask when none of the other pirates did?

She touched Sister Fallyn's arm. "Did ye see the masked man earlier?"

The nun shuddered. "He's a frightening one, he is. Ye should keep yer distance from him."

"Do ye know where he is?"

"Far away, thank the goddesses." Sister Fallyn pointed up.

Brigitta glanced up and her heart stuttered in her chest. She couldn't see him well, for the sun was too bright overhead, but she could make out his tall silhouette against a blue sky that was now devoid of clouds.

He was standing in the crow's nest, facing her. Watching her, she could feel it. He bowed slightly, and her heart leaped into a fast rhythm. Who was he?

Unlike the other bare-chested crewmen, he was wearing a white shirt. She had noticed earlier that the top few buttons were undone, and his neck and chest had seemed tanned . . . and strong. And when he'd held his own weight, his sleeves had pulled tight against the muscles in his arms.

She turned away, not wanting to admit she'd studied him that carefully. But how could she not be intrigued? Her special gift compelled her to uncover secrets, and he was hiding so many. He was even hiding his face.

She shook her head. There had been something off. Something wrong, but she'd been too flustered to figure it out.

His eyes had been a golden color. Amber, and they had twinkled with a smoldering fire. Because of his mask, only the bottom portion of his face had been visible, but it had looked quite attractive. His jawline had been strong and sharply defined, his mouth wide and expressive. When he'd smiled, she'd forgotten to breathe for a moment.

Why would such a handsome man need a mask?

She stiffened with a gasp. *Tall and handsome?* "Oh, no."

"What's wrong?" Sister Fallyn asked her.

"It can't be." Brigitta shook her head again. "Who is the masked man?"

Before the nun could answer, a deep voice whispered, "Ni Rupert."

Brigitta spun around, but no one was behind her. "What was that?"

Jeffrey chuckled. "You have to watch what you say on deck, my lady. Rupert can bring your words to him on the wind and then send his back to you."

A chill prickled Brigitta's arms as she lifted her gaze once more to the crow's nest. The masked man had introduced himself on a breeze. *Ni Rupert.*

"I am Rupert" in the language of Tourin.

Good goddesses, no. He was a pirate and a Wind Sorcerer. He couldn't possibly be her tall and handsome stranger. Even if he was tall. And most likely, very handsome.

Her chest tightened. The Telling Stones were mocking her. For there was no way that her destiny could be linked to the infamous pirate Rupert.

Chapter Four

As Brigitta entered the small cabin, she noted that although it was smaller than the captain's room aboard the Eberoni naval ship, it was just as well furnished. A narrow bed was built into an alcove along one wall. Blue velvet curtains flanked each side of the bed and could be drawn shut for privacy. A sideboard rested along the opposite wall, topped with a tray containing a pewter pitcher and two goblets. At the end of the room, sunlight sparkled through a mullioned window. Beneath it, the window seat looked comfy with a blue velvet cushion. In the middle of the room, a round table sat with four wooden chairs.

She smiled at Jeffrey, who hovered in the doorway, watching her and Sister Fallyn with an expectant look. "'Tis lovely. Thank you."

He grinned. "I cleaned it myself. And I put fresh sheets on the bed, too."

"You did a wonderful job." Brigitta kept smiling, although she wondered if the boy was overworked.

Sister Fallyn circled the room, inspecting everything carefully. "Is there a lock on the door?"

Jeffrey's grin faded. "No." He scratched his head, inadvertently pulling a few strands loose from his short ponytail. "No one's going to bother you, miss. They know the captain would tan their hide if they did."

"And who will watch over the captain?" Sister Fallyn muttered.

Jeffrey looked baffled. "Well, the captain's expecting to watch over you. His cabin's down the hall."

Sister Fallyn stopped with a jerk. "Goddesses protect us," she whispered.

"I'm sure we'll be fine." Brigitta gave the boy a pat on the shoulder. No tingles activated her special gift. He was exactly as he seemed—a sweet, innocent boy.

He stepped back into the hallway. "I'll show you the other cabin now. It's just next door."

Sister Fallyn gasped. "Absolutely not!"

The boy blinked. "But there are two of you. And we have two guest—"

"We will remain together." Sister Fallyn pulled Brigitta back from the door. "That decision is final."

Jeffrey gave her an exasperated look. "But that bed ain't big enough for two."

"We will manage," Sister Fallyn insisted. "I will not leave the princess unattended."

Jeffrey scratched his head again.

"Ye poor child." Sister Fallyn frowned at him. "Do ye have lice?"

His eyes widened with horror. "No! I ain't got no bugs. I took a bath this morning. The captain made me."

Sister Fallyn stepped closer to look him over. "Ye can be honest with me, child. Are they abusing yerself here?"

"No!" The boy took a step back. "Jeepers. I-I'll come back with some food." He ran down the passageway and raced up the stairs to the main deck.

Brigitta winced. "I think ye frightened him."

"This whole situation is frightening!" Sister Fallyn

pulled the door firmly shut. "Why is that poor boy living with pirates? And how will we be safe if we can't lock this door?"

"We were told that no harm would come to us."

"And ye believe a bunch of notorious pirates?" Sister Fallyn huffed. "This is not one of those *overly dramatic* stories ye write where the heroes are young and dashing. The men here are criminals!" She grabbed one of the chairs and wedged it beneath the door latch. "There. That should keep them from coming in."

Brigitta groaned inwardly. She didn't think she was the one being *overly dramatic*. "The only one coming in will be a sweet young boy. I think the captain assigned him to us so we would feel safe."

"Didn't ye hear? The captain's room is right down the hall!" Sister Fallyn paced about the room. "No doubt the rascal is hatching some sort of nefarious plan."

Brigitta picked up the pitcher and filled the two goblets with wine. "He didn't strike me as a rascal." As far as she was concerned, that honor went completely to Rupert. Telling her to wrap her legs around him and squeeze him tight. Ha! Then eavesdropping on her conversation and blowing his voice into her ear. "Scoundrel," she muttered.

"Exactly." Sister Fallyn grabbed one of the goblets and took a gulp. "I'm sure the scoundrel is fully aware of how handsome he is."

"Rupert?"

Sister Fallyn looked shocked. "Nay, the captain. Good goddesses, who would know what that horrid Rupert looks like, what with that hideous mask he's wearing."

Brigitta winced inwardly. Why did she feel so certain that he was handsome? Maybe she *was* being overly dramatic. After all, how could a sorcerer be her tall and handsome stranger? The very notion was ludicrous, and she was letting the Telling Stones make a fool out of her.

This is reality, she told herself. She was surrounded by pirates, not dashing young heroes. If she needed to be rescued, she would have to do it herself.

Sister Fallyn set down her goblet with a heavy *thunk*. "We must be vigilant and remain alert at all times."

"Aye." Brigitta nodded in agreement. Forget the Telling Stones. She would be the author of her own destiny.

"We'll take turns sleeping and standing guard." Sister Fallyn paced about the room. "And no matter what, we must not let them separate us. That would be tantamount to disaster."

Brigitta blinked. "Disaster?"

"Aye." Sister Fallyn stopped to give her a sympathetic look. "Ye poor innocent. Do ye not know what pirates do?"

"They . . . plunder."

"And?"

Brigitta considered. *There's always another village for me to pillage.* "They pillage. And make bad poetry." She took a sip of wine.

"They ravish women."

Brigitta sputtered. "What?" She wiped her mouth.

"I know." Sister Fallyn nodded her head knowingly. "'Tis shocking. But it is the way of pirates. No doubt, they plan to ravish us."

Brigitta inhaled sharply as she glanced at the chair wedged beneath the door latch. Was that what Rupert had meant about being free with his hands? "Are ye sure?"

"Aye." Sister Fallyn resumed her pacing. "Ye saw all those burly, half-naked men. They mean to ravish us for sure. First, they'll seduce us with honeyed words. Then they'll lure us in for a passionate kiss."

"But surely the captain wouldn't let—"

"Oh, he would be the worst!" Sister Fallyn pressed a hand against her chest. "A man like him would never be satisfied with just a kiss."

Brigitta eyed the nun's flushed face. "Are ye all right?"

"I'll be fine." She rummaged through the drawers of the sideboard, but they only contained a few linen napkins. "We need a weapon. And we mustn't let anyone through that door!"

A knock sounded, and Sister Fallyn spun toward the door. Brigitta's heart lurched.

"Ladies?" Jeffrey called. "I've brought your food."

Brigitta exhaled with relief. "'Tis only the boy."

"But he may not be alone," Sister Fallyn whispered.

As the door swung back into the passageway, the chair fell over.

"Jeepers." Jeffrey looked askance at the fallen chair as he stepped around it. "I brought you some food."

"That's very sweet of you." Brigitta rushed forward to relieve him of the tray. "Why, this looks wonderful!" She set it on the table. There was a plate filled with cold sliced beef and cheese, a bowl of fruit, a small loaf of bread, a crock of butter, and some utensils.

"Aha!" Sister Fallyn grabbed the knife. "This is exactly what we need. Ye can spread the word, child, that if any man comes in here, I will gullet him!"

Jeffrey's eyes widened. "With a butter knife?"

"Sister," Brigitta whispered, shaking her head.

"Oh." Sister Fallyn grabbed a fork and checked the sharpness of the tines. "This might work better."

Jeffrey stepped back, watching Sister Fallyn with a wary look. "Why do you want to attack someone?"

"To keep from being ravished, of course."

The boy scratched at his brown hair. "What's that?"

"Never mind about that for now." Brigitta motioned to the rip in her gown. "Do ye think ye could find me some needle and thread?"

"A needle!" Sister Fallyn nodded with a gleam in her eyes. "That would make a good weapon."

Jeffrey frowned at the nun and whispered, "Is she all right?"

"She'll be fine." Brigitta tried to change the subject once again as she led the boy toward the door. "Ye speak the Eberoni language very well."

"Of course. I'm from Eberon," Jeffrey explained. "I grew up in a fishing village called Danport. Rupert buys food for his fleet there."

"*Buys?*" Sister Fallyn scoffed. "Don't ye mean he steals whatever—"

"No!" The boy looked offended. "Rupert always pays for his supplies. And he pays with gold. The villagers call him a hero."

Brigitta blinked, taken by surprise. *A hero?* "But he's clearly a thief. The gold he's paying with was stolen."

"But he only steals from the king because Gunther's a stinking bastard!" Jeffrey slapped a hand over his mouth. "I ain't supposed to say that. You won't tell the captain on me, will you?"

"Nay." Brigitta shook her head. "Of course not."

Sister Fallyn snorted. "I blame the captain for teaching yerself such foul language."

"But it's Rupert who says it." Jeffrey gave Brigitta a sheepish look. "I hope I didn't offend you. I heard the stinking—King Gunther is your brother."

"I'm not offended," she assured the boy and patted him on the shoulder. "I really don't know the man." And if it was true that he'd killed her younger brother, then he deserved something worse than a bad epitaph. But she had to wonder what sort of grudge Rupert could have against the Tourinian king.

"I'll go ask the captain about the needle and thread,"

Jeffrey said, then scampered down the passageway and up the stairs.

Brigitta shut the door and gave Sister Fallyn a speculative look. "Ye grew up in Tourin. What can ye tell me about my family?"

The nun grew pale, then suddenly moved to the sideboard to refill the goblets. "Ye should come and eat. Ye need to keep yer strength up."

Brigitta frowned as she dragged the fallen chair back to the table. Why was Sister Fallyn dodging her question? "Do ye not like to talk about Tourin?"

The nun plunked the two goblets on the table. "Nothing good has ever come from that place."

"We did." Brigitta sat at the table.

The nun smiled as she took a seat. "Aye. That's true. Perhaps I should say no good man has ever come from there." Her smiled faded. "Except one."

"Who was that?"

Sister Fallyn didn't answer, only frowned as she ran a fingertip around the edge of her goblet.

A strong surge of curiosity swept through Brigitta. She ignored it the best she could while she nibbled on a piece of cheese. It had always been this way for her. She could sense hidden or lost things, and once she did, she felt driven to uncover them.

The odd gift had been considered a blessing at the convent when one of the nuns misplaced an item and needed it back. Brigitta had always been able to find lost things.

But she'd discovered several years ago that her gift was not appreciated when a nun was hiding something in her mind. People didn't like having their secrets revealed. Unfortunately, knowing that didn't do much to curb Brigitta's curiosity once it was aroused. She still felt driven to uncover secrets.

And of all the people she had ever touched, no one harbored more secrets than Rupert.

She took a sip of wine and pushed the infamous pirate from her thoughts. It was much safer to turn her insatiable curiosity toward Sister Fallyn. "Ye've been at the convent ever since I can remember."

The nun gave her a wry look. "Then yer memory is poor. Ye were seven when I arrived."

"So ye've been there twelve years."

"Aye." Sister Fallyn's eyes grew misty as a mournful expression stole over her face. "I was seventeen when I came. Poor and brokenhearted. I thought my life was over."

"Why? Can ye tell me what happened?"

Sister Fallyn reached for the small loaf of bread and tore it in half. "Did ye know my father was a baker?"

"Nay." Brigitta passed her the knife and crock of butter. "No wonder ye bake so well. Everyone at home loves yer bread."

The nun grimaced as she examined the loaf. "This is at least two days old."

"I suppose it's hard for pirates to get fresh bread."

Sister Fallyn sighed. "My father wanted me to marry another baker. They planned to consolidate their businesses and have the biggest bakery in Lourdon."

Brigitta wrinkled her nose. "That doesn't sound very romantic."

"The baker was much older than me self. I didn't want to marry him. Especially when I . . ."

"What?"

Sister Fallyn blushed. "I was in love with Kennet, the butcher's son down the street."

"Yes!" Brigitta grinned. "Now, that's romantic."

The nun gave her a dubious look. "This is not one of

yer *overly dramatic* stories where falling in love is all rosy and magical. My father threatened to kill Kennet."

Brigitta winced. "So ye married the old baker?"

"Nay." Sister Fallyn's eyes glistened with tears. "I was young and reckless. Kennet and I ran away."

"Ye eloped?"

"Aye, we went to a port on the coast and married there."

Brigitta clasped her hands together. "How exciting!"

Sister Fallyn shook her head. "We had only a week together before the ruffians my father had hired found us. Poor Kennet. He tried to fight them off, but there were five of them."

"Oh, no." Brigitta's heart sank.

"He told me to run while he fended them off. We were supposed to take a boat to the Isle of Moon in the morning, so I waited for himself at the dock." A tear rolled down Sister Fallyn's cheek. "He never made it."

"I'm so sorry." Brigitta reached over to squeeze the nun's hand.

"I couldn't bear the thought of going back to my father, not after what he did to my poor Kennet, so I went to the Isle of Moon by me self."

"Ye rescued yerself." Brigitta gave her hand another squeeze. "Ye're much stronger then ye think."

Sister Fallyn shook her head. "It's taken me years to stop blaming me self for Kennet's death." She wiped her cheek. "I'm not looking forward to going back to Tourin."

Brigitta winced. "I don't want to go, either. I suppose Rupert plans to hand us over to my brother, Gunther."

"Aye, in exchange for a hefty amount of gold, no doubt." Sister Fallyn sighed as she slathered butter on her bread. "There are no good men in Tourin."

"Except Kennet."

"Aye, but he's gone." The nun gave Brigitta a stern look.

"Ye must be careful with yer heart, lass. Love is a powerful force, and once it's taken ye over, it can cause ye to do all sorts of things ye ne'er imagined."

Brigitta's eyes widened. "Exciting things?"

"Terrible things. Tragic mistakes that can cost some-one's life. 'Tis not like the *overly dramatic* stories ye write. Ye're not guaranteed a happy ending."

Brigitta swallowed hard. "I understand." She already suspected her concept of a dashing young hero was sadly flawed. Why else would she even entertain the notion that the infamous Rupert could be her tall and handsome stranger?

She shoved him from her thoughts once again. "What can ye tell me about Tourin? Ye must know quite a bit, since ye grew up in the capital."

Sister Fallyn shook her head. "Lourdon wasn't always the capital. Many years ago, the capital was up north in the Highlands, and the House of Trepurin ruled the country."

"Isn't that where the gold is mined?" Brigitta asked. "The mountains in the north?"

"Aye. The gold was discovered four hundred years ago by Lord Aelfrid Trepurin, who used his newfound wealth to become the first king of Tourin. He spread the wealth among the Highland clans, so they were always loyal. Fierce warriors, too. Whenever the nobles in the south rebelled, they were crushed."

Brigitta nodded. "I remember from my studies that the country was constantly plagued with civil war."

"Aye." Sister Fallyn grimaced. "The problem was the gold. The northern nobles had it, and southern ones wanted it. Together, they made life miserable for the common folk. They were always taking our healthy young men to fight their battles for them. And every time the south lost, there would be towns burned and lives destroyed." She shuddered. "It was dreadful."

"But wasn't my father from the south? How did he become king?"

Sister Fallyn took a bite of bread and waved a dismissive hand. "It hardly matters. What's done is done."

She was doing it again, Brigitta realized. The nun was dodging questions about her family. "Sister, I need to know. I could end up at the royal court in Lourdon. It would be dangerous for me to go there ignorant."

Sister Fallyn sighed. "Aye, I suppose ye need to know." She took a sip of wine, then gave her a worried look. "I have to warn ye, lass. 'Tis not a pretty story."

Brigitta sat back in her chair. "Tell me."

The nun's eyes grew unfocused as she delved back into her memory. "When I was a child, King Balfrid died and his son Manfrid inherited the throne. Manfrid was the first king to reach out to the south. He spent some of his gold rebuilding towns and bridges. He spread the gold about, hoping to buy peace for the country."

"It sounds like he wanted what was best for Tourin."

Sister Fallyn shrugged. "I suppose. But he also wanted to avoid war because his firstborn son was only four years old and his second son just a babe. The two boys would have been in grave danger if anything happened to himself."

An ominous feeling crept over Brigitta. "But something did happen?"

Sister Fallyn nodded. "After a few years, yer father Garold claimed to have a plan that would bring a lasting peace to Tourin. A way to unite the north and south for all time. A marriage that would bind the House of Trepurin to the House of Grian. All the king had to do was betroth his elder son, Prince Ulfrid, to Garold's baby daughter."

Brigitta's breath hitched. "Me self?"

"Aye." Sister Fallyn gulped down some wine. "King

Manfrid agreed and came south with a small army. He was welcomed everywhere with cheers, for the people desperately wanted peace. The king didn't expect any trouble, not when Garold had sent him his elder son, Gunther, as a hostage."

"Ye mean if King Manfrid was attacked, Gunther would be killed?"

"Exactly. Gunther was only twelve years old at the time, but I'm sure he understood how he was being used. He was illegitimate, after all, so he was probably considered expendable."

Brigitta winced. "So what happened?"

"King Manfrid took his elder son and personal guard to Garold's castle in Lourdon, and there the ceremony took place. The prince was about six or seven years old at the time. Old enough to recite the betrothal vows to yerself."

Brigitta's heart pounded fast. She'd been betrothed? "How old was I?"

"Three months. Everything seemed to be going well . . ."

A chill skittered down Brigitta's spine. Surely her father hadn't . . .

"It happened when the king and his entourage were riding back through the town of Lourdon. Garold had positioned archers along the tops of the buildings."

A wave of nausea swept through Brigitta. *No. Dear goddesses, no.* Her father was a murderer.

"At the same time, a secret army from the south attacked Manfrid's army," Sister Fallyn continued. "The south was victorious, and before the day was over Manfrid's dead body was on display and Garold had crowned himself king."

Brigitta swallowed hard at the bile rising up her throat.

"Garold immediately dispatched assassins to go north to kill Manfrid's queen and their younger son."

"Enough," Brigitta whispered, her hand pressed against her mouth.

"'Tis known for certain that the queen died, but there was a rumor that the younger prince might have survived. Garold always claimed the rumor false. He was much more concerned about the older prince, Ulfrid, who was betrothed to you. Ulfrid's body was never recovered, so Garold was afraid the boy might still be alive and come back someday to claim the throne. The prince's betrothal to yerself became a liability, but Garold solved that problem by announcing that ye had . . . died."

Brigitta blinked. "What?"

Sister Fallyn nodded. "Everyone believed it, too, for ye were nowhere to be found. It wasn't till I arrived at the convent seven years later that I suspected who ye were. I asked Mother Ginessa, and she confirmed it. Garold sent ye there in secret afore ye were four months old."

Brigitta's mind raced. No wonder her father had never sent for her or even bothered to contact her. He'd wanted everyone to believe she was dead. A sharp pain shot through her heart, and she pressed a hand to her chest. *Goddesses, no.* Her father had killed her. In his mind, he had killed her off so her existence couldn't cause him any trouble.

Tears burned her eyes. Her father had murdered the royal family so he could be king. He'd risked the life of his elder son, Gunther. And after he'd used her to lure his enemies to their death, he'd shipped her away for good.

She jumped up so quickly, her chair toppled over. "A monster." She backed away from the table. Her father had been a monster. Even Gunther had proven to be a monster when he'd murdered her younger brother.

"They're all monsters." She hugged herself, digging her fingers into her arms as if she could rip away the bad blood that coursed through her veins. "I come from a family of *monsters*!"

"Nay!" Sister Fallyn ran toward her and pulled her into a tight embrace. "We are yer family, lass. Mother Ginessa, me self, yer sisters." She leaned back and grasped Brigitta by the shoulders. "Ye are loved. Ye're a good soul. *We* are yer family. Ne'er forget that."

Tears ran down Brigitta's cheeks. "I'll try—"

"Ye can do it." Sister Fallyn hugged her once more. "And I'll do everything I can to protect yerself."

With a sniff, Brigitta nodded. "Even if ye have to use a butter knife?"

Sister Fallyn snorted. "Aye. 'Tis like ye said. We're much stronger than we think."

Chapter Five

He wasn't as strong as he had thought. After a few nautical miles, Brody realized he wouldn't be able to match the speed of the pirate ship for much longer.

As one of the Embraced, Brody's special gift was the ability to shift. It was a rare gift, and one that Brody tried his best to keep secret. Most men in power would consider him a threat and want to kill him. That was one of the reasons he had sought out Leofric, the Beast of Benwick, six years ago. Since Leo was also Embraced and considered highly dangerous, Brody had figured his own ability wouldn't seem so threatening. He'd been right, for Leo had immediately hired him as a spy.

In canine form, Brody was able to infiltrate any castle on Aerthlan and listen to private conversations. Being a dog gave him the dual advantage of being almost invisible but still trustworthy. In human form, he'd become one of Leo's best friends. And now that Leo was the king of Eberon, he relied even more on Brody's special abilities.

But Brody wasn't the only versatile shifter on Aerthlan. Eight months ago, he and Leo had come across the

Chameleon, who had murdered and impersonated both the crown prince and the king of Eberon. The Chameleon had come close to stealing the throne before his escape as an eagle.

Brody didn't want to admit it to anyone, but he felt personally responsible for the Chameleon's escape. If only he had known how to shift into a bird, he could have followed the bastard.

But Brody was accustomed to staying in canine form most of the time. People didn't realize that just because he could assume the shape of an animal, it didn't mean he automatically knew how to move, behave, or make sounds like that animal. Since there had always been a few dogs in the household where he'd grown up, he could do a convincing job of behaving like one. And being a dog seemed best suited for his job as a spy.

He could also do a fair imitation of a seal or dolphin. As a child, he'd learned how to swim in the ocean, so he'd spent some time studying sea creatures.

But birds? It was something he'd never attempted before. After the Chameleon's escape, Brody had spent two weeks studying all sorts of birds so he could mimic their shape and build. The difficult part had been getting the wings just right.

Even when he'd finally mastered the correct form, it didn't mean he'd acquired an instinctual knowledge for flight. And of course, there were no books detailing how to fly. It had taken him another two weeks, a painful two weeks with more crashes than he cared to remember. But eventually, he'd learned how to use the wings and judge the air currents just right.

He'd been so exhausted from his training that he'd slept right through Leo's and his wife's coronation. But now, if the Chameleon ever showed up again and tried to escape by turning into an eagle, Brody would be right behind him. *Try getting away from me now, you bastard.*

Unfortunately, his search for the Chameleon seemed nearly impossible. He knew the Chameleon's scent, but had no idea what the bastard's true form looked like.

This latest assignment had seemed easy in comparison. A pleasant cruise to the Isle of Moon and back to make sure Queen Luciana's four adopted sisters arrived safely in Ebton.

But nothing had gone as planned.

Brody had spent years gathering useful information, but even he had been surprised by the news that Brigitta was actually the princess of Tourin. Everyone had long believed the princess to be dead. When the pirates had taken her, Brody had seen a chance to kill two birds with one stone. By following the pirates, he could make sure Brigitta and Sister Fallyn were safe. And for Leo, he could gather information about the most infamous pirate who sailed the seas—the Wind Sorcerer, Rupert.

Tourinian pirates had been plaguing the Eberoni coastline for over a hundred years, and Leo wanted rid of them. While General Harden and the main army were patrolling the northern and eastern borders with Norveshka and Woodwyn, his son, Nevis, had several troops guarding the western coastline, hoping to capture and destroy pirates. Most of the Eberoni naval ships were also hunting for them.

Brody examined the pirate flagship as he swam beside it. There was no way he could gather information or check on the ladies unless he managed to get on board. But he couldn't do it as a human. The other men aboard would wonder why there was suddenly a stranger in their midst. Especially one who had no clothes.

Besides, thanks to a witch's curse, Brody wasn't able to stay human for long. The damned witch had screwed up his shifting ability, forcing him to become human each day before midnight, but never allowing him to remain that way for more than two hours at a time.

In other words, he could never lead a normal life. He was a human who couldn't be human. Doomed to spend most of his life observing and listening. An imperfect existence. But a perfect spy.

He couldn't do much spying here in the ocean, though, so he dove down till the pressure built against his ears, then shot toward the surface as fast as he could. The second he broke through and became airborne, he shifted into a pelican.

Up, up he flew till he was far above the flagship. There he rested, stretching his wings to glide on the steady wind that was filling the ship's sails and pushing it south. He veered to the right so he could glance back. The entire fleet was moving south in a V formation like a flock of geese.

Tipping back to the left, he flew directly over the flagship and scanned the deck below. Brigitta and the nun were nowhere to be seen. They must have been sent below. The captain and helmsman were standing by the wheel on the quarterdeck, although Brody assumed the ship needed little steering as long as Rupert was in control.

Brody had heard the captain introduce himself with the name Landers. So where was the infamous Rupert? The masked man in the crow's nest was the only pirate on board attempting to conceal his identity. He was facing the bow of the ship with his arms stretched out, his palms turned up to the sky. Slowly, he lifted his arms, as if he was gathering the air around him, then rotated his palms and pressed them forward. South, the same direction as the wind.

He had to be Rupert.

Brody dipped down closer. The pirate appeared tall, and his black hair was long and braided. It was hard to tell any more than that because of the hat and mask he was wearing. Why was he taking Brigitta south? If he was intending to ransom her, he should have headed north toward Tourin.

A young boy scampered up onto the quarterdeck to speak to the captain. Brody spiraled downward to make a landing on a nearby railing.

"I have a box with needles and thread somewhere in my cabin," Captain Landers was saying. "I'll go look for it and take it to the ladies."

The boy gasped. "Oh, no, Captain! I'll take it! Y-you're busy right now."

"Not that busy. Besides, I should make sure our guests are comfortable." The captain headed for the stairs.

"Wait!" The boy jumped in front of him, his arms stretched out. "You shouldn't disturb them. Th-they're asleep!"

"How did they ask for needle and thread in their sleep?"

The boy winced. "Just tell me where the stuff is, and I'll take it to them. You should stay here."

Landers leaned over, lowering his voice. "Jeffrey, you don't tell a captain what to do. Move aside."

"But if you go, the nun will gullet you!"

"What?" The captain straightened with a jerk.

"She said if any man came into the cabin, she would gullet him. With the butter knife."

The nearby helmsman chuckled. "She sounds a bit feisty for a nun."

Captain Landers shot him an annoyed look. "It's not amusing that the women don't feel safe."

With a shrug, Jeffrey stuffed his hands into his pockets. "The nun said they were going to be ravished."

"*What?*" The captain spun back to the boy.

Jeffrey's eyes widened. "What does it mean?"

Landers gritted his teeth. "Never mind about that for now."

The boy's shoulders slumped as he muttered, "That's what they told me, too."

Meanwhile, the helmsman lost his struggle not to laugh and a snort escaped.

Captain Landers cuffed him on the head. "Their fear is not unfounded. If any other pirates had taken them—"

"Tucker." A deep voice carried toward them on the wind.

Who the hell was that? Brody noted the helmsman looking up, so he glanced up, too.

The masked man in the crow's nest was staring down at them. Apparently, he'd been listening to the entire conversation. His mouth moved as words sifted toward them on a breeze. "Take a break, Tucker. And not a word to anyone. I can hear everything said on deck, so if I hear gossip about the women, I will know it came from you."

Tucker nodded. "I understand, Admiral. I won't say a word." He bowed his head, then scrambled down the steps to the main deck.

As far as Brody could tell, the women were going to be safe. He hopped down, his webbed feet landing on top of a wooden trunk. Tucking his spindly legs beneath him, he sat down and took a much-needed rest.

Captain Landers removed his hat and ran a hand through his dark, curly hair. "Jeffrey, look in the trunk at the end of my bed. There should be a small lacquer box in there with some sewing supplies."

"Aye, Captain." The boy saluted and headed down the stairs.

"And tell them again that they're safe," Landers called

after the boy, then muttered, "If it will do any good." He plopped his hat back on his head and grabbed hold of the wheel.

Rupert turned to face south and repeated the gesture with his hands to keep the wind moving.

After a few minutes, the captain grumbled, "I won't have it. I won't have women on my ship cowering in fear. I'll tell them myself—"

"Let them think the worst." Rupert's voice filtered down on a breeze as he turned toward the quarterdeck.

Landers lifted his gaze to the crow's nest. "Why?" His voice was barely above a whisper, but apparently Rupert could hear it.

"They're not guests," Rupert replied softly. "They're captives."

The captain's knuckles turned white as he gripped the wheel hard. "I thought I raised you to have a sense of honor."

Rupert turned his back and lifted his arms in the air as if he was unaffected. Brody wasn't entirely convinced, though, not when Rupert's arms moved a bit jerkily and a sudden gust of wind caused the ship to lurch forward.

"They came from a damned convent," Landers growled. "This has to be terrifying for them. Have you forgotten you once took a vow—"

"I have forgotten nothing, Stefan." Rupert whirled to face the captain. "She is the spawn of the bastard who stole everyone and everything from me. She is the enemy."

Brody narrowed his eyes at the level of rage that filled Rupert's voice and radiated from his tense posture. Who the hell was this pirate? And what did he intend to do with Brigitta?

Landers was silent for a moment, his head bowed. "I remember it, too. I was there. I have always been there."

Rupert's shoulders slumped a bit as he turned away. He removed his hat, and Brody was surprised to see that the long black hair was attached. But it remained difficult to tell what the pirate looked like, since he still wore the mask and a red scarf around his head.

As he dropped the hat into the crow's nest, the sails beneath him rippled, no longer full of air. "I am grateful, Stefan. I won't blame you if you wish to leave—"

"No," Landers interrupted. "The choice was mine, and I made it gladly. There's no need for you to feel guilt—" He stiffened. "That's why you're behaving like an arse. You feel guilty for using the girl to—"

"*Enough.*" Rupert lifted his arms, gathering up more air to make another push. The wind picked up and filled the sails once again.

"Captain!" Jeffrey skipped up the steps to the quarterdeck. "I found the box and gave it to the ladies."

"That's a good lad." Landers patted him on the back. "And did you remind them that they're truly safe?"

Jeffrey nodded. "The nun said she feels safer now."

"Excellent."

"'Cause now she can use the needles to poke a man's eyes out."

The captain groaned.

"Did the younger one say anything?" Rupert asked softly, and Brody noticed that the masked man was facing them once again.

"She thanked me for the box." Jeffrey scratched his head. "She looked like she's been crying."

The captain muttered a curse. Rupert turned away, seemingly unconcerned. Even so, Brody suspected his concentration was off. The sails began to sag as the wind died down.

"Jeffrey." Rupert glanced back at the boy. "In the

storeroom, you'll find a blue gown and a bag of women's clothing. Take all of it to the ladies. It might cheer them up."

"Yes, Admiral." The boy saluted.

"Excellent idea." Landers smiled up at Rupert, but the masked man ignored them and increased the wind to the sails.

Brody snorted to himself. It looked like the captain was right and Rupert was feeling some guilt over kidnapping the women. But why did he consider Brigitta an enemy?

Jeffrey headed for the stairs, then halted with a jerk. "Oh, I almost forgot. They want some water now. The nun said the wine is too strong."

"We gave them our best wine," Landers muttered.

"Aye," Jeffrey agreed. "But the nun said they have to keep their wits about them so they won't get ravished."

The captain's hands clenched into fists, and his breath hissed as he took in a long breath. "Take them a pitcher of water."

"Aye, Captain." The boy scurried off.

"Dammit." The captain whisked off his hat as he swiveled in a circle. He caught a glimpse of Brody sitting on the trunk, then did a double take. "What are you looking at? Shoo!"

Brody didn't budge.

"What are you doing so far from shore?"

Brody attempted a small squawk, but it came out more like a belch.

"Trying to get away from a female, aren't you?" With a sigh, the captain plopped his hat back on, then rested his hands on the wheel. "The Light help me. Now I'm talking to birds."

After a few minutes, Jeffrey returned.

"What is it now?" Landers asked softly.

"They need a chamber pot. Should I—"

"Take them to the officers' privy," Rupert called from above.

Jeffrey blinked. "I thought only you and the captain were allowed in there."

"We don't mind," Landers assured the boy.

"Did you take the clothing that Lady Ellen left behind?" Rupert asked.

Jeffrey nodded. "Lady Brigitta thought the gown was beautiful, but the nun told her it must have been stolen from a woman you ravished."

With a growl, Captain Landers threw his hat on the deck. "I'm going to wring her neck."

Jeffrey's eyes widened. "Really?"

"No!" the captain yelled. "They're safe, dammit. From now on, do whatever they ask. I don't want to hear it!"

As the boy scampered off, Brody smirked as well as he could with a pelican beak. The ladies were safe. It was the men who were in danger of losing their sanity.

Up in the crow's nest, Rupert kept calm by surveying his domain. Up here, he was the master. He could sail wherever he pleased, do whatever he wanted, and no one could stop him. Not even a pair of stubborn women belowdecks.

But she was crying. He ejected that thought the second it crept into his head. There was no need to feel guilty. No need to feel anything at all but the satisfaction of knowing he was one step further along on the Official Plan. He would not allow the so-called princess to distract him. Even if she was beautiful. And crying.

Out of sight, out of mind. She could stay belowdecks, and he would remain here. Up here, he was free.

The Great Western Ocean went on as far as the eye could see. Overhead, the endless sky stretched far into the horizon. Most nights, he slept on a pallet on the quarterdeck, so he could feel close to the moons and countless stars.

Others, like Stefan, claimed the enormity of the night sky made them feel small. Insignificant. For Rupert, it made him feel better. The haunting memories, the crushing grief of losing everyone he loved, the years of living in fear—all these things seemed smaller and more bearable when he gazed up at the stars. And the fact that there were so damned many of them made it seem like anything could be possible. Even avenging his family and taking back what was rightfully his. Why shouldn't his chances for success be as limitless as the stars in the sky?

Hope. The vastness of the night sky gave him hope.

During the day, the sky became an enormous workshop, providing him with an endless supply of air that he could shape and turn as he wished. Over the years, he had fine-tuned his gift, so now he could produce anything from the faintest whisper of a breeze to a hurricane-force gale. And he could narrow the wind. Aim it like an arrow. If ten seagulls lined up on a yardarm, he could blow one off its perch while leaving the others untouched.

Control. The vastness of the sky gave him control.

There had been too many years when he'd had no control at all. After losing everything before turning seven, he had spent the next seven years of his life hiding in caves and basements, constantly fearing for his safety. A hopeless, helpless existence, fraught with fear, hunger, and grief.

Even now, the memory of that time shot a spark of rage sizzling through his body. *Never again.* He would never be that weak and hopeless again. He'd learned how to harness the wind, and up here, surrounded by air, he had the power of a sorcerer. He had the control he craved. And the satisfaction of being the master of his own destiny.

Shutting his eyes, he inhaled the fresh, salty air and relished the wind brushing against him. Unfortunately, with his eyes shut, a pretty face came to mind. Blond hair and beautiful turquoise—*dammit*. He opened his eyes and shoved her from his thoughts.

He glanced back to check on the other ships, for they always gave him a great sense of accomplishment. In the seven years since he'd become a pirate, he'd increased his fleet from one to nine.

By the time Rupert had turned fourteen, he had become increasingly rebellious about having to remain hidden. So Stefan had contacted his cousin, Ansel, who was the captain of a merchant vessel. Ansel had agreed to take them on, even though they knew nothing about sailing. Over the next five years, hard work and fresh air had transformed Rupert from a gangly youth into a muscular young man.

During that time, Ansel taught them everything he knew about sailing, while Stefan continued to teach him fencing and archery. Rupert read every book he could find, and with the endless sky around him, he was finally able to practice and master his special gift.

When Rupert was nineteen, the merchant who had owned the trading ship managed to squander away his fortune at the gaming tables. With the ship up for sale, Ansel, Stefan, and Rupert had pooled all their resources and bought it. And that was when the three of them had set the Official Plan into motion.

With their one ship, they attacked a small convoy of Tourinian naval ships carrying gold. Not only did they abscond with some gold, but they took one of the ships. The *Golden Star*. Many of the seamen onboard, frustrated by the measly pay from the royal navy, decided to join Rupert. The officers were put ashore, Stefan became captain, and each sailor on the two ships was rewarded with a gold coin.

Rupert's career as an infamous pirate had begun.

Now he was returning to Danport, where they'd bought supplies two days earlier. They'd traveled south for over an hour. It was time to turn eastward and head for shore.

As he adjusted the wind, Jeffrey's voice filtered up from the quarterdeck. What did the women want now? Was Brigitta crying again? Had she been impressed by the privy he had invented for himself and Stefan?

What do you care what she thinks? Each time Rupert had heard one of the women's complaints he'd gotten distracted and lost his concentration. That had to stop. He needed to get his fleet to Danport as quickly as possible before other pirates attacked the town.

Down below, Stefan was telling Jeffrey to give the ladies some books from his room. They were bored, and Jeffrey hadn't known what to do.

Stay out of it. It's not your problem. With muttered curse, Rupert turned toward them. "The captain's books are all about warfare and navigation. Not what I would call entertaining."

Stefan sighed. "You have a better idea?"

"There's a book in my room about a mermaid and a sorcerer. Take that one to them, Jeffrey."

"Yes, Admiral!" The boy started for the stairs.

"Is she still crying?" Rupert asked, then slapped himself mentally.

"Lady Brigitta?" Jeffrey hesitated. "No. She asked me what you were planning to do with her, but I didn't know. She doesn't want to go to Tourin or see her brother."

Rupert's grip on the railing tightened.

Stefan cleared his throat. "Perhaps we should have a talk with her—"

"Later," Rupert interrupted. He turned back to the bow of the ship and reinforced the wind. She didn't want to go to Tourin? She could be a princess there. Didn't that appeal to her? *She's the enemy. Why should you care what she wants?* With a muttered curse, he yanked the spyglass from his belt. *But what if she's innocent?* He shoved that thought aside while he took a look through the spyglass.

Holy crap! In the distance, there were seven ships. Sails with red and black stripes. The Eberoni Royal Navy.

Dammit, he should have spotted them earlier. Once again, he'd let himself get distracted. "Seven Eberoni naval ships to the east," he called down to Stefan.

"Have they spotted us yet?" Stefan asked.

Rupert didn't think so. Their spyglasses were not as powerful as his. The navy was traveling south, hugging the coastline. No doubt, hunting for pirates. And here he was, a pirate, headed southeast, straight for them.

He adjusted the wind once more, sending his ships south on a parallel course and increasing their speed. With any luck, his fleet could skirt around the navy unnoticed and arrive at Danport first. When he took another look through his spyglass, he spotted three pirate ships far in distance, closing in on Danport. Bloody vultures.

"Three pirate ships to the south," he called down to Stefan. He swung his spyglass back to the navy. *Damn!* They'd spotted his ships and were turning his way.

"Navy's coming in first," he yelled. He shoved his hat on his head as he yanked a red flag from its container inside the crow's nest.

He faced the other ships of his fleet and waved the red flag back and forth. The closest two in the V formation started waving their red flags from their crows' nests, then the next two and next down the line till the whole fleet knew to prepare themselves.

"Jeffrey, make sure the women stay below," Rupert ordered. He couldn't let anything distract him now.

Stefan shouted, "Battle stations!"

Chapter Six

Brigitta removed another item from the bag of women's clothing. A nightgown, snowy-white linen with blue embroidery and a blue satin ribbon drawstring around the neck. Her gowns and nightgowns at the convent had always been plain cream-colored wool. "'Tis very pretty."

"Don't even think about wearing it," Sister Fallyn warned her as she watered down the wine.

"It just makes me wonder . . ." Brigitta's insatiable curiosity was aroused. She fingered the white lace at the edge of the long bell-shaped sleeves. Whoever had owned these clothes must have been fairly wealthy. What had happened to her? Why were her possessions on a pirate ship?

Brigitta smoothed a hand over the linen. Sometimes when she handled objects, she would receive mental clues, a flash of pictures or traces of emotion that would help her understand why the object had been hidden or discarded. But all she could sense from these clothes was a feeling of great relief. "Why would she leave such lovely things behind?"

Sister Fallyn slanted a wary look at the clothing. "Perhaps they reminded her of something terrible. Like being ravished."

Brigitta groaned inwardly. Wherever the pirate Rupert was taking them, it was going to be a long trip.

The sudden blast of horns made her jump. "What was that?" She glanced up at the ceiling as the pounding of feet sounded on deck.

Sister Fallyn made the sign of the moons. "Heavenly goddesses, what will happen to us now?"

Brigitta dashed to the window, but it was hard to see much of anything through the thick mullioned glass. She twisted a handle and opened the window as far as it would go, but that was only about a few inches. Nothing in sight, but now she could hear voices yelling overhead and the blare of horns from other ships in the fleet.

A knock sounded on the door, then Jeffrey peered inside. "I brought you—"

"What's happening?" Brigitta rushed toward him.

"Uh, nothing." Jeffrey offered her a book bound in tooled leather. "I brought this for you to read."

"Thank you." The second Brigitta accepted the book, a small shiver raced up her arms and an instant vision flitted across her mind. A man's hands turning the pages. And somehow, she knew that man was Rupert.

"Ye must tell us what has happened," Sister Fallyn demanded.

"Well . . ." Jeffrey scratched his head. "It's uh . . . nothing much. You just need to stay here."

He started to close the door, but Brigitta caught it with her hand. "Are we under attack? Has the Tourinian navy returned?"

"No, it's the Eberoni—" Jeffrey slapped a hand over his mouth.

"The Eberoni navy?" Brigitta asked.

Jeffrey grimaced. "There's no need for you to worry. Rupert can handle them."

Brigitta's heart raced as an idea popped into her mind. "This is excellent!"

"It is?"

"Aye." Brigitta dropped the book on the bed and grabbed her cloak. " 'Tis the perfect solution for everyone!"

"It is?" Jeffrey repeated.

"Yes!" Brigitta pushed the door open and slipped past the boy into the passageway.

"Where are ye going?" Sister Fallyn called after her.

She darted up the stairs and peered out the door at the main deck. The seamen were busy. She could probably slip past them unnoticed.

"My lady, don't!" Jeffrey clambered up the stairs.

"Come back!" Sister Fallyn yelled as she ventured into the passageway.

Brigitta eased onto the deck and quickly scanned the surroundings. Behind her on the quarterdeck, Captain Landers was shouting orders. To her right, the other ships in the pirate fleet were moving south. To her left toward the shore, there was a group of Eberoni naval ships headed southwest on a collision course with the pirate fleet.

Somehow she had to make contact with them. She ran toward the portside railing and waved a hand in the air. Would they see her? She waved her brown cloak back and forth, hoping they could spot her through a spyglass.

"What are you doing?" A deep voice sifted past her ear on a breeze.

Rupert. She spun around, but he wasn't behind her. She lifted her gaze. There he was, staring at her from the crow's nest. "I need to contact the Eberoni," she said softly, wondering if he would hear her.

He jabbed his spyglass under his belt. "You need to go below where it's safe."

"Nay! I have a plan—"

"To get yourself killed?"

"'Twill be beneficial to both of us."

"Your death?" He slipped on some leather gloves.

"Nay, the plan!" She huffed with annoyance. The man was wasting her time. She turned her back to him and waved her cloak in the air.

"Enough!"

She glanced back just in time to see him slide down a rope and land neatly on the deck. In three long strides he was next to her and ripping the cloak out of her hands.

"Stop that!" She grabbed the cloak back, but he jerked it toward himself, causing her to stumble. To keep from falling into him, she planted her hands on his chest.

"Oof." Even though the soft wool of her cloak had cushioned her hands, she felt like she'd run into a stone wall.

She steeled her nerves in case her gift struck her, but since her hands were only touching her own cloak, she was spared the strong reaction she'd experienced before. She'd actually fainted then. For now, she seemed to be all right. Except that her nose was only a few inches from his bare skin where his shirt was unbuttoned. She could even see a hint of his chest hair.

As her cheeks grew warm, she lifted her gaze to his masked face. His amber eyes were narrowed, watching her so intently that her mind went blank for a moment. Several moments. His rock of a chest budged slightly, expanding as he took a deep breath.

With a small gasp, she came to her senses. "Excuse me." She removed her hands and stepped back.

"What is this plan?" he asked quietly.

What plan? "Oh, aye." She motioned toward the Eberoni ships. "We need to contact them and let them know

I'm here. I know! Ye could shoot one of yer arrows at their mast with a message attached. Like ye did afore."

"Why?"

"To let them ransom me, of course. Their queen, Luciana, is my sister, and she would gladly pay for me. Then I wouldn't have to go to Tourin. I could stay in Eberon with my sisters. And ye would have the gold ye want. Everyone would be happy. 'Tis the perfect solution, don't ye think?"

His mouth thinned. "You think I'm doing this just for the gold?"

"Of course. Ye're a pirate."

His eyes flashed with anger. "Very well. Let's talk about your plan." He stepped closer to her. "One: I don't want Eberoni gold. The only person I rob is your brother, Gunther."

She blinked. "Why? What do ye have against . . ." She retreated a step when he advanced another one.

"Two: In order to reach an Eberoni ship with an arrow, I would have to risk putting my ship within firing range of their cannons. I will not risk the lives of everyone on board."

"Ye shot an arrow afore when I was on—"

"That ship didn't have her cannons ready. These ships do." He stepped closer. "Three: These ships will not be carrying enough gold to pay your ransom. I doubt they even know that you've been kidnapped. In fact, they probably have no idea you're a so-called princess."

"So-called?"

"Four: In order to transfer you to one of their ships, I would have to get too close. The minute you boarded their ship, they would blast me out of the water."

She winced. Apparently, her plan was not so excellent after all.

He moved even closer. "Five."

Would his reasons never end? Her cheeks burned with embarrassment, but she didn't know which bothered her the most—his harsh opinion or his close proximity. Even now she could breathe in the fresh scent of his white shirt and see the individual whiskers shading his handsome jawline. They practically gleamed in the sunlight. *Don't think about that.* "Number five?"

"Never mind." He handed her the cloak. "Go below. You're distracting me."

She was being dismissed. Her embarrassment quickly flared into irritation. How aggravating that this wretched man was now in control of her destiny! Still, she was at his mercy, so if she was going to convince him to send her to Eberon instead of Tourin, she would need to present her case calmly and sensibly.

"When ye have the time, please allow me to discuss my situation with you." She touched his sleeve.

Instantly a shock went up her arm and a series of horrific scenes flashed across her mind. With a gasp, she dropped the cloak. Shouts of pain and screams of terror echoed in her ears as a barrage of arrows zipped through the air and thudded into the backs of men and the haunches of their horses. Blue uniforms turned red with blood. Horses squealed and charged into frantic crowds. A deluge of fear and grief slapped her so hard it knocked her off her feet.

"Brigitta!" Rupert caught her. "What's wrong?"

"I . . ." Good goddesses, she'd never experienced such a powerful vision before. Had she just had a glimpse into his past, a past so painful that he hid it from everyone?

"You're not going to faint again, are you?"

She blinked. He was holding her, supporting her weight as he watched her closely. "I'm fine."

He set her on her feet. "Are you sure?"

Her heart pounded. This man might believe all his secrets were safe, but he couldn't hide them from her. And if this recent vision was any indication, his secret past was very . . . exciting. Much like one of her *overly dramatic* stories.

A sense of elation swept through her. She would uncover his secrets, and it would be the most intriguing challenge she had ever faced. She gave him a bright smile. "I'm quite well, thank you."

His eyes widened as he continued to stare at her. With a small thrill, she realized he was still holding her.

"Rupert!" The captain ran toward them. "What the hell are you doing? They're getting too close!"

Rupert jumped back, releasing her.

An explosion sounded in the distance with smoke billowing into the air. Brigitta gasped as a barrage of cannonballs headed straight for them.

Rupert faced the Eberoni naval ship and pushed his hands forward. A blast of wind whistled toward the cannonballs, slamming into them with enough force that they plummeted into the water several yards short of their mark.

A giant wave of water splashed over the railing, drenching everyone on the portside. Brigitta stumbled back, and the captain caught her. A burst of tingles shot up her arm, and she jumped back. Holy goddesses, he was hiding an enormous number of secrets, too. Just like Rupert.

"My lady." The captain handed her the cloak she'd dropped. "Please go below. If you continue to distract Rupert, it'll be dangerous for us all."

"I-I'm sorry." *How embarrassing!* Rupert had warned her that she was distracting him, but she hadn't listened.

She headed back toward the cabins, making sure not to get in anyone's way. What a fool she'd been! Obviously, this was not one of her *overly dramatic* stories where she could be the heroine. If anything, she'd proven herself to be more of a nuisance. Not only had her plan turned out to be awful, but she'd endangered everyone aboard. If Rupert hadn't stopped those cannonballs in time, they could have all been killed.

But how amazing that he had actually stopped them. She turned around to see what he was doing now.

He'd removed his gloves. His broad chest expanded as he inhaled deeply, and he lifted his arms to the sky, palms up. A small cyclone of wind began over his head, whirling faster and faster, growing larger and larger. Then he pushed his hands forward and the cyclone unraveled, shooting a gale-force wind straight at the Eberoni navy. All seven ships rocked and heaved as the wind buffeted against them. Slowly, the wind turned them till their sails became full.

Rupert pushed again, and the ships shot across the water, headed north. Brigitta's mouth dropped open. His power was incredible! In one day, he'd managed to defeat both the Tourinian and Eberoni navies. And he'd done it without anyone being harmed.

Cheers rang out on deck, but Captain Landers shouted in Tourinian, "We're not done yet! Stay alert!"

Not done? Brigitta hurried toward the door where Jeffrey was waiting. As she stepped through, she blinked to adjust her eyes to the dimmer light in the passageway.

Sister Fallyn was scowling at her from the base of the short staircase. "Look at you, yer gown is all wet. What happened to yerself?"

"There was a big splash from some cannonballs—" When Sister Fallyn stiffened with shock, Brigitta quickly added, "But no one got hurt. Everything's fine."

"It is not *fine*," Sister Fallyn huffed. "What on Aerthlan possessed ye to go up on deck? 'Tis too dangerous!"

"I wanted to let the Eberoni navy know that we're

here. I thought if Luciana paid for our ransom, we could go to Ebton instead of Tourin."

"Oh." Sister Fallyn tilted her head while she considered. "That's not a bad idea."

With a groan, Brigitta shook her head. "It *was* bad. Rupert instantly rattled off five—no, four—reasons why it wouldn't work." Why had he refused to tell her his fifth reason?

Sister Fallyn scoffed. "He's a thieving pirate. What would he know?"

Quite a bit, Brigitta thought as she paused on the second step.

"Come now." Sister Fallyn motioned for her to hurry. "We'll feel safer in our cabin."

"But then we won't know what's happening." Brigitta glanced at Jeffrey, who was hovering behind her in the doorway. "Can we stay here? With the door open so we can hear?"

"I-I suppose." He glanced to the side and laughed. "I can't close the door now. A big fat pelican just sat in front of it."

"Really?" Brigitta peered outside and smiled when she saw the pelican sitting against the door.

She glanced to the portside but could no longer spot Rupert. Where was he? She scanned the deck till she saw his hat. He was indeed tall, for the tip of his hat stood a foot above most of the crew. He was standing close to the mainmast, putting on his gloves. Then he grabbed a rope with one hand and pulled a lever with another.

Suddenly he zoomed straight up into the air till he reached the crow's nest.

Brigitta gasped. "How did he—"

"It's one of his inventions." With a grin, Jeffrey pointed up. "See the pulley up there and the trapdoor? When Rupert pulls the lever, the trapdoor swings open and a heavy weight drops down. The weight's connected to the same rope Rupert's holding. So when the weight goes down—"

"Rupert goes up," Brigitta finished. "But doesn't the weight crash onto the deck?"

Jeffrey snorted. "Rupert designed it so the weight falls into a cargo hole, where it's caught in a net."

Brigitta watched the pirate swing his legs over the railing of the crow's nest and land neatly inside. "'Tis a clever idea."

"Oh, Rupert's really smart," Jeffrey boasted. "He invented the privy down below."

"Really?" Brigitta had been astonished by the sink and toilet that had pipes with running water. There was even an odd thing Jeffrey had called a shower.

"See those tanks over there?" Jeffrey pointed at three metal tanks at the far end of the passageway. "It's my job to make sure they're always full. The water goes down three different pipes to the privy. One for the sink, one for the chamber pot, and one for the shower. Gravity makes the water flow downward and eventually out some pipes into the sea."

Brigitta recalled the levers Jeffrey had shown them. By twisting them up or down, a person could make the water pour out or stop. "What if ye run out of water?"

Jeffrey waved a dismissive hand. "Rupert has it covered. He put a bunch of barrels on deck to collect rainwater."

Indeed, Brigitta thought, the pirate had an annoying way of being quite thorough. He'd certainly blasted her idea full of holes in just a few seconds. Even so, she couldn't help but admire how inventive his mind was.

Tall and handsome. Extremely clever. He certainly seemed like a dashing young hero. Except for the fact that he was a thieving, sorcerer pirate. And that small thing that kept nagging at her. Something about Rupert was off. She just couldn't quite put her finger on it.

"I hate to admit it," Sister Fallyn grumbled, "but the privy was quite impressive."

Jeffrey nodded. "That's what Lady Ellen said. She's the one who left all those clothes."

"A noblewoman?" Sister Fallyn asked. "What happened to her?"

"She was in big trouble," Jeffrey explained. "It was a few years ago when King Frederic was in power. Lady Ellen's husband failed to do something that King Frederic had ordered him to do, so he was executed. The king took his land and ordered Lady Ellen to be executed, too. She fled to Danport and begged Rupert and the captain to help her. We took her to the Isle of Moon where she'd be safe. She didn't have a way to pay for her passage, so she left the clothes behind. Said she wouldn't need them at the convent."

Sister Fallyn exchanged a surprised look with Brigitta. "Sister Ellen!"

"Of course." Brigitta grinned. Sister Ellen had helped Luciana prepare for her role as a noblewoman. "She taught us how to do the court dances."

"Then she's all right?" Jeffrey asked.

"Aye. She's very happy." To be alive. No wonder Brigitta had felt a great sense of relief when she'd touched Sister Ellen's discarded clothing.

These pirates weren't so bad after all, Brigitta thought as she draped her cloak on the second step, then took a seat. They were not only intelligent, but capable of acting with honor and compassion. They'd rescued Sister Ellen, so perhaps they would help her, too. She just needed to explain everything to Rupert.

The thought of spending time alone with him made

her heart beat faster. If she touched him again, would she see more of his secret past? Would she be able to figure out what was bothering her?

Horns suddenly blared again, and Brigitta stiffened.

"Good goddesses." Sister Fallyn made the sign of the moons. "What is happening now?"

Brigitta eased to her feet. "What do the horns mean?"

Jeffrey hesitated before mumbling, "Battle stations."

Sister Fallyn gasped. "Goddesses protect us!"

"Who is threatening us now?" Brigitta asked.

"Pirates," he began but when they gasped, he quickly added, "Don't worry. There are only three of them. Rupert will finish them off before you know it."

"Why are we fighting other pirates?" Brigitta winced when she realized she'd said *we*. Was she siding with Rupert now?

"They're the bad pirates," Jeffrey explained.

Sister Fallyn scoffed. "All pirates are bad."

"No." Jeffrey looked insulted. "We're the good guys. Whenever we buy supplies from a village like Danport, Rupert always pays in gold. The villagers love it, so they never report him to the Eberoni army. It's what Rupert calls a mutually beneficial business arrangement."

Sister Fallyn planted her hands on her hips. "Ye mean he bribes them to stay quiet."

Jeffrey scowled. "They consider him a hero 'cause he protects them. You see, the bad pirates figured out that whenever Rupert leaves a village, there's gold there, so they started attacking the villages after we leave. You wouldn't believe how angry Rupert and Captain Landers were when they found out. Rupert calls them bloody vultures."

"So these bad pirate ships are about to attack Danport?" Brigitta asked.

Jeffrey nodded. "We bought supplies there two days

ago. We were staying close by when Rupert got the message about you, my lady. So we hurried north to get you, then rushed back to make sure Danport was all right."

Outside, Captain Landers shouted, and a thunderous noise vibrated throughout the ship as cannons were rolled into position.

"Goddesses help us," Sister Fallyn whispered.

"I doubt we'll even use the cannons," Jeffrey told her. "Rupert can handle it himself."

What on Aerthlan would he do? Brigitta peered through the open doorway. She could see Rupert in the crow's nest, but couldn't tell what was happening with the three pirate ships.

The pelican took off, flying high into the sky. A bird's-eye view, Brigitta thought with envy, as the door started to swing shut. How could she remain here, not knowing what was happening?

She caught the door before it could close.

"We're supposed to stay below," Jeffrey muttered.

"I know." She didn't want to endanger anyone by being a distraction, but her strong sense of curiosity was compelling her. "Don't ye want to know what's happening?"

When he nodded, she peeked outside. Close to the wall of the quarterdeck and the portside railing, there were three large barrels for collecting rainwater.

"We can stay hidden." She eased outside, staying low and close to the wall of the quarterdeck.

"Brigitta, no!" Sister Fallyn yelled.

Jeffrey followed her and shut the door. Together they scurried along the wall, then hunched down in the narrow space behind the barrels.

She peered over the railing and whispered, "I can see the pirate ships. They have their cannons ready."

"Rupert will have to do something before we get into range," Jeffrey whispered back.

She glanced up at the crow's nest. Rupert was focused on the pirate ships. Slowly he lifted his arms. His fingers were splayed, his palms slightly cupped, his movements graceful and measured, as if he were conducting an orchestra. A whirlwind spun over his head, growing in intensity as he fed it more and more air.

Then suddenly, he struck his hands forward, and the whirlwind unfurled, shooting straight toward the pirate ships.

Brigitta peered over the railing. Two of the ships floundered and skidded toward the rocky shore. Screams sounded in the distance, then a series of loud cracks as the ships crashed against rocks and ground into the sand.

"He ran two of the ships onto the beach," she whispered to Jeffrey.

He nodded. "He usually does that if we're close to a shore. That way, most of the men can survive."

She spotted men scrambling to get ashore. "What about the third ship? The big one?"

Jeffrey chuckled. "Rupert must want that one. Are they waving a white flag yet?"

She peeked over the railing. "Aye. That means they surrendered?"

"Yes." Jeffrey grinned. "Now we'll have ten ships!"

Brigitta glanced up at Rupert. "That's how he increases his fleet?"

Jeffrey nodded. "Most of our ships were taken from the Tourinian navy or other pirate fleets."

"But how can he trust them?"

"He doesn't. He'll make one of his own men the new captain and give the ship a new crew. The old crew will be divided up and spread among the other ships. If they work hard and follow the rules, they'll be rewarded after four weeks with a gold coin. If they cause any trouble, they'll be put ashore."

"I see."

Jeffrey glanced up at Rupert, his eyes gleaming. "He has a fleet as powerful as any navy. And he's destroyed more bad pirates than anyone. No one can beat him."

Brigitta suspected the boy had a huge case of hero worship where Rupert was concerned. But how could he not, she thought, as her gaze settled on the infamous pirate. He'd whisked the Eberoni navy safely out of the way so that he could take on the responsibility of protecting Danport and defeating the bad pirates. And he'd managed to do it all with the least amount of casualties. He was, simply put, an amazing man.

As he lifted his arms to gather more air and push his fleet closer to the lone surviving pirate ship, she noted for the first time how his plaits of black hair stirred with the breeze. Underneath the braids, she could see the red scarf tied around his head.

She blinked. Shouldn't the scarf be on top of his hair instead of underneath? With a small gasp, she finally realized what had been nagging her. The black braids were off. And when she'd seen his whiskers up close, she'd noticed they were a light brown, even gleaming like gold in the sunlight. His chest hair had been brown.

She eyed the black plaits. "They're fake."

"Who?" Jeffrey asked.

"Never mind." Brigitta smiled. *Watch out, Rupert.* She'd figure out all of his secrets, one by one.

Chapter Seven

After watching Rupert handle the three pirate ships, Brody flew in a southerly direction along the shore, searching for Nevis and his soldiers. In addition to being King Leofric's best friend, Nevis was a captain in the Eberoni army. Leo had sent him with a few troops to guard the coastline and capture the Tourinian pirates who were raiding the villages there.

Nevis's father, General Harden, was now Lord Protector of the Realm, which had been Leo's job before he became king. General Harden and the bulk of the Eberoni army were currently guarding the northern and eastern borders of Eberon.

Brody glanced westward, where the sun was lowering toward the horizon. In another hour or so, it would fall beneath the Great Western Ocean, and the twin moons would rise in the east. For the past month, the paths of the two moons had been drawing closer and closer together. Tonight they would eclipse.

Any child born tonight would be Embraced. How many parents would be horrified when that happened? Brody had been fortunate that his family had loved him as he was. Until he'd lost them.

He shoved those thoughts aside, for he'd learned the hard way that he couldn't afford to lose his concentration while flying. After a few minutes, he spotted the small army camp. He swooped down to land behind some bushes, then shifted into his usual canine form. As he trotted into camp, the guards, who were accustomed to seeing him, merely called out a greeting as he passed by.

He scratched at the closed flap of Nevis's tent and gave a loud bark.

"Brody, is that you?" Nevis lifted the flap with one hand, his other hand holding a half-eaten pork chop.

Food. Brody dashed inside. The heavenly scent of freshly cooked meat led him straight to the desk, where a lit candlestick illuminated a tray filled with five different dishes. Nevis was having a huge dinner.

"What are you doing here? I thought you were supposed to be on a ship with—sheesh." Nevis stopped talking when Brody shifted into human form and helped himself to a pork chop. "Put on some breeches, will you?" He tossed him a pair.

Brody caught them with one hand while he continued to eat the pork chop. After hours of swimming and flying, he was starving.

"If you're here, you must have uncovered something important. What is it?" Nevis asked, but Brody kept eating. "Hey, you're eating all my food!"

"And it's delicious," Brody mumbled with his mouth full.

Nevis snorted. "Fine. I'll bring some more."

In between bites, Brody pulled on Nevis's breeches. They sagged around the waist, so he sat in Nevis's chair to keep them from falling down. He was just finishing the last morsel of food when Nevis strode inside the tent with another tray and pitcher of wine.

"Here you go." Nevis set the new tray next to the old

one that was now stacked with empty dishes. "Damn, Brody. Are you sure you're actually human and not a pig?"

With a pig-like snort, Brody pulled at the waist of Nevis's breeches to show how loose they were. "I'm not the one carrying extra pounds."

"This is muscle." Nevis tapped his extra-wide stomach.

"Right." Brody grabbed a loaf of bread off the new tray, tore it in half, and handed a piece to Nevis. "I have news." While he slathered butter on his bread, he explained how one of Queen Luciana's sisters had been kidnapped.

"Damn." Nevis dropped his piece of bread on the tray. "I had no idea Brigitta was a Tourinian princess."

"Neither did I." Brody ate his half of the bread.

"And that bastard Rupert took her," Nevis grumbled. "I've been trying to capture him for months."

"He'll be hard to catch. The local people will protect him. They consider him a hero."

"What? Why?"

Brody downed his cup of wine, then described what had happened with the three pirate ships.

Nevis stiffened. "So two of the ships were run aground? Where?"

"About five miles north of here. The men were scrambling to get ashore."

"Now you tell me?" Nevis shoved the flap of his tent open and yelled at his men to ready their horses. "We ride now!" He dashed about the tent, grabbing his weapons. "Dammit. You should have told me that right away!"

Brody shrugged as he helped himself to Nevis's discarded piece of bread. "I think you should send a message to Leo that Brigitta and Sister Fallyn are safe. I'll go back to the ship to keep an eye on them."

"Write the message yourself," Nevis growled as he buckled on his sword belt. "If all goes well, I can deliver it to Ebton along with some pirates." He ran outside, and soon Brody could hear the sound of his troop charging away on horseback.

Brody refilled his cup with wine, then removed the first tray from the desk so he would have room to write. After a brief description of all that had happened, he added a few lines about Rupert.

I believe he will keep the ladies safe. In fact, he seems intent on keeping all the Eberoni people safe. The only one he steals from is the Tourinian king, whom he hates. I don't know why yet.

I will continue to watch over the women and keep you informed.

Brody signed the letter, then smiled at the food on the second tray. It would be a shame for any of it to go to waste.

Still hidden behind the barrels, Brigitta watched the dinghy from the last surviving ship slowly approach. There were four men on board—two rowers and two sitting stiffly with feathered hats on their heads. They must be the captain and an officer, coming to surrender their ship.

She glanced up at Rupert, who was standing perfectly still in the crow's nest. Apparently, he wasn't going to use his power to move closer to the dinghy and make it easier for the surrendering pirates.

Meanwhile, Captain Landers was busy giving orders. Sails were lowered, the anchor dropped. Was Rupert intending to stop here for the night?

As the dinghy drew near, Captain Landers had the crew line up, all well dressed in clean clothes with sword belts strapped on. A display of power and wealth, Brigitta assumed. She also figured Rupert would be coming down from the crow's nest to meet the newcomers, so she had better move belowdecks before he or the captain spotted her.

"Let's go," she whispered to Jeffrey, and they scurried back along the wall, then slipped through the door.

Sister Fallyn was sitting on the bottom step and jumped up when they descended a few stairs. "Finally! I was so worried. These pirates are having a bad influence on you, lass. Ye're doing things that are far too dangerous."

"No one saw us." Brigitta assured her, then described everything that had happened.

"So the even-more-evil pirates are coming onboard?" Sister Fallyn motioned toward Jeffrey, who lingered at the top of the stairs. "Quickly, child, close that door!"

Jeffrey peered outside. "They've arrived."

"Wait." Brigitta stopped him from shutting the door all the way. "I want to hear them."

Sister Fallyn scoffed. "We mustn't let them see us. They would ravish us for sure!"

"I'll be careful." Brigitta eased close to the crack in the door and heard Captain Landers introducing himself and Admiral Rupert in the Tourinian language.

"I am Captain Wermer," a gruff voice replied, then mumbled something Brigitta couldn't catch. She opened the door a bit wider.

"Don't ye dare go out there," Sister Fallyn whispered. "'Tis too dangerous."

"I know." Brigitta hunched down on the first step next to Jeffrey.

"And this is my first officer," Captain Wermer said. "Commander Stahl."

Sister Fallyn gasped.

"What's wrong?" Brigitta asked, but the nun hushed her and leaned over Jeffrey to listen.

"An honor to meet you, Admiral, Captain," the commander said.

Sister Fallyn gasped again, a hand pressed to her chest. "Nay. It cannot be."

"What?" Brigitta whispered.

Without warning, Sister Fallyn barreled past her and Jeffrey and dashed out the door.

"Wait!" Brigitta ran after her.

The nun darted around the line of seamen, then stopped with a jerk. Brigitta caught up with her and winced at the disapproving glares from Rupert and Captain Landers. The new captain and commander were looking them over with annoying smirks.

"Ladies." Captain Landers strode toward them and lowered his voice. "Please return to your cabins *now*."

"Sorry," Brigitta murmured as she tugged on Sister Fallyn's arm, but the nun remained frozen as she stared at Commander Stahl.

"Kennet," she whispered.

A trace of shock crossed the commander's face before he turned away with an air of indifference.

Brigitta's breath caught. This man was Kennet?

Sister Fallyn's eyes misted with tears as she stepped closer to him and spoke in the Tourinian language. "It is you, isn't it?"

Captain Landers's eyes narrowed on the commander. "You know this woman?"

The commander scoffed. "How would I know a nun?"

Captain Wermer cast him a wary look. "Your given name is Kennet."

"You're alive." A tear slid down Sister Fallyn's cheek.

"Why didn't you let me know? All these years, I thought you were dead!"

"You know this man?" Rupert asked her.

"Yes, I—" Sister Fallyn began, but the commander interrupted her.

"She's confusing me with someone else! She doesn't know—"

"I would know my own husband!" Sister Fallyn cried.

Captain Landers stiffened, then his eyes hardened as he glared at the commander.

Kennet muttered a curse. "That was a long time ago, you stupid wench."

Sister Fallyn flinched.

"Watch your tongue," Captain Landers growled.

"What happened to you?" Sister Fallyn eyed him warily, her expression both injured and confused. "I thought my father's men had killed you."

Kennet snorted. "They paid me to leave you. Why the hell did you become a nun? You were supposed to go back home."

Sister Fallyn stumbled back a step, and Brigitta caught her. "Y-you left me? For money?"

He smirked. "Did you really think I wanted to spend the rest of my life stuck on the Isle of Moon working in a butcher shop?"

Sister Fallyn's face crumpled as tears ran down her cheeks. "How . . . ?"

Brigitta couldn't bear to watch anymore. She wrapped an arm around the nun. "Let's go," she whispered in Eberoni.

With clenched fists, Captain Landers stepped toward the commander. "You abandoned your wife?"

Kennet snorted. "Come now, we're all pirates here. We'll do anything for gold. I got twenty pieces—"

Crack. Captain Landers fist slammed into Kennet's

face, and the man fell back onto his rear. His feathered hat flew off his head, and a sudden breeze blew it overboard.

Yes! Brigitta had been raised to abhor violence, but the sight of Kennet's bloodied lip was oddly satisfying. And she suspected Rupert was responsible for the loss of the commander's fancy hat.

With a grimace, Kennet sat up and rubbed his jaw. "Fine. You avenged her. We'll call it even."

"No, we will not," Rupert said, his voice edged with steel. "If you cannot be loyal to a wife, how can I expect you to be loyal to me?"

"What?" Kennet hefted himself to his feet. "Forget the wench. I'm a good pirate. I'll serve you well!"

Rupert ignored him and turned to Captain Wermer. "I'll accept you and your men, but not your commander. He will be put ashore."

Captain Wermer nodded. "I understand."

"You can't do this to me!" Kennet shouted. "I'll be penniless."

"I'll take him ashore," Captain Landers offered, and from the rage burning in his eyes, Brigitta suspected the captain was planning a little more violence.

Kennet shot an angry look at Sister Fallyn. "This is all your fault, you stupid—"

"Watch it!" Captain Landers raised his fist, ready to strike.

"Oh, I see." Kennet smirked. "You've done quite well for yourself, haven't you, Fallyn? You're not a nun at all, are you? You're the captain's whore."

Sister Fallyn gasped, and Captain Landers struck the commander hard, knocking him out.

"Sister," Brigitta whispered. "We should go below."

"But—" A look of panic streaked across the nun's face. "What should I do? Aren't I still married to him?"

Captain Landers frowned at her. "Do you still wish to be with him?"

"No!" Sister Fallyn cried, and the captain looked relieved.

"Madam," Rupert said. "You should have no trouble getting the marriage annulled due to abandonment."

"Oh." Sister Fallyn cast one last look at the unconscious Kennet, then turned away. She simply stood there, looking dumbstruck, so Brigitta led her back to the stairs.

"Is there anything you need?" Jeffrey asked as he followed them to their room.

"Perhaps some more wine," Brigitta told him, and he rushed off. She shut the cabin door as Sister Fallyn collapsed silently on a chair. "Are ye all right?"

The nun remained silent.

"Ye must have been terribly shocked." Brigitta filled a cup with wine. "I know I was."

Still no reply. Sister Fallyn was staring into space.

"Something to drink?" Brigitta offered her the cup. When the nun didn't budge, she sighed. "Well, at least we know that yer father didn't have someone killed."

Sister Fallyn blinked. "Nay, he just offered Kennet twenty pieces of gold." Her face crumbled. "And he took it! I thought he loved me, but he left me!"

"I'm so sorry."

"He betrayed me! How dare he!" Sister Fallyn grabbed the cup and downed it.

"That's it. Ye should be angry." Relieved that the nun had come out of her shock, Brigitta took the empty cup and refilled it. "I'd have punched him myself if the captain hadn't done it."

Sister Fallyn shuddered. "Such violent behavior. But I suppose it is to be expected from a pirate."

"Actually I found it quite satisfying."

A small smile twitched at Sister Fallyn's mouth. "It was a bit, wasn't it?"

"Aye." Brigitta smiled as she handed her the cup.

The nun drank it, then sighed. "I fear these pirates are a bad influence on us. We mustn't forget our training." She winced. "Am I even a nun? Did my vow count when I was still under the vows of marriage?"

"Yer intent was sincere, so I would think it counted."

With a frustrated groan, Sister Fallyn jumped to her feet. "Why did I ever marry that . . . that . . ."

"Bastard?" Brigitta poured more wine into her cup.

Sister Fallyn looked appalled for a second, then nodded. "Ye're right. He's a bastard." She grabbed the cup and drank it down. "All men are bastards!"

"I wouldn't say that." Brigitta recalled how much she'd enjoyed seeing Rupert reject Kennet.

"Oh, they are." Sister Fallyn strode to the sideboard to refill her cup. "'Tis just as I told you. There are no good men from Tourin."

"I think Rupert and Captain Landers are all right."

Sister Fallyn shook her head. "They're still pirates."

"The captain was very quick to defend yer honor."

The nun paused a moment, her cheeks blushing. "I— we mustn't allow ourselves to be swayed. They're not like the dashing young heroes in the stories ye write."

Brigitta hesitated as an alarming thought crossed her mind. Was she being swayed? She'd already convinced herself that Rupert was an amazing man. Handsome and capable of acting in an honorable manner. And even though he was a Wind Sorcerer, she could hardly blame him for being Embraced when she was, too. But like Sister Fallyn said, he was still a pirate. He'd captured her so he could use her to earn a hefty ransom.

Instead of admiring him, she should be angry with

him. And even though he piqued her curiosity, uncovering his secrets should be viewed purely as a mental exercise. Nothing more. She could never allow herself to trust him. Or be attracted to him.

A knock sounded on the door, then Jeffrey peeked in. "I brought you some dinner."

"Oh, thank you." Brigitta rushed over to relieve the boy of the heavy tray. "Ye should let me know when ye're bringing food. This is too heavy for yerself."

"Oh, I can handle it." Jeffrey smiled. "I want to have big muscles like Rupert."

Brigitta sighed as she set the tray on the table. "His muscles are rather big." *Don't think about him like that.*

"Not any bigger than the captain's," Sister Fallyn muttered. When Brigitta gave her a curious look, she cleared her throat. "Jeffrey, what is happening now?"

He scratched his head. "Not much. Everyone's having dinner. The other ships are busy exchanging crewmen with the new ship. Oh, Rupert wanted you to know that none of the new pirates will be here on the *Golden Star*. He didn't take any 'cause he wanted to be sure you would be safe."

Sister Fallyn scoffed. "He might as well admit that they would want to ravish us."

"Please convey our gratitude," Brigitta told the boy. "Is the ship going to remain here for the night?"

Jeffrey nodded. "The sun will be setting soon. I have a cot at the end of the passageway, so let me know if you need anything."

"Thank you." Brigitta walked him to the door.

After she and Sister Fallyn ate their dinner, they soon grew bored. Brigitta opened the window to let in some fresh air. The sky was turning pink and gold as the sun neared the horizon.

"I suppose Mother Ginessa and the girls will have arrived in Ebton by now," Sister Fallyn grumbled as she poured the last of the wine into her cup.

"Probably so." Brigitta curled up on the window seat and rested her elbows on her knees. Would Luciana be upset when she learned what had happened? "Tomorrow they'll have a birthday celebration for Luciana and Sorcha."

"Oh, that's right." Sister Fallyn sipped some wine. "They were both born on the Spring Embrace."

And Luciana's baby was due in a few days, Brigitta thought. She would miss the birthing. She already missed her sisters. Tears crowded her eyes, but she blinked them away. Feeling sorry for herself wasn't going to change anything. "We should do something."

"Like what?" Sister Fallyn took another sip.

Brigitta frowned. She'd never seen Sister Fallyn drink this much. No doubt the poor woman was still upset. "I know. Let's try on Sister Ellen's clothes!"

"Why bother?" Sister Fallyn mumbled.

"'Twill be fun." Brigitta strode over to the bed to pick up the gown. "'Tis lovely, don't ye think?"

Sister Fallyn shrugged and finished her cup.

"I think it'll fit yerself better than me." Brigitta held it out to the nun. "Come on, I want to see how beautiful ye look."

Sister Fallyn snorted. "Would Kennet have left me if I was truly beautiful?"

"Ye are beautiful, Sister. And we've already established that Kennet is a bastard. I would say ye're much better off without him."

Sister Fallyn nodded slowly. "Ye have a point." She eyed the gown warily. "'Tis much prettier than I've ever worn before."

"Let's do it!" Brigitta laid the gown over the back of a chair, then fumbled through the bag of clothing to find a pretty shift and matching shoes.

Soon Sister Fallyn was dressed. The blue velvet gown fit her perfectly around the waist, but the skirt was a trifle short.

Brigitta clasped her hands together. "Look at you! Ye're truly stunning!"

The nun shook her head, her cheeks pink. "I feel like my breasts are falling out. And my ankles are showing."

"Come, sit down." Brigitta drew her to a chair. "We should do yer hair."

"'Tis not necessary."

"Ye have lovely hair." Brigitta unraveled the long blond braid, then combed through it with her fingers.

A knock sounded on the door.

Sister Fallyn lurched to her feet and nearly fell over. "Good goddesses, my head is spinning."

Brigitta steadied her. "Ye drank a bit more than usual, but don't worry. I'm sure it's only Jeffrey."

The boy peeked inside and blinked at Sister Fallyn. "Jeepers. You look like a queen."

"I—don't be silly." The nun pressed a hand to her chest to cover up the exposed skin.

Jeffrey scurried inside. "I came for your dinner tray."

"Thank you." Brigitta handed it to him, and he headed out the door.

"Oh, good evening, Captain." Jeffrey's voice filtered from the passageway.

Sister Fallyn gasped. "Quick! Close the door."

Brigitta dashed toward the door just as Captain Landers peered inside.

"Good evening, my lady," he greeted Brigitta. Then his gaze landed on Sister Fallyn and his mouth dropped open.

Brigitta glanced at the nun, who was frozen in shock, then looked back at the captain. Oh dear, if she wasn't mistaken this resembled a scene from one of her *overly dramatic* stories. "Captain, how kind of you to drop by."

He didn't seem to hear her.

She cleared her throat. "Captain Landers?"

He blinked. "Ah yes, I-I would prefer that you call me Stefan. I wanted to make sure you were both comfortable."

"We are," Brigitta assured him. "Aren't we, Sister?"

Sister Fallyn suddenly remembered to breathe, and her breasts nearly popped out.

The captain's eyes bulged and he audibly gulped.

"Was there anything else?" Brigitta asked.

Stefan tugged at his shirt collar. "Yes. I-I wanted to assure you that Commander Stahl was taken ashore. You should never have to see him again."

Sister Fallyn nodded.

"Also . . ." The captain withdrew a folded sheet of paper from his coat. "I took the liberty of having the commander write this. He has declared the marriage null and void and vows he will make no future claim on you."

Sister Fallyn's blush faded away as she grew pale.

The captain unfolded the paper and set it on the table. "You are a free woman, Mistress Fallyn."

Tears glistened in her eyes.

"I-I'll be going then." Stefan headed toward the door. "Good evening, Lady Brigitta."

"Good evening," Brigitta replied.

He paused in the doorway to glance back. "Good evening, Mistress Fallyn."

She winced. "'Tis Sister Fallyn."

His gaze grew more intense as the seconds ticked by and he continued to stare at her. "Mistress Fallyn, you will never be a nun to me." He left, closing the door behind him.

Sister Fallyn's knees gave out and she collapsed onto the floor.

Chapter Eight

❧

Luciana, the queen of Eberon, hurried down the grand staircase of Ebton Palace as quickly as she dared. With her belly so huge, she could scarcely see her feet.

"Careful." Her husband, Leo, bounded up the stairs to take her arm.

"Is it true?" she asked. "Has the ship been sighted?"

"They're tying off at the pier right now."

Luciana's heart leaped in her chest. It had been eight months since she'd last seen her sisters. "I'm so happy they're finally here! And so relieved they've arrived safely."

"I'm relieved Mother Ginessa is coming with them," Leo said as he helped her down the stairs. "Your father says she's the best midwife around."

Luciana patted his arm. "Don't worry. The babies and I will be fine." A few months ago, she'd become convinced that she was having twins. Since then, she'd doubled her efforts in order to have enough clothing and supplies for two babes. She was fairly certain at least one of them was a girl. The other, she wasn't so sure. Of course, Leo was hoping for a boy and heir to the Eberon throne.

So far, her pregnancy had gone well, and she'd been blessed with an abundance of energy. Over the past month, she'd had several gowns made for each of her sisters. She'd furnished a bedchamber for each of them in the palace. And she'd arranged for a grand ball to happen tomorrow night, supposedly to celebrate Sorcha's eighteenth birthday and her own twentieth birthday. Her true purpose, though, was to introduce her sisters to some eligible young noblemen.

This time, she would convince Mother Ginessa to let her sisters live with her. For some secret reason, Mother Ginessa thought it would be too dangerous, but Luciana was positive she could keep her sisters safe here at Ebton Palace. After all, who would dare risk the wrath of her husband, the king? Leo was famous throughout all of Aerthlan for his ability to use the power of lightning.

Finally they reached the ground floor and dashed toward the castle entrance that overlooked the Ebe River. Or rather, Leo dashed. Her walk, unfortunately, looked more like a duck waddle.

Leo smiled as he slowed his steps to match hers. "There's no need to hurry. If all goes well, your sisters will be here for a long time."

Luciana nodded. "Definitely." As they stepped outside onto the massive front terrace, she shielded her eyes from the setting sun.

There they were! "Look!" She motioned to the group of young women hurrying down the pier.

"Chee-ana!" Maeve yelled and lifted her skirt to run.

Luciana grinned as more of her sisters sprinted toward her. Leo guided her down the stairs to the pier, and as soon as she arrived, Maeve flung her arms around her. Then Gwennore and Sorcha.

"Look at yerself!" Sorcha stepped back, her eyes widening. "Ye're so huge!"

Luciana laughed. "I'm having twins!"

They all gasped, then hugged her again.

Leo bowed. "Welcome to Ebton Palace." As he continued to chat with them, Luciana wondered why Brigitta was taking her time. She glanced at Mother Ginessa, who was approaching at a slower pace. No Brigitta. She looked at the ship. The captain was disembarking. Alone.

She turned to her sisters. "Where is Brigitta?"

Their smiles faded. Sorcha and Gwennore exchanged worried glances, and Maeve ducked her head, studying her feet.

Luciana's chest tightened. "Is something wrong? Is she ill? Was she unable to travel?"

"There ye are, child." Mother Ginessa reached her and gave her a hug.

"I'm so glad you're here," Luciana told her.

Mother Ginessa rested a hand on Luciana's belly. "Ye seem to be doing well."

"Aye. Where is Brigitta? Has something happened to her?"

With a sigh, Mother Ginessa glanced back at the captain. "Captain Shaw will make arrangements with yer husband to get her back. I think we'd better—"

"What do you mean, *get her back*?" Luciana cried.

Leo ran toward the captain, and they began talking in urgent tones.

Mother Ginessa took hold of Luciana's hands. "Ye must remain calm now—"

"No!" Fear skittered down Luciana's spine, chilling her to the bone. "What's happened to Brigitta?"

"I think we should go inside so ye can sit—"

"Nay!" Luciana interrupted as panic set in. "Ye have to tell me!"

Mother Ginessa drew a deep breath. "First, I should tell ye that Brigitta is the Tourinian princess."

"What?" Luciana's heart stuttered. She should have known this. The last time she'd played the Game of Stones with Brigitta, she'd realized that the blue and gold stones referred to Tourin. And she'd sensed some sort of danger. But as hard as she'd tried, she hadn't been able to discern more than that.

"The Tourinian navy surrounded us at sea," Mother Ginessa continued. "They intended to take Brigitta, but then some pirates stopped them."

Luciana gasped. "Pi-pirates?" The world swirled around her, and she swayed on her feet.

Mother Ginessa grabbed her arm to steady her. "This is too stressful for yerself. We must get ye inside—"

"What—" Luciana struggled to catch her breath. "What happened to her?"

"The pirate Rupert took her and Sister Fallyn," Gwennore said softly.

Luciana pressed a hand to her chest as it became even harder to breathe. Rupert? He was the most infamous pirate of all Aerthlan. Some even called him a sorcerer.

Mother Ginessa motioned to Sorcha to take Luciana's other arm. "Quickly. We must take her inside."

A sudden gush flooded Luciana's legs. With a gasp, she stared down at the growing puddle around her slippers.

"What's wrong?" Maeve cried.

"Not to worry." Mother Ginessa assured them. "The babe has decided to come early."

"There are two of them." Luciana touched her belly. "And I thought I had a few more days."

"They will most likely be born tonight," Mother Ginessa replied. "Sorcha, let's take her to her room. Maeve, inform her husband—"

"Holy goddesses," Gwennore whispered. "Tonight the moons are embracing."

Everyone stilled for a moment as they realized what would happen.

Luciana's children would be Embraced.

Hours later, Brigitta was gazing out the small window in their cabin. There wasn't much else to do. She didn't want to disturb Sister Fallyn, who had finally drifted off to sleep on the narrow bed. And since the sun had set, it was too dark in their room to read the book Jeffrey had left.

With nothing to occupy her thoughts, her mind kept wandering into forbidden territory—Rupert. Who was he really? He seemed well educated, so what sort of circumstances had led him to become a pirate? Why did he disguise himself with a mask and false hair? Had he been forced to leave Tourin because he was Embraced?

There had to be some clues in the vision she'd seen when she'd last touched him. Arrows in the back. Blood and screams. An ambush? Her view of the scene must have been how Rupert had witnessed it, and the flood of grief and terror she'd felt had also been his. What a terrible experience!

Since it was her first vision from him, she suspected it was his most powerful memory. Not only traumatic for him, but a defining moment that had changed his life forever.

It was the strongest vision she'd ever received from anyone. And she'd passed out the first time she'd touched Rupert. Was it because she'd never encountered someone hiding as much as him? Or was there something special about him? *What if he's your tall and handsome stranger?* a small voice inside her wondered, but she quickly rejected that thought.

He'd taken her against her will by threatening the lives of her sisters. He intended to ransom her for gold. According to Lieutenant Helgar of the Tourinian navy, he

was an evil sorcerer, responsible for destroying their ships
and burning the officer.

*But he defended Sister Fallyn. He protected the town
of Danport from the bad pirates. He sent the Eberoni
navy away without harming them. And he helped Sister
Ellen escape to the safety of the Isle of Moon.*

Hero or evil sorcerer? With a groan, she stood and
stretched her legs. She didn't know what to think. Her
emotions waffled between anger and insatiable curiosity.
And something more, something that made her heart race
whenever he was near and watching her with his golden
eyes. Or floating his deep voice to her on a soft breeze
that tickled her ears.

Stop thinking about him!

She needed a diversion, she decided. If everyone was
asleep, she should be able to walk about on deck. She'd
already changed into the pretty nightgown from Sister
Ellen, so she threw her cloak on top, then eased into the
dim passageway. The sound of Jeffrey's soft breathing
emanated from the far end of the corridor. Moonlight filtered in from the open doorway at the top of the stairs,
and she inched toward it, silent in her bare feet.

On deck, she could spot only two sailors at the bow of
the ship keeping watch and a helmsman resting on a
trunk on the quarterdeck. A large pelican was roosting
on top of a closed barrel. She glanced up at the crow's
nest. Empty. Rupert must be asleep somewhere. Good.
The last thing she needed was him staring at her as if he
was trying to read her mind. How embarrassing it would
be if he knew how much he was in her thoughts!

She wandered to the midship port railing. A lantern
was lit there, surrounded in red glass. Over on the starboard side, a blue lantern was lit. As she gazed out to sea,
she saw more red and blue lanterns. Nine of each. This

must be how the ships in Rupert's fleet kept up with one another at night.

A gentle breeze caressed her face with fresh, salty air. The sea lapped against the sides of the ship with soft, swooshing noises. Overhead the twin moons were embraced, the smaller Lessa resting in front of the larger Luna. Together they shone more brightly than usual, and the ocean beneath them sparkled as if jewels had been scattered as far as she could see.

But she was too worried to enjoy the view. What would become of her and Sister Fallyn? And what had happened to the dog, Brody? She could only hope she'd been mistaken and he'd remained on board with her sisters.

"Please be all right," she whispered.

And how was Luciana doing? She must know by now that Brigitta and Sister Fallyn had been taken. If only there was a way to let Luciana know she was safe. Brigitta didn't want her to worry when her baby was due so soon.

A pang of self-pity pricked at Brigitta. She would miss the child's birth. Miss the birthday celebration for Luciana and Sorcha. By the goddesses, she missed all of her sisters something fierce.

Tears burned her eyes as she realized she might never see them again. Even when she was free from Rupert, she'd be under Gunther's control. And since the mainland kingdoms were often at war, she doubted her brother would let her live with a neighboring king and queen. He might not even let her visit.

The words from the Song of Mourning filled her head. Bereaved women from the Isle of Moon sang it whenever they lost their men at sea. Right now, it felt like she'd lost her entire family.

A tear rolled down her cheek, and, with a trembling

voice, she sang, "My true love lies in the ocean blue. My true love sleeps in the sea. Whenever the moons shine over you, please remember me. Please remem—"

Her voice broke, and she wiped away more tears. This wasn't going to solve anything. If she wanted to be the author of her own destiny, she would have to be strong. And smart. And brave.

"Good evening." A deep voice drifted toward her, speaking in Tourinian.

Rupert. Behind her. Her heart sprang into a quick beat. *He's not a hero*, she reminded herself. The scoundrel had kidnapped her. She mustn't appear nervous or flustered in front of him. Even if she was suddenly aware that she had nothing on but a thin nightgown and cloak. She clutched the edges of the cloak together. *Be brave.*

"That was a pretty song." His whisper tickled her ear.

Oh, but there was something about his voice that made her feel weak in the knees. *Be strong.* She responded in Tourinian, "I thought I would be alone. I didn't mean to wake anyone." *Especially you.*

"I was still awake." The deck creaked behind her as he came closer. "I prefer to sleep on the quarterdeck, so I can be under the stars and open sky."

It sounded like he wanted to feel free. But the scoundrel didn't mind holding her captive. *Be smart.* "Enjoy the open sky while you can. Once you're captured, you'll be locked away for good in a dark dungeon. If not worse."

"How could anyone capture me when I can simply blow them away?"

She snorted. He seemed so blasted sure of himself. "Full of hot air, are you?"

He chuckled as he reached the railing beside her.

Still wearing that ridiculous mask and hat with the fake hair, she noted. Did he even sleep with them on? She was tempted to rip them off herself.

He frowned at her. "You've been crying."

"Why shouldn't I? I'm a prisoner here, aren't I?"

His mouth thinned. "I have no wish to harm you."

"Then let me go."

"You will not have any more freedom with your brother."

That was probably true. She groaned inwardly. "Do you know why my brother wants me?"

"No. But I know he wouldn't have sent for you if it didn't benefit him in some way."

How did kings benefit from using princesses? She thought back to her history lessons. "Do you think he has plans to marry me off to gain an ally?"

His jaw shifted as he grabbed on to the railing. "Perhaps."

"According to Sister Fallyn, I'm already betrothed."

His grip tightened till his knuckles turned white. "How . . ." He gave her a wary look. "What else did she tell you?"

Brigitta sighed. "A terrible story. I'd rather not repeat it. Or even think about it. I . . ." She turned away as tears burned her eyes. "I come from a family of monsters."

He was quiet for a moment, then said softly, "Don't cry."

She turned toward him. "Don't pretend to care."

A muscle twitched in his cheek, but he said nothing.

She winced inwardly. How could she convince him to do as she wished, if she irritated him? "I didn't mean to sound harsh. The fact is I dread the thought of going to my brother. I really want to be with my sisters."

"You mentioned them before. How can it be that you have sisters?"

"I grew up with them at the Convent of the Two Moons. We were all left there as babes."

"Isn't that the convent that makes books?"

She nodded. "The best books in the world. Transcribed in all four mainland languages."

"So that's why you speak Tourinian so well." He smiled. "A little bit of an accent, but I like it."

Her heart warmed, then she chided herself. Why should she care what he thought? Or even notice how lovely his smile was? She quickly changed the subject. "Luciana is my oldest sister. We were on our way to Ebton Palace because she's giving birth soon. I'm afraid she'll be worried about me, and it might cause harm to her and her unborn child. If you would just send me there, she would be more than willing to pay my ransom."

His smile faded. "I already told you my reasons for not doing that."

"I know. There were four," she muttered, then gave him a curious look. "What was your fifth reason?"

His gaze narrowed, his eyes a shimmering gold. Her heartbeat quickened and once again, she was acutely aware that she was naked beneath her thin nightgown and cloak. As his gaze wandered over her, her skin tingled as if she'd been laid bare.

He turned suddenly toward the sea. "I don't recall."

He did remember, she was sure of it, but for some reason he didn't want to tell her. She hunched her shoulders, tightening her grip on her cloak. He was definitely the most secretive man she'd ever met.

She eyed the fake plaits, her hands itching to jerk the silly hat off his head. But if she touched him or anything that belonged to him, she might have another vision. *Would that be so bad?* It might give her more clues to figuring out his secrets.

His gaze returned to her, and the heat in his eyes had cooled to clear amber. "Your song was for your sisters then?"

"Yes."

His mouth curled into a teasing smile. "For a moment I thought you might be mourning a lost lover."

She scoffed. "I grew up in a convent. I haven't seen that many men."

His eyes flared with heat again. "A man would need only a glimpse of you to know you are a treasure."

Her heart lurched. "I-I should be going now." She took a few steps toward the entrance to the cabins. "Enjoy the stars and open sky."

"And the embraced moons," he said quietly as she retreated another step. "Today is my birthday."

She halted. Of course. He was Embraced. The two moons aligned twice a year, once in the spring and once in the fall, always around the same time.

Did he have no one to celebrate with? He looked so alone, standing there gazing at the moons. She opened her mouth to say her birthday would be at the Autumn Embrace, but thought better of it. Being Embraced was still a crime in Tourin, so she should keep it secret. "I hope you had a good day."

He glanced back at her and smiled. "It has been one I shall always remember."

Did he mean because of her? Goddesses help her, why did she want to be special to this man? Was it simply her curiosity that drew her to him, or was it more? "So how old are you now?"

"Twenty-six."

Seven years older than her. "I'm—"

"Nineteen," he finished for her.

"How did you know?"

He shrugged.

He wasn't going to tell her. The man was simply too annoying. "You said those Eberoni naval ships wouldn't

know who I was or that I had been captured. So how did
you know the Tourinian navy planned to take me? How
did you know who I am?"

He shrugged again. "I can't say."

She narrowed her eyes. Blast this man and his secrets.

"Let me ask you something." He stepped closer. "Why
do you keep fainting? Are you suffering from some kind
of illness?"

She shrugged. "I can't say."

His mouth tilted up. "Stalemate. It appears we both
have questions we want answered. Perhaps I should warn
you. I'm quite good at detecting secrets."

"Not as good as I."

He stepped closer. "You intend to compete with me?"

"I intend to win." Her heart pounded as she reached
up and yanked on one of his plaits. A vision of a black
horse flashed across her mind, then disappeared, leaving her with an amusing sight. His hat had spun around
sideways, leaving plaits to dangle in front of his face. It
looked so funny, she laughed.

He grabbed his hat to right it. "What the . . . ?"

"There goes one of *your* secrets. Fake hair."

"It's real," he insisted.

"Real horsehair, I would say."

With a muttered curse, he tossed his hat on the deck.
"How did you know?"

She grinned, relishing her victory. "Your hair should be
under your scarf, not over. And I doubt your hair is actually black. The whiskers along your jaw are a golden
brown. Even the hair on your chest—" She stopped with a
wince. Good goddesses, she was saying far too much.

He leaned closer to her and lowered his voice. "Have
you been studying me?"

Warmth invaded her cheeks. "I'm naturally a very
observant person." She lifted her chin. "But that hardly

matters, for I have won the competition, and you have been exposed. You might as well take off the mask, too. Why bother to hide your handsome—" Her face blazed hotter.

His eyes smoldered like molten gold. "You were saying?"

Saying far too much, she was. Whenever his gaze grew heated or he lowered his voice, she became too flustered. She waved a dismissive hand. "I only assumed that you might possibly be handsome. I'm a kind person, so I naturally give people the benefit of the doubt."

His eyes twinkled with amusement. "That is kind of you. Thank you."

"Don't mention it." She cleared her throat. "The point is your disguise is no longer necessary."

"I still need to conceal my identity."

"Why? Everyone knows you're Rupert." A sudden thought occurred to her. "Oh, that's not your real name, is it?"

The muscle in his jaw twitched again.

She grinned. Victory again! Another secret uncovered. "Don't worry. I won't tell anyone."

"You are Gunther's sister," he muttered. "I cannot possibly trust you."

She huffed. "I don't know him. And I don't want to know him. I heard he murdered my younger brother."

"You share his blood. You're from the House of Grian."

Her hands curled into fists as she clutched her cloak. "Sister Fallyn told me what my father did. He was a monster. My brother is a monster, too. I want nothing to do with them!"

Rupert gave her a dubious look. "Don't you want to be a princess?"

"No! I just want to be with my sisters. Why can't I go where I want to? Why can't I control my own destiny?"

He stiffened, a look of shock crossing his face.

She took a deep breath. It didn't help matters to lose her temper. She needed to remain calm. "You control the wind. You control ten ships now and all the people on board. You can whisk away an entire navy. Surely you understand the value of being in control."

He turned away, his hands clenched into fists.

She'd touched on a nerve, she was sure of it. "Why on Aerthlan would you want to control me?"

He shot her an incredulous look. "Since when can I control you? You were told to stay belowdecks, but you sneaked up here to hide behind those barrels."

She blinked. "Y-you noticed that?"

"I notice everything about you, Brigitta."

Her skin prickled as a strange feeling swept over her, a feeling that she was somehow connected to this man. In the past and in the future. But who was he? And why did he say her name as if he knew her?

She had to find out more about him. And there was one sure way to do it.

Steeling her nerves, she planted a hand upon his chest. A wave of images struck her hard, and she reeled back from the intensity. Goddesses help her, it was as if she were there. On a battlefield. Swords slashed, blood sprayed, screams rent the air. Horses shrieked, axes swung, and the smell of blood and mangled limbs nauseated her.

Horror flooded her senses, along with a stab of grief so fierce, her knees buckled. As she collapsed, her heart ached for Rupert. For one thing was certain.

All this horror and grief had been his.

Chapter Nine

"Brigitta!" Rupert grabbed her as she crumpled in front of him. *What the hell?* He swept her up in his arms.

Her head rolled to the side, coming to rest upon his chest. Her eyes were closed now, her face pale, but he'd seen the look of horror and pain flash across her features. And it had happened right after she'd touched him.

Dammit to hell! Was he some kind of poison to her? This was the third time she'd reacted badly after coming into contact with him.

"Brigitta?" He lifted her higher against him, so he could peer at her face. "What's wrong? Do I need to find a healer for you?"

Her brow furrowed as she grimaced, her eyes squeezed shut. "I-I'm so sorry," she whispered.

His chest tightened. "For what?" She'd done nothing wrong. As far as he could tell, she was completely innocent. She didn't deserve to be used by him or her brother. When she didn't answer, he whispered back, "No, I'm the one who's sorry."

Her eyes flickered open, then grew wide as she gazed at his face just a few inches away.

Such a lovely shade of turquoise. Her eyes reminded

him of the sea close to a white, sandy shore. Clear and pure. No guile or cruelty hidden in their depths. Could it be she was nothing like the other members of her family? She'd called them monsters. Claimed to want nothing to do with her brother.

His grip on her tightened. By the Light, he wanted her to be exactly as she appeared. A beautiful, clever, sweet, and caring woman. *His* woman.

His gaze wandered down her body. Her cloak had fallen open, revealing a thin white nightgown that barely concealed sweet feminine lines and curves. His groin reacted. How easy it would be to unravel that blue ribbon at her neckline and expose her breasts. How tempting it would be to slip his hand beneath the hem.

"Put me down."

He glanced back at her face and noted the alarm in her eyes. Holy shit, he must have been eyeing her like a hungry wolf. "Don't worry. I would never harm you."

She regarded him sadly. "Do you expect me to believe the word of a pirate who has kidnapped me?"

At first, he'd wanted her to believe the worst of him, but damn, that was now becoming increasingly hard to bear. There was a part of him that wanted to show her he could be a good and honorable man who was worthy of her. That part was growing, along with the bulge in his breeches.

And he wanted to know what kind of woman his betrothed had become. That had been his fifth reason for not sending her away. Not that he could ever tell her. Hell, he didn't like to admit it to himself. Her father had killed his father. Hunted down his entire family. He should hate her, but apparently he was a fool who wanted to believe that somehow an evil family had spawned an innocent angel.

He set her on her feet. "Will you be all right now?"

"Yes." She gathered her cloak around her. "I should go now. Good night." She hurried toward the staircase that led belowdecks.

He still didn't know why she kept collapsing. Frustration ground at his nerves. The woman was affecting him mentally, emotionally, and physically. "We'll talk tomorrow."

She glanced back, and he was surprised by the sympathetic look in her eyes.

"Happy birthday, Rupert." She descended the stairs, leaving him to stare at the open doorway.

How many years had it been since anyone had offered him birthday wishes? Stefan had raised him well, but without any sentimentality. He'd always known Rupert would need to be tough to survive.

Don't let a few kind words make you soft. She was still the enemy. And she was figuring out too much about him. Damn, if she ever discovered his true identity, he'd have to hold her prisoner indefinitely. He couldn't risk her passing that information on to her brother. If Gunther knew who he was, all his plans would crumble into dust.

Why can't I control my own destiny? Her words jabbed at him. How could he even contemplate imprisoning her?

He knew too well the despair of being confined. For seven years he'd been forced to hide in caves and basements. That was why he now slept under the open sky.

By the Light, he hated the memory of living in constant fear of being caught and murdered. He hated the smothering cloud of grief and anxiety that had caused him to wake in the middle of the night unable to breathe. And most of all, he hated the utter sense of helplessness.

Yes, he knew the value of control. It wiped away the bad memories and gave him hope. He craved control. Without it, he would never achieve his goal of revenge.

But dammit, he hadn't realized Brigitta would feel just

as strongly about controlling her own future. And he was stealing that control from her.

Why should he care? She was the enemy. *Don't pretend to care.* Her words sliced like a knife.

Dammit to hell. He wasn't pretending. The way she kept collapsing had him worried. He picked up his hat and climbed the stairs to the quarterdeck. Tomorrow he would find out why she reacted like that whenever they came in contact. Did it mean he could never touch her? Or kiss her?

Holy shit, where had that thought come from? With a groan, he stretched out on his pallet.

He gazed up at the moons and stars, but they didn't give him the comfort they usually did. And it would be damned hard to sleep with this bulge in his breeches.

Only a fool would lust after the enemy. *Then you're a bloody fool.* He could deny wanting her till the stars fell from the sky, but his hard cock indicated otherwise.

He'd been too long without a woman, that was all. She wasn't any different from any other woman. *Liar.*

He ripped the mask off his face. *Go ahead, you idiot. Lust after her till your balls turn blue. But don't ever trust her.*

Brigitta woke the next day when Jeffrey brought in their midday meal. She'd slept late since she hadn't been able to use the narrow bed till Sister Fallyn had finally woken at dawn. Brigitta hadn't minded, though, for she'd been far too agitated to relax.

Her mind had replayed her conversation with Rupert over and over. And she'd carefully examined her visions. Somehow, Rupert had survived an ambush and a battle. Had someone wanted him dead? Or perhaps they'd wanted his family members dead, and that was why she felt such overwhelming grief connected to his memories. Could the visions explain why he was hiding his identity and living as a pirate?

She still wasn't sure what to think of him. He made her nervous and excited, confused and angry, and even sympathetic when she recalled the horror and grief he'd endured. And she still wanted to know more about him. Nay, she was driven to know more. The man aroused her curiosity more than anyone she'd ever met.

"Good morning, lad." Sister Fallyn greeted Jeffrey and helped him set the tray on the table.

Brigitta sat up, drawing the blanket up to her chin.

Jeffrey grinned at her. "You slept late. We're on our way to Danport."

"To get supplies?" Sister Fallyn picked up the small loaf off the tray and frowned at it. "I hope ye'll get some fresh bread."

"Aye." Jeffrey nodded. "The captain will make sure of it."

Brigitta slipped on her cloak and approached the table. "Didn't ye say Danport was yer hometown? Are ye going to visit yer relatives?"

Jeffrey made a face. "Only my uncle lives there, and I sure don't want to see him."

Brigitta poured herself a cup of water. "Why not?"

"'Cause he's a mean old drunk," Jeffrey muttered.

"Oh, I'm sorry." Brigitta motioned to one of the chairs. "Would you like to join us?"

He glanced back at the door, then took a seat. "I guess I could stay here a little while."

"Of course." Brigitta sat next to him and passed him a slice of cheese.

Sister Fallyn handed him a piece of buttered bread. "Ye poor lad. Have ye lost yer parents?"

Jeffrey nodded as he ate. "About five years ago."

"Ye must have been so young," Brigitta murmured.

He paused with his mouth full and gave them a sheepish look. "I don't really remember them very well. Is that bad?"

"Nay." Sister Fallyn poured him a cup of water. "'Tis to be expected, lad."

"So how did ye end up on a pirate ship?" Brigitta asked.

Jeffrey drank some water. "Rupert and the captain saved me."

Brigitta's curiosity flared. "How?"

"Well, after my parents died, my uncle took me in, but he made me clean chimneys all day, then he spent the money I earned on whiskey. And if I complained, he hit me."

Brigitta winced. "That's awful."

"Ye poor child." Sister Fallyn regarded him sadly. "Did ye run away?"

"No." Jeffrey shook his head. "I didn't have anywhere to go. But one day, after I'd earned a few coins, I went to the market to buy myself some food. And that's when I saw Rupert and Captain Landers. They were buying supplies. But then my uncle saw me eating an apple, and he started beating on me. And guess what? The captain yelled at him to stop, and when he didn't, Rupert pushed him away!"

"With the wind?" Brigitta asked.

"No, with his hands. Then my uncle said he was my guardian and could treat me however he wanted. And Rupert offered him five gold coins for me!"

Brigitta sat back. "He bought you?"

Sister Fallyn shuddered. "I should have known. These pirates are nothing more than slavers."

"No!" Jeffrey looked appalled. "After my uncle took the gold and ran off, Rupert told me I was free to go. And the captain asked if I had family elsewhere who could

take me. But I don't have anyone else, so they said I could
live here. I like it here." His nose wrinkled. "Except when
they make me read boring books and write essays."

"They're educating you?" Sister Fallyn asked with an
incredulous look and Jeffrey nodded.

"Mostly the captain. He has a ton of books. He taught
Rupert when he was growing up." Jeffrey's small chest
swelled with pride. "And now he's teaching me."

"Are ye saying Captain Landers raised Rupert?" Brigitta asked.

Jeffrey scratched his head. "Well, I think he did." He
shrugged. "Rupert says if I study real hard, I could be a
captain someday."

"Is that what ye want?" Sister Fallyn asked.

"Of course! I want to be like Captain Landers." Jeffrey
lowered his voice. "I can't be like Rupert. He has magical powers."

Brigitta nodded. "I noticed."

Jeffrey beamed. "No one can beat Rupert!"

Brigitta suspected that was true, but Sister Fallyn
scoffed. "All pirates come to a bad end. 'Tis only fitting,
given their evil ways."

Jeffrey frowned at her. "They're not evil."

Sister Fallyn snorted. "They're teaching you to be a
pirate."

"They're not bad," Jeffrey grumbled. "They only steal
from Gunther because he's a stinking—" He gave Brigitta an apologetic look. "Sorry."

"'Tis all right." Brigitta thought back to what Rupert
had said. *The only person I rob is your brother, Gunther.*
Why did Rupert hate the Tourinian king? Was it somehow connected to the visions she'd seen?

A whistle sounded overhead, and Jeffrey jumped up
from his seat.

"I should go." He dashed for the door.

"What's wrong?" Sister Fallyn stood. "Are we going into battle again?"

Jeffrey grinned. "No, they're dropping the anchor. We've arrived in Danport."

As quickly as she could, Brigitta washed up and dressed in the privy one deck below. Sister Fallyn insisted on keeping guard outside the door, since she claimed the mere sight of Brigitta in that thin nightgown would make a man want to ravish her.

Brigitta didn't want to admit that Rupert had already seen her in the nightgown. And if the look on his face had been any indication, he'd certainly had some impure thoughts. Her cheeks still burned whenever she recalled that hungry look in his eyes.

But he hadn't harmed her. He'd rescued Jeffrey. And Sister Ellen. He'd protected the village of Danport.

Could it be true? Her instincts said yes.

Rupert was a man of honor.

Perhaps she could convince him to help her. And perhaps, the Telling Stones had not been playing with her after all. For it seemed very possible that he was her tall and handsome stranger.

After she was dressed, Brigitta accompanied Sister Fallyn up on deck to see what was happening. Dinghies were being launched from all ten of Rupert's ships, presumably to fetch food and supplies from the small town. She spotted Rupert's hat with the false plaits and Captain Landers's fancy hat. They were on a dinghy drawing close to the pier of Danport.

Along the shore, the villagers had gathered, and they waved and cheered as Rupert approached.

"They must know they were rescued from the bad pirates," Sister Fallyn observed.

Brigitta nodded. It seemed that Rupert was indeed a hero. But he didn't trust them enough to remove his hat.

With a spurt of satisfaction, she wondered if she was the only one outside of his crew who knew his secret.

She glanced at him. There was only one other rower aboard his dinghy, for Rupert was also rowing. *No wonder he's acquired such strong muscles.* And he didn't consider himself above manual labor.

Her tall and handsome stranger. She smiled to herself. Apparently, her *overly dramatic* stories could actually happen, for she'd found a young and dashing hero.

Captain Landers threw a rope up to a worker on the pier. As the worker tied off the dinghy close to a ladder, a swarm of young women rushed onto the pier. They squealed so loud, Brigitta could hear them from the ship.

"Rupert!" They crowded around the ladder, pushing and shoving so much, Brigitta half expected one of them to fall into the sea.

Her mouth fell open when a few of them lifted their skirts halfway up their calves. Others leaned over to welcome him, and their breasts nearly fell out of their low necklines.

Sister Fallyn huffed. "Such wanton behavior!"

Brigitta winced. Apparently being a hero came with a few perks. More than a few. There had to be at least twenty women competing for his attention.

Sister Fallyn sighed. "Well, I suppose we should consider this a blessing. If the captain and Rupert sate their beastly desires in the village, then they will be less likely to ravish us."

Brigitta groaned inwardly, eyeing the women. It was only last night when Rupert had gazed upon her with a hungry look. No wonder he'd been able to restrain himself. He'd known there would be a handful of willing women in this village. Good goddesses, he might have women in every port!

Anger sizzled through her, then she stiffened with a sudden realization. Goddesses help her. She was jealous.

And that could only mean she was attracted to him. A sorcerer pirate with a hoard of treasured secrets. And she'd only met him the day before.

With a heavy heart, she watched him climb the ladder, then stroll down the pier, surrounded by fawning women. She'd been a fool to think she could be special to him.

Her destiny could not be linked to him after all.

Chapter Ten

❧

"The mayor wishes to thank you," a pretty redhead announced as she blocked Rupert's progress down the pier.

The minute he slowed down, two women latched on to his arms and even more surrounded him. He watched in dismay as Stefan and Tucker kept going, leaving him to deal with the women alone.

The redhead grazed her fingertips down his chest. "I'd like to thank you, too."

It was interesting, Rupert thought, that three women had their hands on him, but none of them appeared ready to faint. So why did Brigitta react so badly whenever she touched him? And why was he not reacting? All these women were vying for his attention, but he felt nothing but slight annoyance that they were in the way.

And how many times had these women pestered him over the years? But none of them had ever figured out that his plaited hair was fake. They fawned over him, because they considered him a hero with magical powers, but they never really saw him. Not like Brigitta had.

The blonde to his right leaned close enough to press the side of her breasts against his arm. "I want to thank you, too. You wouldn't believe how *grateful* I am."

"Not half as grateful as I," the brunette on his left boasted.

"No one is more grateful than me," the redhead announced. "I think it's amazing how you blew those nasty pirates ashore."

The blonde giggled. "You can blow my skirt up anytime you like."

He winced inwardly. Somehow, these women always made him feel like the prize at a county fair.

"If you have a few minutes, I think you would really enjoy how grateful I can be," the brunette said.

"*Minutes?*" The redhead scoffed. "I could be grateful for hours!"

The blonde released his arm to glare at the other women. "I could be grateful all night long!"

The argument escalated, and soon all the women were yelling at one another. Rupert slipped through the crowd and hurried to catch up with his companions.

"Rupert!" the women wailed.

Damn. He'd almost completed his escape. He glanced back and gave them an apologetic smile. "Perhaps another day."

The redhead huffed. "That's what you said last time."

He ran to join Stefan and Tucker at the entrance of the pier. "Dammit, don't leave me alone like that."

Stefan snorted. "Are the ladies too scary for you?"

He arched a brow. "Is a bloody nose too scary for you?"

When Tucker snickered, Stefan shot the junior officer a wry look. "Make yourself useful." He shoved a small bag of gold and a list into Tucker's arms. "Do the shopping."

"Aye, Captain." Tucker saluted, then strode toward the market square.

The mayor approached them with a beaming smile. "We owe you thanks once again."

Stefan shook his hand. "We were glad to help."

"I beached the pirates a few miles south of here," Rupert explained, "but I was worried that the survivors might come here and cause trouble."

"Some of them did," the mayor admitted. "But a troop of Eberoni soldiers captured them."

Rupert stiffened. For a fleeting moment, his old fear gripped him.

"Don't worry," the mayor quickly added. "The soldiers are gone. They left at dawn to take the prisoners to Ebton. You're perfectly safe now."

Rupert nodded. "Thank you." Most people assumed he was worried about being captured because he was a pirate. They didn't realize that his true identity was even more dangerous.

He'd been a few months short of the age of seven when he'd been forced to live with the possibility of being caught and killed. Fortunately, now that he had learned how to harness the wind, he was much better equipped to protect himself and his companions. Even so, the only time he truly felt safe was when he was at sea or on his secret island. And the only people he trusted completely were Stefan and his cousin Ansel. They were the only ones who knew his true identity.

He glanced at the stone tower on the highest bluff above the village. A green flag was waving there. That was the mayor's signal to him that it was safe to come ashore. A red flag meant the Eberoni army was nearby hunting for him. So far, the mayor had proven loyal. But Rupert knew most men had a price, and he could be in deep shit if the Eberoni army ever offered the mayor a larger amount of gold.

"We appreciate your efforts to keep us safe, Your Honor," Stefan said.

"It's the least we can do," the mayor insisted. "We

appreciate your business and your protection. We know that as long as you're safe, we'll be safe from other pirates."

"We'll do our best," Rupert assured him.

The mayor stepped closer and lowered his voice. "I received a message from your associate. He'll be waiting for you upstairs at the Salty Pelican."

That had to be Dryden, one of Rupert's spies. The mayor didn't know Dryden's name, but he passed on messages for the spy. "Thank you." Rupert shook the mayor's hand.

"Of course. I'll try to buy you some privacy." The mayor raised his voice. "Come along, ladies. Drinks are on me!" He led them toward the village tavern.

The women waved as they passed him by. "We'll be waiting for you at the Salty Pelican!"

Rupert and Stefan waited for more dinghies to tie off at the pier. As officers from each ship arrived, Stefan handed each of them a small bag of gold so they could purchase supplies.

"Ahoy there!" Ansel's loud voice echoed across the water as his dinghy approached.

Rupert smiled and waved at the big bear of a man who had taught him and Stefan everything they knew about the sea. Poor Stefan had been only nineteen years old when he'd suddenly found himself responsible for a young, traumatized orphan with a price on his head. But Stefan had never given up on him, and Rupert had always admired him and loved him for that.

With only twelve years' difference in their ages, Stefan had always felt like an older brother or young uncle. Ansel, though, was old enough to be Rupert's father, and he'd willingly taken on that role. Without Ansel, Rupert would still be hiding in the mountainous regions of northern Tourin while Stefan worked odd jobs to support them both. Because of Ansel, Rupert was now an admiral in charge of ten ships, and together, the three of them were working on the Official Plan.

While Rupert waited for Ansel to climb the ladder, a large pelican swooped down and landed on the pier beside him. He glanced at it a second time. Was that the same bird that had been roosting aboard his ship?

"There you are!" Ansel greeted them with his booming voice and pulled Rupert into an embrace. "Ten ships, now, you rascal! You're doing great!" He clapped Rupert on the back, then turned to embrace his cousin.

They looked very similar, Rupert thought, although Ansel's dark, curly hair was now half gray. And Ansel was much broader across his girth.

"How is Wermer doing?" Stefan asked, since the defeated pirate captain had been assigned to Ansel's ship.

Ansel grinned. "Not too pleased that he was demoted to a lieutenant. But I told him he could eventually work his way back up to captain."

Stefan nodded. "If he proves his loyalty long enough."

Ansel chuckled. "Yeah, for about ten years."

"Come on." Rupert motioned toward the village. "Dryden is waiting for us at the Salty Pelican."

The three of them made their way through alleys to the back door of the tavern.

They slipped up the back stairs, carefully avoiding the horde of women in the front room. A blue kerchief was tied around the latch of the third door in the hallway. Ansel knocked softly on the door.

Dryden cracked the door and peered out. A middle-aged man, with a craggy, weathered face, he'd been one of Ansel's most trusted seamen until he'd lost a leg in a shark attack. No longer able to climb the rigging, he'd opted for a land job instead. Now he spent most of his time hanging around taverns close to Ebton Palace, listening in on conversations. Whenever he heard anything useful, he rode to Danport to pass the information on to Rupert.

"There you are, you old codger!" Ansel barged into the room and gave his friend a bear hug. "How are you?"

"Can't complain." The spy shook hands with Stefan and Rupert, then walked toward the round table, his peg leg clunking on the wooden floor.

No fire burned in the hearth, since it was a warm spring day. On the table, a pitcher of ale and four goblets waited. Ansel filled the goblets while Stefan checked under the bed and behind a dressing screen.

Rupert drew back the curtains and blinked in surprise to find a pelican perched on the windowsill. "Shoo!" He blew a puff of air, and it hit the bird with enough force to knock it off the sill.

With a squawk, the bird fell into a rubbish bin.

"Oops." Rupert closed the windowpane and pulled the curtains shut. "It seems like every time I turn around, there's a pelican watching me."

Ansel shrugged. "Those damned birds have always congregated around here. That's how the tavern got its name." He sat next to Dryden. "So, buddy, you have news?"

"Aye." Dryden drew a folded sheet of paper from his jacket. "The Tourinian ambassador at Ebton Palace was passing these out to young noblemen. Since it involved Tourin, I thought you would want to know." He unfolded the paper and set it on the table.

Rupert sat in front of it, and on either side of him, Ansel and Stefan scooted closer so they could read.

NOTICE OF COMPETITION
FOR THE HAND OF
THE TOURINIAN PRINCESS

Attention all young men of noble birth:

His Most Royal Majesty, King Gunther of
Tourin, decrees a competition to begin two weeks
after the Spring Embrace of the moons. All those
who enter will compete against one another in a series of contests designed to show combat skills and
the ability to complete challenging quests.

The winner will be awarded with a betrothal to
the Tourinian princess, Brigitta. If he success-
fully begets a son with her in one year, he will be
allowed to marry her, and his son will become the
heir to the throne of Tourin. If he fails, the second-
place winner will take his place.

The kingdom of Tourin is not responsible for any
deaths that occur during the competition. All those
seeking to compete must arrive in Lourdon before
the competition begins and pay the requisite fee of
three hundred gold coins.

Shock sizzled through Rupert as he read the notice.
Not wanting to believe it, he scanned it a second time,
and his shock ignited into rage.

He jumped up so quickly his chair fell over. "Dammit
to hell!"

"Calm down," Stefan cautioned him.

As Rupert's anger grew, the air in the room began to
swirl, and a breeze ruffled the curtains and coverlet on
the bed. Dammit, he needed to stop thinking about it, but
how could he not face the truth? Brigitta's brother was
planning to use her as a broodmare. If one stud failed to
impregnate her, the next one would be called in.

"I'll kill that bastard!" He slashed his hand through

the air, and a wind knocked the hats off his companions. They grabbed their goblets to keep them from being blown over.

"Control yourself." Stefan righted Rupert's fallen chair. "Do you want to start a hurricane in here?"

Dryden's eyes widened. "He could do that?"

Rupert clenched his fists as he paced across the room. *Control.* He needed to stay in control. It was the one bad side effect of his power. He had become so connected to the wind that it was somehow attached to his emotions. Whenever he grew too agitated, the wind picked up like the tempest that roiled inside him. The last time he'd lost control it had been a disaster.

The Tourinian navy had tried to ambush his fleet in the fog. In his desperation to keep his men alive, he'd caused the naval ships to blast each other with their cannons. Two ships had caught on fire, and men had lost their lives.

Control. He inhaled deeply to calm the racing of his heart. But Brigitta's words still pricked at him. *Why can't I control my own destiny?* Dammit, she would never have a chance. "I'm going to kill that bastard."

"Why is he so pissed?" Dryden whispered to Ansel.

Ansel cleared his throat and gave Rupert a pointed look.

Rupert took another deep breath. Dryden only knew that he carried a grudge against Gunther. He didn't know why. And he sure didn't know that once upon a time, Rupert had vowed to be loyal and true to a baby girl, and to always protect her. *That vow was obliterated, along with your family. She is the enemy.*

So why did the thought of her being abused make him want to commit murder?

"We kidnapped the princess," Stefan explained as he retrieved the fallen hats and deposited them on the table. "She's on board the *Golden Star.*"

"Holy Light." Dryden's eyes widened. "You have Gunther's sister?"

With a chuckle, Ansel set his feathered captain's hat back on his head. "Gunther must be shitting his breeches right now. He's planned this whole contest, but thanks to us, he can't deliver the prize."

Prize? Rupert gritted his teeth. How dare that bastard use Brigitta as a prize?

Ansel swallowed down some ale, then belched. "Damn, but this is excellent timing for us. The more desperate Gunther is to get his sister back, the higher the ransom we can require."

"Don't you see what's he's doing?" Rupert yelled. "The bastard is using her as a broodmare! She'll be forced to bed whoever wins."

Ansel gave him a curious look. "And that bothers you?"

"Of course!" Rupert replied. "The man is arranging his sister's rape!"

Stefan and Ansel exchanged looks.

Dryden shrugged. "Aren't princesses usually married off to strangers?"

Rupert lifted a clenched fist, ready to punch a hole in the wall.

"Sit down, Rupert." Ansel used the same tone he had when Rupert had been a rebellious fourteen-year-old. "We need to discuss this matter calmly."

Rupert didn't budge. "Who are we to decide her destiny?"

Ansel quirked a brow. "Didn't you do that when you kidnapped her?"

Holy crap. It was true. Rupert's frustration and anger turned on himself, and another burst of wind shot across the room, blowing Ansel's hat off once again.

"Dammit, boy," Ansel growled.

"Enough, you two." Stefan lifted his hands. "We need

to go over this announcement. First, the timing. The moons embraced last night, so the competition is set to begin in two weeks."

Ansel nodded, then pointed at the second paragraph. "Did you notice this? That the son would become Gunther's heir?"

"I wondered about that, too," Dryden said. "Gunther had an heir, but the boy died three years ago. Now there's a rumor going around that Gunther can no longer father children. I thought it might be merely gossip, but apparently he was seriously injured two years ago in a battle with the Norveshki."

Stefan grimaced. "I remember hearing about that. A dragon set his breeches ablaze."

"Ouch." Ansel winced. "My biscuits are burning!"

While the men chuckled, Rupert ground his teeth over the irony of the situation. If Gunther had been able to sire his own heir, he would have never sent for his sister. He would have gladly pretended that she'd never existed. But now she was his only hope. "Brigitta is the only way he can get an heir from his own bloodline."

"Aye," Stefan agreed, then turned to Dryden. "Do you know if any men have agreed to compete?"

"I've heard there are a few Eberoni noblemen who are interested. Or rather, their ambitious fathers are interested." Dryden took a drink of ale. "But I'm surprised Gunther is inviting foreigners to compete."

"I'm not," Ansel muttered. "The greedy bastard gets three hundred gold coins from everyone who enters. He's probably hoping for a hundred contestants."

Dryden shrugged. "Even so, I doubt Gunther would let a foreigner win. Most people are saying the whole thing is rigged, that Gunther has three men he favors: his top general, the admiral of the Tourinian navy, and the captain of his personal guard. They say the contest is just to see which of those three men is the strongest, since Gunther wants a strong male heir."

A strong brute forcing himself on Brigitta. "Holy crap," Rupert growled.

Ansel gave him a pointed look. "If you don't like it, why don't you compete?"

Stefan scoffed and jabbed a finger at the paper. "Did you read the fine print at the bottom of this thing?"

"What?" Ansel leaned over, squinting his eyes as he read, "'*Only two contestants will survive the competition, for at the end of each round, the contestant with the lowest score will be put to death.*' Shit!" He sat back.

"Aye." Stefan nodded. "That's why Gunther opened the competition to foreign noblemen. He gets to kill them."

"Bastard." Ansel downed his goblet and slammed it on the table.

"We can't send her back," Rupert announced.

Stefan scoffed. "If we don't send her back, we don't get the ransom."

"Screw the ransom!" Rupert growled. "We captured her so we could upset whatever plans Gunther had, and we have accomplished that. If he never gets her back, he can never have an heir from his bloodline. The House of Grian will die! That's worth more to me than any ransom."

Dryden's eyes narrowed. "Why do you want the House of Grian to die?"

Ansel shot Rupert a pointed look that told him to shut the hell up.

"Here. For your expenses." Stefan handed Dryden a small bag of gold. "We need you to go back to Ebton now, so you can keep us informed."

"Sure." Dryden stood as he pocketed the gold.

"Wait." Rupert rushed over to the desk and wrote a quick note to inform Queen Luciana that her sister

Brigitta was safe, and he would do his best to protect her. "Here. Deliver this to Ebton Palace. And thank you."

"Just doing my job." Dryden plopped his hat back on his head and pocketed the note. "See you later." He left the room, and Rupert listened to the *clump-scrape* of his walk down the hall.

"You wrote to the king of Eberon?" Ansel asked.

Rupert shook his head. "The queen. She's Brigitta's sister and about to give birth. Brigitta didn't want her to be worried."

Stefan exchanged a look with Ansel, then asked, "How did you know about that?"

Rupert shrugged. "She told me. Last night." He peered out the door to make sure the hallway was empty.

"Come sit down," Ansel said.

Rupert locked the door, then took his seat. The other two men were watching him closely. "I know what you're thinking. I said too much in front of Dryden. I need to be more careful."

"You've always been careful." Ansel refilled his goblet. "But today you're different. A lot more emotional."

With a snort, Rupert tossed his hat on the table and pushed back his mask. "I've always hated Gunther with a passion. And the House of Grian. That's nothing new."

"Yes, but Brigitta is from the House of Grian," Stefan said, "and you seem very protective of her."

Rupert shrugged. "I hate to see anyone being used by Gunther."

Stefan sipped some ale. "Perhaps you feel protective because she's betrothed to you."

Rupert snorted. "Given the circumstances, I think we can safely say the engagement was called off."

Ansel tapped a finger on the announcement. "This whole competition has been designed for the purpose of getting the princess pregnant, so Gunther can have an heir."

Rupert gritted his teeth. "That's what I said before. The bastard is using her as a broodmare."

Ansel nodded. "And since we like upsetting Gunther's plans, why don't you beat him to the punch?" He leaned forward. "Seduce the girl and get her pregnant."

Rupert flinched. "What—no!"

"It seems obvious that you're attracted to her," Stefan said.

"*What?*" Rupert scoffed. "Where the hell did you come up—"

"You look ready to commit murder whenever we talk about her bedding someone else," Stefan explained.

"That's ridic—"

"Is the task too hard for you, lad?" Ansel interrupted him, then gave his cousin a smirk. "I thought he was made of sterner stuff."

Stefan grinned. "Nothing but an old windbag."

"Enough!" Rupert rose to his feet and glared at the two men. "I will not abuse her. Nor will I have you talking about her as if she's nothing more than a pawn or a walking womb. She deserves better than that."

Ansel snorted. "You just proved our point, boy. You do care about her."

Rupert blinked. Had they been playing with him? "Look, you bastards. I never said I cared about her."

Stefan shrugged. "But you obviously do."

"No!" Rupert protested. *Holy crap!* Did he care? No, it was just lust. Nothing more. "I—you taught me to have a sense of honor. That's why I object to her being used."

Ansel nodded. "All right. Since you want to be honorable about it, I'll perform the marriage ceremony for the two of you."

"*What?*" Rupert stepped back. Marry Brigitta? "I just talked to her for the first time yesterday!" *And you've been thinking about her ever since.*

"It's not a bad idea." Stefan drank some ale. "After all, the two of you are already betrothed."

"I'm not marrying her!" Rupert paced away. "Dammit, have you forgotten what her father did? He killed my father, murdered my entire family! Stole the throne from us, and doomed me to hiding in the dark for seven years. The House of Grian must be destroyed!"

Ansel shrugged. "Fine. Since she's so awful, we'll ransom her back to her brother. Let some other man get between her legs and—"

"Stop it!" Rupert hissed. "Don't talk about her like that."

Stefan gave him a weary look. "Why don't you just admit that you care about her?"

Rupert took a deep breath. "I can't marry her. But I won't let Gunther abuse her, either. We'll stick to the Official Plan, the one we were doing before we even knew she was still alive. We defeat the Tourinian navy, blockade the coast, and completely cut off Gunther's supply of gold. Once he can't pay his army, his soldiers will desert. With no gold, the economy will collapse, and the people will turn on him. Then we rally our supporters in the north—"

"That's where the plan goes awry, and you know it," Ansel said. "It's been nineteen years since your father died. We can't be sure you have any supporters left."

Stefan nodded. "Gunther killed off any that were vocal about supporting the House of Trepurin."

"They're there," Rupert insisted. "The clans were always close. And loyal. Once they know I'm alive—"

"And what if they want proof?" Stefan asked. "They'll have only our word for it that you're the lost prince. We have no idea where your mother hid the royal seal."

"True." Ansel sipped some ale. "I hate to say it, but it would be easier to use the girl."

"No." Rupert shook his head. "I will not use her. If I did, I would be no better than her bastard brother. The throne is rightfully mine, but I will not lose my honor in order to obtain it."

Stefan gave him a wry smile as he lifted his goblet. "Spoken like a true king."

"Aye." Ansel smiled. "But if he wants to be an honest king, he should learn to admit the truth."

Rupert groaned. "I know how to be honest."

"Then admit you're attracted to her." Stefan downed his drink.

Rupert scoffed. "Are you admitting you're lusting for a nun?"

Stefan sputtered his drink all over the table.

Rupert smirked. "I'll take that as a yes."

Ansel sighed. "Why is my ship so boring? You two are having all the fun."

Chapter Eleven

Brigitta's anger festered the more she thought about Rupert enjoying himself in the village while she was trapped on board. His prisoner.

The scoundrel had threatened her sisters with flaming arrows in order to force her compliance. How could she ever think she was attracted to him?

Yes, she was curious about him, even intrigued by him, but that was merely a side effect of the gift she'd been born with. And no doubt, any attraction she might have felt toward him had been caused by her *overly dramatic* imagination. This sinking feeling in her heart was nothing more than her disappointment over something that had never been real.

The truth was: She should be angry. She should be defiant. Hadn't she vowed that she would not be a willing captive? It was time for her to take control of her own destiny. The Eberoni shore was close by, and she was an excellent swimmer.

The junior officer, Tucker, had returned with the dinghy filled with boxes of supplies. As he tied the dinghy off, other crewmen wheeled a large contraption to the portside. The machine had a series of pulleys and a rope with a giant hook on the end. When a seaman turned a crank, the rope lowered over the side of the ship. Tucker slid the hook under the ropes tied around a box, then the seamen turned the crank to lift the box into the air. Then other crewmen pivoted the contraption to the side so the box could be lowered into a cargo hold.

"Isn't it great?" Jeffrey grinned. "Rupert designed it so it would take only one man to lift something really heavy."

"Aye, 'tis very clever. Excuse me." Brigitta grabbed Sister Fallyn's arm to lead her toward a quiet spot.

"Is something wrong?" the nun asked.

"We should escape," Brigitta whispered, then held up a hand when Sister Fallyn stiffened with shock. "Hear me out. We're close to the shore. We could swim—"

"We're farther away than ye think."

"The tide is going in. As long as we stay afloat—"

"Nay," Sister Fallyn argued. "Our gowns could drag us under." She shuddered. "Or sharks could attack us."

"We have to try!"

"Nay, I will not have ye risking yer life."

"And ye—" Brigitta struggled to keep her voice a whisper. "Ye would let yer life be controlled by some pirates?"

Sister Fallyn hesitated. "I understand yer frustration, but ye'll be safer here. Even if ye make it ashore, how will ye travel all the way to Ebton Palace? Ye could be set upon by brigands." She grabbed Brigitta by the shoulders. "Lass, ye must stay here."

Brigitta groaned inwardly. She could see the shore. *Freedom.* How could she give up?

Sister Fallyn patted her on the back. "Go below and rest a bit. Then ye'll feel better."

With a sigh, Brigitta headed down the stairs to their

cabin. How could she accept defeat? How could she let the Telling Stones, or a sorcerer pirate, or even an unknown brother dictate her future?

She paused at the door, mentally reviewing all of Sister Fallyn's objections. Her gown was definitely a problem, but she didn't want to go ashore in nothing but her shift. If only she could wear breeches—her gaze fell on the door at the end of the passageway. Captain Landers's room. And he was ashore right now. With his breeches off, no doubt. Just like Rupert. Blast him.

She imagined Rupert returning to the ship only to discover that she'd escaped while he'd been busy with all those women. A spark of satisfaction shot through her. Yes, she would do this!

She slipped into the captain's cabin and found an old pair of breeches and white linen shirt. On his dresser was a small bag. She peeked inside. Gold coins! She might need them. Even so, she hesitated, her conscience objecting to her being a thief. *They're pirates*, she argued with herself. The gold was already stolen.

She groaned. What choice did she have? She took the gold and clothing back to her cabin.

The woolen breeches were far too loose around her waist and felt strange and itchy against her bare legs. She stuffed the bottom of her shift into the breeches, then used her own belt to gather up the waist so they wouldn't fall off. Before fastening the belt, she attached the bag of gold to it. The breeches were also too long, so she rolled up the hems to mid-calf. The white shirt was loose, but she was grateful the long length hid her hips and bottom. She buttoned it up to her chin, then rolled the sleeves up to her elbows.

What else would she need? She stuffed her slippers into the pockets of the breeches, along with a dinner knife Sister Fallyn had confiscated the night before.

Once she made it ashore, she would seek out the mayor of the village and beg him to contact the Eberoni army. There were always some troops patrolling the shoreline, searching for pirates. Once she was with the army, they could give her safe passage to Ebton Palace.

She eased up the stairs and peered out the doorway. The crewmen had their backs to her as they used Rupert's pulley machine to unload supplies. She darted behind the barrels and took a look over the portside railing.

Tucker was climbing up the rope ladder as the last box was being lifted. Once he landed on deck, he ordered some of the crew to put the machine away and others to follow him belowdecks. Brigitta assumed they were going to be stashing away the supplies. The only other seamen were far to the front of the ship, where they were busily repairing some sails, so focused on their task that they never looked her way.

Her gaze drifted back to the empty dinghy. Did she dare? She'd never rowed a boat before, but how hard could it be? It was definitely a better option than swimming.

As Sister Fallyn headed toward the stairs, Brigitta slipped out and grabbed her.

"What—" The nun's eyes widened as she looked Brigitta over. "What are ye doing?"

Brigitta put a finger to her lips to signal quiet, then whispered, "We're leaving now."

"What? Why are ye dressed like that?"

Brigitta dragged her toward the railing. "If we hurry, we can take the dinghy." She hefted herself over the railing onto the wooden ladder. Goodness, this was so much easier without a long skirt!

Sister Fallyn gasped. "Have ye lost yer mind?"

Brigitta descended a few steps on the ladder. "Quickly! Afore someone sees us."

The nun glanced frantically about. "We can't—"

"Aye, we can. Hurry!"

Sister Fallyn eyed the ladder, and tears filled her eyes. "I-I don't think I can do it."

Brigitta paused. "I can't leave without you."

A tear rolled down the nun's face, then she nodded. "Aye, ye can. Ye must."

"Sister—?" Tucker's voice sounded on deck. "Who are you talking to?"

Sister Fallyn quickly wiped her face and turned toward him. "Oh, those pesky seagulls. They're always begging for food. Could ye show me where the galley is? Perhaps I could find some stale bread for them."

"Oh, all right," Tucker replied. "This way."

Sister Fallyn waved a hand at Brigitta, a shooing gesture, before she followed the young officer.

Brigitta closed her eyes briefly as tears threatened. Would Sister Fallyn be in trouble for aiding her escape? How could she leave her behind?

But if she did escape, there was a chance that the pirates would simply let Sister Fallyn go. After all, they couldn't earn a ransom with a nun. And if they didn't release the sister, Brigitta would do her best to rescue her.

Aye, she had to do this. She hurried down the ladder to the dinghy and untied the ropes. As the small boat drifted away from the ship, she spent a few awkward moments figuring out how to slip the oars through the rings. Then she realized she was facing the wrong way. It would be easier to row with her back to the shore. As she pivoted around on the bench, she lost her grip on an oar, and it started to slide into the water.

She lurched to the side to grab it and gasped as the boat nearly tipped over. Good goddesses, she needed to be more careful or she would be swimming ashore. She took a deep breath to calm her nerves, then started to row.

Her heart pounded in her chest. She was doing it! She was making her escape.

After another few minutes of discussion, Rupert had finally convinced Stefan and Ansel to stick to the Official Plan and leave Brigitta out of it. She would be allowed to decide her own fate.

Now, with all their decisions made and a few additional supplies bought, they were walking toward the pier. While Stefan and Ansel talked about some needed ship repairs, Rupert's mind wandered back to Brigitta. How was he going to tell her about Gunther's plans? No doubt it would upset her. Perhaps even make her cry, and he hated to see her cry.

Dammit, he did care. A little. Shouldn't any decent man hate to make a woman cry? That was all it was. His sympathy was a natural by-product of his own sense of honor and decency.

And lust, a nagging inner voice reminded him. *So what?* he countered. Any normal man occasionally felt some lust. It was healthy, dammit.

But he hadn't lusted for the women on the pier.

So what? That just proved he had good taste. Not only was Brigitta beautiful, but she was much more clever than any of those other women. She'd seen through his hat of fake hair. And she'd been bold enough to rip it off. Bold, beautiful, and clever.

Dammit. He would never admit to caring about her. No matter how much Ansel and Stefan might try to badger him into a confession. He could never say it. Not out loud. How could he care for the daughter of the man who had destroyed his family?

He would champion her right to control her own destiny because it was the honorable thing to do. Nothing more.

His grip tightened on the package he was carrying. If she decided to side with her brother, Gunther, then she would go down with the bastard. For nothing would stop him from getting his revenge.

The sudden shrill of a whistle jerked him out of his thoughts. One of the ships had sounded an alarm. He broke into a run with Stefan and Ansel right behind him. As he dashed onto the pier, he quickly scanned the horizon. All ten ships were anchored in the bay, their sails furled. Dinghies were traveling back and forth transporting supplies. Nothing seemed out of the ordinary.

The whistle blared once again. One long blast, then one short burst. That meant the *Golden Star*. But he couldn't spot anything wrong with the ship, other than Tucker and some crewmen yelling at something. The dinghy?

His eyes narrowed. Whoever was rowing, his handling of the oars was awkward. He'd passed the bow of the ship and seemed headed for the shore instead of the pier. Was that a long blond braid down his back?

"Holy crap!" Rupert dropped his package on the pier and leaped into the nearest dinghy. "It's Brigitta!" What the hell did she think she was doing?

Stefan tossed him the tether line. "Hurry."

"I will." Rupert pushed off from the pier and grabbed hold of the oars.

"It looks like we argued over nothing." Ansel shaded his eyes as he watched her progress. "You wanted her to decide her own destiny. She's doing it."

"She can't travel alone." Rupert pulled hard on the oars. Dammit, why was she doing something so dangerous? Was she that desperate to get away from him?

As he continued to row, he inhaled deeply and blew air in her direction. The breeze increased in power as it crossed the water till it finally hit her boat and stopped her progress. She didn't give up. Bending over the oars, she heaved hard and once again moved toward the shore.

He'd have to use a stronger wind. With his hands, he gathered up some air and blasted it toward the *Golden Star*, taking his dinghy with it. As he skipped across the surface headed toward her, the wind shoved her boat back toward the ship. Using an oar, she jabbed at the side of the ship, trying to push away.

"Brigitta, stop!"

She twisted around, half standing, to see who was calling her. Waves, caused by his wind, rocked her boat hard.

"No!" He cut the wind off, but there was no way to stop the waves. Her boat tipped, dumping her into the sea.

"Brigitta!" *Dammit.* Did she know how to swim? Even if she did, the waves could slam her against the side of the ship or cause the dinghy to crash on top of her.

He yanked off his jacket, hat, and boots, then dove into the water. The impact shoved his mask askew, and he tore it off. Swimming furiously, he reached her in a matter of seconds, although each second that ticked by seemed an eternity.

He spotted her blond head breaking the surface a second time. She reached for the dinghy but couldn't get a good hold on it.

"Brigitta." He reached for her and managed to grab an arm.

She stiffened with a gasp, her eyes wide with shock, then she went limp and sank underwater.

"Brigitta!" He pulled her up. *Dammit.* Why did she always react like this? He held her close and patted her face. "Brigitta." Her eyes were closed, her face pale.

He stroked her cheek, then eased a finger between her lips. With her mouth slightly open, he leaned close. "Don't leave me." His lips grazed hers as he blew gently into her mouth.

Her eyes flickered open.

"Are you all right?" He skimmed a hand over her wet hair. "Did you hit your head?"

"Nay, I. . . ." She still looked stunned.

"No injuries?" He ran his hand down her back.

With a small gasp, she reacted, arching against him. "Y-ye can let me go." She started to tread water, but when her legs brushed against his, she grew still.

He tightened his hold on her. "You scared me. I thought I'd lost you."

A pained look crossed her face. "Ye've lost before. Everyone ye loved."

He stiffened. "How would you—" He stopped when she touched his face.

"Yer mask is gone."

"Hard to swim with it."

Her hand skimmed up his cheek to his temple, where she slipped a thumb beneath the sodden scarf tied around his head. "Ye might as well take this off, too."

He stopped her and pressed her hand against his chest. "Sweetheart, are you eager to undress me?"

Her mouth fell open, and he thought about kissing her again. Properly, this time. But just as he leaned forward, she shoved him back. "Haven't enough women undressed you today?"

"What? What women?"

"I saw you. With all yer . . . admirers." She pulled away from him and swam toward the ladder.

"Wait." He followed her. "You think I . . ." Water splashed into his mouth, and he spit it out. "Dammit to hell, woman. You think I bedded them all?"

She grabbed on to the rope ladder and glared at him. "Isn't that what pirates do?"

He grasped the rung closest to her. "Have you forgotten that I've been keeping my identity secret? How could I bed a woman without risking the loss of my disguise?"

She blinked. After nervously tucking some wet strands of hair behind her ear, she gave him a shy glance. "Then ye didn't . . ."

"No. I didn't bed anyone." As her cheeks grew pink, he eased closer. "Were you worried about that?"

"Nay, of course not." Her cheeks bloomed brighter. "I just keep hearing about all this ravishing ye supposedly do. Seducing women and stealing passionate kisses. 'Tis all Sister Fallyn can talk about. I've grown quite tired of hearing about it."

"Then would you prefer to do something about it?"

She gasped. "I have no idea what ye . . ."

"Were you jealous?"

"Nay!" She looked aghast, then lifted her chin. "If I cared, would I be trying so hard to escape?"

Damn. That hit home. He scowled at her. "How could you risk your life like this? I told you I'd never harm you."

"Ye're holding me against my will. That is harm."

His chest tightened as a stab of guilt struck him hard. How could he explain without revealing too much? The urge to confide in her was starting to overwhelm him, but he had to ignore it. He could never trust her.

She closed her eyes briefly, then gave him a weary look. "I was so close to getting away. Why did ye have to stop me?"

He could say he needed her for the ransom. Or claim he was helping her because she would be worse off with her brother. Or he could explain how dangerous it would have been for her to travel alone with no protection. But the yearning in his heart overpowered all his logical thoughts, so instead, he whispered, "Reason number five."

Her eyes widened.

He wanted to spend more time with her. He wanted to get to know her. And dammit, he suspected he simply wanted her. He motioned toward the ladder. "Ladies first."

She grabbed a rung, but the weight of her wet clothes made it difficult for her to climb. He planted a hand on her bottom to give her a boost up to the next rung.

"Stop that." She turned toward him, and his heart stuttered in his chest.

Her breasts were now above sea level, and the white linen shirt was glued to them, blatantly showing the sweet round contours, the extra plumpness of her nipples, and even the tips as they hardened in reaction to the cooler air. A sound escaped him, somewhere between a moan and a gasp.

"Oh!" She dropped back into the sea.

He glanced up and spotted Tucker and some other crewmen staring down at them. "Get back to your jobs!" As they scattered, another face peered over the railing. The nun. "Sister, please fetch her cloak."

The nun nodded and ran off.

Next to him, Brigitta groaned, her hand pressed against her chest.

"Don't worry. I'll carry you up, so no one can see. Just climb onto my back." His mouth quirked. "And wrap your legs around me and squeeze me tight."

She snorted. "That again?"

"Just trying to help."

"No thank you." She started up the ladder again. "Be a gentleman, if you can, and try not to stare."

"As you wish." He stared at her nicely rounded rump as she ascended.

When she reached the top, she slipped over the railing and Sister Fallyn wrapped her up in a cloak. By the time he reached the railing, they had disappeared belowdecks.

He glanced toward the dinghy he'd abandoned. His hat was there, and his jacket with the notice about Gunther's competition. His mask was floating a few feet away.

Stefan and Ansel were in another rowboat, approaching the abandoned dinghy. They would tow it in, along with the boat Brigitta had used for her escape.

If only she had waited. He was determined now to let her decide her own destiny. But apparently, she didn't trust him, either, so she'd felt compelled to take matters into her own hands. He would have to be careful she didn't uncover any more of his secrets. She knew his face now, but she still didn't know his true identity.

Ye've lost before. Everyone ye loved. Her words came back to him. Did she know more than he thought?

And why did she go limp every time he touched her? She'd scared the shit out of him when she'd sunk underwater. He had to know what was going on. Hell, he wanted to know all of her secrets.

But he needed to figure them out, without telling her any of his.

Chapter Twelve

❧

He was indeed handsome.

Don't think about him, Brigitta told herself as she peeled off her wet shirt in the privy. If it hadn't been for Rupert's interference, she would have escaped. Blast him!

She unfastened her belt and let the baggy breeches slide to the floor. *Sweetheart, are you eager to undress me?* Good goddesses, had he really said that to her?

Stop thinking about him!

The minute she'd landed on deck, Sister Fallyn had flung a cloak around her and whisked her down the steps to their cabin, all the time thanking the goddesses for her safe return. After gathering up her cream-colored convent gown and one of Sister Ellen's old shifts, they'd headed down to the privy.

And now, Sister Fallyn was standing guard outside the door. "Wash up quickly!" she yelled. "We can't have ye catching a cold."

"Aye, Sister!" Brigitta dropped her sodden shift on top of the white shirt and breeches. He was indeed very handsome. And in his hurry to rescue her, he'd taken off his mask. Did that mean he cared more about her than preserving his secret identity?

Who was he really? She suspected his real name wasn't even Rupert.

She undid her braided hair, then slipped inside the stall that Jeffrey had called a shower. Perhaps it would be like a rain shower? Whoever Rupert was, he was very clever with all his inventions.

On a shelf, she found a jar of soap. She lifted it to her nose and sniffed. A woodsy, smoky scent. Very masculine. Like Rupert. *Don't think about him.*

She pulled a lever and gasped when a barrage of cool water cascaded over her head.

Gooseflesh broke out over her skin. Brr, she would definitely need to be quick about this. She lathered up her hair, then remembered how he'd smoothed a hand over her head, checking for injuries. He'd touched her face and her mouth.

With a shiver, she recalled the brush of his mouth against hers and how his breath had brought her back to her senses. He must have thought she was unconscious, but she hadn't been. The minute he'd touched her, another vision had struck her hard, sucking her down into memories so dark and painful she'd thought she might drown.

She shook her head, determined not to dwell on him any longer. But when she lathered her breasts, how could she not remember the way he'd looked at them? Even now, just thinking about it, her nipples grew tight, and her breasts felt full and achy. And the sound he had made, somewhere between pain and desire. *Don't think about it!*

When she soaped up her hips, she recalled his hand on her rump, giving her a boost. And when she washed her legs, she could almost feel his legs brushing against hers.

Dear goddesses, she felt . . . strange, as if some sort of desperate need was overwhelming her, leaving her hot and breathless.

She pulled the lever to let a gush of water cool her down and bring her back to her senses.

But she still couldn't wash away the vision that had shot through her the second he'd touched her.

Don't leave me, he'd whispered to her before pressing his mouth against hers. The words had served as an eerie echo to the first voice she'd heard in her vision.

"Mother," a young male voice, a younger Rupert, had cried as he'd leaned over, resting his face against a stone crypt. "Don't leave me."

"I'm so sorry." An older male voice had sounded like Captain Landers. "How did she die?"

Another man had answered, "We all believed her husband and eldest son had been brutally murdered. She knew the same fate awaited her and the younger boy if they were captured. When the soldiers came for her, she ran up the nearby mountain. They chased her until she . . . she fell off a cliff to her death."

Brigitta had felt Rupert's reaction like a knife to the heart. Pain so fierce, it had dragged her underwater.

"What about the younger brother?" Captain Landers had asked.

"No one knows," the other man had replied. "He may have died with her, but if so, his body seems to have vanished. If you know what's good for you, you'll make sure this boy vanishes, too."

"Don't leave me," the adult Rupert had whispered, then he'd ended the vision by sharing his breath.

And she'd opened her eyes to see his face. His handsome face. Why had he been forced to vanish from Tourin? Was that why he'd become a pirate?

In the shower stall, a chill crept over her, prickling her skin. The ambush she'd seen, or perhaps the battle—that must have been when his father had been brutally murdered. She shuddered. Rupert had seen his father die. And then he'd lost his mother, too.

Don't leave me. Dear goddesses, her heart ached for him. Even though he was holding her captive, how could she hate him when he'd suffered so much?

"Brigitta!" Sister Fallyn pounded on the door. "Are ye all right? What's taking ye so long?"

"I'll be right there." She yanked the lever again so more water would rinse her off.

After toweling dry and getting dressed, she wrapped the wet clothes in the towel and met Sister Fallyn in the passageway.

"All that wet hair." The nun shook her head. "We'll be lucky if ye don't get sick. I asked Jeffrey to bring some hot soup to our room."

They hurried up the stairs to their cabin and arrived just as Captain Landers did with a tray loaded down with a big tureen of soup, two bowls, and a basket of fresh bread.

"Oh! Ye needn't have troubled yerself, Captain." Sister Fallyn tried to relieve him of the tray, but he brushed past her and set it on the table.

"I thought it would be too heavy for Jeffrey," he told the nun, then turned toward Brigitta. "Are you all right, my lady?"

"Aye." With a wince, she set the rolled-up towel on the table. "I apologize for taking yer clothes. I'll return them after I wash—"

"Jeffrey can wash them," the captain interrupted. "And no need to apologize. We're the ones who kidnapped the two of you."

Sister Fallyn snorted. "If ye're truly sorry, ye'll take us to Ebton Palace, where we belong."

"I would like to discuss the matter with you." He

stepped closer to the nun. "Perhaps you would have dinner with me tonight?"

Sister Fallyn's face turned pink. "Certainly not. I will not leave Brigitta unattended."

His mouth thinned. "I assure you, no harm will come to her on my ship."

Sister Fallyn scoffed. "That horrid Rupert nearly drowned her!" When Brigitta objected, the nun quickly added, "He made yer boat tip over. I saw it!"

Brigitta sighed. If she had simply sat still, she doubted she would have fallen overboard. "Captain, I have something I need to return to you." She rummaged through the pile of sodden clothes. Her slippers fell out of the pockets of the breeches, along with the dinner knife. They tumbled onto the floor, nearly missing her bare feet.

She jumped back.

"Careful!" Sister Fallyn quickly swooped up the knife. After drying it, she stuffed it under the pillow on the bed.

Captain Landers scowled at her. "Mistress Fallyn, there is no need for you to stash weapons about the cabin. I have told you repeatedly that you are safe here."

"We must be prepared in case someone tries to ravish us," the nun insisted. "And I have told you repeatedly to call me *Sister* Fallyn."

"And I have told you to call me Stefan."

She glared at him as he glared back.

"Here it is." Brigitta located his pouch of gold coins. "I shouldn't have taken it, but—"

"Keep it." He gave them both a weary look. "It is the least I can do." With his shoulders slumped, he shuffled out the door.

"I think we hurt his feelings," Brigitta whispered.

Sister Fallyn's cheeks bloomed a brighter pink. "He's a pirate. Why should we care how he feels? Now sit down and eat." She ladled soup from the tureen into the two bowls.

As Brigitta sat, she noticed the nun's hands were trembling. Was the captain affecting her? Hardly surprising, Brigitta thought. For Rupert was certainly affecting her.

A few minutes into their meal, a loud, grinding noise echoed throughout the ship.

Sister Fallyn gasped. "Whatever could that be?"

"I think they're raising the anchor." Brigitta rushed to the window to look out. "We're starting to move."

"Oh dear goddesses. What will become of us now?" Sister Fallyn ladled more soup into their bowls. "We must keep up our strength. Come back and eat some more."

Brigitta was halfway through the bowl when Jeffrey knocked on the door. "I have a package for you." He came in, holding a bulky bundle wrapped in cloth.

"Set it on the bed." Brigitta started to stand, but Sister Fallyn jumped up first.

"Finish yer soup," the nun ordered. "I'll take care of this." She rushed to the bed to open the package.

"Rupert and the captain bought this stuff for you in Danport," Jeffrey explained.

"Where are we headed now?" Brigitta asked.

Jeffrey shrugged. "We won't go far. We just left some gold in Danport, so we'll stay close by for a few days."

Brigitta nodded. Rupert wanted to make sure the village was protected.

"'Tis clothing," Sister Fallyn said as she removed items from the package and laid them out on the bed.

"Really?" Brigitta wandered over to the bed for a closer look. There were four new shifts, two nightgowns, and two new outfits that consisted of a dark-green woolen skirt, a white linen blouse, and a dark-green velvet vest that laced up the front. "They bought us new clothes. How nice of them!"

Sister Fallyn scoffed. "They only did this because they feel guilty."

"If they were truly bad men," Brigitta countered, "they wouldn't feel guilty."

"That's right," Jeffrey agreed. "They're not bad at all."

Sister Fallyn opened a drawstring pouch and removed the contents onto the bed. A hairbrush with a carved wooden handle, two toothbrushes with engraved silver handles, a small mirror made of polished silver, and a pottery jar tied shut with a ribbon.

Brigitta untied the ribbon and looked inside. "'Tis soap." She took a sniff. Roses. It smelled so heavenly, she was tempted to take another shower.

Sister Fallyn picked up the hairbrush. "I was wondering how we would untangle yer wet hair." She sighed. "'Twas thoughtful of them, I admit, but it makes me wonder how long they intend to keep us here."

"Oh, that reminds me." Jeffrey turned to Brigitta. "Rupert wants you to eat dinner with him."

Brigitta's heart started to pound.

"Absolutely not!" Sister Fallyn declared. "She will not be alone with that man."

"But he gave you all these nice presents." Jeffrey gave Brigitta a hopeful look. "He just wants to talk to you."

Sister Fallyn huffed. "Does he think we are easily swayed by a few trinkets?"

Brigitta winced. Perhaps she was being too easily swayed. "I have nothing to say to him until he agrees to release us."

"Exactly." Sister Fallyn gave a curt nod. "We must stand firm."

Jeffrey's shoulders slumped. "All right. I'll tell him." He wandered from the room.

With a groan, Brigitta trudged back to the table. She

should have at least told Jeffrey to pass on their gratitude for the presents. "We might be hurting his feelings."

"He's a pirate and a sorcerer," Sister Fallyn mumbled. "Why should we care how he feels?"

Why, indeed? Brigitta collapsed in a chair. She shouldn't care. It would be foolish to care for her own kidnapper.

Don't leave me. The voice of a younger Rupert haunted her. All the terror, grief, and despair she'd felt from his memories had now become memories of her own.

And somehow, he'd survived all that pain. He'd become a powerful man with an entire fleet at his disposal and the sheer force of the wind at his command. He'd become a man who rescued the innocent and protected his allies. He'd become a man of honor.

Goddesses help her, she did care.

"Well?" Rupert asked while Jeffrey fidgeted at the door to his cabin. "Did they like the presents?"

"I-I think so."

"And did Brigitta agree to dine with me?"

Jeffrey hung his head and mumbled, "She said she has nothing to say to you until they're released."

Rupert stiffened, stunned for a moment. Brigitta was refusing him? Why? Was she that angry that he'd foiled her escape? He'd only done it to keep her safe.

He winced. *Safe?* He'd blown her into the water and nearly drowned her. And all because he felt an overwhelming need to protect her. *Dammit.* That vow he took as a child didn't count anymore. There was no need for him to care so much.

But he did.

He dragged a hand through his wet hair. What should he do now? After Brigitta had finished washing up in the privy, he'd taken a shower and put on fresh clothing.

During it all, he'd wondered why she reacted so badly every time he touched her. And he'd considered the best way to tell her about the competition Gunther was planning.

But now she was refusing to see him. Didn't she care about her own future?

"Wait a minute," he told Jeffrey, then strode toward his worktable. He shuffled through drawings of future inventions till he found a blank sheet of paper. After dipping a quill into an inkwell, he wrote: *It is imperative that we talk. I thought you wanted to be in control of your own destiny. What happened to that?*

He waved the paper in the air while he strode back to the door. With the ink dry, he folded it. "Deliver this to her right away."

"Yes, Admiral." Jeffrey scampered down the passageway, knocked on their door, then slipped inside.

Rupert paced barefoot about his cabin. She would agree to see him now. She had to.

His cabin was on the starboard end of the passageway, whereas Stefan's room was on the portside. Their cabins occupied the back corners of the ship, with large windows overlooking the sea.

During the day, a great deal of light shone in, so Rupert liked using the room as a workshop. The long table was covered with drawings, metal parts, and tools. The large bed was mostly ignored, for he preferred to sleep under the stars. After seven years of living in caves and basements, he couldn't bear the feeling of being cooped up.

A knock sounded at the open doorway and he whirled about. But it wasn't Jeffrey with a response.

Stefan was standing there, holding his boots, hat, and mask. "You left these behind."

"Thanks." Rupert tossed the boots onto the floor.

Stefan handed him the hat and mask. "I think you should continue with the disguise."

"She's seen my face."

"Lady Brigitta has, but Mistress Fallyn probably didn't get a good look at you. And neither of them has seen the color of your hair. Besides, there are too many new crew members on the other ships. They might spot you through a spyglass. We can't trust them yet, so you should still be careful."

"Fine." Rupert dropped the hat and mask on his bed, then rummaged through a dresser for a clean scarf.

"We've moved out to sea, circling close to Danport to keep an eye out for pirates," Stefan said.

"Good." Rupert wadded up the new scarf in his hand and threw it on his bed.

Stefan's eyes narrowed. "Is something bothering you?"

"No, of course not." Rupert peered out the doorway to see if Jeffrey was returning yet. No sign of him.

"Expecting someone?" Stefan asked.

"No." Rupert noticed the dubious look on his friend's face. He wasn't fooling Stefan. "I'm expecting a reply." He gritted his teeth. "She refused to have dinner with me."

Stefan sighed. "I know the feeling."

The door to the ladies' cabin opened and Jeffrey came out.

"What took so long?" Rupert demanded.

Jeffrey winced. "I had to fetch her a quill and ink." He handed Rupert a sheet of paper.

He unfolded it. It was the same paper he'd written on.

It is imperative that we talk. I thought you wanted to be in control of your own destiny. What happened to that?

And underneath his words, she'd written:

I was in control until you stopped me. Take me to Ebton, and I will convince King Leofric that you are harmless, so he need not hunt you down in the future to destroy you.

Rupert scoffed. Was she threatening him? And since when was he harmless? He was the most powerful man on the ocean. He strode to his worktable and wrote another message beneath.

Whether you wish to make a deal or issue useless threats, you should have the courage to do it to my face.

He marched back to the door and shoved the folded note into Jeffrey's hands. "Give her that!"

"Aye, Admiral." The boy walked slowly back to the ladies' cabin.

Stefan arched a brow. "Are you arguing with her long-distance?"

Rupert clenched his fists. "You're right. I should go there myself—"

"No." Stefan planted a hand on Rupert's chest to keep him from moving. "Nothing will be gained from seeing her in anger. Leave her be."

"I need to talk to her. I need to explain what her bastard brother is planning to do to her." Rupert grimaced. "It's going to upset her. I don't want to . . ."

"I know." Stefan gave him a sympathetic look. "You nearly caused a tornado when you found out. Wait a few hours till you can be calm."

Rupert took a deep breath. Stefan was right, as usual. Both he and Brigitta were too agitated right now.

Jeffrey exited the ladies' cabin and trudged toward them. "Here."

Rupert unfolded the paper as he walked into his room.

A man who hides behind a mask shouldn't talk about courage.

Damn, she knew how to hit hard. His mouth curled up in a smile. What a strong and fearless woman. She reminded him of the wildcats that roamed the mountains of northern Tourin.

He dipped his quill and wrote:

I will have the courage to show you my face on the quarterdeck tonight. If you have the courage, join me beneath the stars. I will be waiting.

He folded the letter and handed it to Jeffrey. "There is no need for a reply."

"Thank the Light," Jeffrey muttered as he headed down the passageway.

"Well?" Stefan asked.

With a sigh, Rupert leaned against the doorframe. "Either she'll see me tonight. Or she won't."

Stefan lowered his voice to a whisper. "Are you falling for her?"

"Don't be ridic—"

"It's a legitimate question that could change everything. Are you falling for her?"

"It changes nothing." Rupert glanced at the ladies' door as Jeffrey went inside. "No matter how I feel, I dare not trust her."

Chapter Thirteen

❦

A few hours later, just as Brigitta was finishing her supper, a clap of thunder sounded overhead.

Sister Fallyn dropped her knife and fork with a clatter. "Oh dear goddesses, a storm is coming."

Brigitta ran to the window and peered outside. Dark clouds were gathering in the sky, blocking out the setting sun. In the dim light, the ocean looked dark and agitated. A few drops of rain blew through the narrow opening to land on her face.

Blast. How could she meet Rupert on the quarterdeck now? Their meeting would have to be postponed.

She winced when a crack of lightning shot through the dark sky. "If this storm moves to the mainland, the lightning will strike Luciana's husband."

Sister Fallyn jumped to her feet. "We must pray it doesn't strike us and set the ship ablaze!" She made the sign of the moons.

"I'm sure we'll be all right." The ship rocked suddenly, causing Brigitta to fall onto the window seat.

"We'll be sick if we eat any more." Sister Fallyn stumbled toward the bed. "I need to lie down. And pray."

As the nun crawled under a blanket, Brigitta closed the

window and secured the latch. Rain now pattered against the glass at a much faster rate, but at least the rocking of the ship wasn't too bad. So far.

She'd never been at sea before during a storm. Surely, since Rupert could control the wind, he would keep them safe. It was odd, though, that when the rain had started, her first thought had been that she wouldn't see him tonight. Instead of feeling concern for their safety, she'd felt disappointment.

A knock sounded at the door, and Jeffrey came in with a lantern. "The captain wanted me to tell you that everything was fine, that you shouldn't worry."

Sister Fallyn sat up in bed. "Thank the goddesses."

"Rupert thought you might want some light." Jeffrey stood on a chair to latch the handle of the lantern over a large hook in the ceiling.

The lantern swayed with the rocking movement of the ship, and Brigitta realized it was the safest way to keep a lantern from tipping over and starting a fire.

She moved to the table to gather the dishes onto the tray. "Is it possible for Rupert to blow the storm away?"

Jeffrey shrugged. "I suppose he could, but right now he's happy for the rain. We have all the barrels open to collect water."

"Oh, I see."

Jeffrey leaned close and lowered his voice. "Rupert says you should stay belowdecks tonight."

Brigitta nodded. Their meeting was indeed canceled. Her disappointment was quickly followed by a jab of anger. Why was she letting the man affect her so much?

Jeffrey glanced at the bed, where Sister Fallyn was apparently being rocked fast asleep. "If you want a bed of your own, remember there's an empty cabin next door."

"Thank you." Brigitta held the door open so Jeffrey could leave with the tray.

As the minutes ticked by and Sister Fallyn's snores grew louder, Brigitta grew restless. She folded the new clothes and stashed them away in the sideboard. Then she took the jar of soap and toothbrush down to the privy, where she washed her face and brushed her teeth. Back in the cabin, she changed into one of the new nightgowns.

What could she do now? There was enough light to read the book Rupert had loaned her. She tensed as she picked the book up, expecting to see a vision. But no images came to mind, only a strong feeling of loneliness. And sadness.

Poor Rupert. He'd lost his parents so violently. Both of her parents were gone, too, but she had no memories of them. She'd heard that her father, Garold, had been killed in battle with the Norveshki, but she had no idea how her mother had died. Her younger brother had been murdered by her older half brother, Gunther, but she didn't know how. She didn't even know her little brother's name.

Since she'd been raised in ignorance of her family, she'd never experienced fear and loneliness like Rupert. She'd grown up in a safe place, surrounded by people who loved her.

As she read the book, she realized it was a different world, an imaginary one filled with mermaids and sorcerers. Had Rupert's world been so sad and painful that he used this book to escape? She checked the last page to make sure he had at least been comforted with a happy ending.

No, the mermaid died, and the sorcerer drowned trying to save her.

With tears in her eyes, she closed the book.

I won't let this happen. She rubbed her weary eyes. *I will control my own future. We will have our happy ending.*

She sat back. *We?*

What was she thinking? Did she truly believe that Rupert was her tall and handsome stranger?

She shook her head. She couldn't sit here all night thinking about him. Why not go to the cabin next door so she could sleep?

She slipped on her cloak, and as the ship rocked, she stumbled into the passageway. Dim light filtered down from the deck, and she noticed the pelican curled up on a dry step of the stairwell. She edged down the passageway, trailing her hand along the wall to keep her balance and search for the next door.

It was farther away than she'd expected, practically at the end of the passageway. When she eased quietly inside, she was surprised by the size of the bed to her left. It was large with a canopy overhead and thick velvet curtains along the head and foot of the bed.

This couldn't be right.

The room was lit. It was dark and shadowy here beside the bed, but there had to be a lantern somewhere, perhaps on the other side of the bed curtains.

She inched toward the light, then heard a clanking sound, metal striking against more metal. Her heart stilled. This room was occupied.

As she spun back toward the door, the floor creaked beneath her foot.

"Jeffrey, is that you?"

Rupert. She rushed to the door and fumbled with the latch.

"Brigitta?"

She whirled around to find him at the corner of the bed, staring at her. Her heart pounded. His head was uncovered, but it was hard to see the color of his hair in the dim light. It was long, though, down to his shoulders.

His shirt was unbuttoned and loose at his sides, leaving his chest bare. Such a broad chest. And what were those ridges on his stomach? Muscles?

A lightning flash suddenly brightened the room, and she gasped. His hair was a light brown, shot through with gleaming gold. Much like the color of his eyes.

He stepped toward her. "Are you all right? Were you worried about the storm?"

She shook her head. "I'm fine. I-I didn't know this was yer room. I was searching for the spare bed—I mean, cabin. I thought ye slept on deck."

"Not when it's raining." He shifted his weight and ran a hand through his hair. "So . . . did you like the gifts?"

"Yes." She wrapped her cloak more tightly around her. "I'm wearing one of the new nightgowns."

"I noticed."

Her face grew hot as she turned her back to him and reached for the latch. "I should be going. 'Tis not proper for me to be here."

"Who's going to know?"

A chill skittered down her back. Her grip tightened on the latch, but she didn't turn it.

"I was working on something. Would you like to see it?"

Blast him. Did he know her weakness was an insatiable curiosity? She glanced over her shoulder. "Ye're inventing something?"

He nodded and motioned toward the back of the room. "I'm making a windmill. Want to see it?" He walked out of view.

She followed slowly, stopping at the back corner of the bed. So this was his cabin. A long worktable was covered with papers, tools, and metal parts. Paned glass windows stretched along the upper half of the back wall. The bottom half was filled with dressers and bookcases. Another large window ran across the side of the room. Beneath it was a long window seat, padded with blue velvet cushions that matched the curtains around his bed.

He stopped in front of his latest invention and gave the blades a whirl. "I'm going to install it at the top of the foremast. The plan is to transfer the power of the wind to a machine."

She stepped closer. "What kind of machine?"

He shrugged, bringing her attention back to his broad shoulders. "I'm not sure yet. I'm considering a machine that could wash dirty clothes."

She snorted, then covered her mouth to keep from laughing.

He gave her an annoyed look. "It could also do sheets and towels."

A chuckle escaped her mouth.

He arched a brow. "You find it amusing that I run a clean ship?"

"I didn't realize pirates could be so tidy." She grinned. "I thought you were planning some sort of awesome war machine, a powerful weapon that would strike terror into the hearts of yer enemies."

"I don't need a weapon for that. I *am* the weapon."

Her breath caught. Good goddesses, he looked like a weapon. But she shouldn't let him intimidate her. She affected a shudder. "Oh, I'm scared."

He took a step toward her, his eyes gleaming. "You should be."

She moved back. "Aye, the tidy pirate might capture me and wash my clothes."

His mouth twitched. "I'd have to remove them first."

Another flash of lightning lit the room. The air between them felt charged, as if some sort of energy was sizzling between them.

"I should be going." She turned toward the door.

"Why do you react so badly whenever we touch?"

She halted with a jerk. "I-I don't know what ye're—" When he grabbed her arm, a shock went through her. A surge of grief and despair so overwhelming, it made her knees buckle.

"Brigitta! Dammit." He swept her up in his arms.

She was in another place. A dark room. Chilly and dank. A cellar? She was trapped there with a young Rupert, trapped in his mind, living his terror. It was cold, but he didn't dare light a fire, for someone might discover him and turn him over to the soldiers who hunted him day and night. It was dark but he didn't dare use a candle, for someone might notice the light through the window.

So afraid. So bereft. So lonely. It made her heart ache for him.

Rupert, how did ye survive?

"Brigitta," he whispered. "Don't leave me."

Her eyes flickered open. Goodness, she was lying on his bed. Had he put her here?

He was standing next to the bed, frowning. "What is it that I'm doing to you? How can I make it stop?"

"'Tis nothing. I'm fine." She scrambled out of bed and lunged toward the door.

"You're not fine." He slammed a hand against the door to keep her from opening it. "Tell me!" When she didn't answer, he planted his other hand on the door with her trapped in between. "I can touch other women without harming them, so why do—"

"Then touch them." She turned to glare at him.

"I don't want to." He moved closer till their bodies were a few inches apart. "What happens when we touch? Does it cause you pain?"

She shook her head. The pain was all his.

"Look at me."

Her eyes met his, and the intensity of his gaze took her breath away.

"I want to touch you." His gaze dropped to her mouth for a few heated seconds before returning to her eyes. "But I don't want to hurt you."

He was the one who was hurting. Lonely and bereft. Her heart filled with a need to comfort him, to hold him and tell the young boy inside him that he wasn't alone.

"May I touch you?"

She nodded, then braced herself mentally for another vision. But when his fingertips stroked her cheek, she saw nothing. She stared him, surprised for a moment, then a wave of emotion hit her so hard, it flattened her against the door.

Yearning. He wanted her.

She inhaled sharply as her heart lurched into a rapid pace. This was no young boy in need of comfort. This was a powerful, grown man, and he wanted her something fierce.

His eyes narrowed. "You felt something. What was it?"

She turned her face away. "Nothing."

"Brigitta." His fingers skimmed down her neck to her shoulder as he leaned toward her. The tip of his nose brushed across her cheek, and she felt his warm breath and the slightest touch of his lips. He paused by her ear and whispered, "You're lying."

She planted her hands on his chest and pushed. He stepped back, taking her hands and moving them beneath his shirt so she was touching his bare skin. His eyes burned an amber gold, and his heart pounded against the palm of her hand.

She swallowed hard. "I'll tell you my secrets, if ye will tell me yers."

His mouth thinned. "I have nothing to tell."

"Rupert." She repeated the words he'd used. "Ye're lying."

He squeezed her hands. "Then we've both been caught."

They stared at each other for a few sad seconds, then he released her and stepped back. "I'll fetch a lantern and take you to the spare cabin."

She slipped into the dark passageway and took a deep breath to calm her nerves. Good goddesses, now she knew how much he wanted her. But she didn't dare give in to her own feelings of attraction. How could she, when he didn't trust her enough to tell her his secrets? And she didn't trust him enough, either.

She glanced back to see him coming toward her, holding a lantern in one hand while stuffing a paper into a pocket of his breeches with the other.

"This way." He led her down the passageway.

"I thought the spare room was supposed to be next door to us."

"It is." He glanced at her with a smile. "On the other side."

"Oh." She followed him into the second guest cabin. It was smaller than the one she and Sister Fallyn had been using. Other than the narrow bed, the only other furniture was a table and two chairs.

"I'll leave you this." He reached up to hang the lantern on a hook in the ceiling.

"Thank you." The room grew quiet except for the pattering of rain against the small window. She adjusted her grip on the edges of her cloak to keep her nightgown from showing. Why wasn't he leaving? He was scowling at the floor, seemingly lost in thought.

"Is something wrong?" she asked. Had he reconsidered and decided to divulge his secrets?

He took a deep breath. "Earlier today, when I was in Danport, I learned why your brother wants you back."

"Oh." Her chest tightened. By the look on Rupert's face, the reason wasn't good.

"I've been wondering all day how to break the news—"

"Is it that bad?"

With a grimace, he removed the paper from his pocket. "I'll let you judge for yourself."

She unfolded the sheet of paper and stood underneath the lantern to read it. A competition. Her hands trembled.

"Seven suitors vying for my hand," she whispered.

"Seven?" Rupert took the paper and looked it over. "I don't recall there being a number—"

"It's coming true." She pressed a hand against her pounding heart. Luciana's prediction was coming true!

Rupert gave her a confused look. "What . . . ?"

"I didn't want this to happen!" She paced across the room. "Holy goddesses, I don't—I can't be a prize!" It was even worse than she had feared. The men would be competing not for her hand, but for her body.

She leaned over, gasping for air. The winner would have the right to rape her.

Rupert set the paper on the table. "I'm sure this must be upsetting—"

"You think so?" she cried. "My brother is a monster! How can he treat me like a-a . . ."

"Broodmare."

A chill skittered across her bones, and she wrapped her arms around herself.

Rupert cursed under his breath. "I know it stinks. I debated whether I should even tell you—"

"Oh, no!" A horrible thought crossed her mind. "Ye're planning to send me to that monster, aren't you? So ye can get yer pile of gold. How could you?" She raised a fist to hit him, but he caught her by the wrist.

A vision flashed through her mind, the image of a baby

in a crib, but in her distress, she pushed it aside. "Let me go!"

He tightened his grip. "I will protect you."

She blinked. "What?"

"You want control of your own destiny. I will protect that."

Her jaw dropped. "Th-then ye're not planning to send me to my brother?"

"Only if you want to go." He released her wrist and motioned toward the table. "Let's go over your options."

"What? Are ye saying ye're willing to give up on my ransom?"

He sat at the table and gave her a wry smile. "I have other ways of stealing Gunther's gold."

Her heart softened. "Thank you." He *was* her tall and handsome stranger, after all. As she sat beside him, she realized the Game of Stones could have only referred to Rupert. He'd come into her life, not to kidnap her from her brother, but to rescue her.

She took a deep breath. "I would like to go to Ebton Palace to live with my sister, Luciana. She could pay—"

"I don't want Eberoni gold."

"Only Gunther's?" When he nodded, she wondered once again what sort of grudge he had against her brother.

Rupert tapped a finger on the paper. "Gunther needs you. Or rather, he needs your womb."

She grimaced. "Disgusting pig."

"After a fiery battle with a Norveshki dragon, Gunther is no longer able to father children. You are his only hope of having an heir from his own bloodline. That means he will be desperate to get you in his court and under his power. Desperate enough that he could attack Eberon and—"

"Luciana could be in danger?" Brigitta sat back in her

chair. She couldn't cause any harm to come to her sister or Leo or the baby.

"If the two countries go to war, there will be many lives lost—"

"Fine." Brigitta jumped to her feet and paced across the room. "Then I won't go there. I'll go back to the Isle of Moon."

"Gunther could attack the convent—"

"Fine!" She couldn't endanger any of the sisters. "Is there any safe place I can go?"

Rupert shrugged. "You would probably be safe with Gunther. After all, he needs you healthy."

She scoffed. "Are ye serious?"

"You would have pretty gowns and balls to attend. Doesn't every girl want to be a princess?"

She grabbed a pillow off the bed and clobbered him upside the head.

"Hey!" He gave her an indignant look. "That wasn't very princess-like."

She lifted the pillow again, ready to strike, but his smile stopped her. With a groan, she tossed the pillow back on the bed. "Should I hide somewhere? Change my name? Wear a disguise like yerself?"

His mouth twitched. "Do you want to be a lady pirate?"

With a huff, she crossed her arms. "I know nothing of the sea."

He shifted on the chair, his smile fading. "There is a place that only I and my most trusted crew members know about."

"Really?" She sat beside him. "Where?"

He tapped his fingers on the table. "The location is a secret."

She snorted. "Of course."

"It's a small island we've been going to for about five years now. Some of the men took their wives there and built homes, so we now have a small village. A few farms, a miller, a bakery, a smithy."

"What do ye call it?"

He shrugged. "I never named it, but the others call it Rupert's Island."

She stood and wandered across the room. "Ye're willing to take me there?"

"I will do whichever option you want."

"Thank you." With a quick breath, she made her decision. "It would be safer for everyone if I hide on yer island."

"Very well." He stood. "We'll set sail at dawn."

She nodded. So she would hide. Was that taking the coward's way out? But what choice did she really have?

"Good night, then."

Tears burned her eyes. When would she ever see her sisters again? "Is there a way to let my sisters know where I am? And that I'm all right?"

A pained look crossed his face. "It would be best for you to simply disappear. No one can know where you are. And I can never let anyone know where the island is. Not even you."

She blinked away tears. She was banishing herself from the rest of the world, going to an island that would eventually feel like a prison. But it was the only way to protect her sisters and the nuns who had raised her. "How long will I have to stay there?"

"You will not be safe until Gunther dies."

Her breath caught. "Th-that could be years."

In the dim light, Rupert's face grew harsh. "Trust me. It will not be long now."

Her heart grew still. "What are ye planning to do?"

He turned toward the door. "Good night."

"Wait!" She ran toward him. "I know ye have a grudge against him. And ye like to steal his gold. But . . . please don't . . ."

He gave her a stern look. "Are you sympathetic to your brother?"

"No! He's a monster."

Rupert turned back to the door. "Then you need not be concerned."

"My concern is for you." She grabbed his arm and was instantly flooded with a wave of rage: *Fury.* "It is one thing for you to be a thief, but please don't be something worse. Even if he deserves to be murdered, please don't . . . don't do this to yerself. Ye're a man of honor!"

He stiffened, staring at her with a stunned look.

"Rupert—"

"No. I will have my revenge, and even you will not stop me." He left, closing the door in her face.

Chapter Fourteen

The next morning, a scream woke Brigitta from a fitful slumber. She jumped out of bed and ran to the door just as she heard Sister Fallyn shriek again.

"Brigitta!"

She dashed into the passageway. "I'm here!"

Sister Fallyn whirled around, her face stricken with panic. "Oh!" She stumbled, colliding with the wall. "Oh, dear goddesses, ye scared me to death."

"I'm fine." Brigitta patted her on the back.

Footsteps pounded on the nearby stairs as Rupert raced down them. He halted with a jerk when he saw them.

Brigitta's heart squeezed at the frantic look on his face. He must have heard the scream. "I'm fine," she repeated.

Sister Fallyn slumped against the wall as if she was too weak from shock to support herself. "I woke up and ye were gone. Where were you?"

Brigitta glanced over the nun's shoulder to see Rupert watching them. He was wearing a scarf on his head again, but no hat or mask. He now had boots on his feet, and somehow he'd managed to button his shirt. That was a shame.

What was she thinking? Her cheeks grew warm. "I was sleeping next door."

"Ye should have woken me! I would have gladly given you the bed." Sister Fallyn pressed a hand to her chest. "Dear goddesses, I thought someone had dragged ye off to ravish you!"

Brigitta's face blazed with more heat. Should she tell the nun that a potential ravisher was standing right behind them? She glanced at him once again.

One side of his mouth had curled up in amusement. He tilted his head as his gaze slid down her. All hint of a smile disappeared. Her skin prickled as she recalled the emotions she'd felt from him last night. Yearning. Desire.

Good goddesses, she had nothing on but a sheer night-gown!

"Come." She grabbed the nun and bustled her into their cabin. With the door shut, she quickly changed into her convent gown.

When they ventured into the passageway to go to the privy, she noted that Rupert was gone.

After returning to their room, she peered out the window. The rain had stopped, and a brilliant sun sparkled on blue water. The ship was moving, cutting smoothly through a calm ocean. None of the other ships were in sight. That seemed odd, since the fleet usually trailed behind the *Golden Star*.

Jeffrey knocked on the door with their breakfast.

"What happened to the other ships?" she asked as he set their tray on the table.

"Oh, they're staying close to Danport," Jeffrey explained. "In case some pirates come."

Brigitta helped him unload the tray. "But they won't have Rupert's special powers to defeat the pirates."

Jeffrey nodded. "They would have to fight the old-fashioned way. But that's not a problem. Captain

Ansel can handle it. He'll be in charge while we're away."

Sister Fallyn frowned. "Then where are we going?"

Jeffrey scratched his head. "I'm not supposed to say. That's another reason the other ships stayed behind. They have too many new crew members, and Rupert doesn't trust them yet." The boy gave them a sheepish look. "He doesn't want you to know which way we're headed, either, so you're supposed to stay belowdecks."

The nun's eyes widened with shock. "What is he planning to do with us?"

"Don't worry," Brigitta assured her. "We're just going to a secret place. Rupert told me about it last night."

Sister Fallyn looked even more upset. "Ye talked to him alone?"

"I'll explain after breakfast," Brigitta said.

Sister Fallyn huffed as Jeffrey made a quick exit.

After a few bites of oatmeal, the nun set down her spoon. "I must know what's happening."

"Very well." Brigitta fetched the paper from the next room. When she returned, the nun was nervously pacing about. "Here."

Sister Fallyn quickly read the notice, then dropped it on the floor and backed away as if it were poisonous. Her hand fluttered to her chest, then her mouth. "I-I think I may be sick."

"We'll be all right." Brigitta patted her shoulder. "Rupert has agreed to take us to a secret place where my brother will never find me."

"But what about the gold he would make with yer ransom?"

"He's willing to give it up, so we'll be safe."

"Oh, my." Sister Fallyn collapsed in a chair. "These pirates are surprisingly . . . noble."

"Aye," Brigitta agreed. "I believe Rupert and the captain are honorable men." She didn't want to mention the revenge that Rupert might be planning. She'd tossed on the narrow bed half the night, trying to figure out why he would hate Gunther enough to kill him.

Was it somehow connected to the visions she'd seen? Rupert's father had been murdered, then his mother had been driven off a cliff. Both of them had died, an eerie echo of the ill-fated deaths that had befallen the hero and heroine in the book Rupert had loaned her. Had the deaths of his parents inflicted a wound on him so severe that he was now drawn to tragic endings? Did a happy one seem impossible to him?

And why did Rupert want her brother dead? In her visions, Rupert had been a child when he'd lost his parents. So it seemed doubtful that Gunther had been responsible. He was only a few years older than Rupert.

Sister Fallyn suddenly rose to her feet. "I have made a momentous decision."

Brigitta blinked. "Ye have?"

"Aye." Sister Fallyn nodded. "Ye're a princess, so ye must remain pure and untouched. And it is my sworn duty to protect you, no matter what."

"I don't think I'm in any danger—"

"And so—" Sister Fallyn clasped her hands together at her chest—"when the captain comes to ravish us, I will offer myself."

Brigitta gasped. "Sister, I don't think—"

"I will make the supreme sacrifice!" The nun's eyes glimmered with tears. "It is my duty. Ye must allow me to do this for you."

Brigitta winced. "All right. Thank you."

"Good." Sister Fallyn sat back down to finish her breakfast.

Brigitta sighed. She'd only agreed because she seriously doubted such a scenario would ever come to pass.

And Sister Fallyn had seemed so adamant that Brigitta hadn't wanted to diminish the nun's act of bravery.

Even so, she had a strange feeling that Sister Fallyn might actually be disappointed if the proposed ravishment never occurred.

By that afternoon, Brigitta and Sister Fallyn were tired of feeling cooped up in their room. With nothing to do, the only chore they could come up with was washing the clothes they'd been wearing for three days. When they asked Jeffrey about it, he returned with good news. Captain Landers had given them permission to come on deck to do laundry.

They changed into their new shifts and gowns, then headed up the stairs with their clothes from the convent. Brigitta inhaled deeply, enjoying the fresh sea air after the stuffiness of their cabin.

Jeffrey was on the portside, filling a tub with fresh water and soap. "Here you go. After the rain, we have plenty of water."

"Thank you." Sister Fallyn dropped their clothes into the tub. "We can take over from here."

While the nun swished their clothes in the soapy water with a paddle, Brigitta looked around the ship. Captain Landers, or Stefan, as he wanted them to call him, was on the quarterdeck with a helmsman. Rupert was up in the crow's nest, facing forward. The sails were full, though she couldn't tell if the wind was natural or caused by him.

"I wonder why he's still wearing the scarf," she murmured.

Sister Fallyn shrugged. "Who knows?" She ventured a glance toward the quarterdeck.

"It keeps the sun off my head," Rupert's voice tickled Brigitta's ear.

She glanced up at the crow's nest to find him now focused on her. His mention of the sun reminded her that she should be able to tell which direction they were headed. Since it was midafternoon, the sun would be slightly to the west. That meant they were currently headed north?

"Are you trying to figure out where we're going?" Rupert's voice filtered toward her on a breeze.

"North," she whispered.

"At the moment, yes. But as long as you're on deck, we'll be going in circles." With a movement of one hand, he shifted the wind.

On the quarterdeck, Stefan yelled out orders, and crewmen adjusted the sails. The ship veered slowly toward the east.

So they didn't think she could be trusted. Why? Because Gunther was her brother? How could she have any loyalty to a family member who had ignored her existence until he needed to use her? Brigitta shot Rupert an annoyed look, then turned her back to him and took the paddle from Sister Fallyn. "Let me do it awhile." She gave the clothes a stab.

The nun frowned at the large tub. "This is a lot of work for only a few clothes. Perhaps I should see if . . . someone else has some laundry they would like done?" She glanced again toward the quarterdeck.

"Ye mean Stefan?" Brigitta whispered. "I suppose it wouldn't hurt to ask."

Sister Fallyn took a tiny step toward the quarterdeck, then stopped. "Nay. It wouldn't be proper to mix a man's clothes with ours."

"I don't think he would mind."

Sister Fallyn bit her lip. "He might think I'm terribly forward—"

"There's no harm in simply talking to him."

Sister Fallyn nodded. "Actually, I should thank him for rescuing us from the clutches of yer evil brother. That would only be well mannered of me."

"Exactly." Even though Brigitta considered Rupert the main rescuer. She smiled to herself as Sister Fallyn cautiously approached the quarterdeck.

Normally, she would never approve of a relationship between a man and a nun, but Sister Fallyn's life was no longer normal. She and Brigitta could end up stranded on Rupert's Island for years.

Once again, a jab of disappointment pricked at her. No matter how she thought about it, running away to hide seemed a bit cowardly. But what choice did she have when her brother was planning to use her so abominably? Or when he could use his army or navy to attack those she cared about.

She also felt guilty that Sister Fallyn would be forced to share her self-imposed exile. But if the sister was able to find some happiness in the midst of this turmoil, then Brigitta would be delighted for her. And relieved that she wasn't destroying the nun's life.

She glanced toward the quarterdeck. The captain and Sister Fallyn were talking to each other quietly. He looked just as nervous as she did. With a smile, Brigitta swirled the paddle around.

"Happy?" Rupert's voice filtered down.

She tilted her head toward the quarterdeck.

"Perhaps we should do the same," he said. "Would you like to come up here?"

She grimaced. "Good goddesses, no. I would be too afraid to climb that high."

"No need to climb. I have a pulley system that will whisk you up here in a few seconds."

"That sounds even more frightening."

He smiled. "Not if we did it together. If it scares you, you can hang on to me."

She scoffed. Next he would be telling her she could wrap her legs around him and squeeze him tight. When he didn't, she felt almost . . . disappointed. Blast him. She turned her attention back to swirling the clothes.

"Then I shall come to you."

Her disappointment vanished. In fact, she felt quite breathless as he swung his legs over the side of the crow's nest and slid down a rope. He landed neatly and strode toward her, removing his gloves.

She tried not to think about the way his biceps had bulged as he'd controlled his descent of the rope. Or the swagger of his long-legged stride as he approached her. Instead, she focused on the laundry.

She stirred so briskly, some water sloshed over the side of the tub and landed on his boots. "Oh, sorry."

"No problem." He reached for the paddle. "Shall I take over for a while?"

"Nay, I'm fine. Did ye have any . . . shirts ye wanted to add?"

He stepped closer and lowered his voice, "Are you still trying to undress me?"

She snorted and gave him a wry look. "Perhaps some-day, someone will invent a machine for this."

"No doubt, it would take a genius."

She laughed.

"You doubt me?" He grinned. "Now I will definitely have to invent one."

"Brigitta!" Sister Fallyn rushed down the steps. "Ye shouldn't be alone with him."

"He's helping us escape my brother," Brigitta said, coming to his defense. "And there's no need for you to worry. He's perfectly harmless."

"Excuse me?" Rupert growled.

"I know he's helping, and I appreciate that." Sister Fallyn slanted Rupert an apologetic look. "I am sorry, young man, but ye must understand that she's a princess—"

"Sister," Brigitta objected.

"'Tis true, whether ye like it or not," Sister Fallyn said.

"I understand." Rupert gave Brigitta a mocking bow. "Thank the Light I'm too *harmless* to cause any danger to Your Most Royal Highness."

Brigitta huffed. "This is ridiculous."

"I shall console myself tonight under the stars," Rupert continued as he slipped his gloves back on. "Even though the moons will have separated from their embrace, they will still be almost close enough to touch." He gave Brigitta a pointed look. "And that will give me hope."

A shiver ran down her arms. He was asking her to see him tonight, she was sure of it. She inclined her head. "I'm sure it will be lovely."

His eyes gleamed a golden amber as his mouth curled into a smile. "Indeed." He strode back toward the mast, grabbed a rope, and with a yank on a lever he shot back up to the crow's nest.

Tonight. Brigitta smiled to herself. As soon as Sister Fallyn was fast asleep, she would see Rupert again.

Would she come?

Rupert stood alone at the wheel. He'd dismissed the helmsman, so there would be no one else on the quarter-deck. And he'd ordered the other crewmen on duty to stay toward the bow of the ship. Only the silly pelican remained close by. With most of the sails furled and a minimum breeze, he was advancing the ship very slowly. If she did come, he doubted she would be able to detect their north-western heading.

His hands gripped the wheel. He would miss her once

she was left behind on the island. *It won't be for long*, he promised himself. With her safe, he could immediately set the Official Plan into action.

First step, seek out the Tourinian navy and destroy it. Hopefully, he'd be able to crash the ships without losing too many lives. He was, after all, the rightful king, so he didn't relish the prospect of killing his own countrymen. Only Gunther and his supporters needed to die.

His thoughts returned to Brigitta's plea that he not kill her brother. *Ye're a man of honor*. Dammit. It was a matter of honor that he avenge his family and take back the throne.

But if he killed Gunther, would she be able to love him? *Dammit to hell*. Why should he care how she felt? Since when did he even want her to love him?

He curled his hands into fists and pounded one against the wheel. Of all the stupid things—he was falling for her. Falling for the daughter of the man who had killed his father and destroyed his family. Falling for a woman who was impossible for him to trust.

She didn't trust him, either. She refused to confide in him. He gritted his teeth. That had to stop—

"Good evening," she said softly as she ascended the stairs to the quarterdeck.

He swallowed hard. Why was she so damned beautiful?

"Is something wrong? Ye were frowning something fierce."

He took a deep breath and spoke to her in Tourinian. "I wasn't sure you would come."

"I'm here now," she answered in the same language. She looked up at the sky and smiled. "The stars are as bright as diamonds tonight. And the moons so full and pretty, side by side."

Why did he love the way she spoke Tourinian so much? Her voice was soft and almost musical with its island lilt. How sweet she would sound on a dark night as she lay in his arms, her long legs entwined with his. *Dammit.* Why did he want her so badly? "Why don't you trust me?"

She blinked and gave him a surprised look.

"I'm taking you to a safe place. I agreed that you should decide your own destiny." He scowled at her. "You should trust me."

She shifted her weight. "Trust has to be earned."

"I could have earned ten thousand gold coins for your ransom, but I gave it up."

Her eyes narrowed. "Are you saying I owe you something in return?"

"No!" He gritted his teeth. "Yes, dammit. You should trust me."

"I've known you only three days!"

But he'd known her since she was a babe. "Brigitta, all I want is for you tell me what happens to you when you touch me." When she opened her mouth, he quickly added, "And don't tell me it's nothing. You fainted the first time I touched you. You nearly drowned yesterday when I grabbed you in the water. Am I hurting you somehow? Am I poisonous to you?"

"No! You're not . . . hurting me."

"Then tell me, dammit. Because I want to be able to touch you." He lifted a hand to caress her face, but hesitated an inch away. "I like touching you."

Her eyes glittered with tears as she stepped back.

Was she going to leave? "Brigitta." *Don't leave me.*

Her eyes met his. There was so much emotion in her eyes and face. A mixture of fear, nervousness, sympathy, and did he dare hope? Desire.

"Why do you say my name as if you know me?" she asked.

He winced inwardly. "There are things I dare not say."

"Then our distrust is mutual."

"I trust you enough to show you my face." He pulled the scarf off his head and tossed it on the deck. "And no one, other than my own crew, is allowed that much. You know enough about me to endanger my life if you ever tell—"

"I would never do that!"

"I believe you." Rupert gave her a pained look. "I trust you that much. So please, tell me."

She drew in a shaky breath. "I-I suppose it would be safe. After all, you're the same way."

"The same what?"

"But you have to understand, I've been warned my entire life not to ever tell anyone. People like us are killed on the mainland, so I—"

"Holy crap. You're Embraced?"

She hesitated, then nodded. "Yes."

He remained stunned for a few seconds. He'd never met anyone before who was Embraced like him, so the idea had never occurred to him.

"Damn." He ran a hand through his hair as his mind raced. When he'd first met her, that horrific day, it had been winter, and she'd been about three months old. "You were born on the night of the Autumn Embrace?"

"Yes." She wandered toward the starboard railing to gaze up at the twin moons. "Growing up, I always assumed that my parents had sent me to the Isle of Moon for my own protection. But now I know that my father wanted rid of me. I was a loose end after he . . ."

Killed my father, Rupert mentally finished her sentence.

"I want nothing to do with my family," she whispered. "I hate to even think of them as family. They're monsters, and to think I share their blood . . ." She shuddered.

"You're not like them."

She turned toward him with tears in her eyes. "Thank you."

The Light help him, he wanted to grab her and hold her tight. He wanted to show her how beautiful she was. He wanted to revel in her sweet innocence and kiss away all her self-doubt.

He joined her at the railing. "What is your gift as one of the Embraced?"

She wrinkled her nose. "It's not nearly as exciting or useful as your gift."

"It causes you to faint whenever a handsome man touches you?"

She snorted. "Are you calling yourself handsome?"

He smiled. "It was you who said it. You said I shouldn't be hiding my handsome face."

"Oh." Her cheeks grew pink.

"So what is your gift?" He leaned close. "Show me yours and I'll show you mine."

She huffed. "I've already seen yours."

"Are you sure?"

"Of course. It was very impress—" When he laughed, she gave him an annoyed look. "Are we still talking about gifts?"

"Are we?"

"Are you going to answer everything with a question?"

"Am I?"

She swatted his arm, then grew still, her face pale.

"What?" He grabbed her shoulders. "What happened?"

"I—sometimes, I see things. Images. Sometimes, I just feel emotions." She regarded him sadly. "I saw you hiding in a cave. So lonesome and afraid. I'm so sorry."

He released her and stepped back. "What are you—you're eavesdropping on my mind? Invading my thoughts?"

She winced. "I don't know what you're thinking. Though I can guess by the look on your face that you're not at all pleased."

He swallowed hard. How much did she know?

"Let me explain," she quickly added. "My gift enables me to find lost or hidden things. At the convent, it came in very handy whenever a sister would lose or misplace an item. All I had to do was touch her while thinking about the item, and then I would see it in my mind."

He narrowed his eyes. "So if I say I've lost my . . . hat, you could tell me where it is?"

"I doubt it's actually lost."

"Humor me."

"Fine." She touched his sleeve. "It's on the bed in your cabin."

"Amazing."

She snorted. "Not really. I only knew it was your bed because I've seen your room before. Otherwise, it could be any bed in the world."

He frowned. "How many beds do you think I've been to?"

"I didn't mean . . ." Her face flushed. "Let me put it this way. You accidentally drop a coin overboard. I might see a vision of it at the bottom of the sea, but that wouldn't help you find it. Not when it could be anywhere in the ocean. So you see, it's not always a very useful gift."

"But why did you see me in a cave? I didn't lose anything there."

She winced. "I don't just see lost things. I see things that have been hidden. Usually, my reaction is very mild, but with you . . . well, I've never met anyone who is hiding as much as you."

He stiffened. "You see hidden . . . memories?"

She nodded. "One time when I was about twelve, I was

running to the dining hall for dinner, and I tripped and fell over. Sister Marian helped me up, and I saw her crying and holding a baby who had just passed away. Without thinking, I blurted out how sorry I was that she'd lost her baby. She went deathly pale, then burst into tears and ran back to her room. The next day, she acted normal again, but from then on, whenever she saw me, this pained look would cross her face, and I knew I was causing her to remember her grief, over and over again."

"That's a sad story," Rupert murmured.

Brigitta nodded. "Sister Marian had never told anyone at the convent her secret, because she'd wanted to escape the painful memory and make a new life for herself, but I messed it up for her. That's when I realized that people don't always keep secrets because they're being dishonest or deceitful. Sometimes we push memories into a dark hole because they're too painful to live with day after day. Sometimes we have to keep secrets just to survive."

A chill ran down Rupert's back. Had she been seeing his secrets?

Brigitta sighed. "After that, I had my own secret. I didn't tell anyone I could see their hidden memories. After all, it doesn't help anyone. It only makes them uncomfortable. If people are desperate enough to keep a secret, then they don't want it to be exposed."

He gripped the railing hard. "So every time we touched, you saw something?"

She nodded. "But I would never tell any—"

"What did you see?"

She winced. "An ambush. A battle. A dark basement. The crypt where your mother is interred. A—"

"Enough." He stepped back. She knew way too much.

"I could feel your emotions, too." She turned toward

him with tears in her eyes. "So much grief and despair. My heart ached—"

"Enough!" He retreated another step, his hands clenched into fists. "I'm not that child anymore."

"I think you are."

"No!" He gritted his teeth. "You should go now."

Her shoulders slumped. "I shouldn't have told you. I'm sorry." She wandered toward the stairs.

When she glanced back, a tear was rolling down her check, and he felt like a complete ass.

"Your secrets are safe with me," she whispered, then hurried down the stairs.

Crap! He wanted to pummel something. He wanted to beat something till his knuckles were bloody and raw. She knew too much. And if they kept touching each other, she would know even more. *Dammit.* No matter how much he longed for her, he couldn't touch her again.

Chapter Fifteen

He was avoiding her.

Brigitta paced about the cabin. She should have known this would happen. After she'd blurted out Sister Marian's secret, the nun had been careful to avoid her.

Why had she thought Rupert would be different? Even though he was attracted to her, that didn't mean he wanted to share his secrets. She'd learned from her visions that he'd spent years of his life hiding in dark places, afraid of being captured. He'd been forced to keep his identity secret in order to survive. So it only made sense that he wouldn't want her to discover who he really was.

Unfortunately, her curiosity refused to quit. She was even more compelled to figure him out. Who was this sorcerer who monopolized her thoughts and made her heart squeeze with longing? How could she gain his trust? How could she convince him that his secrets were safe with her?

A whole day had passed, and she'd seen him only once. After the midday meal, she and Sister Fallyn had ventured out on deck for some fresh air. While the nun had chatted with Stefan, Brigitta had approached the crow's nest where Rupert was standing.

"Good afternoon," she'd said softly, knowing he would be able to hear her if he wanted to.

No reply.

"I could meet you tonight under the stars," she'd suggested. Silence had stretched out while she'd grown increasingly tense.

His whisper had finally filtered down. "Not tonight." Then he'd grabbed a rope and swung through the air to the next mast, where he'd dropped a few feet to land neatly on a yardarm. After grasping another rope, he'd swooped down toward the bow of the ship, disappearing from her view.

Normally, such athletic feats would have made her breathless, but she'd been too mortified to appreciate it.

He was avoiding her. She should have known not to tell him the truth.

But she'd wanted to be close to him. She'd wanted to forge a bond with him where they could share their secrets, thoughts, and burdens. She'd wanted to be special to him.

It hurt. Blast him. His rejection hurt. And that could only mean she truly cared for him.

She'd fallen for him.

Now she was back in their cabin, pacing about. How on Aerthlan had she fallen for a man when she didn't even know who he was?

But she knew his heart. She knew he was good and honorable, responsible and clever, strong and handsome. She knew his pain and heartache. His grief and fear. She'd felt his desire for her. His yearning.

Hadn't she? Good goddesses, had she just imagined his desire out of wishful thinking?

"Will ye sit down for a minute?" Sister Fallyn fussed. "Ye're going to wear holes into yer slippers."

With a groan, Brigitta collapsed in a chair. "Aye. We

could be stuck on that island for years, so I may never have another pair of slippers."

Sister Fallyn scoffed. "Why are ye being so negative? 'Tis not like you."

Brigitta shrugged. How could she gain his trust if he refused to see her?

"Stefan has told me all about the island," Sister Fallyn continued. "They're growing oats and barley. And raising sheep. They even have a few milk cows. And he said we could use his cottage. I think it will be quite lovely."

Brigitta nodded.

"And Stefan said they'll come to visit every month or so and bring us whatever we need. So if ye need new slippers, ye'll only have to ask."

Brigitta sighed. "Ye don't think it's cowardly of me to hide?"

Sister Fallyn scoffed. "Would ye rather have yer brother condemning you to a life of abuse?"

A knock sounded on the door.

"That must be our dinner." Sister Fallyn stood. "Come in!"

Jeffrey opened the door to reveal Stefan holding an enormous tray of food.

"May I join you?" Stefan walked in to deposit the tray on the table. Jeffrey put a jug of wine on the sideboard then scampered away.

Sister Fallyn blushed. "I suppose it would be all right." She busied herself unloading the tray.

"Thank you." Stefan slanted a tender look toward the nun that she didn't see, but Brigitta did.

And her heart hurt even more. "I'm not very hungry. I think I'll lie down in the cabin next door."

Sister Fallyn gave her a worried look. "Are ye ill?"

"I'm fine. I just didn't sleep very much last night." That much was true. Brigitta had hardly slept a wink, for she'd kept replaying her confession to Rupert in her mind and remembering the horrified look on his face.

She blinked her eyes to keep tears from gathering. "Good night." She hurried from the room and dashed into the smaller cabin next door.

The sun was setting outside, so only a little light filtered through the small window. And the lantern had long since run out of oil. She lay on the bed, watching the encroaching shadows until she finally fell asleep.

Sometime later, a knock on her door awakened her. Was it Rupert? She jumped out of bed and fumbled toward the door in the dark. "Yes?"

The door opened and Jeffrey peered inside. "I brought you some food."

"Oh." She opened the door to let in more light from the passageway. The scent of roast beef made her mouth water. "Thank you."

Jeffrey set the tray on the table, then hurried back out. "I'll bring you a lantern."

In a few minutes he was back, and Brigitta held a chair for him to climb up and replace the old lantern on the ceiling hook.

"There." He jumped down from the chair. "Rupert heard you didn't have any dinner, so he told me to bring you something nice."

Brigitta's heart did a little leap. Rupert might be avoiding her, but he hadn't forgotten her.

With her appetite back, she sat down to eat. What could be so important about his secrets that he couldn't let anyone know? Did it have something to do with his plan of revenge against her brother? Why did he hate Gunther so much?

Gunther was twelve years older than her. Rupert was seven years older, or six and a half to be precise. Any way she looked at it, it seemed like Gunther would have been too young to have killed Rupert's father, yet he was the one Rupert had targeted for revenge.

She replayed the vision of the ambush in her mind. The men had been on horseback. Some wearing uniforms. Guards? Others had been richly clothed in velvet with fur-lined capes. *Nobles.*

Rupert's father had been a nobleman.

If Gunther hadn't killed Rupert's father, then—Brigitta dropped her fork with a clatter. No, not her father.

Her heart pounded as she tried to stop where her thoughts were going. Had her father killed Rupert's father? Good goddesses, no!

She jumped to her feet. *No, no.* She didn't want to believe it.

But she knew from her history lessons that Tourin had long been plagued with uprisings and civil war. It was not uncommon for a king to demolish a noble family if he considered them traitors. If Rupert did come from nobility and his entire family had been wiped out, who but a king would have had the power to do that?

She paced about the room. This couldn't be it. She was mistaken. There had to be some other explanation. She just needed to reexamine all the visions. There had to be a way to fit the puzzle pieces together so they would construct an entirely different picture.

For how could she live with the notion that her father had killed Rupert's father?

"It can't be true." She stopped with a jerk. If it was true, Rupert would know.

Her knees gave out and she collapsed on the floor.

He would hate her.

The next day, when Jeffrey came to their cabin to collect their luncheon tray, he announced, "The captain said you could go on deck now. We're approaching Rupert's Island."

"Oh, how exciting!" Sister Fallyn leaped to her feet and ran toward the open doorway.

Brigitta helped Jeffrey stack their plates and bowls on the tray.

He gave her a worried look. "You didn't eat very much. And you hardly ate anything last night."

She attempted a smile. "I'll be all right."

Jeffrey didn't look convinced. "The island is a nice place. If I didn't want to be a sea captain someday, I would be happy to live there."

"I'm sure it will be lovely." Tears threatened once again, and she blinked them away. She'd cried enough last night. Self-pity wasn't going to change anything. It couldn't change the fact that she was going to spend her life in hiding. It couldn't reunite her with her sisters. It couldn't make it possible for her and Rupert to have a happy ending.

Sister Fallyn huffed outside the door. "Are ye not coming?"

Brigitta followed the nun up the steps. On deck, a cool breeze helped wipe away some of the grogginess of a sleepless night. Her gaze lifted automatically to the crow's nest. Rupert was there, his back to her, and she was surprised to see him wearing his mask, scarf, and hat once again. Good goddesses, he even disguised himself on his own island? Did the man trust no one?

He'd let her see his face and hair. He'd given her that much trust. Did he now regret it?

"Brigitta, look!" Sister Fallyn called from the starboard railing.

As she approached the railing, she saw an emerald-green island rising out of the blue sea. Seagulls cawed

as they swooped back and forth along the rocky coastline.

"Isn't it beautiful?" Sister Fallyn made the sign of the
moons. "Thank the goddesses we have found a safe ref-
uge."

An exile, Brigitta thought, although she had to admit
the island was lovely. The coastline was jagged with dramatic cliffs and rock formations.

"Look!" Sister Fallyn pointed at a waterfall that cascaded over a cliff. Where the water plunged into the sea,
a shimmering rainbow arched over a cloud of mist.

"Do you like it?" Rupert's voice tickled her ear as it
swept past her on a breeze.

Her heart squeezed. He was talking to her again. "'Tis
beautiful."

"It's very pleasant during the summer, but the winters
can be a bit harsh," Rupert said.

Brigitta nodded. The breeze here was cooler than what
she was accustomed to on the Isle of Moon. This island
had to be situated farther north.

Up on the quarterdeck, Stefan called out some orders,
and crewmen rushed about, lowering some sails and ad-
justing others. Brigitta saw the reason why as the ship
sailed past a rocky peninsula that jutted into the sea. Just
on the other side, a wide bay stretched out before them.

Instead of cliffs, the land sloped gently to a sandy
beach. Several whitewashed stone buildings had been
built along the shore close to a wooden pier. More stone
cottages dotted the green fields.

A horn sounded on the ship, and Brigitta watched as
people stopped working in the fields or along the shore.
Cottage doors opened and more people peered outside.
Soon, they were all waving their arms and running toward
the pier.

As the ship moved farther into the bay, Brigitta noticed

that most of the people on the pier were women and children. Meanwhile, on deck, Stefan continued to call out orders. With the sails lowered, they crept forward slowly. Anchors were dropped, and the ship shuddered and groaned as it finally came to a stop.

Crewmen wheeled out the pulley system Rupert had invented for loading and unloading supplies. He slid down a rope to direct the crewmen. Stefan joined him as he decided which supplies to load into each dinghy.

Eventually, Stefan walked over to them. "I apologize for the delay. We'll take you ashore as soon as possible."

"There's no hurry," Brigitta assured him.

Sister Fallyn smiled at him. "The island is every bit as lovely as ye said."

He smiled back. "I think we're doing something wonderfully new and different here. For the first time in their lives, these people are not working fields or living in houses that are owned by a nobleman."

"Ye mean Rupert hasn't claimed that the island belongs to him?" Brigitta asked.

Stefan shook his head. "We call it Rupert's Island because he discovered it, but when our crewmen asked if they could bring their families and settle here, Rupert told them he would not be their landlord. They would be the lords of their own lands and decide their own destiny."

Brigitta's heart squeezed in her chest. How could she not fall in love with such a man?

"But what if there is disagreement among the people?" Sister Fallyn asked. "Surely someone must be in charge."

"They vote for someone to be the village chieftain," Stefan replied. "For the last few years, that's been Granny Hargraves. She's considered the oldest and wisest."

"A female chieftain?" Sister Fallyn exchanged a smile with Brigitta. "This may not be that different from the convent."

"Oh, it's different." Stefan motioned toward the crewmen who were rushing about on deck. "These men are in a hurry to get ashore. Those are their wives and children on the pier. Granny Hargraves will be watching over the children this afternoon while the men—" He stopped with a wince. "Well, it's not a convent."

Sister Fallyn blushed.

Brigitta smiled to herself. "And ye were never tempted to marry, Captain?"

His gaze slid to Sister Fallyn. "I've been waiting for the right woman. Excuse me." He inclined his head. "I'll see about getting you into a dinghy."

As he strode away, Sister Fallyn pressed a hand to her chest.

"Are ye all right, Sister?" Brigitta asked.

"Is it all right for me to feel this way?" Sister Fallyn whispered.

"You like him."

She nodded and tears glimmered in her eyes. "I'm falling for him. How can that be when I'm a nun?"

Brigitta sighed. It was a problem, she had to admit, but it didn't seem as daunting as the problem keeping her and Rupert apart. If her father had actually killed his—she pushed aside that horrible thought. "Why did ye take yer vows?"

Sister Fallyn hung her head. "I thought I had caused Kennet's death. So I thought I should spend the rest of my life in atonement for my sins."

"But Kennet is alive. Ye never did anything wrong."

"I disobeyed my father."

"He was using you for his own financial gain."

Sister Fallyn sighed. "I followed my heart and did something reckless."

"Ye did it for love. Even if it was a one-sided love, how can love be wrong?" Brigitta patted the nun's shoulder.

"If you and Stefan love each other, I think ye should grab on to it and never let it go."

A tear ran down Sister Fallyn's cheek, and she quickly wiped it away. "We shall see." Taking a deep breath, she turned toward the island. "I have a feeling we will soon know which paths we are to take."

"I hope so." For right now, Brigitta was feeling very lost.

It seemed like the more joyous everyone was, the more Brigitta felt a sense of upcoming doom.

After rowing them to the island, Stefan had proudly shown them his stone cottage.

"'Tis lovely!" Sister Fallyn exclaimed with a grin.

"You are both welcome to live here as long as you wish," Stefan claimed. "I can bunk down in Rupert's house."

Rupert had a house? Brigitta's heart sank a bit more. She hadn't been invited to see it.

While Sister Fallyn busied herself cleaning the dusty cottage, Brigitta wandered about the small village. The reunions on the pier had been joyous with the men hugging their happy wives and tossing their laughing children in the air. But it hadn't taken long for the men to whisk their wives off to the cottages. Some had even carried their wives over the doorsteps.

Brigitta sighed. She didn't even know where Rupert was. Up in a field, the children were running about, playing tag, while Granny Hargraves sat on a rock, keeping an eye on them as she knit. Over time, Brigitta figured she would learn everyone's name, and eventually it might feel like home. Instead of an exile.

She walked in a southerly direction down the beach, then found a log to sit on. A pelican swooped down and sat beside her.

"I guess it's just us," she muttered, and the bird gave a small squawk.

The bay faced west, so she had a lovely view of the sun lowering in the sky, painting the sea with shimmering shades of pink and gold.

She heard voices in the distance and saw people emerging from their houses. After a while, she realized they were setting up a celebration on the shore. A fire was built, and they began roasting a lamb on a spit. Tables were carried out, along with plates and goblets. A cask of ale was rolled out. Canopies were erected on poles and lanterns hung.

The children arrived, accompanied by Granny Hargraves. A man began playing a fiddle, and another, some sort of pipe. Brigitta spotted Sister Fallyn and Stefan joining the party. She looked so happy.

Rupert was nowhere in sight.

With a groan, she glanced at the sun. It sat on the horizon now, as if it were melting into a sea of red fire. And her feeling of doom grew heavier.

After all the thinking she'd done, she hadn't been able to rearrange the puzzle pieces. Every time she replayed the visions in her mind, she came to the same conclusion. Rupert was from a noble family. A noble Tourinian family. And most likely, her father was responsible for the deaths of his loved ones.

She picked up a stick and stabbed at the sand. That had to be why Rupert found it so difficult to trust her. He considered her family the enemy.

Who was he exactly?

She stood and used the long stick to scratch letters in the sand. *Ni Rupert.* "I am Rupert" in Tourinian. That was how he had introduced himself. As she crossed the last *t*, she looked back over the words. Backward.

She gasped, and the stick tumbled from her hands.

Trepurin.

"No," she breathed. The House of Trepurin? The house that had given Tourin its first king and a long line of kings?

The house her father had destroyed.

Her mind raced back to the terrible story Sister Fallyn had told her. King Manfrid had come south with the prince. The lost prince!

"Rupert," she whispered as tears burned her eyes. Just like the cogs and wheels of one of Rupert's inventions, all the clues fit neatly together and locked into place.

The ambush had been her father's plan to kill the rightful king, Rupert's father. The wheel in her mind turned and clicked onto the next vision. The battle had been her father's army attacking the king's army. *Click.* Rupert had cried over his mother's grave, the queen's grave. *Click.* Rupert had hid in caves and basements because her father's soldiers wanted to kill him. *Click.* All the grief and despair that Rupert had felt, it had all been caused by her father.

With a cry, Brigitta fell to her knees. Tears ran down her face as more memories made sense. That was why Rupert had referred to her as a *so-called princess.* He knew her father had stolen the throne.

That was why he said her name as if he knew her. Another one of his hidden memories flitted across her mind. A baby in a crib festooned with white lace.

She doubled over as if she'd been struck in the stomach. It was her. That baby in Rupert's mind was her.

"No." She dug her fingers into the sand, then hurled a clump of sand into the sea. "No!" She grabbed the stick and dragged it back and forth across the letters to erase what she had done. The pelican stood nearby, its head cocked as if it had been reading what she'd wrote.

But she couldn't erase what her father had done. He'd

destroyed Rupert's family. Only Rupert had survived. He was the lost prince.

No. Her heart stuttered. He was the rightful king.

Dear goddesses, no wonder he wanted revenge.

She collapsed forward onto her knees and elbows. Rupert had been betrothed to her. She had been the excuse to lure Rupert's family to their doom.

How could he ever trust her? Or love her?

With a cry, she realized any future with him was impossible. And now that she knew it could never happen, she was suddenly aware of how much she wanted it. She wanted his love.

Goddesses help her, she was in love with him.

Chapter Sixteen

❧

"Child, what are you doing here alone?"

Brigitta looked up to find Granny Hargraves leaning over her. The old woman was holding a small earthenware pitcher in her hands.

"Ah, you've been crying." Granny Hargraves watched her sadly.

Brigitta sat up. She wasn't sure how long she'd been crouched over the sand. A cool breeze stung her face and brought her back to the world around her. Only a sliver of light colored the sea a glowing red where the sun had set. Darkness had descended unnoticed.

She'd been numb, she realized. Withdrawn into a miserable, small place filled with gloom and despair. Now she could hear the music and laughter of the celebration in the distance. People were eating and dancing.

"Why are you crying?" Granny Hargraves straightened. "Ah, perhaps you don't speak Tourinian."

"I do," Brigitta croaked, then cleared her throat.

"Heartbroken, are you?" The old woman waved a bony hand when Brigitta stiffened. "No point in denying it. I've endured enough heartbreak in my life to recognize it when I see it. So why are you here alone?"

Brigitta eased back onto the log and stretched her cramped legs in front of her. The pelican was still nearby, watching them. "I didn't feel like celebrating."

"I don't mean them." Granny Hargraves motioned toward the party. "Why aren't you with the one you want to be with? Did he not come to the island with you?" Her voice softened. "Has he passed away?"

"He's fine." Brigitta glanced at the celebration. "I suppose he's here somewhere. But it is not possible for us to be together."

"Is he married?"

Brigitta shook her head. At least, she assumed he wasn't. Surely if he had a secret wife stashed somewhere she would have seen that in a vision. "It's just not possible."

"I see." The old woman settled her thin frame on the log and set the earthenware pitcher in her lap. "Did you know I was the daughter of an earl? I fell in love with a sailor, and of course, everyone told us it was not possible."

Brigitta turned to face her. "What happened?"

Granny Hargraves smiled. "We married and had five children and twenty-three grandchildren." Her smile faded. "He passed away two years ago. His grave is not far from here. I was on my way to see him when I spotted you."

"I'm so sorry."

"No need to be. We had fifty-four wonderful years together." Granny Hargraves lifted the pitcher. "I was taking this to his grave, so I could share it with him."

"You were together a long time."

"Aye." The old woman snorted. "But looking back, it doesn't seem long at all. Life is too short to live with regrets. And you never know what's truly possible until you try. Is your man not worth a try?"

Brigitta sighed. "He's worth everything I could ever give him."

"So why are you alone?"

Brigitta's eyes burned with tears. "I'm afraid he would never be able to love me back."

"Ah. Well, you'll never know if you don't ask." With a groan, Granny Hargraves hefted herself to her feet. "Love is a more powerful force than you think, child. You should believe in it and believe in yourself. If he's a smart man, he will see your true worth."

The old woman headed farther south down the beach, and Brigitta sat alone, wondering what Rupert actually thought of her. He had to know what her father had done, and he'd spoken of revenge, but he'd never directed his anger at her. That one time when she'd felt his emotions, she'd sensed desire. Yearning.

He'd been desperate to make sure he could safely touch her. *I like touching you.* And when she'd lamented that she came from a family of monsters, he'd said, "You're not like them."

She rose to her feet. Could he accept her as she was?

With a wince, she realized that even if he said it didn't matter who her father was, it would still matter to her. She would still feel guilty. Unworthy. The true problem here was that she couldn't accept herself. How could she bear to face him, knowing that her father had destroyed his life?

"I have to make it right," she whispered. She couldn't sit back and do nothing when it was her family that had started this mess. She had to get off this island and fight for Rupert. Somehow, she needed to help him regain his throne.

Words of love wouldn't be enough. If she truly loved him, she needed to act. And it was only through her actions that she would earn his trust. And feel worthy of his love.

She squared her shoulders. "You can do this."

Determination pounded through her with each step

she took toward the village. She scanned the crowd, but couldn't spot Rupert anywhere.

"Brigitta!" Sister Fallyn approached her, carrying a plate of food. "Come and eat. The lamb is wonderful, but the bread . . ." She wrinkled her nose. "I think I'll have to help them out in the bakery."

"Do ye know where Rupert is?"

"Oh. He went somewhere with Stefan." Sister Fallyn motioned to the hilly coastline on the north side of the village. "Stefan said he owns that land. They'll return soon enough. Ye could have a bite to eat while we wait."

Brigitta spotted a lantern far in the distance. The conversation she needed to have with Rupert was best done in private. "I'll be back later."

She ignored the nun's objections that it was too dark and too chilly and hurried to the outskirts of the village. There, with the light of the stars and two moons, she could make out a narrow path that wound up into the hills.

Long grass brushed against her skirt as she climbed, following the flickering light of the lantern.

"She saw your past memories?" Stefan tripped over a clump of grass and nearly fell over.

Rupert snorted. "I reacted about the same way." He lowered the lantern to better illuminate their path.

"Damn," Stefan muttered. "I've never heard of a gift like that."

"I know. She saw the ambush, the battle—"

"Shit. Does she know who you are?"

"I don't know." Rupert gritted his teeth. "I feel like I'm losing my mind, trying to figure that out. She knows her father is a monster. But I don't know if she's ever heard the story about my family."

"Then you don't know if she's ever heard about the lost prince?"

Rupert groaned with frustration. "I can't very well ask her."

"No, that would make it too obvious."

"She has a clever mind. Eventually, she'll figure it out."

"Then she needs to stay here, out of the way."

Rupert scoffed. "I can't hold her prisoner."

"We would let her go as soon as you gain the throne."

Rupert groaned again. "Oh, I'm sure she would appreciate that."

Stefan stopped. "Then what do you want to do?"

Rupert's heart clenched in his chest. He wanted the impossible.

"Have you fallen for her?"

Yes. "I can't possibly trust her." He quickened his pace.

Stefan trailed behind. "Maybe you should reconsider Ansel's suggestion. Deliver her to her brother already pregnant."

"No," Rupert growled as he whipped around. "I will not abuse her for my own gain. And I will not endanger her. Have you considered how her bastard brother might react if she showed up pregnant by a pirate? He could punish her or torture her until she lost the child. Hell, he might forgo the competition altogether and let his favorites rape her."

Stefan winced. "You have a point. Then there's nothing we can do but leave her here."

With a sigh, Rupert resumed his walk along the path. He felt like a complete ass. Brigitta believed she had decided her own fate, but he'd knowingly steered her toward exile on this island. *Dammit.* He'd just wanted to keep her safe. But now that he knew how dangerous her gift was, her exile seemed more geared toward keeping himself safe.

No matter what he did, he couldn't escape the feeling that he was using her. If only he could tell her the truth. If only he could trust her.

He could wait until he regained the throne to tell her who he really was, but by then she probably would have figured it out. Even if she hadn't, she would hear the news that the lost prince Ulfrid had returned. And then she would know that he hadn't trusted her. She would know that he had waited until she was no longer a threat before revealing the truth.

It was cowardly. Unworthy. How could she ever love him if he treated her like that?

Dammit, he wanted her to love him. But did he want it enough to risk losing the throne? Or jeopardizing his plan for revenge?

The path veered left toward the coast, and Rupert quickened his pace.

"I've decided to marry," Stefan announced.

"What?" Rupert glanced back. "You courted a nun that quickly?"

Stefan shot him an annoyed look. "All I can do is propose. It would be her decision whether she can accept me."

Rupert nodded. "Then I'll wish you luck."

"I came to pick out a ring for her."

Rupert snorted. They were headed to the secret cave where they hid most of the gold and jewels taken from Gunther's naval ships. "I'm not sure she'll appreciate a stolen ring."

"Well, I could buy her one, but I'd be using stolen gold to pay for it, so what's the difference?"

Rupert shrugged. He didn't actually consider the gold stolen, not when the mines had originally belonged to his family. It was the House of Grian that was stealing the gold, and he was simply taking back what was rightfully his.

They reached the cliff. The ocean before them was a black pit with only a glimmer here and there where the stars were reflected on the dark surface. Waves crashed on the rocks below. To their right, a narrow path descended sharply to the beach. Rupert took the lead on the narrow trail. One false step here and he would plummet to the rocks below.

"Are you picking up a trinket for Brigitta?" Stefan asked.

"I hadn't planned to." Rupert frowned. Somehow he didn't think a string of pearls was going to make it any easier to talk to Brigitta. Especially when he didn't know what to say. "I'm going to the grotto for a swim. I need to think."

The lantern was gone.

Brigitta stopped in dismay as it flickered out of view. What should she do now? She glanced back at the village. The fire on the beach and all the lanterns served as a beacon that would easily guide her back. But she'd come too far to give up.

She narrowed her eyes on the last spot where she'd seen the lantern. Nothing but darkness. Close by, the moonlight gleamed off the tall grass, painting it silver. The path was easy enough to detect, since it made a trail of black cutting through the grass. She moved forward slowly, for the ground would slope up, then suddenly dip without warning.

Behind her, the village grew smaller and smaller. Eventually, the land leveled out, and she realized she was on top of a plateau. The wind was much stronger here, and it whipped at her skirt and loosened her hair from its braid.

She slowed down even more as the path veered toward the coast. The sound of the ocean grew louder, and her heart pounded faster. In the dark, it would be hard to see where the land ended and the sea began.

The grass became shorter, the wind stronger. She crouched down to feel the path in front of her.

Rocks. She'd reached a cliff. To the right, she spotted a light down on the beach. It wasn't bright, but between it and the moonlight, she could see the golden sand of the path leading down to the shore. She eased down the trail, keeping her shoulder pressed against the rock wall to her right. When a series of steps began, she sat and eased herself down on her rump.

The beach. She exhaled with relief as she stood on the narrow strip of sand between the cliff and the ocean. The light seemed to be coming from a cave.

She peeked inside. Several torches had been lit, illuminating a wide, rocky tunnel. No one in sight.

"Hello?" she called softly. No answer. But she could see boot prints in the sand. Rupert and Stefan had to be here somewhere.

She slipped inside. The walls of the cave shot straight up so high she couldn't see the top. A narrow stream meandered toward the cave entrance. The water seemed to be trickling out to sea, although she assumed there were times when the sea would roll into the cave.

She gulped. Surely it was safe at the moment. Rupert and Stefan wouldn't be here if it wasn't.

A crunching noise sounded in the distance. Footsteps.

She whirled around, wondering if she should hide. But she wasn't doing anything wrong. Was she?

Stefan came around a bend, holding a brass candlestick with a lit candle. "My lady? What are you doing here?"

"I-I came to see Rupert." She brushed back some tendrils of hair that the wind had whipped free from her braid. "He's here, isn't he?"

Stefan gave her an incredulous look. "How did you get here?"

"I could see your lantern in the distance."

"Do you know how dangerous it is to be close to the

cliffs at night? And this entire area is riddled with caves. The ground above us isn't safe. There are holes in the surface where you can fall into a cave and break your neck."

"I didn't realize . . ."

He scoffed. "The villagers know it's not safe. They should have stopped you." He stuffed a ruby ring in his pocket. "I'll take you back to the village."

"No." She lifted her chin. "I'm not leaving until I see Rupert. It's important."

Stefan hesitated. "I suppose you two have some talking to do." He gave her a stern look. "You'll have to follow my directions carefully. One wrong turn and you could be lost in the tunnels forever and never found."

She gulped. "I understand."

He motioned with his candle. "You see this path that goes along the stream? If you follow it, you'll reach the grotto."

Grotto? "Is that where Rupert is?"

"Yes. Here." Stefan handed her the candlestick holder. "I'll take one of the torches back to the village."

"Thank you."

Stefan removed a torch from a bracket on the rock wall. "Don't venture off the path. Even if you see another one, don't take it. Follow the stream till you reach the grotto."

"I understand." She nodded. "Thank you."

"Good evening, then." He inclined his head and strode through the entrance of the cave.

She was alone. Brigitta steeled her nerves. Lost in tunnels forever? But it seemed simple enough if all she had to do was follow the stream.

Slowly, she walked deeper into the cave, making sure the stream was always to her left. The sand gave way to gravel, and the cave grew more narrow. As she went around a bend, it became much darker. The torchlight at the cave's entrance was no longer visible.

The light flickered on her candle, and with a wince, she cupped a hand around the flame. If it went out, she'd be surrounded by darkness. It was odd, though, that the breeze seemed to be going toward the sea. Perhaps the wind was coming from those holes in the ground that Stefan had mentioned.

After a while, she heard the tinkling sound of running water. As she rounded a curve, she saw where a pile of rocks had dammed up the stream. A small waterfall was slipping over the rocks, but behind it, there was a pool of water. And more light in the distance.

Was that the grotto? She started toward it, then noticed another path that veered off to the right. A series of stone steps leading up to another room.

Don't venture off the path, Stefan had warned her. She could get lost. But surely, as long as she could retrace her steps to the stream, she would be all right. Her insatiable curiosity poked at her. The room was close by. What would be the harm of a little peek?

She climbed the short flight of stone steps and peered into the cave room. It was long and narrow. She crept forward a few feet, then stopped with a jerk as something flickered into view.

A trunk. A long line of trunks. She opened the first one and gasped. It was full of gold coins! The next one had even more gold coins. The next one was filled with sparkling jewels—rings and necklaces made of precious stones and pearls. She lifted the candlestick high and spotted more trunks against the other wall. Holy goddesses, she'd discovered the secret place where Rupert hid his horde of treasure.

No wonder Stefan had warned her not to take this

path. No wonder Rupert only allowed those he trusted to know that this island existed.

She peered at the far end of the room, wondering how far it went and how many more trunks there could be. Was she just imagining it, or was there a dim light at the end of the room? She eased toward it and realized the floor was sloping slowly downward. The room suddenly ended with a rock wall, but to her left, there was a narrow opening. And that was where the light was filtering through.

She peered outside and gasped. Holy goddesses, this was the grotto! A cavernous room stretched out before her, big enough to fit a three-story house inside. Below her, a large pool of water shimmered in the moonlight. She glanced up and saw a ragged hole way up in the ceiling. Long trails of ivy dangled from the hole, and stars twinkled in the sky.

It was breathtaking. She stood still for a moment to admire the view. A lantern was sitting on a flat rock that jutted out over the pool. The rock walls were green with moss and clumps of ferns. To the right, there appeared to be a hole in the wall, a sheltered ledge. Inside she could see a pile of furs and blankets. Did Rupert sleep there? In front of the ledge, a rope ladder descended into the pool of water.

She heard a splash of water. Was Rupert in the pool? It was a tight fit, but she managed to slip through the narrow opening. A steep path led straight down to a narrow strip of sandy beach.

Another splash.

She scanned the water and spotted Rupert swimming toward the ladder. If she followed the sandy path around the pool, she could meet him close to the ladder. She eased down the path, wincing as her feet skidded a few inches in the loose gravel.

Rupert reached the ladder, then turned to dive under-water, flashing a naked rump in the moonlight.

What? The candlestick holder tumbled from her hand. As she made a grab for it, her feet slid out from beneath her. With a squeal, she skidded down the steep incline. *Bam.* She hit the beach hard and fell forward onto her knees, her hands and face splashing into the water.

"Brigitta!"

She sat up, sputtering as she pushed wet hair out of her face.

"Brigitta, what are you doing here?" he yelled in Tourinian.

"I—" The water had been surprisingly warm. She blinked as she spotted him coming toward her. "Wait!"

He paused with the water up to his navel. "Are you all right? How did you get here?"

"I . . . walked." She scrambled to her feet and dried her wet hands on her skirt. "I saw Stefan at the cave entrance, and he said you were here."

Rupert scoffed. "What the hell was he thinking? He should have walked you back to the village."

"I told him I had to talk to you. So he said it was all right . . ."

"It's not all right! Dammit." He turned around in the water while dragging a hand through his wet hair. Water sluiced down his broad back, meandering over the bulges of his muscles.

Her heart lurched, and she nearly fell back onto her knees.

He faced her once again. "Are you all right? Did you trip on something?"

"I'm fine." Her knees stung, but she wasn't about to lift her skirt to take a look at them.

His eyes narrowed. "You took the path along the stream, right?"

"I—" With a wince, she noted the trail she'd been instructed to take. Rupert was going to be angry when he realized she'd discovered his secret stash. How could she convince him to accept her help if he was angry with her? "Perhaps we should talk later. You seem to be busy right now."

"You can't go back to the village without a light. It's too dangerous."

She glanced back at him. Good goddesses, he'd moved closer and the water level was down to his hips. She focused on a nearby rock.

"Did you follow the stream?"

She hesitated. Even if she made him angry, wouldn't it be better to be honest with him? How else could she ever earn his trust?

"Brigitta—"

"I won't tell anyone about the treasure."

"*Crap!*" His head fell back and he lifted his hands to run them through his hair.

Her mouth dropped open. With his bulging muscles and broad shoulders, he looked like a mythical sea god emerging from the ocean. "I really won't tell anyone. I'm on your—"

"Are you sure you're not a spy? You should be 'cause you're damned good. Now I'll have to find another cave."

"I swear to you I will not tell another soul."

He scoffed. "How can I believe you when you followed me here?" He slapped the surface of the water as he made a noise of frustration. "What am I going to do with you?"

Did he see her as nothing but a problem? That irked her. She planted her hands on her hips. "The real question here is what can I do for you? How can I help you make things right? We need to sit down and have a serious talk."

"Fine, let's talk." He strode toward her.

She gasped as more of his abdomen was revealed.

"No!" She held up her hands to cover her eyes. "Don't come any closer!"

"I thought you wanted to talk!"

She squeezed her eyes shut behind her hands. "I can't talk to you naked."

"You're not naked. I am."

"Don't come any closer!"

He made another noise of frustration. "What are you afraid of? It's a damned cock! It's not a creature from the deep!" There were some splashing noises. "Fine. You can look now. I retreated."

She peeked through her fingers. The water was back up to his navel now.

"Dammit." He glanced down with an annoyed look. "Can you throw me my breeches?" He motioned to a large boulder. "They're over there."

"Yes, of course." She rushed over to the boulder. Next to his boots, his shirt and breeches lay folded neatly. She picked up the folded breeches and tossed them toward him.

To her horror, they simply unfurled in the air and plopped onto the water a few feet from where she stood.

"Are you kidding me?" He gave her an incredulous look. "You call that a throw?"

She winced. "I thought they would go farther."

He glanced down and grimaced.

"Don't worry." She kicked off her shoes. "I'll push them toward you." She waded into the water.

"Stop!" He held up a hand. "I-I think you should stay there. I'll get them."

"But—"

"Just turn around if you don't want to see." He gritted his teeth. "We can't have my cock leaping out of the water to attack you."

She gasped. "It *leaps*?"

"I was kidding!" He winced. "A bit. Turn around."

She did. Water splashed as he waded toward the breeches. She winced at the sound of a few muttered curses. Perhaps she shouldn't have admitted to finding the treasure. But she wanted complete honesty between them. "Is it safe now?"

He snorted. "It was always safe." After a moment, he said, "You can turn around."

She swallowed hard. The time had come for her to admit everything she knew. And once she told him, there was no going back. With her heart pounding, she clenched her skirt in her fists.

"Is something wrong?" He'd moved to the flat rock where the lantern was, and he was sitting there, watching her as he leaned forward, his elbows on his knees.

She took a deep breath. "I know who you are."

Chapter Seventeen

❧

He immediately sat up, a wary look in his eyes. "What do you know?"

Her heart thudded loud in her ears. Was this a mistake? She'd been so eager to help him and atone for her family's sins that she'd come straight here without realizing that her confession might be the last thing he wanted to hear. He had no reason to trust her, not when it was her family who had caused all his grief. It was a wonder he could even bear to look at her.

"I know . . . you must hate me. I know why you need revenge." Tears burned her eyes. "And I'm so very sorry for everything my father did to you and your family."

A look of alarm crossed his face as he rose to his feet. "Then you know . . . ?"

"You're the lost prince."

He stiffened, his hands clenching into fists.

She winced. From the look on his face and the tension radiating off his body, she could tell she'd given him an unwanted shock. "It will be all right, really. I would never tell anyone."

He scoffed, then wandered into the water.

She watched with increasing alarm as he went deeper and deeper into the pool. "Rupert, what are you doing?"

He glanced back at her, a tortured look on his face. "Nineteen years. I kept my identity a secret for nineteen years. Only Stefan and Ansel knew." With a grimace, he pounded a fist through the water. "Dammit to hell! You figured it out in five days!"

He'd gone from shock to anger. She didn't know which was worse. "Well, I . . ." She attempted a placating smile. "I tried to warn you about my gift. I'm very good at finding lost things. Even lost princes."

With a frustrated groan, he slapped the water again. A wind whistled through the grotto, churning up the water. "Dammit." He closed his eyes, and his chest expanded as he took deep breaths.

He was truly her tall and handsome stranger, Brigitta thought. The moonlight shone down on him, illuminating the sharp lines of his jaw and the wide breadth of his shoulders. The golden strands in his light-brown hair gleamed with starlight. And all those muscles—he looked so incredibly strong, yet at the same time so alone and vulnerable. Her heart ached for him. If only he could accept her in spite of who she was.

His eyes opened and he regarded her sadly. "I don't know what to do with you."

Her heart squeezed and tears gathered once again. "That's all right. I know what to do." She stepped toward him, her bare toes reaching the edge of the water. "That's why I came here tonight. I want to offer my services. I'll go with you and help you set things straight."

He gave her an incredulous look. "I'm not letting you endanger yourself."

"I have to help you. It's the only way I can atone for the crimes of my family. Please let me—" A tear rolled down her cheek, and she impatiently brushed it away. "It nearly kills me to think how much you've suffered because of my—"

"Stop," he growled. "You've done nothing wrong."

"But I have to do something! What my family did to you was unforgivable. I'll help you with your revenge, and I'll earn your trust. I swear it." With trembling legs, she lowered herself onto one knee. "Your Majesty."

His face went pale. "Shit." He plunged into the water and swam toward the left side of the grotto.

That was not the reaction she'd hoped for. With a sigh, she plopped down onto the beach and watched him swim. He was doing laps back and forth from the left wall to the right one, where the rope ladder was hanging. Perhaps he just needed to think. Or work off some tension.

She still needed to persuade him to let her help, but she had a bad feeling that he would not be easily convinced. What she needed was a plan. As he swam, her mind raced with ideas of what she could do.

He finally stopped in front of the ladder, his hands gripping a rope rung while he leaned forward to catch his breath. She followed the sandy path around the pool till it ended with a flat rock that jutted out a few inches above the water.

She settled on the rock, not far from him. Then she lifted her skirt just enough to dangle her feet into the pool. "I can see why you like this place. The water is so nice and warm."

He scowled without looking at her.

"Are you ready to talk now?" she asked. "I've been thinking, and I have a few ideas how—"

"I've been thinking, too. You'll need to stay here on the island."

"But I have a plan—"

"I will not let you risk yourself." He turned to face her,

the water up to his chest. "You don't owe me anything. What happened was not your fault."

"I was used to lure your family to their doom. So I will help you, whether you like it or not."

"Dammit, Brigitta! Don't make me force you to stay here!" Another breeze swept through the grotto.

"Then don't!" She scooted forward till she was sitting on the edge of the rock with her lower legs immersed in water. "You said I had the right to decide my own destiny."

With a wince, he turned to the ladder and muttered a curse.

"My decision has been made," she continued. "I expect you to honor that."

He dragged in a deep breath and turned toward her. "I cannot bear for you to be in danger. And I will not use you to further my cause. When you were a babe, I made a vow that I would protect you."

Was he still trying to keep the betrothal vows after everything her father had done? Tears collected in her eyes once again. "I was too young then to return the vow, but I can make one now. I will help you regain the throne. And I will earn your trust." A tear rolled down her cheek. "How could I ever betray you when I'm in love with you?"

His eyes widened with a stunned look.

She sat back, hastily wiping her cheeks. Good goddesses, that was more than she'd intended to confess. Mortified, she pulled her legs out of the water.

His hand shot out to grasp her ankle.

She gasped as a surge of emotion blasted through her body. *Desire. Longing.* He wanted her. He wanted her something fierce.

He moved closer. "Are you all right? Did you have another vision?"

"Nay, I . . ." she answered in Eberoni, then switched

back to Tourinian. "I didn't see anything." Since she knew his identity now, she doubted she would see any more of his memories. But why had she felt his emotions? Normally her gift only worked with things that were hidden.

Of course. The answer clicked inside her. He'd been trying to keep his feelings for her a secret.

"Ack!" she cried out when he suddenly hauled her into the pool. "What are you—"

His mouth clamped down on hers.

She was so surprised she didn't know what to think or how to respond. With a strangled cry, she broke the kiss. "Wait." She gasped for air. "Why . . . ?"

He cradled her face in his hands. "You said you loved me."

Her cheeks grew hot. She could hardly deny her own words. "That doesn't mean you should—" She glanced down and saw her green skirt up to her armpits, floating around her in the water. "Oh goodness." She tried pushing it down.

"Allow me." He pushed the skirt down in the back and fumbled with the drawstring.

"What are you—" She huffed when he lifted the wet skirt over her head and tossed it onto the rock. "I didn't say you could—"

"This, too." He quickly unlaced the green velvet vest and dragged it down her arms.

With her arms pinned down momentarily, she glanced down and winced at the wet blouse and shift now molded against her breasts. She ducked down a few inches. "Rupert, I thought we were going to talk."

"Sweetheart." He threw the vest onto the rock. "Don't you know when you're being ravished?"

Her mouth fell open. "I don't recall agreeing to that."

"Then I'll ask." He pulled her tight against him.

Her hands landed on his bare chest, then she withdrew them a few inches, curling them into fists.

"Brigitta." He cupped his hand around the back of her head while he planted soft kisses across her brow. "Sweetheart." The tip of his nose glided down her cheek, then he nibbled a path to her ear.

She shivered, and her hands slowly uncurled.

He nipped at her earlobe, then whispered, "Would you like to be ravished?"

Her knees grew weak, so she grabbed on to his shoulders.

"Is that a yes?" His nose brushed back across her cheek toward her mouth.

"I-I'll consider it."

"Take all the time you need." His mouth took hers, gently savoring and coaxing her until the world swirled around her, and time seemed to slow to a halt.

All that was left was Rupert. His mouth against hers, sweetly molding her and making her melt. His hands touching her neck, stroking her back, and sending delicious shivers along her spine. His chest pressed against her, making her breasts feel so achy and full that she finally gave in to a desperate need building inside her. With a moan she rubbed her breasts against his chest.

He groaned against her mouth. His hand moved down her shift all the way to her rump, then he pulled her hard against him.

She gasped as something hard jabbed at her. But as soon as her mouth opened, his tongue slipped inside.

"What?" She pulled back. "What was that?"

His eyes glimmered with a golden heat. "Shall we continue with the ravishing?"

"I . . ." Did he intend to do more than a passionate kiss? "Are you planning to do more strange things with your tongue?"

His mouth twitched. "Definitely."

"I—" She glanced down. "I think there's something in the water. A turtle, perhaps. I'm afraid it'll bite me."

"It's a damned cock. It doesn't bite."

She inhaled sharply. That was him? Her cheeks blazed with embarrassment.

"Would you like to investigate for yourself?" He took her hand from his shoulder.

"No!" She jumped back, pulling her hand away. "I mean, I'm not ready . . ." She paused when she realized his gaze was riveted to her chest. Unwittingly, she'd moved into shallower water, and now her breasts were showing. Her wet blouse and shift were glued to her skin, the nipples tight and protruding.

"Come here," he growled, pulling her back into another kiss.

Longing. She felt his emotions flow through her, mixing with her own desire until she could no longer tell which of them was the more desperate.

When he deepened the kiss, she opened her mouth, and this time she welcomed his invasion. He explored and stroked her tongue, encouraging her until she was kissing him back. Heat built inside her until she dug her fingers into his shoulders and squirmed against him.

He clamped a hand on one of her breasts, squeezing and flicking a thumb over the hardened nipple. When she shuddered, he whispered, "Do you want more?"

"Aye."

He grasped the hem of her shift, then pulled it and the blouse over her head. The wet clothing landed with a plop on top of her skirt.

Good goddesses, she was naked. She barely had time to acknowledge it before he tugged her back into an embrace. Her breasts against his chest, bare skin touching, sent a wave of sensation hurtling through her. Each breath he took pressed against her.

He planted his hands on her rump and lifted her off the pool's rock floor. "Wrap your legs around me."

"What?" She grabbed on to his shoulders as he kept raising her higher. Her breasts were now abovewater, completely exposed. Her nipples pebbled in the cool air, the tips tight and aching to be touched.

"Wrap your legs around me," he repeated. "And squeeze me tight."

Tentatively, she hooked her right leg around his hips, just above the low waistband of his breeches.

"And the other one." He slid one arm under her rump to support her, while using his other hand to drape her left leg around his waist.

He pulled her hard against him, and she cried out when her private parts came in contact with his hard abdomen. Her gaze met his, and she melted at the fierce yearning in his golden eyes.

He placed his fingertips on her shoulder, then dragged them down the upper curve of one breast till he reached her nipple. When his thumb rasped against the hardened tip, she shuddered.

"Sweet," he whispered, gliding his hand beneath the breast to test its weight, then returning to tease her nipple. His gaze moved to her other breast, then he leaned close and drew that nipple into his mouth.

She cried out, raking her fingers into his hair and holding him close. With each flick of his tongue, she tightened her legs around his waist. When he suckled hard, she could no longer bear it. Digging her heels into his back, she ground herself against him.

With a groan, he nuzzled his face against her breasts. "You're killing me."

"I don't mean to."

"I want to touch you. But that's as far as I can go. I cannot risk getting you with child."

Her thighs tightened involuntarily, and his gaze met hers.

"But I want you. I want you so bad it hurts." He looked around, then carried her over to the rope ladder. "Here." He moved her hands to a rung above her head. "Hold on tight."

"Why?" She curled her fists around the rope.

"I'm going to play with you until you scream." He plunged a hand between them, and she jolted when his hand cupped her.

Good goddesses, it was hard to breathe. With a moan, she squeezed her eyes shut and hung on to the rope. His fingers moved over her, stroking gently.

"Rupert," she groaned.

"Keep holding." His fingers grew bolder, exploring until she was panting and squirming.

When he inserted a finger, she cried out, the rope twisting in her hands. He waggled the finger inside her while his thumb rubbed against a spot that made her quiver all over.

"Rupert!" She tensed suddenly as if she were on the edge of a waterfall. Her grip on the rope failed, but he pulled her toward him just as a wave carried her over the falls. Her scream echoed around the cave. She was crashing, soaring, tumbling through a wild tempest. She squeezed him tight and felt herself throbbing against his hand.

"Sweet," he whispered once again.

As her eyes slowly came into focus, she realized he was still holding her, his hand now gently stroking her back. She wasn't sure why her body had shattered like that, or if it was even normal, but one thing was clear.

When she was with Rupert, she thoroughly enjoyed being ravished.

An hour or so later, Rupert glanced up at the ledge where Brigitta was. It was quiet, so he assumed she'd fallen asleep on the pile of furs.

After their lovemaking, he'd suggested she climb up the ladder to the ledge so she could rest. Then he'd busied himself in the grotto, trying to take his mind off a painful erection.

First he'd stacked some driftwood and dry grass in the fire pit and used the lantern to set it ablaze. Once the fire was well established, he'd extinguished the lantern to save the oil. He and Brigitta would need it later in order to leave the cave. Then he lay out her wet clothes on rocks not too far from the fire, hoping the heat would help them dry.

While he worked, he considered what to do now that Brigitta knew his true identity. After nineteen years of trusting no one, it was difficult to trust her. He wanted to. Deep inside, he suspected that was one of the reasons why he'd jumped her. It had been his way to lay claim to her so she wouldn't betray him.

He doubted she would betray him intentionally, but he couldn't risk her being around her brother. If Gunther thought she knew the true identity of the infamous pirate Rupert, he would stop at nothing to wheedle that information out of her. Knowing too much made her a danger to herself as much as to him.

Her offer to help had tugged at his heart, but how could he, in clear conscience, allow her to assist him? His plan involved battles and bloodshed. Much too dangerous for her.

He peeled off his wet breeches and stretched them out to dry next to Brigitta's clothes. Then he swam over to the ladder and climbed to the ledge.

She was there, wrapped in a blanket, sound asleep, and his heart squeezed at the sight of her. He couldn't risk losing her. When she'd confessed that she loved him, a startling realization had shot through him.

If he lost her, there would be no victory. Even if he won his revenge and gained the throne, it would all be meaningless without her.

And so, he'd reached out to her. And she'd responded so beautifully, melting in his arms and shattering with his touch. Even now, he wanted to rip off her blanket and make love all over again.

He winced as his cock swelled once more. He'd had more erections in the past five days than his entire life. He pulled a blanket up to his waist, then stretched out beside her. Just a short rest, he told himself, while their clothes dried.

As he drifted off, he realized he was still torn. Part of him wanted to keep her here on the island where she would be safe, but another part was tempted to ignore the danger. He wanted to grab on to her and never let go.

Somehow, in just a few days, she'd become as important to him as his quest for revenge.

Chapter Eighteen

❦

When Brigitta woke up, she discovered the pillow beneath her head was Rupert's shoulder. With a gasp, she sat up. Her blanket fell to her hips, and she jerked it back up to her chin.

Good goddesses, she'd been sleeping with him naked. Her mind raced, trying to remember what had happened, but she only had a dreamy recollection of some sweet snuggling in the dark.

"Don't leave me," he mumbled, pulling her back down.

She landed on his chest. "Rupert, wake up."

He cracked open one eye, then closed it and smiled. "Good morning."

Morning? She sat back up, holding the blanket against her breasts. Sure enough, there was sunlight beaming through the hole in the cavern. "We slept through the entire night? Sister Fallyn will be worried sick!"

He blinked sleepily at her, then tugged at her blanket. "Why are you hiding from me?"

She scooted out of his reach. "It's daylight."

"I know. I want to see everything I fondled last night."

She huffed. "Honestly, we have more urgent matters to attend to."

He smiled slowly. "I'm more urgent than you realize."

She wasn't sure what he meant, but then her brain was having a hard time thinking when he was smiling at her, stretched out on a pile of furs with his gleaming amber eyes, tousled hair, and sharp jaw shaded with whiskers. And then there were his gloriously muscled arms and chest, his skin the color of golden honey. Her gaze dropped to his navel and the narrow trail of hair that disappeared beneath a blanket that looked oddly like a tent.

The tent suddenly twitched.

She gasped. "It does leap."

"It's a damned cock." With a wince, he dragged a hand through his hair. "If you keep staring at it, things will get messy."

She frowned at him. "Why do you keep cursing your own . . . manhood? I'm sure it's perfectly nice."

"Nice?"

From the annoyed look on his face, she gathered she'd used the wrong word. How had he referred to her private parts? "More than nice. Sweet."

"*Sweet?*" He sat up. "Holy crap."

She groaned inwardly. Apparently, he was rather sensitive about his manhood. "Look, we have more important matters to address. We need to make plans for regaining your throne and—"

"I already have plans."

"And first, I need to reassure Sister Fallyn that I'm all right."

He waved a dismissive hand. "She'll have other things on her mind. Stefan was planning to propose to her last night."

"*What?*" Brigitta scrambled to her feet, still holding the blanket against her.

"That's why Stefan came here to the cave. He was

picking out a ring for her." Rupert's mouth twitched. "They may have been too busy last night to even notice we were gone."

"Oh, dear goddesses. I have to hurry back!" Brigitta rushed over to the ladder. Sister Fallyn must have been shocked! Had she said yes?

With a wince, Brigitta realized she would need to drop her blanket in order to climb down the ladder. She motioned to Rupert. "Turn around."

"I saw you last night."

"It was dark. Please. I'm not comfortable with this yet."

Rupert sighed, then flopped back onto the furs. "Fine." He turned his back to her, taking his blanket with him and leaving his rump entirely exposed.

Her mouth dropped open as she eyed the long length of his muscular back, all the way from his broad shoulders down to his bare feet. When she dropped the blanket, she was tempted to crawl toward him.

She shook her head. What was wrong with her? "Give me enough time to get dressed before you come down."

As she made her way down the ladder, more memories from last night came to mind. Good goddesses, a few kisses from the man and she'd let him take liberties with her. Mother Ginessa would definitely not approve. Sister Fallyn would be scandalized.

Or would she? Brigitta suspected the nun was madly in love with Stefan. He might have taken liberties, too.

Halfway back to the village, Rupert let Brigitta take the lead so he could trail behind and adjust his breeches. They had dried well, along with Brigitta's clothes, but they were too damned tight in the crotch.

"Damned cock," he muttered.

"Are you cursing yourself again?" She glanced back, then quickly looked forward when she caught him re-arranging his load.

He snorted. She should try living a week with blue balls. And watching the sway of her hips wasn't helping. "By the way, *nice* and *sweet* are not the words a man wants to hear describing his cock. Just so you'll know for future reference."

She slanted a dubious look back at him. "You think I'll be referring to your manhood in the future?"

"Oh, you'll be doing a lot more to it than referring."

She scoffed. "Sure of yourself, are you?"

"Cocksure."

She shot another look at him. Her attempt to look scandalized didn't quite work when she was trying hard not to laugh. "You're incorrigible."

"Thank you."

"Then which descriptive words would you prefer?" She glanced back, her turquoise eyes glinting with humor. "Something like . . . cocky?"

He grinned. Just saying the word had made her blush. "Rugged would be good. Or well-tempered steel."

She covered her mouth to keep from laughing.

"Relentless. Powerful." He waved a hand in the air. "Magnificent."

She snorted. "Sounds cocky to me."

"Ha! Come back to the grotto with me. I'll show you some cocky." He made a grab for her, and she squealed, then ran down the hill, giggling.

He caught up with her, grabbed her around the waist, and twirled her around while her laughter filled the air. Setting her down, he planted a kiss on her pretty mouth.

She grinned up at him. "You may be in big trouble."

"Why?"

With a shrug, she resumed her walk along the path. "Now I'll be expecting magnificent."

He followed her. "You think I can't deliver?"

"Oh, I'm sure it'll be . . ." She glanced back with a sly look. "Sweet."

He narrowed his eyes. "Now you're asking for it." When she laughed, he found himself grinning like a fool.

He took her hand and walked by her side. No doubt they would soon be arguing over her future role in his plan for revenge and conquest, but for now, for these few minutes as they crossed the green hills beneath a bright-blue sky, it was the happiest time in his life.

When they crested the last hill before the village, he spotted Sister Fallyn pacing in front of Stefan's cottage, situated behind the village on another hill.

"There she is." Brigitta waved her arms in the air. "She looks upset."

The nun saw her and waved back. Stefan peered through the cottage door, then followed the nun as she ran toward the village. Brigitta lifted her skirt to hurry down the hill.

The village and fields were mostly empty. Rupert suspected the celebration had lasted long into the night with a great deal of drinking. So most of the islanders were sleeping in this morning. The fire on the beach had been extinguished, leaving a pile of blackened wood and ash. The tent canopies were still up, shading the long tables and empty chairs.

"Brigitta!" Sister Fallyn stopped in front of the tavern just as Brigitta reached the edge of the village.

Within seconds, they were embracing each other.

The nun's smile quickly faded as she took Brigitta by the shoulders. "Don't ever do that again. Ye scared me self something terrible."

"I'm perfectly fine," Brigitta assured her. "I meant to come back earlier, but I fell asleep, and the next thing I knew, it was morning. I'm so sorry ye were worried."

"Humph." Sister Fallyn aimed a suspicious glare at Rupert as he approached. "He should have brought ye back. 'Tis not fitting for a princess like you to be out all night."

"Good morning," Rupert told the nun, noting her hands on Brigitta's shoulders. No ring.

"Come here." Sister Fallyn dragged Brigitta toward the pier. "I need some privacy to talk to you."

Stefan sighed as the nun walked right past him without a look. With a frown, he approached Rupert. "I should clobber you."

"The proposal didn't go well?" Rupert asked.

"It went well enough," Stefan grumbled, casting a forlorn look at Sister Fallyn in the distance. "She was surprised, but happily so, I think. She said she needed to be alone to consider it, so I left her at my cottage and went to your place. Then about an hour later, she was banging on the door, frantic that Brigitta hadn't returned. I assured her that the girl was safe because she was with you. Then she went into a full panic." He paused, aiming an inquisitive look at Rupert.

He shrugged. "And then?"

Stefan snorted. "Fallyn insisted I retrieve her before a ravishment could happen. She even threatened to never marry me if I didn't rescue the princess from your evil clutches. I told her the tide would roll in during the night, making it impossible to reach you."

Rupert nodded. "Well, that's true."

"For a few hours, yes, but not the entire night." Stefan glowered at him. "I saved your ass, and now Fallyn isn't speaking to me."

"She'll get over it." Rupert winced when Stefan punched his arm. "Once I have the throne, she'll approve of me."

"That could be months," Stefan growled.

"It may happen sooner than expected." Rupert shifted his weight. "We'll need to adjust the plan. Brigitta knows everything."

Stefan stiffened. "You . . . you told her?"

"No, she figured it out on her own." Rupert glanced over at the two women, who were whispering by the pier. With a movement of his hand, he brought their words to him on a breeze.

"That pirate will never be suitable for you," the nun was fussing. "Ye're a princess."

"He's an honorable man," Brigitta insisted. "And I love him."

Rupert smiled.

Sister Fallyn looked appalled. "Heavenly goddesses, child, did he use his sorcerer powers to seduce you?"

"I . . ." Brigitta brushed her hair back from her face. "I want to know about you. Did ye accept Stefan's proposal?"

The nun huffed. "I'm not talking about that man."

"She's Gunther's sister, and she knows everything?" Stefan asked, breaking Rupert's concentration. "Do you realize how dangerous that is? What are we going to do? Hold her prisoner here until—"

"She wants to come with us," Rupert said quietly.

Stefan snorted. "How can we possibly trust her?" He lowered his voice. "Is that why you spent the night with her? Are you going with Ansel's plan to get her pregnant?"

"No." Rupert glared at him. "I will not use her." A barking sound drew his attention. A shaggy black-and-white dog was loping down the beach, headed for the women.

Brigitta stiffened, her hand pressed to her chest. "Brody?"

Sister Fallyn turned to look at the dog and stumbled back in shock. "Heavenly goddesses, it can't be."

The dog barked as it came to a stop before them. With a grin, it sat down and lifted a foreleg.

"Brody!" Brigitta lunged at the dog, pulling him into her arms. "Oh, Brody, I was so worried about you."

"What the hell . . ." Stefan mumbled.

How on Aerthlan did a dog get on this island? Rupert strode toward the animal with Stefan by his side. "You know this dog?" he asked in Tourinian.

"Yes!" Brigitta laughed, rubbing the dog's ears. "It's Brody!" She cradled his long face in her hands. "I was afraid we'd lost you."

"How?" Rupert asked. "Where did you lose him?" The dog glanced at him, and Rupert was momentarily taken aback by the sharp intelligence in the dog's blue eyes.

"He was on the Eberoni ship with us," Sister Fallyn explained. "He belongs to King Leofric and Queen Luciana. They sent him on the voyage to guard us."

"When you kidnapped us, I thought I saw him jump overboard," Brigitta added. "But when I couldn't see him in the water, I thought I must have imagined it." She patted his head. "Poor baby, did you swim all this way?"

Sister Fallyn made the sign of the moons. "It's a miracle."

Stefan snorted, and Rupert exchanged a look with him. There was no way the dog could have stayed alive in the ocean for a week or managed to swim a long distance to an island no one else knew about.

Brigitta rose to her feet, still patting the dog. "You must be starving!"

The dog barked in reply, then grinned at her, his tongue lolling out.

"There's some leftover lamb in Rupert's cottage," Stefan suggested. "We could take him there."

"Brigitta, you should come with us," Rupert told her. "So we can have our talk."

She nodded. "I need to fetch something from Stefan's cottage. Then I'll come."

Sister Fallyn huffed. "I can't allow you to be alone with them."

"This is important," Brigitta whispered to her. "It's about our future."

"Fallyn, you didn't sleep at all last night," Stefan said. "Why don't you get some rest?"

"Since when am I talking to you?" Sister Fallyn shot him an annoyed look, then grabbed Brigitta's arm. "Come with me." She marched off to Stefan's cottage with Brigitta in tow.

"I'll be along in a moment," Brigitta called back.

"Nay, ye will not," Sister Fallyn hissed back in Eberoni.

"I will, too," Brigitta argued.

With a groan, Stefan trudged toward Rupert's cottage. "She's taken over my house and won't even speak to me."

Rupert followed him. "You think that's bad, Brigitta wants to help me gain the throne."

Stefan gave him an incredulous look. "How on Aerthlan would she do that?"

"I don't know, but she thinks she has to atone for her father's sins."

"It's not her fault her father was a murderous bastard."

"I know." Rupert opened the door to his cottage, and to his surprise the dog scampered right inside.

Stefan snorted. "Making himself at home, I see."

Rupert followed Stefan inside. "There's something really fishy about that dog." As he closed the door, he noted that the dog had trotted over to the empty hearth.

He was a fairly large dog with long fur in black and white splotches. There was a large black spot over one eye.

"I'll get him some food." Stefan wandered over to the table.

The dog barked as if he wanted their attention. Rupert stepped closer, then halted with a jerk as the dog's form suddenly began to shimmer.

"What the . . ." Stefan dropped a knife on the table with a clatter.

The dog's form wavered more violently as it grew taller. The dog's snout receded, along with his fur, until the shape of a man could be seen. Then, just as suddenly, it was over and a new form had locked into place.

A naked young man stood before them.

He stepped behind a chair and gave them a smile. "Good morning. My name is Brody. Do you have any clothes I can borrow?

"Holy crap," Rupert whispered.

Chapter Nineteen

❧

Brigitta steeled her nerves before knocking on Rupert's door. No doubt he would object to her plan of action, so she would have to remain firm and convincing.

When Rupert let her in, she noted the tense look on his face. "Is something wrong?"

"We have a guest." He motioned toward the hearth.

There was a tall young man standing there, looking down as he quickly buttoned his shirt, his long black hair falling forward to conceal his face. He wore breeches, but no socks or shoes. He glanced up, shoving his shaggy hair back from his face, and smiled. "Hello, Brigitta."

This man knew her? She glanced at Rupert, who had crossed his arms over his chest while studying the young man with a wary demeanor. Even Stefan was eyeing him with suspicion.

The man's blue eyes seemed familiar, but other than that, she couldn't recall ever seeing him before. "Excuse me, but have we met?"

"You were patting his head a few minutes ago," Stefan grumbled.

Brigitta blinked. "What?"

"I'm Brody," the young man announced.

"*What?*" Brigitta stepped back.

"He's the dog," Rupert muttered.

Brigitta moved closer to him and whispered, "He's not a dog."

"He *was* a dog," Rupert insisted. "And now he's human. Or at least, I assume he's human."

Brody rolled his eyes. "I am human. I'm Embraced, like the two of you. Shifting is my special gift."

"I've never heard of anyone who can shift," Stefan said.

Brigitta shook her head. "I don't believe it. Are you playing a jest on—"

"It's no jest," Rupert interrupted her. "We saw him shift."

Brigitta frowned at the young man. "I still don't believe it."

Brody sighed. "I could show you, my lady, but I would need to undress—"

"Not happening," Rupert growled, then turned to Brigitta. "Believe me, the man can turn into a dog."

Brody cleared his throat. "Actually, I've spent most of my time lately as a pelican."

"Oh, crap." Rupert turned around, dragging a hand through his hair.

"What the hell?" Stefan shouted. "You're the pelican?"

"Oh, my . . ." In a daze, Brigitta wandered toward the table and sat in one of the chairs.

Stefan collapsed in the chair beside her. "I've been talking to the damned pelican."

"Why were you on my ship?" Rupert asked.

"Luciana asked me to watch over her sisters as they traveled to Ebton Palace," Brody explained.

Brigitta rubbed her brow. "So Luciana knows that you're a . . . ?"

"Shifter, yes." Brody nodded. "When you were kidnapped by pirates, I thought I'd better stay close to you to make sure you were safe. And I knew Leo would want more information on the pirate Rupert—"

"You're a spy!" Rupert charged toward Brody. "You're working for King Leofric, aren't you?"

Brody lifted a brow. "A dog's got to eat."

"Damn you." Rupert grabbed Brody's shirt and yanked him forward.

"Don't hurt him!" Brigitta jumped to her feet. "He's Luciana's pet!" When Brody shot her an annoyed look, she winced and sat back down. "This is all very strange."

Rupert released Brody and stepped back. "It *is* strange. You could have remained a pelican and no one would have ever known what you were doing. Why have you revealed yourself?"

Brody smoothed down his shirt. "Because last night I figured out who you really are." His mouth curled up with a hint of a smile. "Ulfrid from the House of Trepurin, the rightful king of Tourin."

Brigitta's breath caught. The pelican had been right beside her when she'd written *Ni Rupert* in the sand.

"Damn," Stefan muttered. "Does everyone know now?"

Rupert had gone very still, his gaze still locked on Brody. "What do you intend to do with that information?"

"We'll have to keep him prisoner on the island," Stefan said.

Rupert shook his head. "I doubt we can. Not when he can change into a bird and fly away."

Brody lifted both hands in surrender. "I mean you no harm. I revealed myself to see if you're interested in an alliance with King Leofric."

Rupert's brows lifted. "Go on."

Brody sauntered over to the table. "It's no secret that the current king of Tourin is an ass. Gunther is so greedy for gold that he's been sending raiding parties across the border into Eberon to steal the golden orbs out of village churches. And he's done nothing to stop the Tourinian pirates who have been pillaging along the Eberoni coast. I'm sure Leo would prefer an honorable king in Tourin. Especially one who would value peace as much as he does."

Rupert followed him to the table. "Do you know King Leofric well enough to speak for him?"

Brody nodded. "We're friends. He trusts me and my advice." He motioned to the platter of meat and loaf of bread. "I'm really tired of eating fish."

"Help yourself." Stefan slid a pewter plate in front of an empty chair. Then he put silverware, goblets, and a pitcher of wine on the table.

"Thank you." Brody sat and transferred a huge slice of mutton to the plate, then grabbed the loaf of bread and tore off a hunk.

Rupert sat in the fourth chair, across from Brody. "Can Leofric offer military support to help me usurp the throne?"

"Probably so." Brody buttered up the bread, then took a bite. "Is that your plan? A military takeover?"

Rupert nodded. "First we defeat the navy and completely cut off Gunther's supply of gold. When he's unable to pay his soldiers, we're hoping some of them will desert and come to our side. I'm also counting on some nobles from the north."

Brody forked a bite of mutton into his mouth. "So you plan to fight the king's army? What if he stays holed up in the royal palace in Lourdon? Will you attack the capital city?"

A muscle in Rupert's jaw twitched.

Brigitta realized this was a weakness in Rupert's plan, so she spoke up. "Can you expect the Tourinian people to swear loyalty to a new king if he's just killed off their family members in battle?"

Rupert's mouth thinned. "I realize the plan has its faults, but there is no other way."

"I believe there is." Brigitta took a deep breath as all three men at the table focused on her. "First, I should mention that my sister, Luciana, inherited the gift of foresight."

Brody nodded as he ate. "I've heard that her mother's family were witches who could see the future."

"That is true," Brigitta continued. "When we were young, my sisters and I would play a game with Telling Stones. We gathered up forty pebbles from a nearby beach and painted them with colors and numbers. And then we used the stones to make predictions. And that's when we discovered that Luciana could see the future as accurately as the Seer."

Brody snorted.

"What does this have to do with us?" Rupert asked impatiently.

"Luciana's prediction about herself came true," Brigitta explained. "So I asked her to use the Telling Stones to foresee my future. She picked blue and gold, which she said represented the colors of Tourin. This was eight months ago when we didn't know I was the Tourinian princess. She also picked the number eight, saying I would meet a tall and handsome stranger in eight months." She gave Rupert a pointed look.

His eyes softened. "I'm delighted you think I fit the bill, but it's still a coincidence."

"We've played the Game of Stones several times since then. Every time I grabbed a handful of stones, without fail the blue and gold ones would be in my hand. But the number eight stone would change. Five months ago, I picked the stone with the number five. Four months ago, I picked number four. One month ago, it was number one. Do you call all of that a coincidence?"

Rupert frowned.

Stefan shuddered. "I call it damned spooky."

Brody bit off more bread as he watched them all.

"Are you saying we were fated to meet?" Rupert asked.

Brigitta nodded. "Yes. I believe it is my destiny to help you regain what you lost."

Rupert sighed. "I've always believed that our futures are of our own making."

"I agree to a certain extent. It will be our actions that will see you take the throne. But sometimes, things do happen that we can't control." Brigitta looked down at her clenched hands on the table. "Like what my father did to your family."

"That wasn't your fault," Rupert said quietly as he rested a hand on hers. "Your father's actions affected you, too. You were sent away, abandoned by your family."

"But I gained a new family. I grew up surrounded with love and happiness. You . . ." Brigitta heaved a sigh. "You lost everything."

He squeezed her hands. "Aye, I have lost too much. That's why I want you to stay here where it's safe."

She shook her head. "There was another stone that Luciana selected, and I picked it every time, too. The number seven. Luciana said it meant there would be seven men vying for my hand."

Rupert released her hands as he sat back. "You mean . . . ?"

"The competition." Brigitta retrieved the notice from her skirt pocket. This was what she had gone back to Stefan's cottage to fetch from her small bag of belongings.

She set the notice on the table. "This was meant to happen. And this is how I will help you retrieve what you have lost."

"What is this?" Brody turned the notice around so he could read it.

Rupert shook his head. "I can't let you do it, Brigitta. Whoever wins that contest will assault you."

"Then you'll have to enter and make sure that you win." She shot him a challenging look. "Are you afraid you'll lose?"

He scoffed. "I would win."

She smiled. "Then it's not a problem."

"Yes, it is!" Stefan growled. "Did you read the fine print?"

"I did." Brody pointed at the bottom of the page. "The loser of each round will be executed."

"Exactly." Stefan sat back, crossing his arms. "Rupert is not doing that damned contest!"

Brody shrugged. "It seems to me if he goes to war against the Tourinian navy and army, he'll be risking his life just as much."

"That's true!" Brigitta agreed. "But if he enters the contest, he can have safe access to the capital and the palace. He won't have to kill his own countrymen in battle."

Brody nodded as he tapped his finger on the notice. "I like this plan better. I'm sure Leo will prefer it, too. We won't have to risk a bunch of people's lives. The only one in danger will be you." He looked at Rupert. "Can you handle that?"

Rupert snorted. "I'm not worried about myself. It's Brigitta who will be in danger. Didn't you read the notice? Her brother wants her pregnant by the man of his choosing. He will definitely not choose me. Even if I win the damned competition, there is no guarantee he won't have her raped by his favorite. She's safer here on the island."

Brigitta swallowed hard. There was a risk, she had to admit it, but she couldn't live with herself if she hid here like a coward. "You can't force me to stay here."

Rupert gritted his teeth. "Watch me."

She slapped her palm on the table. "Then you're willing to go into unnecessary battles and watch your own men die and kill your own countrymen? What kind of king do you intend to be?"

Rupert stood so quickly, his chair toppled over. He paced across the small room.

Brigitta's heart pounded as she clutched her hands together. "I know you're an honorable man, Rupert. I simply wish to prove myself an honorable woman."

He stopped his pacing and dragged a hand through his hair. "You'll be in danger."

"I'm willing to risk it," she said. "I can insist my brother treat me fairly in exchange for my full cooperation. I can pretend to love the contest. I can lie and manipulate all I need to in order to stay safe. I will not be going in there as a meek, helpless lamb!"

Rupert looked at her, his eyes softening. "I know you're clever. I know you're brave. But I cannot bear any harm to come to you."

"I will go with her," Brody offered. "As her personal guard dog. No one will be able to attack her."

Stefan sighed. "I suppose this plan is doable."

Rupert winced. "It is true I am reluctant to battle my own people. I want prosperity for Tourin. And peace."

Brigitta's heart stuttered. "Then you agree? We'll do the competition?"

Rupert frowned at her. "I'm giving you a blade, and on the way to Eberon, I'll be teaching you how to use it."

She grinned. "Yes!"

His frown deepened. "This is not a game, Brigitta. If you are forced to defend yourself, you will have to kill the bastard. Wounding him will only cause him to become more violent."

She gulped. "I understand."

"Once you win the contest, how do you get the throne?" Stefan asked Rupert. "Could you assassinate Gunther during the final ceremony?"

Rupert shrugged. "I'm not sure. Too many unknowns. We'll have to play it by ear."

"I thought we could imprison him," Brigitta suggested. She winced at the dark look Rupert gave her. "I don't want you to live with that stain on your soul."

Stefan leaned toward her. "Are you sure you won't be sympathetic toward Gunther? He is your brother, after all."

"Just because I'm reluctant to have him murdered doesn't mean I'm on his side. You can trust me." Brigitta glanced at Rupert. Didn't he trust her?

He looked away with a grimace. "Gunther cannot be allowed to live. He would represent a continued threat to the throne."

Brigitta swallowed hard. How could she stop the man she loved from committing a cold-blooded murder? "Like you said, we'll play it by ear."

"We'll finish making plans, then set sail this afternoon." Rupert set his chair upright, then took a seat.

Brody pointed to a line on the notice. "The contest is scheduled to begin a fortnight after the last embrace of the moons."

Rupert counted the days in his mind. "This is the beginning of the sixth day. I can put a strong wind behind us so we can reach Eberon on the eighth day."

Stefan winced. "We're cutting it close. We'll have less

than a week to return Brigitta and have you ready to compete."

Rupert nodded. "And I can't compete as Rupert or the lost prince, so I'll need a new identity."

Brody buttered up more bread. "Leo can help with that. Since you speak Eberoni fluently, you can pass as an Eberoni nobleman. As soon as we get close enough to shore, I'll fly to Ebton Palace and finalize the plans there."

"Good." Rupert poured himself a goblet of wine.

"Lady Brigitta," Stefan whispered, leaning close to her. "May I have a word with you in private?"

"Of course." As Brigitta followed the captain out the front door, her heart raced. She'd done it! She'd convinced Rupert to follow her plan. She wouldn't have to hide here on the island like a coward. No, she would be taking an active part in deciding her own future.

How odd that for months she had dreaded the idea of a competition, fearing that it might be forced on her whether she liked it or not. But now she actually wanted it to happen.

She looked at the *Golden Star* where it lay anchored in the bay. This afternoon, they would set sail and follow their destiny. She made the sign of the moons with a silent prayer that they would all remain safe.

Stefan closed the door and cleared his throat.

Brigitta turned toward him. "Yes?"

He glanced toward his cottage. "I wanted to ask you about Fallyn. You may have heard . . ."

"That you proposed to her?" Brigitta prompted.

He heaved a long sigh. "Am I being a fool? Am I expecting more from her than she's able to give? I love her. I love her enough not to force her to follow a path that will cause her pain." He grimaced. "Is it hopeless for us?"

Brigitta paused, not sure what to say. She couldn't see

the future like Luciana. "I think Sister Fallyn does care for you. Very much."

"I don't know what the rules are at a convent that worships the two moons. What kind of vows did she take?"

"We worship the twin goddesses there, so the convent has always served the purpose of being a safe haven for women. The only vows are faith in the goddesses, fidelity to ourselves, and loving support to other women."

Stefan's eyes narrowed. "That's it? No vows of chastity or poverty?"

"No." Brigitta shook her head. "We must be true to ourselves. That is a matter between us and our goddesses. Sister Fallyn is very faithful."

"That's all right." Stefan's eyes lit up with hope. "A faithful woman is a rare treasure. If you'll excuse me." He bowed his head, then strode toward his cottage.

With a smile, Brigitta let herself back into Rupert's house. If they were going to continue making plans, she wanted to be a part of it.

Chapter Twenty

❧

"Thank you for your help," Rupert told the pelican Brody. "And please convey my gratitude to King Leofric. I'm looking forward to meeting him."

Brody bobbed his head in acknowledgment.

It was late afternoon of the next day, and the *Golden Star* was now close enough to the Eberon coast for Brody to fly to Ebton Palace and make plans with Leofric.

Rupert's head swirled with a mixture of emotions. Excitement that finally he was moving forward with his quest for revenge. Fear that Brigitta would be exposed to danger. And a sudden sense of trepidation. For years, he'd been so focused on the act of revenge that he'd never thought past it.

What kind of king do you intend to be? Brigitta's words had hit him hard. Gaining the throne was not the end of his life's work, but the beginning. It would all be for naught if he didn't prove to be a worthy king.

"Brody!" Brigitta dashed onto the deck. "I heard you were leaving." She hunched down in front of the pelican.

Rupert had enjoyed teaching her how to defend herself. Unfortunately, those few hours yesterday and this morning were the only times he had seen her. Sister

Fallyn had watched them like a hawk, ready to screech whenever his touch had lingered longer than necessary.

They'd been forced to explain everything to the nun before leaving the island. Otherwise, she had refused to let Brigitta participate in a contest that would end with sexual assault. Once Sister Fallyn had understood that he was the lost prince, and that he would be winning the contest, she had condoned their plan. And when Brody had assured her that he would be going along to guard Brigitta, the nun had insisted on coming, too.

But as soon as they'd set sail, Sister Fallyn had announced that there would be no ravishment on board. Even if he was a prince, instead of a pirate, he would not be allowed to seduce Brigitta until he married her. The nun had even posted the dog Brody outside Brigitta's door that night to stand guard.

Brigitta patted the pelican on the head. "Be sure to tell Luciana and Mother Ginessa and all my sisters how much I love them and miss them. If Luciana has given birth, I doubt she'll have recovered enough to come see me. Please tell her not to feel bad about that. Tell her you'll be guarding me in Tourin, and I'll be perfectly safe."

Brody nodded and shifted his weight on his webbed feet.

"I think he's ready to go," Rupert said.

"All right." Brigitta straightened on her feet. "Oh, and if you see the newborn baby, give him a big kiss from me."

Brody made a grunting noise.

Rupert snorted. He didn't think that last part would happen. Brody ran forward, flapping his wings until he began to soar higher and higher.

Brigitta watched him go. "It must be interesting to fly, though I would be afraid of crashing."

"Would you like a bird's-eye view?" Rupert asked her. "I'll take you up to the crow's nest."

She shuddered. "Too scary."

"I'll be with you the whole time."

She glanced over her shoulder to check on Sister Fallyn. The nun was on the quarterdeck talking to Stefan. Whenever Brigitta came on deck, the nun came, too, to make sure Rupert behaved himself. "I suppose you would have to hold me to keep me safe."

"Definitely." He took her hand and led her toward the rope-and-pulley mechanism next to the mainmast.

"Brigitta!" Sister Fallyn yelled from the quarterdeck. "Stay where I can see you."

"I will," Brigitta shouted back, then whispered, "How do we do this?"

Rupert wedged his left boot through the tight loop, then put on his gloves. "You'll have to wrap your legs around me and squeeze me tight."

She scoffed. "There you go again."

"I mean it." He lifted her so she could wrap her legs around his waist. "You'll have to hold tight."

She nearly choked him.

He grasped the rope with his left hand. "Ready?" When her head nodded against his cheek, he pulled the lever with his right hand, then held on to her as they shot upward.

She squealed, squeezing him tight. When they reached the top, he hooked his right boot around a wooden slat of the crow's nest and pulled them up against the railing.

"You'll have to let go now," he whispered, and she shook her head. "I still have you." He set her bottom on the railing. "But you'll need to swing your legs over the railing."

He helped her slowly turn and ease her feet over the railing. With one hand still clutching him, she reached for the mainmast. He slipped over the railing to stand next to her. She was hugging the mainmast with her eyes shut.

"You did it," he whispered in her ear.

Her eyes opened and she took a quick look around. "Oh, sweet goddesses. We're at the top of the world."

"Brigitta!" Sister Fallyn screamed.

Rupert turned just in time to see the nun faint into the waiting arms of Stefan.

Brigitta winced. "Oh, dear."

She didn't seem ready to let go of her grip on the mainmast, so Rupert hugged her from behind, resting his chin against her temple. "Finally. I've been wanting to hold you since we left the island."

She leaned against him. "It never frightens you to be up so high?"

"No. I like the vastness of the sky. It makes me feel like anything is possible."

She sighed. "I suppose anything is possible. Here you are hugging me, when you should hate me."

He kissed a path along her neck to her ear.

"You must have always known I was Garold's daughter. Why didn't you hate me?"

"I tried." He nuzzled his cheek against hers. "I thought I should hate you, but from the beginning . . . everything about you touched me."

She turned in his arms. "I suspected right off that you were my tall and handsome stranger. But I was terribly shocked that my hero could be a sorcerer and a pirate."

He smiled. "I think I started falling for you the minute you surrendered in order to keep your friends safe from the flaming arrows."

She thumped his chest. "I'm still angry over that."

"I wouldn't have hurt them." He took her fist and kissed the knuckles. Her hand opened and he laced his fingers with hers. "From the beginning you showed that you're brave and beautiful. When you helped Sister Fallyn up the ladder, I knew you were kind and humble. And when you first gave me a piece of your mind, I knew you were bold and clever. You're everything I ever wanted or needed. How could I have possibly hated you?"

"Oh, Rupert." Her eyes glimmered with emotion.

He leaned down for a long, leisurely kiss, and she melted against him.

"Brigitta!"

He broke the kiss. Apparently, Sister Fallyn had recovered.

"Brigitta, come down from there this instant!" the nun yelled.

Rupert sighed. "I'll take you down."

Brigitta looked up at him, her eyes still soft and dreamy from their kiss. "Was this your fifth reason? When you didn't want to release me, you had a fifth reason that you wouldn't tell me."

"I wanted you near me, yes. I wanted to know what kind of woman my betrothed had become."

Her eyes widened. "But you couldn't have considered me your betrothed, not after what my father did."

"I considered the engagement broken, yes." He kissed her brow. "But not anymore."

She drew in a quick breath.

"Brigitta!" Sister Fallyn yelled again.

He smiled as he lifted her up in his arms. "Wrap your legs around me and squeeze me tight."

"That again?" With a grin, she hugged him.

He lifted them over the railing and slid down the rope. Sister Fallyn was waiting close by and the minute Brigitta's feet hit the deck, she snatched her by the arm and glared at Rupert.

"I will not have you ravishing the princess!" Sister Fallyn marched off with Brigitta, who glanced back with a cheerful wave.

He waved back, smiling. Tonight, he would sneak into her cabin.

By the next morning, Rupert had maneuvered the *Golden Star* close to the Eberoni shore. The pelican Brody landed on deck, then hopped into Rupert's cabin and shifted into human form.

Rupert handed him a pair of breeches. "What did Leofric say?"

"He and Luciana are delighted to be of assistance." Brody pulled on the breeches. "Shouldn't Brigitta hear about this?"

Rupert winced. After sneaking into Brigitta's cabin last night, he'd discovered her tearing an old sheet into strips. With a blush, she'd admitted that she'd started her monthly courses. He'd seen no reason to leave, claiming he would be happy just to sleep with her in his arms. But the nun had burst into the room and thrown a fit. "Sister Fallyn has forbidden me to see her for the rest of the voyage."

Brody snorted. "The nun takes her job seriously."

"Aye," Rupert agreed. "I would complain, but I'm actually glad that she's so fierce about watching out for Brigitta. Between you and the nun, I feel much better about Brigitta going to Lourdon Palace."

Stefan entered the room, carrying a tray of food. "You have news?"

"Yes," Brody replied. "Since this ship is too large to sail up the Ebe River, Leo and Luciana are traveling down the river on the royal barge. They'll meet us at the small village of Ebport at the mouth of the Ebe."

"The queen is coming?" Rupert cleared an area on his

worktable so Stefan could set down the tray. "I thought she was supposed to be giving birth about this time."

"She had the twins early." Brody grabbed a slice of cheese off the tray and popped it into his mouth.

"Twins?" Stefan poured him a cup of wine.

Brody nodded as he chewed. "A boy and a girl. Born on the night the moons embraced."

They would have magical powers then, Rupert thought. And they shared his birthday.

"So we need to go to Ebport," Stefan said.

"Yes." Brody took a sip of wine. "Luciana's father, the Duke of Vindalyn, is coming, too. He was at Ebton Palace for the birth of his grandchildren, so we included him in the meeting. He has provided Rupert with a new identity for the competition."

He'd been Rupert since the age of fourteen. Twelve years. It would feel strange to be anyone else now, even his true identity. "Who will I be?"

"One of the duke's barons recently died without an heir," Brody explained. "The duke has revealed that you are a distant cousin, and he's awarded the title to you. You will be Umberto Vintello, the new Baron Suffield. His Grace is bringing the paperwork to prove it. That way, if Gunther has you investigated, you will appear legitimate."

Stefan performed a deep bow. "Lord Suffield."

Rupert snorted.

"Congratulations." Brody smiled at him. "You temporarily own some land and an excellent manor house."

"Maybe Sister Fallyn will like me better now," Rupert muttered, and Stefan chuckled.

Brody finished his cup of wine. "Leo has already sent an envoy to Lourdon to announce Brigitta's rescue from the notorious pirate Rupert. Leo's best friend, Captain

Nevis Harden, is bringing several troops of soldiers down the river. Everyone will believe they're providing protection for the royal barge. But Nevis and one of his troops will take Brigitta to the Tourinian border to meet her brother. I'll be her guard dog."

"Thank you." Rupert refilled the shifter's cup.

"You will go to Ebton Palace as Baron Suffield," Brody continued. "That way, the Tourinian ambassador and his spies will see you as an Eberoni nobleman. You'll be outfitted in suitable clothing and given a small troop of guards and servants to accompany you to Lourdon."

"I'm going with him," Stefan insisted.

Rupert's heart swelled. Stefan had stayed by his side since that tragic day nineteen years ago. As a young soldier from one of the loyal northern clans, Stefan had been given what was considered a prestigious assignment—guarding the prince and heir to the throne. But Stefan had soon found himself raising a traumatized young orphan who was being hunted by an entire army. Through it all, he had remained true. "Thank you, old friend."

Stefan waved a dismissive hand as if he didn't care, but his voice was gruff with emotion. "What else would I do?" He looked away, blinking. "I'd better get this tub headed toward Ebport." He quickly left the room.

Brody took a bite of bread. "The royal barge will arrive in Ebport by noon. Can we make it by then?"

"Yes." Rupert glanced at his worktable. This had been his room for seven years now. He gave the windmill one last twirl. No more tinkering on his inventions here. No more pirating. His days as Rupert were over.

A new life lay in front of him, but he was no longer that frightened orphan. And he didn't have to face the future alone. Stefan would be by his side, along with his new allies from Eberon.

And most of all, there was Brigitta.

"Look!" Brigitta pointed at the royal barge in the distance. She'd been waiting excitedly by the ship's railing as they'd drawn closer to the village of Ebport. Now she could see the pier that ran along the Ebe River and the large barge tied off beside it. A brightly painted cabin had been built on top with long windows and an outside staircase leading to the flat observation deck on the roof. Flags in the Eberoni royal colors of red and black flapped in the breeze that swept in from the ocean.

"I can see women on deck," Sister Fallyn said with a grin.

"Ye can?" Brigitta held up a hand to shield her eyes from the bright sun. "Oh my, I think they're all there!" She waved an arm, and the women waved back.

"Praise the goddesses." Sister Fallyn made the sign of the moons.

"But how can this be?" Brigitta asked. "I thought Luciana would be giving birth now."

"She went into labor a week ago," Brody said as he joined them by the railing.

Brigitta glanced at him, surprised to see him in human form. "I didn't know ye were back."

"We were talking belowdecks," Rupert said as he strode toward them.

Brigitta blinked. Why was Rupert wearing his old disguise? "Is everything set?"

"Yes." Rupert handed her his spyglass. "Would you like to use this?"

"Oh, aye!" Brigitta pushed aside all worries about the upcoming dangerous adventure as she focused the spyglass on her sisters. "I see them!" They were like a rainbow, each one dressed in a different-colored beautiful gown. "There's Maeve and Sorcha! And Luciana!"

Sister Fallyn *tsk*ed. "She shouldn't be traveling so soon after childbirth."

"Traveling by barge is fairly easy," Brody said. "I'm sure she was resting inside the cabin for most of the trip."

"Oh! There's Mother Ginessa!" Brigitta continued to look through the spyglass. "And she's holding the baby!"

"Let me see!" Sister Fallyn reached for the spyglass.

"Wait!" Brigitta stiffened. "Oh my goddesses, Gwennore is holding a baby, too."

"Oh, right," Brody said. "Luciana had twins."

Brigitta lowered the spyglass to stare at him. "Now ye tell me?"

"Are they healthy?" Sister Fallyn demanded. "Are they both girls?"

Brody shrugged. "They're loud. I suppose that means they're healthy."

"One boy and one girl," Rupert added.

"What are their names?" Brigitta asked.

Brody gave her a blank look. "I . . . didn't ask."

She gave him an incredulous look, then turned to Rupert.

He shrugged. "Is it important?"

With a huff, she exchanged a look with Sister Fallyn. The nun shook her head and muttered, "Men."

"Here." Brigitta offered her the spyglass.

"Oh dear goddesses," Sister Fallyn murmured as she looked at their friends. "I was afraid I'd ne'er see them again."

"Ye can stay with them if ye want," Brigitta whispered. "Ye don't have to come with me."

Sister Fallyn handed her the spyglass with a tearful look. "I know, lass, but 'tis the right thing for me to do.

We're both Tourinians, so we should go together. And from now on, we should only speak in Tourinian."

Brigitta nodded and switched languages. "You're right. Thank you."

"I see you're ready to go," Rupert said.

"Yes." Brigitta returned his spyglass. At her feet, she had a small bag stuffed with their meager belongings—their convent gowns, several nightgowns and shifts, two toothbrushes, and a hairbrush. The last items had all been gifts from Rupert. "I'm going to miss you."

He gave her a sad smile. "I'll miss you, too. I should arrive in Lourdon the day before the competition begins. We'll have to pretend not to know each other."

She nodded. "I understand." And she would have to watch him risk his life in the competition without showing how terrified she was.

Tears burned her eyes. Their ship was now close enough to Ebport that she could easily see her sisters at the bow of the barge. Luciana's father was with them. Off by himself, Leo stood at the back. As far as Brigitta knew, only Luciana could touch him and live. Did that mean the poor man was unable to hold his own babies?

Luciana broke off from the group of women and walked toward her husband. Leo took her in his arms.

Brigitta blinked to keep from crying. She'd always written her *overly dramatic* stories with happy endings, but now she feared there was no such thing as a perfectly happy ending. As much as she wanted Rupert to gain the throne that was rightfully his, it would mean the death of her brother. How could she continue to love Rupert if he committed a cold-blooded murder?

"Are you all right?" Rupert asked.

She wiped her cheeks. "I-I think I'm going to miss being at sea with you."

He nodded. "I've been at sea since I was fourteen. And the *Golden Star* has been my home since I was nineteen."

"What will happen to the ship?"

"Tucker will sail her west to meet up with the rest of the fleet. Then Ansel will be in charge. They're going to sail north and be close to Tourin in case we need them."

In case something went awry and they had to escape? Brigitta took a deep breath.

A loud noise filled the air as the anchor was dropped, and the ship groaned and shuddered as it came to a stop.

Stefan joined them by the railing as crewmen lowered the dinghy and a rope ladder.

"I'll go first." Brody climbed down to the dinghy.

As Sister Fallyn and Stefan each descended the ladder, Brigitta watched her sisters crossing a wide plank from the barge to the pier. At the end of the pier, a troop of soldiers waited.

"Your turn." Rupert helped her over the railing, and she slowly descended to the dinghy.

She settled on a bench next to Sister Fallyn, who took her hand and squeezed it. Stefan sat across from them and caught her bag when Rupert tossed it down.

Rupert joined them in the dinghy and pushed them off from the *Golden Star*.

A part of Brigitta wanted to jump back on board with Rupert and sail away to live happily ever after. But how could they be happy if they ran away from their destiny?

As Rupert and Stefan rowed them ashore, she turned to face her sisters. They were waving and Maeve was crying. Poor Maeve.

"I won't be able to hold this form for much longer," Brody told her. "But I wanted to assure you that no matter how it might look, Leo is on your side."

"All right." With tears in her eyes, Brigitta waved at her sisters.

"We have to make it look authentic," Brody added. "So when—"

"I missed you!" Brigitta called out to her sisters as the dinghy drew close to the pier.

"Brigitta!" her sisters cried out. "Sister Fallyn!"

Luciana's father tossed a rope to Rupert, and he tied the dinghy off.

Sorcha and Maeve grabbed Brigitta to help her off the small boat, then pulled her into an embrace. Sister Fallyn followed, and soon they were all laughing and hugging.

"I was so afraid for you." Luciana broke into tears as she held Brigitta close.

"I'm fine. I'm perfectly fine," Brigitta assured her.

"I know." Luciana wiped her cheeks. "I swear I cry at the drop of a hat these days. Let me show you the twins."

Mother Ginessa proudly displayed one with a shock of red hair. "This is Eric."

"And this is Eviana." Gwennore showed off a sleeping baby with soft features and even softer black hair on the crown of her head.

"Oh, they're beautiful." Brigitta admired them and was so busy talking that she barely noticed Rupert and Stefan meeting Leo. But she stopped in midsentence when the troop of soldiers suddenly came charging down the pier.

Leo pointed at Rupert. "Arrest him!"

"What?" Brigitta gasped and started toward them.

Luciana grabbed her arm. "Don't."

"But—" Brigitta watched in horror as the soldiers ran after Rupert.

Stefan tried to stop them, but four of the soldiers jumped on him and pinned him down. At the end of the pier, a soldier caught Rupert by the arm. He planted a fist in the soldier's face, knocking him out. Five more soldiers grabbed Rupert and wrenched his arms behind his back.

"No!" Brigitta cried.

Sister Fallyn fell to her knees, a hand pressed to her chest.

The troop's captain marched up to Rupert and punched him in the jaw. "I've been trying to capture you for months!"

Rupert glared at him and spit out a mouthful of blood.

"Don't hurt him," Brigitta pleaded with tears in her eyes, but Luciana hushed her.

"Rupert, you are charged with piracy," Leo announced. "The sentence is death."

Chapter Twenty-One

❦

"Why are ye doing this?" Brigitta cried as she watched the troop of soldiers dragging Rupert and Stefan toward the village. "Where are ye taking them?"

"Come with me." Luciana led her toward the barge.

"No!" Brigitta pulled away so she could follow Rupert.

Luciana grabbed her and leaned close to whisper in her ear, "The arrest was playacting. No one will be hurt."

"What?" Brigitta asked.

Luciana sighed. "Brody was supposed to warn you."

Sister Fallyn scrambled to her feet and joined them. "Will Stefan be all right?"

Mother Ginessa frowned at her. "Ye're concerned for that pirate?"

The nun blushed. "I-I'm thinking about marrying him."

All of Brigitta's sisters gasped.

Mother Ginessa's eyes widened with shock. "We need to talk."

"Did ye fall in love?" Maeve asked.

"Aye, we want to hear all about it," Sorcha demanded.

"We'll leave you here for the moment," Luciana told them, then led Brigitta onto the barge. "So Rupert is the tall and handsome man I predicted with the Telling Stones?"

"Aye."

With a thoughtful look, Luciana opened the cabin door and motioned for Brigitta to enter.

Inside, Brigitta was impressed by how comfortable it was. There were deeply padded armchairs and settees, a table with six chairs, and a long sideboard covered with trays of food and pitchers of wine.

"Are you hungry?" Luciana asked as she closed the door. "Help yourself."

"I want to know what's happening to Rupert and Stefan. Where are ye taking them?"

"It's all part of the plan, so don't worry." Luciana eased into an armchair. "Nevis and his most trusted soldiers are taking them to a secluded cabin in the woods."

"Who is Nevis?" Brigitta planted her hands on her hips. "Is he the bastard who punched my Rupert in the face?"

Luciana's mouth twitched. "I see Brody is right. You're quite smitten with this Rupert. But there's no need to be angry with Nevis. He's a good man. He's Leo's best friend and a captain in the army."

Brigitta snorted, but Luciana ignored it and continued, "At the cabin, one of Nevis's men will don Rupert's disguise. Then Nevis will have one of his troops escort the false Rupert to Ebton Palace, where he will be kept in a private room in the dungeon. From there, the story will be that Rupert attempted an escape and was accidentally killed while being recaptured. His disguise will be posted publicly as proof that the infamous pirate Rupert is dead."

Dead. Brigitta sat across from her sister. She would miss the Rupert she knew.

Luciana sighed. "Brody really should have warned you."

"I think he did. I just didn't hear it." But Rupert must have known. He could have blown those soldiers away and escaped if he'd wanted to. But he had played along. And that was why he had worn the old disguise. So now Rupert would be dead. Brigitta shook her head. "I don't know what to call him. He'll always be Rupert to me."

"You must be careful," Luciana warned her. "You can never call him by that name in public."

"Is he coming back here? When will I see him again?"

Luciana hesitated a moment before speaking. "My father is traveling with them. At the cabin, Rupert will change into the clothes of a nobleman. Then my father and Rupert will ride to Ebton Palace together as the Duke of Vindalyn and his vassal, Baron Suffield. That way, my father can introduce Rupert at court. It's the best way to validate Rupert's new identity. And it's very important that the Tourinian ambassador and his spies see him as the baron."

Brigitta nodded. "I see. So we're taking the barge back to the palace? I'll see Rupert there?"

With a sigh, Luciana sat back in her chair. "You won't see him again until he arrives in Lourdon for the competition."

"What?" Brigitta jumped to her feet. "But we didn't get to say good-bye."

"We can't risk anyone seeing you with Baron Suffield," Luciana explained. "You're not supposed to know him."

Brigitta frowned. "Do we really have to be that careful? Surely, there's a private place—"

"You don't know what's been going on since Leo and I became king and queen. For the most part, our people seem really happy with us, but unfortunately, there is a faction that wants to kill us and take over the throne."

Brigitta's eyes widened. "Are ye in danger?"

"Nevis and his father, General Harden, are doing their best to keep the peace. And Leo's lightning power keeps us safe. The problem is the royal order of priests who used to work as spies for the crown. We disbanded them. Our people are delighted that they no longer have to live in fear. But the priests hated losing the power they wielded over everyone. Their leader is Lord Morris, who was chief counsel to the late king. Lord Morris and the disgruntled priests have allied themselves with your brother, King Gunther of Tourin."

Brigitta sat back down. "I don't like to think of him as a brother."

Luciana nodded. "By all accounts, he is a cruel man. He's been hoarding gold for years while his people starve. And he's using that gold to pay Lord Morris and his priests to spy on the Eberoni people and cause unrest."

Brigitta winced. "No wonder ye want rid of him."

"Gunther has provided the priests with enough gold to pay for information all over Eberon. The end result is there are very few people left whom we can trust."

"So that's why you staged that show?"

"Yes. The villagers saw our soldiers capturing the pirate Rupert and dragging him away. The news will spread, and Gunther will hear about it." Luciana sat forward. "Are you sure you want to go through with this? Gunther is a dangerous man."

"Brody will be with me. And Sister Fallyn."

"But I won't be there." Luciana winced. "When I picked those Telling Stones eight months ago, I sensed danger. I kept hoping I was wrong. I didn't tell you because I didn't want you to spend all those months worrying about it."

Brigitta gave her a wry smile. "I worried anyway. I didn't want to be the prize for a contest."

"You could still back out. You don't have to do this."

"I know. Rupert could take the throne by force. When I thought fate was forcing the competition on me without my consent, I was thoroughly opposed to it. But now I realize it is a choice, and it's the right choice. It will save lives. I can right the wrongs done to Rupert by my family. And I can prove to him that he can trust me."

Luciana's eyes glimmered with tears as she rose to her feet. "I'm so proud of you. I know you'll do well."

Brigitta jumped up and gave her a hug. "Thank you."

"I've missed you so much." Luciana wiped away a tear, then motioned to a small trunk next to the sideboard. "I've packed a few of my gowns for you to use."

"Thank you. I missed you, too."

"Nevis and his second troop will take you to the Tourinian border. Gunther will meet you there."

Brigitta took a deep breath. "All right. When do I leave?"

"As soon as Nevis returns." Luciana squeezed her hand. "Today."

That evening, they arrived at the appointed meeting place, a bridge that crossed the Norva River at its narrowest point. The Norva began in the mountains of Norveshka, then flowed west toward the ocean, marking the border between Tourin and Eberon.

Brigitta was relieved that the uncomfortable ride in the small carriage was over, for the constant jostling had made her stomach ache. But her relief was short-lived. One look at the Tourinian army camped across the river, and her stomach lurched.

Nevis ordered his men to set up camp, while he ventured onto the bridge. The Tourinian officer in charge met him halfway. Then Nevis returned with the news.

Her brother had not yet arrived. So she and Sister Fallyn retired to their tent to rest. And wait. They ate supper and still waited. Finally, they stretched out on the cots Nevis had provided and tried to sleep. But it was hard to sleep when such an unknown future loomed before them.

The next morning, Sister Fallyn helped Brigitta dress in one of the gowns that Luciana had loaned to her. It was made of lovely turquoise silk with a matching scarf of sheer gauze. Instead of wearing the scarf over her head, Brigitta wrapped it around her shoulders to cover up the low neckline. Since the gown appeared brand-new and was the same color as her eyes, she suspected her dear sister had actually had it made for her.

She missed her sisters already.

Nevis invited them to his tent for breakfast, and Brody was there in human form. They sat around a small portable table.

"One of my men bought these at a local farm," Nevis explained as he passed Brigitta a bowl of strawberries to go with her oatmeal.

"Thank you." Brigitta forced herself to eat a few bites. Her appetite was gone, but she knew she needed to keep up her strength. "Do you think my brother will arrive today?"

"The lieutenant across the river thinks so," Nevis replied as he filled their goblets with apple cider. "He confirmed that Gunther is on his way."

"He's making you wait on purpose," Brody added between bites of oatmeal. "It's his way of showing you he's in charge."

"He's a royal ass," Nevis muttered, then gave Brigitta an apologetic look. "No offense."

"None taken." Brigitta gave him a wry look. "Although I was upset when you hit Rupert so hard."

Nevis winced. "Sorry. It was part of the show."

"A part you thoroughly enjoyed," Brody added with a smirk.

Nevis scowled at the shifter. "You don't have to tell her that. Why don't you go chase a squirrel?"

"There aren't any," Brody replied. "They all took one look at you and ran away."

Nevis scoffed. "So you already checked for them this morning."

Brigitta smiled to herself. Their bickering reminded her of being with her sisters. But before she could see them again, she would have to survive the ordeal with her brother. "Is there anything you can tell me about King Gunther that might be of help?"

"Ah." Nevis ate a strawberry while he considered. "He's a typical bully, so I would advise you not to appear weak in front of him. He will respect you more if you're strong. At the same time, you mustn't offend him. I've heard he has a terrible temper." He turned to Brody. "Didn't you tell me that?"

Brody nodded as he finished his bowl of oatmeal. "After his son and heir died from a fever, he went into a rage and blamed his wife for not taking good enough care of the boy. That night she accidentally fell down a flight of stairs and broke her neck."

Brigitta gulped. "You mean he killed his wife?"

Brody shrugged. "There are some in the Tourinian court who believe so."

"Goddesses protect us." Sister Fallyn made the sign of the moons, then quickly clenched her hands together. "I must remember not to do that anymore."

"True," Nevis told her. "And be mindful of your speech. Worshipping the twin goddesses is forbidden in Tourin."

Sister Fallyn nodded. "We'll be careful."

"Rupert told me my brother was unable to father children. Is that true?" Brigitta asked.

"Aye." Nevis made a sour face as he finished his breakfast. "A few years ago, he had his breeches burned off in a battle with a Norveshki dragon."

Brody nodded. "According to gossip at the Tourinian court, he's unable to . . . perform in bed."

Nevis shuddered. "I would pity the man if he wasn't such an ass. No offense."

"None taken." Brigitta's mind raced. Her brother's misfortune could be considered good news for her. If she was the only way Gunther could have an heir, then he would have to keep her alive and healthy. "How do you know what people in the Tourinian court are saying?" she asked Brody.

Nevis snorted. "He slinks around the royal courts of Aerthlan as a dog."

Brody arched an eyebrow. "I don't slink. And I bring back a great deal of valuable information."

"And a great number of fleas," Nevis muttered.

Brigitta smiled. "I think he makes a very cute dog."

Brody shot her an annoyed look. "Cute?"

Nevis laughed. "Watch out. He bites."

"Only your favorite boots." Brody smirked.

A sudden blast of horns made Brigitta and Sister Fallyn jump in their seats. Nevis and Brody darted to the tent entrance to take a look across the river.

"The royal ass has arrived," Nevis muttered.

Brigitta's heart pounded as she rose to her feet.

"Dear godd—" Sister Fallyn stopped herself.

"Go back to your tent and gather your things." Nevis gave them a worried look. "Don't trust Gunther or any of his minions. Don't say anything to each other or Brody that you don't mind being overheard, for believe me, he will have spies around you."

Brigitta nodded. "I understand."

"Do you have a weapon?" Nevis asked.

"I have a knife strapped to my thigh," Brigitta replied. "Rupert taught me how to use it."

Brody winced. "If you mention him from now on, you must do it with disdain toward the wretched pirate who kidnapped you."

Brigitta nodded, her heart thudding in her ears. She knew they were trying to help, but they were making her more nervous. "We'll meet you at the bridge in a few minutes."

She and Sister Fallyn hurried back to their tent. The night before, she'd added her bundle from the ship to the small trunk of clothes that Luciana had given them.

Two soldiers carried the trunk as she and Sister Fallyn approached the bridge.

"We can do this," she whispered, taking the nun's hand.

Sister Fallyn squeezed her hand. "Aye, we can."

Chapter Twenty-Two

❧

He looked older than his thirty-one years, Brigitta thought the minute she spotted King Gunther standing on the north bank of the Norva River. He was richly clothed in black leather breeches and a tunic and cape that shimmered like gold in the morning sun. A golden crown set with jewels rested on his head, and another bejeweled, golden necklace made a wide circle around his shoulders. The clasp of his leather sword belt was gold, as well as the ornate scabbard that held his sword.

But in spite of all his finery, he was not a man who could ever look refined. His face was ruddy and bloated from excess drinking, his skin riddled with pockmarks and scars, his mouth thin and cruel.

She suppressed a shudder as his sharp blue eyes narrowed on her.

"Will you be all right?" Nevis whispered as he led her onto the bridge.

"Yes." Thank the goddesses she didn't have to face this alone. Sister Fallyn was right behind her, and Brody trotted beside her in dog form.

Nevis motioned for the soldiers to set down her trunk at the midway point across the bridge. "I'll have to leave you now." He inclined his head. "May the Light be with you."

"Thank you." She watched him return to the south bank, then with a deep breath, she turned to face north where her destiny lay.

Her brother was still looking at her, his cold, calculating eyes going over her slowly as if he was searching for flaws.

She needed to play her role convincingly. This was her long-lost brother, the only family she had in the world. She sank into a deep curtsy, then as she straightened, she beamed an excited smile at him and gave him a little wave.

A corner of his mouth tilted up for a few seconds before his expression returned to its normal arrogant sneer. With a wave of his hand, he motioned to an officer standing nearby.

The officer, dressed in an elaborate blue-and-gold uniform, strode onto the bridge. "Your Highness." He removed the plumed hat off his head, sweeping it in front of him as he made a grand bow. "I am Captain Mador, in charge of King Gunther's personal guard."

She gave him a bright smile, even though he looked like a younger, leaner, and crueler version of her brother. "I'm delighted to meet you, Captain."

His gaze drifted slowly down her body. "Have you heard about the competition? I'll be one of the top contenders vying for your . . . hand."

He looked much more interested in her breasts than her hand. Brigitta's smile froze. "How exciting! I'm so looking forward to this contest."

Captain Mador's heavy-lidded eyes met hers. "Are you?"

"Of course." She waved a hand in the air. "How often does a girl get a dozen men competing for her?"

He snorted. "At last count, there are six."

"Oh. Oops." She touched her mouth, pretending to be embarrassed. "Well, six will be enough, I think. I'll be sure to find someone I fancy."

His mouth twisted with an arrogant sneer that he must have learned from her brother. He motioned for some of his men to take her trunk.

"Why do you have a nun with you?" He scowled at Sister Fallyn, who was wearing her convent gown.

"She is my dear friend," Brigitta explained. "I asked her to serve as my maid and chaperone. And of course, I can't go anywhere without my pet dog." She gave Brody a fond look, and he played his part, lifting a foreleg and grinning at her.

Captain Mador scoffed. "They're not coming. His Majesty will provide you with servants."

Brigitta's smile became brittle. "Perhaps you didn't understand. I don't go anywhere without my friend and pet. I'm sure my brother would understand the importance of keeping me happy and healthy."

The captain's eyes narrowed. "Why would he care?"

"Because happy and healthy women give birth to happy and healthy babies."

Captain Mador stared at her a moment, then smirked. "I'm glad you realize your purpose here." He motioned to one of his men. "Take the nun and the dog to Her Highness's tent."

Sister Fallyn exchanged a worried look with Brigitta as she and Brody were led across the bridge. They were taken to a tent with a blue-and-gold pennant flapping above the entrance.

King Gunther turned on his heel and disappeared inside a much larger tent.

Was that it? Brigitta wondered. Would she be lucky enough not to have to talk to her brother?

"I'll take you to His Majesty now," Captain Mador announced.

Not so lucky after all. She winced inwardly as Mador seized her elbow and steered her toward her brother's tent. "Oh, how wonderful!" She feigned excitement. "I've been looking forward to meeting him."

"Piss him off and you'll be sorry."

Her smile wobbled. "Why would I do that? He's the only family I have."

"Don't speak to him unless he speaks first. And don't even try to lie." The captain gave her pointed look. "We will always find out."

"I understand."

He shoved her inside the tent. Her brother was seated behind a table, pouring wine from a golden pitcher into a golden goblet. She immediately sank into a deep curtsy.

King Gunther set the pitcher down. "You can go, Mador."

"Yes, Your Majesty." The captain bowed, then left.

Brigitta's gaze wandered about the tent as she straightened. The rug was thick and glimmered with gold threads worked into an ornate pattern. Cloth of gold had been draped along the inner walls of the tent. Enormous candlestick holders, thick and five feet high, appeared to be made entirely of gold. Why on Aerthlan would he travel with those? They had to weigh a ton. But then, why would he care if he was making life difficult for the servants?

On top of the candlesticks, white pillar candles were lit. A small fire in a solid gold brazier provided more light, making all the gold in the tent gleam.

An ominous feeling crept down her spine. Her brother's lust for gold had escalated beyond a normal level of greed.

He rose from his chair and wandered toward her.

Slowly he circled her, examining her with those cold eyes.

She was sorely tempted to say something to break the awkward silence, but she wasn't supposed to speak until he did. She remembered Nevis's advice. *Don't appear weak. And don't offend him.*

Gunther stopped in front of her. "Are you a virgin?"

She blinked, caught by surprise. "I-I was raised in a convent."

"That's not what I asked." He glowered at her. "You were held captive on a pirate ship for a week. Did they pass you around? Or did you spend the entire time in that bastard Rupert's bed?"

"I was not harmed. I appreciate your concern—"

He suddenly grasped her by the chin, forcing her to look him in the eye. "Don't think I'm concerned about your virtue. I don't give a rat's ass how many men you fuck."

She flinched, but his grip tightened, his fingers digging into her neck.

"I'm only asking because you'll be in serious trouble if you're pregnant." He moved closer. "I won't have some pirate's whelp passed off as my heir."

"I'm a virgin."

"Really? I can have a physician examine you."

She shuddered at the thought. But thank the goddesses Rupert had known to stop when he had. "I'm not pregnant. I'm having my monthly courses now." Her cheeks burned for being forced into such a personal conversation with a stranger.

He released her, shoving her back a few steps. "Good. I'll have the servants verify it."

She took a few deep breaths, then looked him in the eye. "I was not molested. The pirates knew they could earn a bigger ransom if I was returned unharmed."

His eyes narrowed. "Why did Rupert return you to Eberon instead of Tourin?"

"He feared the Tourinian navy would blast his ships out of the water," she lied. "My sister Luciana offered to pay my ransom, and Rupert believed it would be safer to deal with Eberon than with you."

Gunther scoffed. "The coward. I hear the Eberoni army captured him and took him to the dungeons of Ebton Palace. I haven't received more information yet. Do you know anything?"

She shook her head. "I just hope he gets the punishment he deserves."

"That would be death." Gunther stepped back, eyeing her once again. "What is this rag you're wearing?"

"My sister Luciana loaned it—"

"First." Gunther pointed his index finger at her. "You will no longer refer to the Eberoni queen as your sister. I am your only family. Don't forget that."

"Yes, Your Majesty." Brigitta inclined her head.

"Second." He jabbed two fingers in the air. "The Tourinian princess will not be seen wearing secondhand clothes from another country. Especially a poor one like Eberon. You will be dressed in gold and jewels."

She clasped her hands together, smiling as if she were delighted. "Oh, thank you, Your Majesty."

His arrogant sneer returned full force. "Have you heard about the competition?"

"Yes, Your Majesty. It sounds very exciting."

He sauntered back to the table and sipped some wine from his goblet. "It will begin five days from now in the Lourdon stadium. You will be seated next to me in the royal box, where everyone can see you. You must look and act like a princess. I'll expect a different gown each day."

She nodded. "I understand."

"Whenever we are seen in public, you will look delighted that you've been reunited with your long-lost brother. We will appear to be the happiest of families."

"Of course, Your Majesty." She gave him a shy smile. "I am very happy to discover I have a brother."

He snorted. "Perhaps you should occasionally slip and call me 'dear brother.' Or 'brother dearest.' I like that one. And then you could be flustered and apologetic."

"Yes, brother dearest . . . I mean, Your Majesty."

He barked a laugh. "Stay amenable like that, and we'll get along fine."

"Actually, brother dearest, I have a few concerns about the competition."

He waved a dismissive hand. "No need to be concerned. The top three contenders are my favorites. You will end up with one of them."

"Of course. But even so, I would like to give the competition my wholehearted approval. In order to do that, I would ask for a few concessions."

He stared at her a moment. "Are you threatening me?"

"No! Of course not. How could I?" She pressed a hand to her pounding heart. "I simply wish to beg for a few favors that would make me feel more comfortable."

He crossed his arms over his chest. "Go on."

"I would like to be able to participate—"

He snorted. "You wish to join in the swordfight? You would be killed."

"I don't mean anything that drastic. For example, if one of your favorites asks for a token of my support, I would like the freedom to bequeath it or not, according to my wishes. I would like to feel like I'm taking an active role in the process."

Gunther shrugged. "All right. As long as you accept the winner, that shouldn't be a problem."

"Thank you. And speaking of the winner, I would feel more comfortable if I were to marry him before . . ."

"Bedding him?" Gunther smirked. "If it makes it easier for you to fornicate, by all means, say a few useless vows in front of a priest. But if you don't get pregnant in six months, the marriage will be annulled, and you'll be reciting your vows to the second-place winner."

"I understand."

"Good." He sat behind his table and drank some wine. "I'll have my physician concoct a tonic for you to ensure you give birth to a boy. You'll start taking it tonight in preparation for the winner's seed."

She winced inwardly. The winner had better be Rupert. And that tonic would be poured down a privy hole. "I also wanted to ask you about the clause at the bottom of the notice, the one stating that the loser of each round would be executed."

"That is not negotiable." Gunther refilled his goblet. "I can't have a bunch of sore losers roaming about the country, whining and stirring up trouble. Better to just kill them."

A royal ass, for sure. She cleared her throat. "Yes, but I was hoping you could delay the executions? Perhaps do them all together at the end of the competition?"

He snorted. "You want a mass execution on the day of your wedding?"

She shrugged. "It would be very dramatic, don't you think? Everyone would always remember my wedding."

His mouth curled into an actual smile. "You sound like a Grian, after all. Welcome home, sister."

She returned his smile. If all went well, she would marry Rupert, her brother would be imprisoned, and the losers of the contest would be pardoned when Rupert took the throne.

They left for Lourdon at noon, then arrived at the palace the following evening. Over the next three days, Brigitta was not allowed to leave her suite of rooms at Lourdon Palace. Her brother had meant what he'd said about her not being seen in a gown from Eberon. At least her prison was spacious and beautifully furnished, and Sister Fallyn was allowed to sleep in a small room that adjoined her suite.

Brody roamed freely about the castle with other dogs, listening in on conversations and bringing back information to Brigitta. Her brother was busy finishing renovations to the stadium. The plain wooden benches for the public were receiving a new coat of varnish. Meanwhile, the royal box was being encased in gold. A blue velvet canopy with golden fringe would stretch overhead, while blue velvet curtains would surround them on three sides. Two huge chairs were being upholstered with cloth of gold.

Brigitta was assigned a secretary named Hilda, an older woman with beady eyes who watched her like a hawk. Brody confirmed that everything Brigitta did and said in Hilda's presence was passed on to the king. Not that there was much to report, since Brigitta was kept so isolated.

Each day, a small army of seamstresses was hard at work in a room across the hall from Brigitta's suite. She only saw them when they came over for fittings, and Hilda was always there, watching them.

The seamstresses had completed seven capes for Brigitta before she'd even arrived at Lourdon Palace. Since the capes were voluminous, the seamstresses hadn't needed her measurements. But now that she had arrived, they were in a rush to finish seven gowns to match the capes.

Bored out of her mind, Brigitta had begged the seamstresses to allow her to help. She and Sister Fallyn had made their simple gowns at the convent, so even though they didn't know how to produce anything fancy, they were capable of simple tasks such as hemming skirts.

On the third day, around noontime, Hilda brought over two seamstresses for the final fitting of the fifth gown. This one was midnight-blue silk embroidered with gold thread. Each gown had gold in it somewhere. Brigitta suspected her brother had selected all the fabric, for he was strangely obsessed with gold.

While the two seamstresses, Norah and Marthe, helped Brigitta into the new gown, she motioned to the empty pitcher on the nearby table. "I've completely run out of wine. Would you mind bringing me some more, Hilda?"

With a frown, the older woman peered inside the pitcher. "You drank it all already?"

Actually, she'd poured half of it down the privy hole when Hilda had gone to check on the seamstresses an hour earlier. "I was thirsty. And I'm hungry, too. All these fittings wear me out. Could you bring us some food? Please?"

Hilda huffed. "Very well." She gave the seamstresses a stern look as she headed for the door. "No gossiping. Stay on task."

"Whew." Brigitta heaved a sigh when Hilda the spy left. At last she could fish for some information. Of course there was no guarantee that the seamstresses weren't spies, too. Even the guards outside the door were probably listening. Good goddesses, she was becoming paranoid. She would have to do her fishing very carefully. "I hope the contestants will like this gown."

"Oh, I'm sure they will." Marthe tugged at the laces on the back of the bodice. "You look beautiful in it."

"I can't believe the competition begins tomorrow morning," Brigitta continued. Shouldn't Rupert be arriving soon? "I'm so looking forward to it."

Sister Fallyn exchanged a look with her, then continued hemming a white silk shift. "I heard there are six contestants."

"That's what I heard." Norah knelt on the floor to pin the hem of the skirt. "But only the first three matter. They're the king's favorites. No one will be able to defeat them."

Brigitta tugged at the bodice, wishing the neckline wasn't cut so low. "They must be very strong."

"Oh, yes," Marthe agreed. "The first one is the captain of the king's personal guard."

"Oh, you mean Captain Mador?" Brigitta feigned a smile. "I've met him. Who are the others?"

"The second one is the head general," Norah replied as she worked her way around the skirt. "And the third one is the admiral of the king's navy."

"Then who are the other three contestants?" Brigitta asked.

Marthe waved a dismissive hand. "Don't worry about them. I heard the king doesn't even want to acknowledge their names. So all the men will be given numbers during the competition. It's supposed to keep it anonymous and fair, but of course, everyone knows who the first three are. The last three will simply be Four, Five, and Six."

"I see." Brigitta drew a deep breath. So when Rupert arrived, he would be called Seven. And just as the Telling Stones had predicted, she would have seven suitors vying for her hand. "I know the other contestants can't win, but I can't help but be curious about them. After all, they're risking their lives."

Norah nodded. "They must be very brave."

Sister Fallyn shook her head. "Or foolish."

Marthe placed the matching headdress over Brigitta's hair, then made some adjustments. "I suspect their fathers have forced them into it. After all, the winner gets to be the father of the heir to the throne. There are plenty who would risk their lives to be powerful at court."

Hilda burst into the room, followed by two servants carrying trays of food. "That's enough talk." She stopped to eye the gown. "That one will do for this evening. Marthe, have it finished in two hours."

"Yes, madam." Marthe inclined her head.

Brigitta swallowed hard. "Is there something happening this evening?"

"His Majesty is hosting a feast to celebrate the competition that begins tomorrow morning," Hilda explained. "King Gunther plans to present you to the court, so you must look your best. I have requested several maids to see to your bath and arranging your hair. I suggest you eat quickly before they arrive." She shooed the two servants who had brought food out the door. "Marthe, remove that gown from her and get back to work."

"Yes, madam." Marthe untied the laces while Norah gathered up their supplies.

Brigitta's heart raced. "Will the contestants be at the celebration?"

"Of course." Hilda pursed her lips in disapproval. "But there will be seven now. A foreigner has arrived at the last minute."

Rupert. Brigitta took a deep breath, careful not to show any reaction. But inside her heart was pounding.

Rupert was here, and she would see him tonight.

Chapter Twenty-Three

Rupert hoped Brigitta had a better room than he did. He and Stefan had been relegated to a small room in the basement of the older west wing. But the first part of the mission was accomplished. He was safely ensconced in Lourdon Palace, and no one had questioned his identity.

When he had arrived with a small troop of soldiers and servants, he'd been immediately taken to the office of Lord Argus, who was King Gunther's chief counselor and the man in charge of the finer details of the competition.

Argus had examined Rupert's papers, written by King Leofric and the Duke of Vindalyn and introducing him as Baron Suffield, an Eberoni nobleman from the Duchy of Vindalyn.

"You are qualified enough to enter," Argus had said while returning the papers. "But can you afford the entrance fee?"

Rupert had brought quite a bit of gold with him from the island, so he plunked down a bag filled with gold coins.

Argus's eyes had lit up when he'd counted out the gold. "Excellent." He slid a paper across the desk. "Sign here that you have agreed to abide by our rules, which are subject to change at any moment."

Rupert had suppressed a snort. So he was agreeing to be executed if he lost a round? He signed as Umberto Vintello, Baron Suffield.

"Excellent." Lord Argus retrieved the paper. "You will be given quarters inside the palace for you and one servant. The rest of your entourage will have to stay at an inn. At your expense."

That meant they wanted to separate him from his soldiers and make it difficult for him to escape. No doubt they also wanted to separate him from more of his gold. "I understand."

"There will be a feast tonight where you will meet His Majesty and the other contestants. Oh, and the princess will be there, too." Argus had waved a hand to dismiss him. "My servant will show you to your quarters."

Now that Rupert was resting in the small room, his thoughts turned once again to Brigitta. Hopefully she had been treated well. If not, he might have to kill her bastard brother before the competition even got started.

Stefan paced back and forth, frowning. "I wonder how Fallyn is doing."

Rupert stretched out on the bed. "Go fetch some food from the kitchens."

Stefan snorted. "You want to eat now? You get to go to a feast in a few hours. Was I invited? No. I have to play the lowly servant."

"Bring back food for yourself. And while you're there, see if you can find out where the princess has her room."

"Oh, right. That's where Fallyn would be." Stefan hurried out the door.

He returned later with a huge basket filled with food and wine. "They were extra generous when I gave them a few gold coins. And very talkative. The princess has a whole suite of rooms one floor up on the east wing. She even has a large balcony overlooking the Loure River."

Rupert smiled. Before making his invention that swept him up to the crow's nest, he'd spent years climbing to it. A balcony one floor up would not present a problem.

An hour later, he had washed, shaved, and dressed in expensive clothes he'd received from King Leofric. A servant led him up some stairs and through a curtained-off doorway. Immediately his surroundings changed. Now he walked on gleaming marble floors, surrounded by gilded mirrors, long windows, thick marble columns, and enormous portraits. A high ceiling arched over him, covered with paintings of naked women lounging about on a green pasture, eating grapes. If women actually did that, he'd somehow missed it.

No doubt, the luxurious décor was intended to leave him in a state of awe, but it did the opposite. It had taken him two days to ride to Lourdon, and he'd seen how the average people in Tourin lived. Half starved and crowded into mud huts. It hadn't been like that when he was young and his father had ruled. All those years when he'd been hiding or living at sea, his countrymen had suffered. And now that he saw proof that the bastard Gunther had been spending all the country's wealth on himself, he was filled with rage.

Instantly, his gift of wind power merged with the sudden surge of emotion, feeding off the excess energy to grow stronger. A gust of air burst down the hallway, stirring the gold brocade curtains and rattling the portraits. Candles snuffed out, causing the hallway to darken. The servant stumbled as his cape swirled around him and his cap blew off his head.

"What the hell?" He grabbed the cap off the floor and cast a wary look down the dim hallway. "Did someone leave a window open? I don't see one."

Rupert tamped down on his power. *Control.* This was not the time to unleash his fury. "Perhaps the palace has ghosts."

The servant's eyes widened as his face went pale. He ran to a door and with trembling hands, jerked it open. "You're supposed to wait here until the feast is served."

As Rupert approached the room, he noted it was dark, lit only by a fire in a hearth. Dark paneling lined the walls, and three well-dressed men were inside.

The servant closed the door after him, and his pounding footsteps sounded as he ran away. Rupert turned to face the other three men.

One of them, who looked Tourinian with his blond hair and blue eyes, gave him a wry smile. "Welcome to the losers' club."

"You must be number Seven," a dark-haired young man said with a slight accent.

Rupert bowed. "Baron Suffield at your service."

"You can forget about having a name here," the blond one muttered. "We're just numbers to them. I'm Five."

"Four." The dark-haired one raised a hand.

"I'm Six," the shy-looking one mumbled.

Rupert frowned. "I would prefer to know you as real people."

Four snorted. "What's the point? We might as well be numbers. Our days are certainly numbered."

At the sideboard, Five began filling cups with wine. "At least tonight, we have a reason to celebrate. I heard they're going to wait till the end of the competition to execute us, instead of killing us one by one."

Four retrieved a filled cup and raised it in the air. "Thank the Light for small favors."

With a sad look, Six took a cup.

"Here." Five offered Rupert one. "Have a drink."

He took a sip. "If you all expect to die, why are you here?"

Four sighed. "My father insisted. Said he would disown me if I didn't win and make his grandson the next king of Tourin." He shook his head. "I'm from northern Eberon, along the border, and the Tourinian army keeps invading our land to steal the golden orbs from the village churches. My father thinks he's can use me to get back at Tourin. I told him it was impossible, but he wouldn't listen."

"So you didn't want to do this?" Rupert asked.

"No." Four drank some wine. "I'm more interested in making improvements to our farmland. I've been studying how to enrich the soil and achieve a better yield of wheat. There are too many hungry people in the world."

"I agree." Six spoke up. "There is too much hunger and too much war. I've spent most of my life studying the different languages and cultures on Aerthlan. We can never hope to achieve a lasting peace with our neighboring countries if we can't communicate with them or understand them. I-I had always hoped to be a statesman someday." He hung his head, blushing.

A farmer and a scholar? Rupert groaned inwardly. No wonder they knew their days were numbered. "And you?" he asked the blond number Five.

"I'm from the north of Tourin, from the Trevelyan clan."

Rupert's breath caught. At one time, the Trevelyans had been staunch supporters of the House of Trepurin.

"My father owns a silver mine," Five continued. "I've been trying to invent equipment to make it safer for the miners."

A fellow inventor? Rupert's curiosity was piqued. "I'd like to see what you've come up with."

Five shrugged. "I don't think my ideas will ever be built."

He expects to die. Rupert winced. These were all men who could make valuable contributions to the world, feeding more people and keeping them safe, or working for peace among the different nations. These were the kind

of men he would need once he was king, for they would
be the ones who could help a country and its people be
secure and prosper.

"So you're from Eberon, too?" Four asked.

Rupert nodded. "From the south, the Duchy of Vindalyn."

"That's a long way from here." Five, the Trevelyan,
narrowed his eyes. "You speak Tourinian very well."

Did he suspect something? Rupert inclined his head.
"Thank you."

"So do you have vineyards on your land?" Four, the
farmer, asked.

"Yes," Rupert replied. He'd been well coached by
Luciana's father. "And a few groves of olive trees."

"Sounds nice," Six mumbled.

"Why are you here?" Five asked. "Did your father
force you, too?"

Rupert shook his head. "I wanted to come."

Four gave him an incredulous look. "Don't you know
we're going to die?"

Rupert took a sip of wine. "I intend to win." He was
met with a chorus of snorts and disbelieving looks. "And
when I do, I'll make sure that each of you lives."

Four scoffed. "I appreciate the thought, but it won't
happen."

Six gave him a shy look. "Can you really do that?"

Five leaned close to whisper, "Don't repeat that to anyone else. You'll never live to see the competition."

Rupert nodded and lifted his cup. "To us."

The men clinked their cups against his and drank.

The door opened, and Lord Argus strode inside. "The
feast is ready to begin. I'll take you to the ballroom."

Brigitta grew increasingly nervous as she accompanied
Hilda down one corridor after another, headed for the

Great Hall. Her midnight-blue silk gown and soft leather slippers hardly made a whisper as she walked on the gleaming white marble floor. Behind her, she could hear the constant clunk of heavy boots. The two soldiers who normally stood guard at her door were now following her.

Did Gunther think she would attempt an escape? For now, she was determined to play the role she had adopted for this mission. A shallow princess who loved her new clothes and enjoyed having men risk their lives in competition for her.

This corridor was lit with candles in gold sconces along the walls on each side. Each sconce had three branches entwined with golden strands made to look like ivy. Mirrors reflected the candle flames, making the hallway even brighter. Ancestors she'd never heard of stared at her from enormous portraits.

She followed Hilda, turning right into another hallway. This corridor was even grander than the last one, although it was darker. A group of servants jumped when they first spotted her and Hilda, then they quickly resumed their task of lighting candles, all the while muttering about ghosts.

Finally, Hilda led her into a grand foyer with massive marble columns that supported an arched ceiling painted with a bloody battle scene. A flash of memory skittered through Brigitta's mind. This battle looked much like the one in Rupert's memory. Had her father had this painting done to commemorate his defeat of Rupert's father's army? Good goddesses, was Rupert going to see this?

She gripped her hands together and took a deep breath. *Stay calm and remember your role.* Lifting her skirts, she climbed the short staircase to the huge golden doors that opened into the Great Hall.

There, at the entrance, she stopped, stunned for a few seconds by the opulence before her. The large, rectangular room gleamed with an abundance of gold. Three massive gold-and-crystal chandeliers hung from a ceiling that was plastered and painted to look like a sky filled with golden suns and stars. Long windows stretched from the floor to the ceiling. In between the windows, long mirrors had been installed, each one bordered with multiple golden sconces so that the flames of a dozen candles would be reflected. Every inch of wall space was decorated with curlicues of plaster painted in gold leaf. With all the gold, mirrors, and candles, the room sparkled.

Two long tables extended down the length of the room. In between the tables, there was enough room for the well-dressed courtiers to mingle. Brigitta scanned the crowd, but couldn't see Rupert. Gunther was easy to spot with his gleaming gold tunic and cape. More gold and jewels adorned his crown, necklace, and multiple rings. No one else was dressed in gold. Perhaps her brother had reserved the color strictly for the royal family. He had made sure that each of her gowns had a little gold.

At the far end of the room, a large dais was topped by a golden canopy. Two golden chairs sat in front of a table, covered with cloth of gold. It was too much, she thought. No doubt her brother would eat gold if he could.

"Her Royal Highness, Princess Brigitta," a footman announced at the door.

Her brother strode toward her, and she sank into a deep curtsy.

"Not bad," he murmured as he took her hand. "I'll introduce you to the men who will be competing for you."

As he led her down the room, the courtiers parted to allow them a wide path through. They bowed and curtsied as Gunther and Brigitta passed by.

"Shouldn't I meet these people?" she whispered.

"Don't bother." He gave them a disdainful look. "They'll just betray you someday, and then you would feel a little miffed about having to execute them when you thought they were friends. So you see, when I keep you isolated, it's for your own good."

"Thank you, brother dearest—Your Majesty."

He chuckled, then stopped in front of three men, who doffed their hats as they bowed. "Here they are."

Brigitta curtsied.

Gunther motioned to the one on the right. "You've met Captain Mador before. He'll be competing as number One."

The captain gave her his usual sneer. "A pleasure to see you again."

Brigitta forced a smile. "Thank you."

"This is General Tarvis." Gunther gestured toward the man in the middle. "He's the commander of the royal army and will be competing as number Two."

"But I'll finish as number One," the general added with a smile.

Mador snorted. "Over my dead body."

"Exactly." General Tarvis gave him a wry look.

"And number Three," Gunther continued. "Lord Admiral Aevar, commander of the royal navy."

"Delighted to meet you, Your Highness." The admiral bowed his head. "I regret that my men were unable to stop that bastard Rupert from kidnapping you. I assure you, the men were duly punished."

"Thank you, my lord," Brigitta replied. "And thank the Light that horrid pirate was captured when he attempted to take the ransom money in Eberon."

"Ah, that reminds me," Gunther said. "You'll be happy to hear the latest news. Rupert is dead."

Her heart lurched, but she quickly recovered and pasted on a big smile. "Oh, that's wonderful. Did they execute him?"

Gunther shook his head. "According to the report, he was killed while attempting an escape. But since he comes from Tourin, I think I should have my ambassador demand that the body be returned to me. I won't believe the bastard is dead until I see it."

"A wise decision, Your Majesty," Mador said.

Gunther nodded. "I'll tell Argus to send an envoy. You three should get better acquainted with my sister."

As Gunther walked away, Brigitta scanned the crowd again. No Rupert in sight.

"Are you looking forward to the competition, Your Highness?" the lord admiral asked.

"Oh, yes," she replied. "Are the other contestants attending the feast tonight?"

Captain Mador waved a dismissive hand. "They'll be here soon. There's no point in you getting to know them."

"True," the general agreed. "They're just going to die."

"I think we should lay bets on which one goes first," Mador said.

General Tarvis scoffed. "Too easy. It'll be whoever has the least experience at riding a horse." He glanced at Brigitta. "Tomorrow's contest will be a horse race."

Mador sneered at the lord admiral. "You might be the one to lose. I doubt you've ridden any horses all those years you were at sea."

A spurt of alarm shot through Brigitta. Rupert had been at sea almost half of his life. Would he be able to survive the first round of the competition?

Admiral Aevar shrugged. "Not a problem. I grew up on horseback. I could jump hedgerows better than anyone on my father's estate."

General Tarvis rolled his eyes. "Hedgerows? One time, when I was on horseback, I jumped across the Loure River."

Brigitta blinked. She could see the Loure River from her balcony. "Isn't the river too wide for that?"

The general waved off her objection. "I jumped halfway across onto a moving barge, then jumped to the other side. Nothing to it."

Mador snorted. "I once jumped off a cliff onto the back of dragon, slit its throat, then dove into a lake and swam ashore."

The admiral shook his head. "That's nothing. One time I harpooned a whale, and it dragged me off the ship and across the ocean, but I climbed up the rope onto the whale's back and stabbed it to death with my sword."

Brigitta frowned. "You killed a whale?"

The general glared at him, then turned to Mador. "One time I jumped onto the back of a dragon and slit its throat, too, but then another dragon attacked, breathing fire. So I leaped onto the back of the second dragon while I was ablaze and strangled it to death with my bare hands."

"That seems rather unlikely," Brigitta began, but Mador interrupted her.

"Oh, everybody's done that. One time I killed *three* dragons in midair, while I was on fire, then hurtled to the ground and broke both legs, but I still made it back to camp."

A movement by the entrance drew her attention, and she spotted Lord Argus arriving with four men. *Rupert.* He was keeping his face cold and expressionless, but she could feel his rage as if it stirred the air around her. He must have seen the painting of the battle.

Gunther strode toward Lord Argus and dragged him aside for a private talk, ignoring the four men who bowed as he passed them by. No doubt he was telling Argus that he wanted Leo to send back Rupert's dead body, not knowing that the real Rupert was only a few feet away.

Rupert shot them a wry look. He must have heard the conversation. Then he turned toward the crowd and his gaze immediately fastened on her.

Her heart pounded. *You don't know him*, she reminded

herself. She turned back to the top three contenders, but they were so intent on out-bragging each other, they seemed completely unaware of her presence. She backed away slowly, then headed across the room. Courtiers parted as she wove through the crowd till she was standing in front of the last four contenders.

They bowed. A blond who looked Tourinian introduced himself as Five, and the others as Four, Six, and Seven.

She smiled at them, trying not to look at Rupert any longer than the others. He was keeping his gaze cool, though for a second, when their eyes met, she felt a surge of heat.

"I wanted to wish you good luck for tomorrow's contest. It will be a horse race. Hopefully, you are all accustomed to riding." She shot Rupert a questioning look.

He inclined his head. "I'm sure we'll do well. Thank you for your concern."

As the other men assured her they would do their best, her heart wrenched in her chest. Rupert had to win the competition. She didn't want any of these men to be harmed.

"The stars should be very bright tonight," Rupert said. "I wager they'll look beautiful over the Loure River."

Was he telling her to go onto her balcony tonight?

"Brigitta!" Gunther stormed toward her and grabbed her by the arm. "What are you doing with the losers?" he growled as he led her away.

"Oh, I didn't realize . . ." she murmured.

Gunther led her onto the dais, and from there he faced the crowd. "Tomorrow morning, the competition for Princess Brigitta begins!"

The crowd clapped and cheered.

Brigitta's cheeks grew warm as she stood there, feeling like the grand prize at a county fair. The top three contenders watched her with smug, self-assured looks.

"Let the feast begin!" Gunther sat down, and everyone else followed suit.

The top three were sitting at the first table close by. Her gaze drifted to the last table at the back of the room. Rupert's eyes met hers, and she felt the longing between them sizzling through the air.

She focused on her food while her mind repeated the same thought over and over. Tonight she would see him.

Chapter Twenty-Four

❧

"You look exhausted," Sister Fallyn told Brigitta as she laid the midnight-blue silk gown on a shelf in the dressing room. "You should go straight to bed."

Brigitta slipped a robe over her sheer nightgown. It was well past midnight, since the feast had gone on and on. By the fifth course, she'd felt stuffed, but there had still been five more courses to go. "I think I'll go onto the balcony for some fresh air."

She tied the sash and strode into her bedroom. Hopefully Rupert would spot her white robe in the dark, and then he would know which balcony was hers.

Sister Fallyn followed her into the bedroom. "I don't think you should—" A bark interrupted her.

Brody was back? Brigitta hurried to the door that opened onto the sitting room and spotted the black-and-white dog sitting by the settee. One of the guards must have let him into her suite.

"What have you been up to?" She smiled as he trotted up to her. "Do you have news?"

Brody yipped in response, then headed toward the dressing room. Brigitta had stashed some clothing for him there.

Sister Fallyn sighed. "As I was saying, I don't think you should go onto the balcony. The last time you did, Hilda fussed at you. And she could arrive any minute now."

With a wince, Brigitta realized that was true. Hilda would be showing up soon with the nightly concoction that she was forced to drink. She had intended to pour the stuff down the privy hole, but Hilda always waited to make sure she drank it.

Blast. She'd been so excited about seeing Rupert again that she hadn't wanted to admit it was too dangerous.

"Brody," she called the dog over and hunched down in front of him. "Can you find you-know-who and tell him not to come here?"

Sister Fallyn gasped. "Oh, dear godde . . . do you mean he . . . ?"

Brody tilted his head, studying the balcony door. Then he trotted over to the door and scratched a paw against the glass pane.

Sister Fallyn shook her head. "Surely, you-know-who wouldn't come here."

A dark shadow moved in front of the glass, and Brigitta's heart lurched. "He's here."

The door opened, and Rupert slipped inside. He was dressed all in black with a black scarf tied around his head, looking so much like her infamous pirate that her heart filled with joy. No matter who he truly was, he would always be her Rupert.

"Oh my godde—" Sister Fallyn made the sign of the moons, then quickly pressed her hands to her chest. "You can't be here! It's too dangerous."

"Shh." Brigitta held a finger to her lips as she glanced through the open bedroom door into the sitting room. The door to the hallway was far enough away that she doubted the guards outside could hear. But still, Hilda could walk in at any minute.

"I won't stay long," Rupert whispered. "I just wanted to make sure you're all right."

"We're fine," Sister Fallyn insisted. "Now go before you get us killed!"

"I brought a letter for you from Stefan." He offered her a folded piece of paper.

"Oh." The nun snatched the paper. "I'll leave you alone then." She ran into the dressing room.

Brigitta gave him a wry look. "Well played."

"Thank you."

His smile and twinkling eyes were making her want to rush into his arms. But it was truly too dangerous. "You really can't stay. Hilda will be arriving soon."

"Who is she?"

"The spy who watches me and reports to my brother. She has a bad habit of just barging into the sitting room without knocking. Oh—" Brigitta turned to Brody. "Could you wait by the door and warn us when she comes in?"

Brody yipped and trotted into the sitting room.

Brigitta closed the bedroom door. Her heart pounded as she faced Rupert.

He smiled. "Alone at last."

She fiddled with the sash of her robe. "How did you get to my balcony?"

"I climbed a drainpipe a few windows down, then jumped from one balcony to the next until I found the right one."

"Are you trying to kill yourself?" She attempted a disapproving glare, but was much too happy to pull it off.

His mouth twitched as he approached her. "I needed to see you. I missed you."

Her heart squeezed. "I missed you, too. But I won't have you endangering yourself just to see me."

He swept her sash up in his hand and tugged at it to

bring her closer. "I was hoping to do more than just see you."

Scoundrel. She rested her hands on his black shirt. "Have you been all right? How was your trip here?"

"Lonesome. I missed you." He brushed her hair back and caressed her cheek.

"Will you be able to manage the race?"

"I rode all the way to Lourdon. I'll be fine." He leaned close, his nose touching hers. "I missed you." He kissed her cheek.

Her hands slid up to his neck. "Did they give you a room here in the palace?"

"A little one." He glanced around her suite. "Not nearly as fancy as—damn, is that your bed? It's huge."

She looked over her shoulder at the enormous four-poster surrounded by red velvet curtains. The curtains had been drawn back on one side to give her access to the mattress covered with red silk. "This suite is basically my prison cell, but a very nice one."

"Hmm." His eyes gleamed as he glanced from her to the bed.

She pushed him back. "Don't even think about that. I've already been interrogated over my virginity."

He grinned. "My, what a naughty mind you have. I was only thinking about a little innocent snuggling."

"Ha!" Her cheeks grew warm. "I doubt that."

He sauntered over to her bed and pressed a hand against the mattress.

"You're not getting on my bed," she warned him.

Brody barked in the sitting room.

"Hide!" In a panic, Brigitta shoved Rupert onto her bed, then shut the curtains.

She rushed to the bedroom door just as Hilda called out, "Your Highness?"

"Coming." Brigitta took a deep breath and slowed down so everything would appear normal. She opened the door, then decided to leave it half open as she sauntered into the sitting room. After all, if she closed it, it might look like she was hiding something. "Good evening."

Hilda set a tray down on the table. As usual, the tray contained a bottle of tonic, a cup, and a pitcher of water. "Here you are." She uncorked the small bottle, then handed it to Brigitta.

There wasn't anything she could do but drink it. The first night Hilda had brought the tonic, she'd made it clear that she would call the guards into the room if necessary to force the stuff down Brigitta's throat. Fortunately, it only tasted like a rather bitter wine.

She downed it, then set the empty bottle on the tray.

Hilda looked her over carefully. "It's been a few days now that you've taken it. You should be feeling some effect."

Brigitta narrowed her eyes. "What do you mean? I thought it was to help me give birth to a boy."

"True." Hilda poured some water into the cup. "But since you're a virgin, your brother feared you would have trouble accepting the winner in your bed. So part of the tonic is a potion to increase your desire."

"What?"

Hilda sneered as she offered the cup of water to her. "With each day, you will feel hotter, your breasts will feel heavier and more sensitive, and your—"

"*What?*"

"No water? Well, perhaps later." Hilda set the cup down. "Anyway, by the time the winner is announced, you should be quite the eager one in bed." She picked up the empty bottle and smiled. "Extremely eager, according to the physician. As frantic as an animal in heat."

Appalled, Brigitta stepped back. How dare her brother do this to her? It had to be nonsense. How could any tonic have such an effect?

With a whine, Brody flopped onto the floor and covered his ears with this paws.

Oh, dear goddesses, this was embarrassing. And what if Rupert was hearing all this? Her cheeks flushed with heat as she glanced toward the bedroom.

"Ah." Hilda gave her a knowing look. "It has begun."

No! Brigitta pressed a hand to her chest.

"I shall return at dawn to make sure you are ready for the grand opening of the games." Hilda inclined her head, then hurried toward the door.

Brigitta groaned inwardly. No doubt the older woman was in a rush to tell Gunther that the tonic was working.

"Oh." Hilda stopped with the door half open. "You may hear some chanting in the hallways tonight. Don't be alarmed. There were some reports of ghosts, but His Majesty has called in the priests to clear them out."

Brigitta blinked. "Ghosts?"

"Yes." Hilda shrugged. "This sort of thing happens from time to time. It's to be expected with the number of tragic accidents that have occurred in the palace."

"Accidents?"

Hilda nodded. "Gunther's wife fell down a staircase. And your mother was trampled by a horse."

Brigitta swallowed hard. Had her mother been murdered? "What happened to my younger brother?"

"Brannoc?" Hilda's eyes gleamed with malice. "He tripped and fell off the highest tower. An accident, of course."

Brigitta clenched her hands together. Now she knew his name. Poor Brannoc. With his mother gone, there had been no one left to protect him.

"But not to worry," Hilda assured her. "The ghosts will be exorcised. There's one thing His Majesty never tolerates, and that's ghosts in the palace." As she left, Brody slipped through the door before she closed it.

Apparently, Brody wanted to investigate the ghost situation. And it made sense that Gunther wouldn't want any ghosts lingering about. There were too many of them that he had killed.

She trudged back into the bedroom and shut the door.

Rupert drew back the curtains and gave her a worried look. "Are you all right?"

She approached him slowly. "How much did you hear?"

"This and that." He patted the bed beside him. "I'm sorry about your mother and younger brother."

She sat beside him. "You lost your mother and brother, too."

He nodded. "My mother was chased off a cliff. I'm not sure what happened to Bjornfrid." He took her hand and squeezed it. "But don't worry. Gunther will get what he deserves."

She sighed. The king did deserve to die, but she still dreaded the thought of Rupert being the one to kill him.

"So is it true?" Rupert whispered.

"What?"

"Are your breasts heavier?" He reached toward her.

"Stop that!" She pushed him back, and he grinned. Her face burned with embarrassment. The rascal had heard everything.

"If you find yourself feeling *extremely eager*, I would be willing to help you find some relief." He pressed a hand to his chest. "Out of the kindness of my heart."

She scoffed. "How noble of you."

"And the tonic will cause you to give birth to a boy?" He leaned close. "Perhaps we should give it a test?"

"Go away." She shoved him again.

With a quick move, he grasped her by the shoulders and pushed her back onto the bed. He paused, his face a few inches from hers.

Her heart thudded loud in her ears, and goddesses help her, she did feel hot. Her breasts did feel heavy. And she wanted him something fierce.

"Do you still love me, Brigitta? Does your heart yearn for me?"

Tears filled her eyes as she nodded yes.

With a small smile, he leaned down to nuzzle her neck and kiss her cheek. "Do you desire other men?"

"No." She slipped her hands around his neck. "Of course not."

"Then don't worry." He gave her a quick kiss. "The tonic has no effect on you. I am your one and only true love."

"Rup—" She stopped when he placed a finger on her lips. With a smile, she whispered against the touch of his finger, "You-know-who, I am madly in love with you."

"Brigitta." He took her mouth with his.

She melted as his mouth moved over hers, tender at first, then rapidly becoming more demanding and hungry.

"Brigitta!" Sister Fallyn hissed.

Rupert broke the kiss.

Sister Fallyn huffed. "I leave you alone for a few minutes, and he starts ravishing you?"

"I beg your pardon." Rupert scrambled to his feet. "I will take my leave now. Sleep well."

Brigitta rose to her feet. "Be careful tomorrow."

"I will." He winked, then let himself onto the balcony.

With a sigh, she sat back down on the bed. "I feel so helpless." Would she have to watch Rupert risking his life, day after day, while she did nothing? She needed to be more than just a pawn in this game.

The next morning, a small army of maids made sure she looked radiant in gold silk with touches of blue. The royal colors of Tourin, Hilda explained. So her golden gown had blue ribbons crossing the bodice and a blue silk sash around the waist. Her golden skirt was embroidered with bluebells, and blue sapphires twinkled around her neck and on her small golden tiara. Even her slippers were gold and tied around her ankles with blue ribbons.

Hilda and her guards delivered her to the palace entrance, where she waited by the enormous double doors for her brother to arrive. He was so covered with gold and jewels, she wondered how he was able to walk.

She sank into a deep curtsy.

He pulled her up and gave her a warning look. "Remember we are being watched today."

"Of course." She gave him a beaming smile. "You look absolutely divine, brother dearest . . . I mean, Your Majesty."

With a laugh, he led her out the door. Along the outer gate, a crowd gave a cheer. "You see?" He waved at the crowd. "They all want to see the long-lost princess. Make sure you act properly appreciative."

She tucked a hand around his arm and leaned against his shoulder. "Indeed, I am grateful for all the beautiful clothes."

"Of course." He patted her head the way she patted Brody when he was in dog form. "Let's go."

They climbed into the waiting open-air carriage that was covered with gilt. Six white horses with golden riggings and white plumes pulled the coach, handled by a driver dressed in white and gold.

"Do you see the flags there?" Gunther pointed to the large blue-and-gold flags across the courtyard. "That's where the race will begin."

"Oh." Brigitta scanned the area. Groomsmen were readying seven horses, but none of the contestants were in sight. "I thought it would happen in the stadium."

"It will finish there, but first, they'll race through the town. They'll be taking the same route that we are."

As their carriage passed through the entrance gate, she noted the blue-and-gold flags marking the sides of the wide road. Soldiers were stationed along the route to keep the townspeople from venturing onto the course.

"Wave to the people and smile," Gunther said as he held up a hand. "It will make their day."

"Of course." She waved at a mother and her young children, all dressed in rags, and her smile wobbled. No doubt they would be more impressed by a good meal.

She looked around as they rode down the long street. The buildings were old and run-down, and the stench of poor sanitation hung in the air.

After a while, the coach turned onto a narrower street, still outlined with blue-and-gold flags.

She froze, her hand in the air and a brittle smile on her face. Good goddesses, this was the street she'd seen in Rupert's memory. The ambush had happened here.

Her gaze flitted along the tops of the tall buildings. The arrows had come from there. Rupert's father had died on this street. And Rupert would have to ride down this street for the race.

Her eyes burned with tears. He would be forced to re-live his worst nightmare.

"What's wrong with you?" Gunther growled.

"Oh." She beamed a smile and waved enthusiastically. "I was just overcome for a moment. By my good fortune."

Her heart thudded. Rupert would have to be strong. If he lost this round, it would be a disaster. She grew increasingly tense as the carriage continued through the town and across a bridge spanning the Loure River.

The huge stadium rose before them. Oblong in shape and four stories high. There had to be at least thirty flags along the top, flapping in the wind. Their carriage drove into a wide tunnel at one end.

"The horses will come through here," Gunther explained. "The royal box is on the other end, so we'll have an excellent view."

As the carriage emerged from the tunnel, Brigitta's heart stuttered at the sight of so many cheering spectators. The carriage started down the middle of the field, headed for the far end, where a golden box gleamed in the morning sun.

"See the hurdles?" Gunther yelled over the noise.

She noted there were three hurdles crossing the dirt raceway, each one a bit higher than the last.

"Each horse will have to jump those hurdles," Gunther explained. "Then the rider has to grab one of the spears from that rack." He pointed at a rack on the far end of the field below the royal box. "After they've hit one of the straw targets over there, they're done."

She spotted three straw figures that looked like men.

"So you see," Gunther boasted with a smile. "It's a test not just of speed, but of strength and accuracy, too."

The carriage pulled to a stop beneath the golden box, and Gunther led her up the stairs while a hush fell over the stadium and everyone bowed and curtsied.

As they settled in their golden chairs, the carriage drove away and disappeared through the tunnel. The crowd settled onto their benches, and the noise grew loud once again as everyone made their bets.

Brigitta clenched her hands together in her lap and sent a prayer to the twin goddesses to watch over Rupert.

Loud horns blasted in the distance.

The race had begun.

Chapter Twenty-Five

❦

As the contestants raced down the wide main street of Lourdon, Rupert kept his horse in the middle of the pack. The pounding of hooves on cobblestone mixed with the shouts of people who lined the streets and leaned out windows from the upper floors of ramshackle buildings.

"You can't come in last," Stefan had told him repeatedly. "But don't come in first, either. It's not about winning right now, but surviving till the end."

Rupert had agreed. It wasn't hard to make sure the top three contenders stayed in the lead. Each contestant had his number pinned on his back, so he could clearly see One, Two, and Three charging ahead. They had obviously been given the best horses from the stable.

He had decided to aim for fourth or fifth place, and the plan was working well until they turned onto a narrow road. And then it hit him.

Flashes of memory spun around him. This was where his father had died. Sweat broke out on his brow, and he found it hard to breathe. This was where his horse had reared after being shot by an arrow. This was where he'd fallen, and Stefan had yanked him up on his horse.

And the alley over there was where Stefan had raced away with the young prince in his arms.

"Seven!" Four shouted at him, and he reeled back to the present. His horse had slowed to a walk.

"What the hell are you doing?" Five yelled.

The contest. "Let's go!" Rupert spurred his horse into its fastest speed. If he wanted revenge for his father, he had to survive each round. If he wanted to protect Brigitta, he had to win the last round.

He glanced to the side to see Five keeping up with him. Four and Six followed closely. They'd looked out for him. They hadn't left him behind.

By the Light, he would not let these men die.

They charged across the bridge. In the distance, he could see the top three entering the tunnel to the stadium.

He urged his horse to go faster.

By the time they entered the stadium, the top three had already cleared the hurdles and were throwing their spears. Number Two, the general, hit his target first, and the crowd roared.

Rupert soared over the first hurdle. Five, Four, and Six followed. They made it over the second hurdle, although Six's horse knocked the top bar off.

The third hurdle was the highest. Rupert cleared it and was halfway to the rack of spears, when he heard a crash and the excited jeers from the crowd.

Six had fallen, and his horse was wandering away. Rupert raced after the horse and caught its reins, then led it back to where Six was slowly rising to his feet.

"Get on!" Rupert ordered.

Six gave him a forlorn look. "I've already lost."

"You're not a loser! You're finishing the race. Get on!"

Six scrambled onto the horse, and Rupert slapped the horse on its rump to get it running toward the rack of spears. Four and Five had already taken the remaining spears, and they tossed the last two to Rupert and Six.

Four and Five raced toward the finish line, hurtling their spears and each hitting a straw dummy. As soon as they moved off the track, Rupert and Six threw their spears.

Six's spear landed a few feet short of the mark. But Rupert had put a strong wind behind his spear and it shot across the field with so much power, it pierced straight through the straw dummy and knocked it off the pole. The straw target flew back six feet, slamming into a wooden wall in front of the spectators, with the spearhead embedded in the wood.

The crowd went wild.

A short time later, the seven contenders were led onto a raised platform at one end of the stadium, next to the tunnel. Rupert and his companions had been warned about this. The long platform had seven trapdoors, and they were painted on top with the numbers One through Seven. At the end of each round, the contestants were supposed to stand on their number and wait for one of the trapdoors to open. The one who fell through would be the loser and immediately taken to the dungeons where he would await execution.

As Rupert climbed the stairs to the platform, he noticed One, Two, and Three already in place, glaring at him.

Damn, he shouldn't have used so much wind. He'd let his fear of losing get the better of him. Losing would spell disaster for Brigitta, and he was desperate to keep her safe.

He stood on the trapdoor marked with the number seven. Across the stadium in the golden box, he spotted Brigitta, sitting next to the king. She looked pale. Lord

Argus was there, talking to the king. No doubt, they were determining the loser.

When his companions passed by, Five gave him a speculative look. "I've never seen anyone throw a spear like that. How did you do it?"

"It was amazing," Four whispered. "Everyone is talking about you."

Six gave him a shy smile. "Thank you for not giving up on me."

"I don't leave men behind," Rupert whispered. "No matter what happens, I won't let any of you die."

Six's eyes glistened with tears as he took his place over the sixth trapdoor. Four and Five moved into their positions.

A hush fell over the stadium as the crowd waited to see who had been doomed to death.

Brigitta clenched her hands together as she listened to her brother and Lord Argus talking.

"Who is this number Seven?" Gunther grumbled.

"A nobleman from Eberon, from the Duchy of Vindalyn," Argus replied. "He appears to be quite wealthy."

Gunther's eyes narrowed as he examined the men on the platform. "We can't let a damned foreigner win."

"Of course not," Argus said. "But I suggest we keep him around for a while. The crowd seems to have taken a liking to him, and it always works in our favor to keep them happy and entertained."

Gunther's mouth twisted. "Fine. Let them have their hero for a few days. Give everyone who attends the games a loaf of bread, and make sure they know it comes from me."

"Of course, Your Majesty. The people will know you are the true hero here."

Gunther nodded. "Exactly. Pull the lever then."

Brigitta drew in a sharp breath. She could see Rupert standing on the platform, looking at her. She would need to warn him that he'd drawn Gunther's attention.

A horn blasted, and the crowd began to count along with the blasts. After six blasts, there was a hush, while everyone waited to see if a seventh blast would occur.

It didn't. Trapdoor number six fell open and Six tumbled through.

The world swirled around her as she leaned over to catch her breath. The roar of the crowd deafened her ears.

Rupert was safe for now. And he would make sure that Six came to no harm.

After enduring a celebratory luncheon with King Gunther and the top three, Brigitta was sent back to her suite. The seamstresses were still working on the sixth and seventh gowns, so she spent the afternoon being fitted.

The two seamstresses, Marthe and Norah, were giddy from the latest gossip they'd heard from other servants.

"So the general won," Norah said as she pinned up the hem on the sixth gown. "And Captain Mador came in second."

"True." Brigitta lifted her arms for Marthe to adjust the bodice.

"But it's number Seven that everyone's talking about," Norah continued. "They say he's incredibly strong. And very handsome."

"I heard he's a foreigner from Eberon," Marthe said. "And very rich. His servants have been spending gold all over Lourdon. They ate at my uncle's pub last night."

"Really?" Brigitta asked.

Marthe nodded, smiling. "My uncle said everyone is very impressed by Seven's generosity."

Brigitta winced inwardly. She wasn't sure if it was

wise for Rupert to become too popular among the people. Gunther wanted all the praise for himself, even though he treated everyone abominably.

"What do you know of him, Your Highness?" Norah asked.

"I . . . I only met him briefly at the feast last night," Brigitta replied. "Do you know what kind of contest will happen tomorrow?"

"I heard it will be archery. There." Norah finished putting in the last pin and rose to her feet. "All done."

Brigitta sighed with relief as the two women helped her out of the gown. Archery would not be a problem for Rupert.

After dinner, Hilda came in with the tray containing her daily tonic. As the older woman marched through the door, Brody slipped inside. Eager to hear Brody's news, Brigitta quickly downed the tonic and wished Hilda a pleasant evening.

With Hilda gone, Brody trotted into the dressing room to shift and put on a shirt and pair of breeches.

Brigitta and Sister Fallyn waited impatiently in the bedroom.

When Brody emerged from the dressing room, barefoot and buttoning the shirt, Brigitta asked, "Do you have news?"

"Yes." He looked around. "Do you have any food?"

Sister Fallyn ran into the sitting room to fetch the bowl of fruit.

"Did you see you-know-who?" Brigitta whispered. "Is he all right?"

"Is Stefan all right?" Sister Fallyn asked as she passed him the bowl.

"Stefan's been fussing at you-know-who that he's drawn too much attention to himself." Brody tossed a grape into his mouth.

"I was afraid of that, too," Brigitta muttered. "Even the king was asking about him."

Brody winced. "He shouldn't have sent that straw dummy flying."

"You saw it?" Brigitta asked.

"Bird's-eye view." Brody bit into an apple.

"You were a pelican again?" Sister Fallyn asked.

He shook his head. "Eagle."

"Oh, my." Sister Fallyn pressed a hand to her chest. "Do you know where Stefan is staying?"

"They have a small room in the basement of the west wing." He gave Brigitta an apologetic look. "You-know-who wants you to know that he's sorry, but he can't come see you tonight. After that performance today, the king is having some guards watch his every move."

Brigitta nodded. "I understand. I heard tomorrow's contest is archery, so at least we can be assured that he'll be safe for another round."

Brody snorted. "He could win if he wanted. But Stefan has warned him not to show off anymore. We can't have the top three seeing him as a threat."

Brigitta swallowed hard. If the top three contenders believed Rupert was in their way, they wouldn't hesitate to kill him.

Chapter Twenty-Six

❧

Boom.

A large kettledrum was hit, the deep sound reverberating across the stadium. The crowd grew quiet.

Rupert nocked his arrow.

Boom. The second strike sounded.

It was the following morning, and the archery contest had begun. There would be a total of ten drum strikes, and within that time all six contestants needed to shoot one of their arrows. Each of them had a target one hundred yards in front of him.

Rupert drew back his bow and waited.

Boom.

One, Two, and Five released their arrows. With a resounding *thud*, all three arrows hit the red center of the bull's-eye.

Boom.

Rupert smiled to himself. With three perfect hits, it wouldn't matter if he added one more. He glanced at number Five, who stood beside him. The northern Tourinian appeared to be more than an inventor. He handled a bow and arrow as well as any soldier. If there were more men like him in the north, could they be counted on if Rupert needed an army?

Boom.

Three and Four shot their arrows. Each one hit the target, but an outer ring.

Boom.

Rupert let his arrow fly. It zoomed straight for the bull's-eye, striking it with a loud *thwack.*

The crowd roared, and some began to shout. *Seven! Seven!*

He glanced over at Stefan, who was in the stands along with Brody in human form. Brody's gaze was scanning the crowd as if he was searching for someone. Stefan crossed his arms over his chest and scowled at Rupert.

He sighed. Being tied for first place with three other men wasn't showing off. He glanced at the golden box where Brigitta sat next to Gunther. Today she was dressed in gold and purple. How long would he have to wait before he could see her again?

A trumpet blared to signal the beginning of round two.

Boom. The first strike of the drum.

Let's just get this over with. Rupert nocked an arrow and let it fly. When it hit the outermost ring of the target, the crowd grumbled. They'd expected better.

Boom.

One and Two hit their second bull's-eye. The crowd went back to cheering.

Boom.

Three and Five just missed the center circle. Four muttered a curse when his arrow fell to the ground three feet away from the target.

Rupert winced. It looked like the Eberoni farmer was going to lose today's contest.

The horn gave a short blast to mark the beginning of the third and final round.

Boom.

Several arrows flew. Four's arrow fell short again, but One managed to hit his third bull's-eye. The crowd roared as he pumped his fist in the air.

Rupert snorted. So Captain Mador thought he was going to be the winner. Didn't he realize number Two, the general, could hit another bull's-eye and tie him?

Boom.

Rupert took aim and hit the ring next to the red center. There, that should make Stefan happy. He was neither winning nor losing.

Boom.

He glanced over at number Two. For some reason, the general was still aiming and hadn't taken his shot.

Suddenly the general turned toward Three and fired his arrow straight into the admiral's chest.

As the admiral fell onto his back, the crowd shrieked and jumped to their feet.

Blood spread across the admiral's white shirt, completely covering the number pinned to his chest. He lifted a trembling hand to the arrow, then his arm fell slack at his side. His head turned slightly, his eyes glazing over.

Damn. Rupert caught Captain Mador and General Tarvis exchanging a smirk. So the first two had planned this together. And since the competition allowed for the top two contestants to remain alive at the end, they probably figured they had it made.

Stefan gave him a pointed look and Rupert nodded. Message received. *Don't be a threat to numbers One and Two, or they will remove you.*

Brigitta suppressed a shudder when the admiral's body was unceremoniously dumped on top of the third trapdoor. The other contestants took their places on the platform.

"Announce Captain Mador as today's winner," Gunther told Lord Argus.

"Yes, Your Majesty." Lord Argus smirked. "I guess it's obvious who the loser is."

Gunther nodded. "I suspected something like this would happen, but I thought it would take longer for them to bare their claws." He chuckled. "Mador and Tarvis have definitely impressed me."

"Quite so," Argus agreed. "You've taught them well."

Gunther waved a dismissive hand. "I can't help it. I'm naturally a good influence on people."

Brigitta pressed a hand to her mouth. She didn't know whether to cry or throw up.

"Finish it," Gunther ordered.

Lord Argus scurried off to give instructions to the trumpet player.

The blast of his horn echoed through the stadium, and the crowd responded with a shout. "One!"

The second blast. "Two!"

A third blast. "Three!"

The third trapdoor opened and the admiral's body fell through.

As the crowd cheered, Brigitta tried not to think about the murder she'd just witnessed. Instead, she focused on Rupert. He was watching her. Slowly, he lifted two fingers to his lips, then smiled.

A kiss. She smiled back.

"I see you're enjoying it." Gunther chuckled. "Wait till tomorrow. I designed the obstacle course myself. It's going to be very exciting!"

The next morning, Brigitta rode to the stadium with Lord Argus. He explained that King Gunther had left before dawn to oversee the completion of the obstacle course.

"We started building it yesterday after the archery contest," Lord Argus explained. "I haven't seen His Majesty this excited in years. There will even be a wild boar!"

Brigitta gasped. "A boar?"

"Yes!" Lord Argus's beady eyes gleamed with excitement. "We'll just have to hope that one of the contestants falls into the boar pit. I'm sure the crowd would find it very entertaining."

"Of course." Brigitta swallowed hard. "I've never seen an obstacle course before. How does it work?"

Argus smiled proudly. "Even though His Majesty designed the course, I came up with a way to determine the winner. The drummer will pound out a steady beat. Then I have servants who are assigned to each of the five contestants. They will count how many beats it takes for each one to finish the course."

"So the fastest one wins the contest?"

Argus nodded. "Yes, but it's more than a test of speed. There's strength and agility factored in. You see, there are three main walls. To reach the top of the first wall, the contestant must climb a rope. Between the first and second walls, there will be a grid made of ropes suspended ten feet over the ground. The holes in the grid are large enough that a man could fall through. The ground below has been made into a giant pit of mud, so if anyone falls through—"

"He gets all muddy," Brigitta finished.

"Exactly." Argus chuckled. "It should be very entertaining."

Brigitta nodded. "So where does the boar come in?"

"The boar pit is between the second and third wall. There will be nine stone columns, three rows of three, and each column will be seven feet high and topped with a small wooden platform. The runner will leap from one platform to another. If he goes in a direct line, he'll land on only three platforms before jumping to the third wall. Then he climbs a pole and rings a bell to finish the course."

"I see." Brigitta took a deep breath. This sounded like something Rupert could do. After all, he had years of experience climbing ropes and maneuvering down yardarms.

"The winner will be the one with the fastest time," Argus added. "And the loser will either have the slowest time or fall into the boar pit and be gored to death."

She winced. Clutching her hands together, she sent up a silent prayer to the twin goddesses to keep Rupert and his companions safe.

He'd pulled a long straw.

Rupert glanced at the other contestants to see what they had ended up with. Since the obstacle course couldn't handle five at once, they would be running it in two teams.

Numbers Two and Five had short straws. They would do the course first. Numbers One and Four had long straws like Rupert. The three of them would run the course together.

Number One shot an arrogant sneer at him and his companions. "Before the day is done, one of you will be feeding the boar."

Rupert drew Four and Five aside. "Watch out for One and Two. Stay as far away from them as you can."

Five frowned. "You think they'll try to throw us into the boar pit?"

"Only if you're close enough that they don't have to sacrifice too much time. Remember, the winner is judged on speed, so do the course as fast as possible. That way they won't have time to deviate off course to attack you. They'll be forced to go straight through in order to beat you to the bell."

Four and Five nodded.

"Run across the grid if you can," Rupert continued. "If you go too slowly, you could lose your balance and fall through. Use your forward momentum to your advantage."

Five gave him a wry look. "You don't sound like a guy who grows grapes."

Rupert smiled and shook his hand. "Good luck."

Five lined up beside Two and waited for the trumpet blast that would signal the start of the race.

The horn sounded and the general dashed for the middle rope hanging from the wall. Five ran to the one on the left.

Boom. The kettledrum sounded the first strike.

Two and Five climbed, walking their booted feet up the wooden wall as they hauled themselves to the top.

Boom. Second strike.

The men started across the grid.

Rupert gritted his teeth. From his vantage point on the field, he could no longer see how Five was faring. All he could make out were the two poles at the end of the course, since they were higher. The cheers from the crowd remained at a constant level, so it appeared that nothing drastic was happening. Still, he didn't trust Two to behave honorably. The general had committed murder yesterday.

He counted the number of drum strikes, and on the twentieth one, he saw Two climbing a spike-studded pole to ring the bell. Five started up the second pole.

"He did it!" Four exclaimed with a grin.

Rupert heaved a sigh of relief. Five had gone fast enough that Two had been hard-pressed to beat him. Indeed, Two rang his bell only a few seconds before Five.

And Rupert was now more convinced than ever that Five had been well trained for combat.

The officer in charge on the field told the second team

to line up. Rupert made sure to place himself between One and Four. If One wanted to cause trouble, he'd have to go through Rupert first.

The trumpet blared, and they took off.

Rupert reached a rope at the same time as One, but he climbed faster and was the first to reach the top. He glanced at Four to make sure he was climbing all right, then took off, running across the grid, his feet landing firmly on one rope after another.

The crowd roared, then started to chant *Seven!*

He was almost across when the ropes suddenly heaved underfoot, throwing him off balance. He fell forward and landed facedown on the grid, which was now undulating like waves on the ocean.

A yelp sounded to his left. Four had fallen through the grid, but had caught a rope with his hands, leaving his feet to dangle over the mud pit.

Rupert glanced to his right. One was behind him, facedown and jerking the ropes on purpose to make the grid unstable. *Asshole.*

He looked back at Four. The Eberoni farmer was dangling underneath the grid, but still managing to move forward, hand over hand, as he made his way to the second wall.

With the grid heaving up and down, the best Rupert could do was move forward on all fours. Luckily, he didn't have far to go.

He reached the second wall. One was now frantically trying to catch up.

Rupert scanned the pit in front of him and spotted the boar running about, desperately searching for a way to escape. The strange surroundings and the noise of the crowd had agitated the animal to the point it was ready to attack.

He jumped to the first platform. Then the second one.

And the third. By this time, he had too much momentum built up, and he nearly skidded off the edge of the platform. He fell back and grabbed on.

The crowd resumed its chant: *Seven! Seven!* He rose to his feet. One more jump and he'd be on the third and last wall. A simple climb up the spike-studded pole to ring the bell, and he'd be done.

He glanced back to check on Four's progress. One and Four had both reached the second wall. Four was focused on a platform, preparing to leap, when One ran at him and pushed him into the pit.

With a screech, the crowd leaped to their feet. The boar reacted to the noise, snorting and scurrying about.

Four ran for the first column to try to climb up to the platform, but the columns were smooth stone and there was nothing to hold on to.

Dammit. Rupert moved toward him, jumping from one platform to another. While he was going in the wrong direction, One leaped across the platforms, headed toward the third wall.

Four cried out in terror as the boar spotted him. Rupert reached his column and lay flat on the platform, hooking his boots over one end as he stretched an arm down to Four.

"Grab on!" Rupert shouted.

As the boar started to charge, Four latched on to Rupert's arm.

Seven! Seven! The crowd chanted.

Rupert strained to pull the man up onto the platform.

Seven! Seven! The crowd erupted in a cheer when Rupert hauled Four safely onto the platform.

"Are you all right?" Rupert asked.

Four lay there, breathing heavily. "You saved my life."

"We're not done yet. Can you jump?"

Four nodded. "I'll be fine. You go first."

As Rupert stood, the bell rang. One had finished the course. He waved his arms in victory, but the crowd didn't seem to notice.

As Rupert leaped across the platforms, the chanting started again. *Seven! Seven!*

He landed on the third wall and glanced back to make sure Four was all right. When Four made it to the wall, Rupert scrambled up a pole, rang the bell, and jumped down.

The crowd went wild.

Holy shit. He ran a hand through his hair. Stefan was going to be pissed.

Up in the royal box, Brigitta heaved a sigh of relief while her brother let loose a long string of curses.

"Who does this Seven bastard think he is?" Gunther growled at Lord Argus. "Mador and Tarvis had excellent runs, and no one even noticed!"

"We could disqualify Seven for going backward on the course," Lord Argus suggested, then his skinny shoulders slumped. "But we might end up with a riot on our hands."

Gunther snorted. "The crowd acts like he's some sort of damned hero."

Because he is, Brigitta thought. As the crowd continued to shout *Seven*, a shocking thought jumped into her mind. The Telling Stone marked with the number seven! All this time, she'd thought it referred to the contest of seven men competing for her. But it meant much more than that. It meant Rupert, himself, for he was number seven.

She took a deep breath to steady her nerves. Surely if the stones had predicted Rupert, that meant he would survive and they would have their happy ending.

Her skin suddenly prickled with an odd feeling that she was being watched. She looked around, but couldn't spot anyone.

Her attention snapped back to Lord Argus when he told her brother, "The crowd already knows that number Four had the worst time. They could get violent if we don't make him the loser."

Gunther huffed. "Seven must be a damned idiot. Why did he bother to save Four's life? All the losers will end up dead, anyway."

Argus nodded. "It was a ridiculous waste of time."

Gunther waved a dismissive hand. "I've had enough of this Seven. What is the contest tomorrow? A swordfight?"

"Yes, Your Majesty," Argus replied. "The four remaining contestants will be paired up for two swordfights. It will be Captain Mador and General Tarvis against numbers Five and Seven."

Gunther smiled. "Tarvis is the best swordsman in the country. Make sure he's paired with Seven tomorrow."

"Yes, Your Majesty." Argus's eyes gleamed.

Brigitta's breath caught. She would have to warn Rupert.

Gunther chuckled. "And tell Tarvis that I have grown tired of Seven. He can take care of Seven just like he did the admiral."

Chapter Twenty-Seven

He'd been given an inferior sword. Rupert ran his hand along the porous steel and thumbed the dull edge of the blade. *Dammit.*

Yesterday, after the obstacle course, Brody had passed on a warning from Brigitta. She had overheard the king's plan to be rid of the annoying number Seven. Gunther had arranged for him to fight the general.

Gunther's decision had not come as a surprise to Rupert or Stefan. After all, Rupert was posing as an Eberoni nobleman, and he'd become the crowd favorite. That was something the Tourinian king would never accept.

Brody had given them an additional warning, although Rupert didn't know what to make of it. For the last two days, Brody had caught the scent of the Chameleon in the stands. But since there was a least a thousand people in the stadium and Brody didn't know what the Chameleon looked like, he hadn't been able to detect him.

Rupert and Stefan had never heard of the Chameleon, so Brody had explained how the bastard had attempted to take over Eberon by assassination and impersonation before escaping in the form of an eagle. Since he had failed to steal the Eberoni throne, his sudden appearance in Tourin could only spell trouble.

Now, the following morning, Rupert pushed aside all thoughts of the Chameleon. His first concern had to be surviving today's swordfight.

He examined the field before him. The obstacle course had been removed, but the mudhole still remained. The boar had been killed and served at a celebratory feast last night.

General Tarvis and Captain Mador were nearby, boasting about the feast and making sure Rupert and Five heard about how they had courted the princess while Five and Seven had been kept under guard in the basement.

Rupert glanced up at the royal box. Even from here, he could see how pale Brigitta looked. She was frightened.

Hell, she had every reason to be frightened. Stefan had warned him that General Tarvis was rumored to be vicious with a sword.

"Use your powers," Stefan had urged him. "Blow him away. Do whatever you have to do to stay alive."

"But you can't afford to be obvious about it," Brody had quickly added. "Being Embraced is a crime here in Tourin. They could kill you for it."

Rupert glanced down at his shoddy sword. He might be forced to use his power.

"Are you making your peace with the Light?" General Tarvis smirked as he approached Rupert. "You should before it's too late."

Rupert squared his shoulders. "Is it true what they say? That you're the best swordsman in all of Tourin?"

The general shrugged. "It's a well-known fact."

"Then why have I been given an inferior sword? Is the prospect of a fair fight too scary for you?"

The general's eyes blazed with anger. "Mind your tongue, Seven, or I'll cut it out before I deliver the final blow."

"When this sword breaks in half on the first strike, the crowd will know you were too cowardly to—"

"Enough!" General Tarvis bellowed, his face turning a mottled red. "Guard!" he yelled at a nearby soldier. "Get him a good sword."

Yes! Rupert tossed the inferior one on the ground.

Tarvis sneered. "Don't think it will make any difference. You will still die today." He marched off to complain to number One.

When the guard handed Rupert a decent sword, he said, "Thank you. Can you give Five a good one, too?"

The guard winced. "He already has a good one."

Rupert snorted. Perhaps he should be flattered that he was the one they most wanted to kill.

The guards handed each of them a white tunic to put on over their shirts. Each tunic was emblazoned on the front and back with their number.

As the crowd grew increasingly noisy and impatient for the match to begin, Rupert wandered over to Five. "If you're in danger of being wounded or killed, surrender."

With a grimace, Five whispered, "The north has surrendered enough to these bastards."

Rupert looked around to make sure no one could hear them over the noise of the crowd. He rested a hand on Five's shoulder and leaned close. "I need you alive so we can make things right."

Five's eyes narrowed. "Who are you, Seven?"

Rupert squeezed his shoulder. "Stay alive."

A horn blasted, signaling the king's wish for the match to begin. The four contestants put on their helmets.

The kettledrum pounded, escalating the tension in the air as the four swordsmen strode onto the field.

Rupert glanced at Stefan and Brody in the stands. They both looked worried, but gave him a thumbs-up.

The contestants paired off on either side of the mudhole—Five fighting Captain Mador, and Rupert facing General Tarvis. They took their stances, their swords raised and pointed at their opponent.

The trumpet blared.

Rupert charged, figuring a bold attack would catch Two by surprise. The general had probably assumed that Rupert would adopt a more defensive posture.

Their swords clashed, the ringing noise echoing about the stadium as the crowd began to chant *Seven! Seven!*

The fight continued for a few minutes until Rupert shot a small burst of air toward his opponent to make him stumble back. The surprise on Two's face gave Rupert hope. If he kept using just enough power to undermine Two's confidence, he might make the bastard desperate enough to make a mistake.

With a shout, Two attacked, his sword striking with speed and incredible strength. Rupert was hard-pressed to parry each move. Eventually, he pushed the general back with another gust of air.

Two breathed heavily, cursing under his breath. No doubt he was confused as to how Rupert was managing to repel him.

Without hesitation, Rupert charged. The general retaliated and came close to slicing Rupert's arm. Rupert leaped to the left, but his opponent kept slashing at him. Rupert blew him back to take a small break.

And that's when he realized they had turned enough that Two's back was now to the mudhole. On the other side of the mud, One was forcing Five into a retreat.

Two charged toward him, his sword raised. Rupert blocked the downward swing aimed for his head. With a growl, Two strained, pressing hard against Rupert's sword.

Rupert's arms burned, but he managed to shove Two back and keep attacking until Two was forced to retreat toward the mud.

Two slipped, his arms flailing as he tried to regain his balance. Rupert jumped and kicked him in the chest, causing Two to crash into the mud with a loud *smack*.

The crowd roared, *Seven! Seven!*

Before Two could get up, Rupert planted a boot on his chest. With both hands on the hilt of his sword, he held the sword with the tip aimed for the general's heart.

"Surrender!" Rupert yelled.

"Never," General Tarvis growled.

"I surrender!" Five yelled, and Rupert quickly glanced at the other pair. Captain Mador had pinned Five to the ground, his sword raised just like Rupert's was over the general.

With a laugh, Mador lifted his sword high, ready to plunge it into Five's chest.

"No!" Rupert let loose a blast of wind that knocked Mador's sword aside enough that it hit the ground beside Five's shoulder.

Five rolled away, safe for the moment.

The general grabbed Rupert's leg that was pinning him down and wrenched him off balance. As Rupert fell on his rump, Tarvis struggled to get to his feet in the slippery mud. With the flat edge of his sword, Rupert knocked Tarvis's feet out from underneath him. The general fell down with another splat just as Rupert jumped to his feet.

He kicked the sword out of Tarvis's hand, then planted his foot on the general's neck. With a growl, Tarvis threw a clod of mud at Rupert's face.

Rupert spit it back onto the general and lifted his sword once more. "Surrender!"

The horn blasted, signaling the end of the match. Armed guards ran onto the field.

"Step back!" one of them ordered Rupert.

Rupert glanced up at Gunther. So the king wanted to save his general from the disgrace of surrendering. No doubt Rupert's victory would be ignored, while One would be named today's winner. Since Five was the only one who had surrendered, he would be the loser.

Tossing his sword aside, Rupert stepped back.

General Tarvis scrambled to his feet and snarled, "I'm going to kill you, Seven. In the next contest, you die."

Rupert removed his helmet. "You're welcome to try." As the crowd continued to chant *Seven*, he smiled. "But apparently, everyone wants you to lose."

"Don't worry," Rupert whispered to Five as they mounted the stairs to the platform with the trapdoors. "I'll make sure you and the others survive."

Five gave him a wry look. "I'm starting to believe you can."

"You have my word." Rupert patted him on the back as he moved toward trapdoor number five.

Mador and Tarvis stood at the far end of the platform, glaring at him.

The horn sounded, the crowd counting along till five blasts had been completed. Five's trapdoor opened, and he fell through.

After the roar of the crowd quieted down, the horn blared again. King Gunther stood, and everyone jumped to their feet. A hush fell over the stadium.

Gunther swept an arm toward the platform. "Good people of Tourin," he shouted. "You see before you the three best warriors in the land. And so, it is only fitting that they confront our country's worst enemy. The next round will be a noble quest, and the winner will be the one who first delivers to me the head of a dragon!"

Rupert stiffened as a thousand gasps echoed around the stadium. *Holy crap*. How could he kill a dragon?

That night, Brigitta paced in her bedroom, waiting for Brody to emerge in human form from the dressing room.

"Try to remain calm," Sister Fallyn said quietly.

"Calm?" Brigitta cried. "How many times must I watch Rup—you-know-who risk his life? The swordfight was bad enough, but now he has to face a fire-breathing dragon?"

Brody strode from the dressing room, wearing breeches and an unbuttoned shirt. "Is there anything to eat—"

"Did you see him?" Brigitta demanded. "Is he all right?"

"I couldn't see him." Brody gave her a sad look. "After the swordfight, the guards took him to the army barracks. They won't even let Stefan see him. They claim if they don't keep him under watch, he might try to escape."

Brigitta sank into a chair. Any man in his right mind would try to escape Gunther's ridiculous quest. "I think the king is using them for revenge. He must hate the dragons for what they did to him."

Brody nodded. "Probably so. Tomorrow, Gunther and several army troops are taking the three contestants to the Norveshki border. They expect to arrive before nightfall. The following morning, the three contestants will cross into Norveshka to hunt for dragons."

Brigitta took a deep breath. For four days now, she'd been forced to sit still, looking pretty while Rupert risked his life. No more. If she wanted a say in her own destiny, she needed to act.

"Here." Sister Fallyn passed Brody a tray of food leftover from dinner. Brigitta had hardly been able to eat.

"You were closer to the field," she said quietly. "You could see him better than I. Was he all right?"

"He's fine. Not a scratch." Brody ate a slice of ham. "Stefan went back to their room in the basement to pack up their things. He's rejoined the other guards and servants from Eberon, who have been staying in town. They plan to follow the troops tomorrow at a discreet distance."

Brigitta nodded. "That sounds good."

Brody sighed. "It's not all good. I shifted into a bird and landed on a windowsill close to where Captain Mador and General Tarvis were having a discussion. Once they cross the border into Norveshka, they're not even going to attempt to kill a dragon."

"But then they'll lose the round," Brigitta said.

Brody shook his head. "There can be only one loser. They intend for it to be Seven. Instead of hunting a dragon, they plan to ambush—"

"Rup—" Brigitta pressed a hand to her mouth. Of course, if Rupert was brought back dead, he would automatically become the loser. The captain and the general would become the last two.

"From their position, it's a great plan," Brody muttered. "They won't have to risk their lives fighting a dragon." He bit off a piece of cheese. "I wanted to pass the news on to you-know-who, but I couldn't get near him. I tried slipping in as a dog, but the guards shooed me away. Even if I made it inside the barracks, I would have to shift to talk to him, and the soldiers would see it."

"We have to warn him." Brigitta rose to her feet and paced across the room. "And we need to be close by in case he needs us." She stopped in front of Sister Fallyn. "Pack some clothes. We're going with the troops in the morning."

Sister Fallyn gasped. "What? I don't think the king will allow it."

"If he tries to refuse me, I'll remind him that he agreed that I could participate as I desired. I need to be there to congratulate the winner when he returns."

"The king might still refuse," Brody muttered. "He's not exactly known for keeping his word."

Brigitta shrugged. "If he does, we'll travel with Stefan and his group. I will not stay here, doing nothing!"

Brody smiled. "Fine. I'll travel along as your dog. Or even fly overhead as a bird."

"Excellent." Brigitta's heart pounded. Rupert would not have to face this quest alone. Even if she had to follow him into Norveshka, she would do it.

For this was her destiny, too.

Chapter Twenty-Eight

❧

The following evening, Brigitta was pacing once again, but this time in a tent by the Norveshki border. Luckily, Gunther hadn't objected to her and Sister Fallyn coming along. He'd actually been pleased by her apparent support of his dragon hunt. And since he normally traveled with a dozen wheeled carts and two dozen servants, the addition of one more carriage hadn't fazed him.

Brigitta's sack of clothes had looked puny compared with Gunther's six trunks that filled one cart. Two carts were filled with tents and rugs, then another two carried the furniture Gunther wanted in his tent. It took another cart to transport the five-foot-tall golden candlesticks he insisted on having. The rest of the carts were filled with cooking supplies and food.

Stuck inside a carriage all day, Brigitta hadn't been able to see Rupert. She'd spent the day gazing out the window at the homeland she'd never known. Rolling farmland, cut into squares and outlined with rock walls. Small villages built around a chapel of Enlightenment.

As they traveled east, the land had grown increasingly hilly, the farms replaced by large forests and pastures of sheep. The last several miles had proven difficult, for the horses had strained to pull the heavy carts up inclines that had become too steep. Eventually, the caravan had halted in a green valley close to a meandering stream. When Brigitta had finally emerged from the carriage, stiff and sore, she'd stared in amazement at mountains so high they were topped with snow.

So now she was pacing in her tent, worrying about the ambush. The night before at the palace, she'd written a note for Rupert. She reached into the bodice of her gown to retrieve it.

Sister Fallyn lifted the flap to enter the tent. "The servants say he'll be sleeping among the soldiers."

"All right." Brigitta carefully palmed the folded note in her hand. "Are you ready?"

Sister Fallyn winced. "If we get caught—"

"We won't. Brody will be watching over us. Let's go." Brigitta strode from the tent with Sister Fallyn following close behind.

There were four lines of tents where the two troops of soldiers would be sleeping. As Brigitta approached, the soldiers stopped what they were doing and bowed.

She nodded her head imperiously. "Good evening."

One of the soldiers, a lieutenant, stepped toward her. "Your Highness, is there something we can do for you?"

"Yes." She let her gaze wander over the tents. "I would like to wish Seven good luck. He's here, isn't he?"

The lieutenant winced. "He's not supposed to see anyone."

Brigitta sneered much like her brother would do. "I'm not just anyone. The man has risked his life to win my hand, so it is only fitting that I acknowledge his efforts." She lowered her voice. "What's the harm in a few words? The man will probably die tomorrow."

The lieutenant shifted his weight. "That is true."

"So where is he? I'm curious to see the man who inspired so much cheering at the stadium."

"This way." The lieutenant led her down the third row of tents and stopped in front of one. "Seven, come out."

The tent flap opened and Rupert emerged with a guard, who immediately bowed.

Rupert's eyes widened a fraction, then he lowered his gaze and bowed. "Your Highness."

Brigitta quickly looked him over. He didn't seem injured in any way. "So this is the man everyone was chanting about?" She leaned close to Sister Fallyn. "He seems quite ordinary, doesn't he?"

Sister Fallyn nodded, then gasped and pointed at the sky. "Good heavens, is that a dragon?"

While the soldiers turned to look, Brigitta grabbed Rupert's hand and pressed the note against his palm.

He squeezed her hand, his gaze meeting hers for a heated second, then he released her, curling his fist around the note.

"It's just an eagle." The guard turned toward them.

"Really?" Brigitta glanced up. It was Brody, ready to swoop down and attack if they needed a distraction.

"Oh, what a relief." Sister Fallyn pressed a hand to her chest. "I'm so afraid one of those awful dragons will attack us."

"Don't worry, madam," the lieutenant boasted. "We're here to protect you."

Brigitta smiled at the soldiers. "How marvelous of you." She turned toward Rupert. "I doubt we'll meet again, sir, but I wanted to wish you good luck."

He gave her a wry look, then inclined his head. "You are too kind, Your Highness."

"Yes, I know." As she sauntered off, she heard Rupert telling his guard he needed to piss. No doubt he was seeking a moment of privacy to read the note. "Thank you, Lieutenant." She waved a hand in the air without bothering to look back.

Sister Fallyn trailed along behind, playing the role of a devoted servant. When they reached the privacy of their tent, they both heaved huge sighs of relief.

"Oh, thank you." Brigitta hugged the nun. "I couldn't have managed without you."

"What did the note say?" Sister Fallyn asked.

"It was short and simple. *'After you cross the border, One and Two will try to kill you.'*"

Sister Fallyn winced. "I suppose that is all we can do for now. I'll go fetch us some dinner."

"Thank you." Alone in the tent, Brigitta resumed her pacing. Hopefully by now, Rupert would have read the note.

A bark sounded outside. Brigitta lifted the tent flap, and Brody, now in dog form, trotted inside.

"Here." She set a pair of breeches on her cot, then stepped outside to let him shift in private.

The sun was lowering in the sky, so numerous torches were being lit around the camp. The scent of wood smoke and roasting meat was thick in the air.

Gunther's tent was unmistakable, since it was huge and topped with a dozen banners in blue and gold. The sound of male laughter emanated from within. He was enjoying a meal with Captain Mador and General Tarvis. She'd been invited, but had declined, saying she was too tired from the day's travel.

Her skin prickled as once again she had the odd feeling that she was being watched. She scanned the camp, but everyone seemed busy at their tasks.

"You can come in now," Brody whispered, and she ducked back into the tent. "I have news. Stefan and the others have camped two miles from here."

"That's good. I managed to pass a note on to Seven."

"Excellent." Brody nodded. "Tomorrow when he leaves, I'll follow him as a bird. Stefan will be able to see me, so he'll follow on horseback. We'll watch his back."

"I'm coming with you."

Brody stiffened. "No, you're not. Seven will have my hide if I endanger you. Once we cross the border, we'll be dragon bait."

"I'm still going with you."

"I've heard the mountains are treacherous, and snow can fall at any time, even in the summer. The forests are full of bears, wolves, and wildcats, and they're actually tame compared with the Norveshki warriors. The valleys have bubbling cauldrons of mud and geysers that shoot hot steam. The land around them is barren and scattered with the bones of animals that ventured too far onto the hot surface."

Brigitta took a deep breath. "No matter what you say, I am going. I can speak Norveshki. Can any of you?"

Brody winced.

"If we're captured by the Norveshki warriors, you'll need me."

Brody heaved a sigh. "Fine. You make a good point. I'll take you."

She smiled. "Thank you."

With a groan, he shook his head. "You-know-who is going to be pissed."

Her grin faded. "I can deal with his anger. What I can't handle is the possibility of him being injured or killed."

The next morning, Brigitta watched as One, Two, and Seven were lined up in front of Gunther's tent. The three men sheathed the swords they were given, then soldiers handed each of them a bow, a quiver of arrows, and a spear.

Brigitta's heart pounded, knowing that Captain Mador and General Tarvis planned to use those weapons on Rupert.

Gunther and a local nobleman strolled in front of the three men, inspecting them.

"You will follow the path along the stream," the nobleman explained. "It will take you into Norveshka."

"Yes, my lord," all three men replied. The captain and the general shot an annoyed look at Rupert that he had dared to answer with them.

"One final note," Gunther announced as he stared at the three contestants. "Don't think you can weasel out of this quest by simply killing one of your companions. I have requested the head of a dragon, and you will deliver. If you're too cowardly to kill a dragon, I'll kill you myself!"

One and Two gulped. Seven's eyes narrowed.

"You will avenge me for what those dragons did to me!" Gunther bellowed, his eyes seething with rage. "Do you hear me? I need revenge!"

Rupert's hands fisted, and a strong gust of wind shot down the valley, shaking the tents and snapping the pennants.

Was Rupert causing this? Brigitta's gown whipped against her legs, and her cloak billowed in the air. The wind kept coming, growing stronger and stronger.

Servants cried out in alarm as they stumbled against one another. Campfires blew out, cooking spits tumbled over, and large pots crashed to the ground. Dark clouds moved in, casting the valley into shadow. Horses whinnied as they trotted nervously about their enclosure.

As the wind grew more powerful, the soldiers' tents began to uproot from the ground, and the objects inside flew into the air. The soldiers who tried to save their tents were blown into one another and pummeled with flying objects.

Thunder cracked overhead, and servants screamed, running for the nearby woods for shelter. Horses crashed through the makeshift fence and charged through the camp, causing more chaos.

Brigitta grabbed Sister Fallyn, and they hunched down as a tremendous gale-force wind struck Gunther's tent.

He screamed in rage as his tent flapped about like a rag doll. "Save my tent!"

Soldiers rushed to help as One and Two grabbed on to Gunther's tent.

Brigitta saw Rupert easing away, unnoticed in all the chaos. He jumped on a horse and charged away, headed on the path to Norveshka.

The dark clouds opened overhead, letting loose a deluge of rain. Brigitta and Sister Fallyn dashed for their tent, which was lopsided but still in place. She ran inside to gather the small bundle she intended to take with her.

"You're soaked through," Sister Fallyn said. "You should change."

"There's no time." She slung the strap of the bundle over her shoulder. "He's already left."

"Goddesses be with you." Sister Fallyn's eyes filled with tears.

"When they notice I'm gone, tell them I was so afraid of the storm that I ran into the woods, and I must be lost."

Sister Fallyn nodded. "I'll be praying for you."

Brigitta hugged her, then exited. One of the oilcloth tarps used to cover up supply carts had blown up against her tent. She draped it over her head to keep the rain off, then made a dash for the woods.

When Brody barked, she spotted him on top of a

ridge. She scrambled up the hillside and found Stefan waiting there with two horses.

"He's already gone!" She folded up the oilcloth, for it was barely raining on the ridge. "He took the path to Norveshka."

"Then we need to go." Stefan led her toward one of the horses and wedged the oilcloth between the saddlebags.

She gulped. "I don't really know how to ride."

"Then I guess you'll learn fast." Stefan hefted her onto the saddle. "Just stay on. I'll lead your horse."

She nodded, her heart pounding. This was much higher off the ground than she'd expected. She grabbed the saddle horn.

Stefan mounted his horse, and they moved at a slow trot along the ridge. Brody ran in front of them, then shifted into an eagle and soared into the air. He soon disappeared from view as he went in search of Rupert.

After a while, the path from the valley merged with the path on the ridge. Brigitta glanced back to see the camp in disarray.

As the path curved to the left, she lost all sight of the valley. She was now surrounded by rocks and scraggly trees.

"This is one of the few mountain passes into Norveshka," Stefan explained as the path grew more steep and narrow.

Soon the horses slowed to a walk as they eased along a cliff. Brigitta glanced to the side and winced. That was a long drop down. She could hear the sound of rushing water in the distance.

"There's a waterfall ahead," Stefan called back. "It feeds into the stream close to where you camped."

"How far to the border?"

"It's about a mile up from the waterfall. At the highest

point of . . ." Stefan's voice faded as the sound of rushing water grew louder.

They rounded a bend, and the noise was thunderous. Water shot through a hole in the mountainside, sending mist into the air. Stefan slowed their horses even more, since the path was damp in places. Brigitta was curious how far the water fell before crashing into rocks, but didn't dare look down into the gorge for fear she would fall.

The path continued its upward climb and became more dangerous, riddled with rocks and boulders, as if nature itself were warning them to turn back. At times, she had to bend completely over, her nose against the horse's neck, for an outcropping of granite would jut over the path. The wind whistled through the pass, making her shiver in her damp clothes.

Up and up they climbed till finally they reached the top, their horses easing through a narrow gap, surrounded on each side by walls of granite. As they emerged onto a promontory, Brigitta gasped.

It was a world she'd never imagined. A high mountain valley stretched before her with a green pasture surrounded by thick forests and mountain peaks covered with snow. In the distance, the green pasture turned white and barren, and geysers of hot water shot into the air.

Green vibrant life, then the white ash of death. The juxtaposition of beauty and horror was startling.

"Welcome to Norveshka," Stefan said.

A screech sounded overhead, and Brigitta glanced up. A dragon was circling far above them, its scales gleaming purple and green in the sun.

"They know we're here," Stefan muttered. He directed their horses down the path, and they descended into the valley.

The path cut through the middle of the valley with a rushing stream to their right. The air was a bit chilly, but at least the bright sun was drying out her clothes.

Stefan pointed at the stream. "This meets up with another stream at the head of the valley, then goes through the rock wall to become the waterfall we saw earlier."

She twisted in the saddle, looking around. They seemed to be alone in the valley, except for the dragon watching them overhead. "Why can't we see Rupert ahead of us? And where did Brody go?"

Stefan slowed to a stop. "Of course."

"Of course, what?"

"Rupert knows he's a target. He'll stay hidden and take to the high ground. This valley is too exposed." Stefan glanced back at the promontory at the head of the valley. "If One and Two go through the pass, they'll see us. Come on."

He led their horses across the stream, then headed for the forested slope along the south side of the valley. As the horses trotted, Brigitta winced as her rump bounced painfully against the saddle.

After they reached the shelter of the forest, Stefan dismounted. "Wait here."

"Where would I go?" she muttered, shifting her weight.

Stefan snapped off the branch of a bush, then ran back to the stream and erased the tracks left by their horses on the muddy riverbank. When he rejoined her, he tossed the branch to the ground, then remounted.

Brigitta gritted her teeth as they continued on and on down the valley, weaving through the trees. An occasional breeze stirred the trees and ruffled the ferns, and she shivered, since her clothes were still slightly damp. With the leafy canopy blocking most of the sun, a chill began to set in her bones. Every now and then, beneath the shade of a tree, she spotted a small pocket of snow. Brr, no wonder she was cold.

The ground was thick with fallen leaves and pine needles, so their horses made little sound. Far above them, she heard the occasional screech of the dragon. Was it still watching them?

Stefan suddenly stopped and quirked his head, as if straining to listen. Then he dismounted and eased toward the edge of the woods.

Brigitta managed to slip off her horse. *Ouch.* She hobbled toward him, her legs and rump objecting to being on a horse for several hours. She hunched down next to Stefan and peered around a bush.

Captain Mador and General Tarvis had reached the Norveshki valley, their mounts galloping down the path next to the stream. The dragon screeched overhead, and Mador shouted back, his voice echoing through the valley. Tarvis yelled, too, shaking his spear at the dragon.

"Fools," Stefan muttered, then motioned for her to follow him back to the horses.

A powerful wind shot down the valley, shaking the trees. Was a storm coming, or was that Rupert? Had he noticed the arrival of One and Two?

Brigitta shivered. "Can we walk for a while?"

"It will slow us down."

"I think the exercise will help warm me up."

He sighed. "Fine. I have to admit that I'm starving. It must be past noon now." He fumbled around in a saddlebag and retrieved a wineskin and two apples.

They ate and drank as they walked the horses through the woods. Luckily, the wind seemed to have died down. They fed two more apples to the horses.

"How is Fallyn doing?" Stefan asked.

"Very well," Brigitta replied. "Do you think Rupert will actually kill a dragon?"

Stefan shook his head. "I don't know. It's not like him to kill for no good reason. I'm sure he couldn't care less about avenging your brother."

She thought back to how Gunther had referred to his need for revenge. Had that inflamed Rupert's own yearning for revenge? "Rupert caused the storm, didn't he?"

Stefan nodded. "If he gets upset, his emotions can create some powerful winds. But I believe today's storm was intentional, so he could escape without being ambushed."

"So there have been times when it wasn't intentional?"

Stefan winced. "One time, the Tourinian navy sneaked up on us in the fog during the night. We could have lost all our men and ships. Rupert was so frantic to save their lives that he unleashed too much power. The naval ships ended up blasting each other, and some men died."

This must have been the incident Lieutenant Helgar had talked about, Brigitta thought. The Tourinian naval officer had ended up scarred for life.

"We tried to save as many as we could," Stefan continued. "Some of them joined us, but the officers demanded to be put ashore." He shrugged. "And then there was the time in Danport when . . ."

"What happened?"

Stefan snorted. "When Rupert found out about Gunther's competition, he nearly caused a tornado inside a room."

Her mouth twitched. "Really?"

Stefan chuckled. "After that, Ansel and I kept hounding him to admit that he cared about you. But he wouldn't."

Her smile faded. He'd never confessed to her, either, even though she'd told him that she loved him. "I suppose it's hard for him to admit."

Stefan nodded. "He's lost everyone he loved. And then for years, I kept telling him the same thing—don't trust anyone. So it's not easy for him to trust."

"Especially when my father killed his father," she muttered.

Stefan gave her a wry look. "There's that, but I don't think he ever blamed you for it."

No, he just wanted to kill Gunther. After he killed a dragon. She groaned inwardly. There had to be a better way.

Every now and then, they checked on Mador's and Tarvis's progress. The two horsemen weren't too far ahead. They'd been forced to slow down when the path in the valley began meandering between piles of white ash and bubbling cauldrons of mud. Every now and then, a breeze would bring the stench of rotten eggs to Brigitta, but for the most part the forest smelled of fresh pine and rich earth.

After a while, a small grassy clearing opened up on the hillside. A small waterfall trickled down the mountain, snowmelt from the white-covered peak.

"Oh, how lovely." Brigitta sauntered onto the meadow, dotted with wildflowers. This was heaven compared with the hellish scene of hot cauldrons and geysers in the valley.

Without a canopy of leaves overhead, she could see the sky. An eagle flew overhead, and she waved in case it was Brody.

It was! He landed by the edge of the meadow where Stefan was standing by the horses. Stefan pulled some clothes from a saddlebag.

"Oh." Brigitta backed away. "I'll leave you alone for a moment." She hurried across the clearing so she could relieve herself behind some bushes.

After she was done and she could hear two male voices, she ventured back into the meadow.

Brody waved at her, then finished buttoning his shirt.

A screech sounded overhead, drawing her attention. The dragon was circling. It screeched again. Was it trying to communicate? She gave it a big smile and wave.

"Did you find Rupert?" she asked Brody as she leaned over the stream to wash her hands.

"Yes," Brody replied. "He's close to the canyon at—"

A huge roar sounded behind Brigitta, and she straightened with a jerk.

Stefan held up a hand. "Don't move."

Her heart lurched. What was behind her?

Stefan quickly nocked an arrow in his bow, and Brody palmed a spear. She slowly turned her head.

A bear! With a huge jaw and enormous claws. It stood on its hind legs and growled.

Panic slithered ice-cold down her veins.

"Don't run," Stefan ordered. "Hold steady."

Tears filled her eyes. Was she going to die?

Suddenly a burst of fire shot down from the sky, hitting the ground hard enough that it trembled beneath Brigitta's feet. With a gasp, she fell to her knees.

A wall of fire rose up between her and the bear. Close enough to the bear that she could barely make out his form through the flames. With an angry roar, the bear turned and charged up the mountain.

Stefan and Brody ran toward her to make sure she was all right, but she hardly heard them. Stunned, she sat back on her rump. The green meadow swirled before her eyes, and she peered up at the sky. The fire-breathing dragon screeched. She lifted a hand toward him. *Thank you.*

Stefan and Brody quickly emptied saddlebags and filled them with water from the waterfall. Soon they had managed to extinguish the fire.

With trembling legs, she rose to her feet.

"We should go," Stefan said, glancing up at the dragon.

"We're too exposed here. It could shoot more fire and roast us alive."

Brigitta shook her head. "It won't hurt us. It saved me."

Brody snorted. "It may have been trying to save the bear. We're the invaders here."

"We should go." Stefan reloaded a saddlebag.

Brigitta glanced up at the sky as the dragon disappeared from sight. Was it true what they said, that the dragons stole children? But this one had saved her, she was sure of it. Could she stop Rupert from killing one of them? But if he didn't, he would fail the quest and be executed, along with the other losers who were waiting in jail cells back in Lourdon. He would also lose his chance to win back the kingdom. And she would be forced to marry either Captain Mador or General Tarvis.

She wandered back to the horses. "We need to talk to Rupert."

Brody winced. "He doesn't want to see you."

She jolted to a stop. "What?"

"I told you he would be pissed," Brody muttered. "He wants us to take you back to Tourin. He said it was an order."

Brigitta scoffed. "I'm not very good at following orders."

Brody smiled. "Neither am I, actually."

Stefan shook his head. "If he ever becomes king, he'll make you eat those words."

"We have to keep him alive for him to be king." Brigitta took a deep breath. "Then we keep going?"

"Aye." Stefan mounted his horse. "Let's go."

Chapter Twenty-Nine

❦

High up on a cliff, Rupert watched Captain Mador and General Tarvis urge their horses up the ridge on the northern side of the valley.

He'd been happy when Brody had appeared earlier and grateful to hear that Stefan was following him. But when Brody had mentioned that Brigitta was also coming, Rupert had immediately reacted with shock, then anger. So much anger that he'd caused a strong wind to whistle down the valley, shaking the trees.

Even now, on the cliff, he fumed whenever he thought about how much danger she would be exposed to. Had Stefan and Brody lost their minds? *Dammit.* Dead leaves fluttered on the ground as his power threatened to erupt with the full force of his fury.

Control, he warned himself. If he lost control here on the mountainside, he could cause a rockslide or avalanche. And that would endanger Brigitta even more.

There had to be a dozen reasons why she shouldn't have come. Wild animals, dragons, Norveshki warriors, and dangerous terrain that either could smother her with snow or boil her with hot mud or steam. And what would

Gunther do to her if he suspected she had allied herself with Seven?

Dammit, didn't she realize that putting herself in danger would terrify him? He'd already lost everyone he loved. He couldn't bear to lose—

He stiffened with a jerk. *Holy crap.* He loved her.

All the yearning he'd been feeling for her, all the joy he felt in her presence, all the desperation to protect her—it should have been obvious to him days ago.

He loved her.

With a groan, he lowered his head. Loving her just made all of this worse. She believed he was an honorable man, but in all likelihood he would be forced to kill a dragon. When the captain and the general tried to ambush him, he would have to kill again. And then when he returned to Tourin, he would have to murder Gunther. Hell, he would have to kill everyone who stood in his way of taking the throne.

Holy crap. For years, avenging his father had seemed like a noble quest, but now . . . he wasn't sure what to do. If he murdered his way to the throne, then he was no better than Garold—who had destroyed his family.

And Brigitta was here in the valley. How could he be this person in front of her?

Dammit, she had to leave. If he didn't lose her to the dangers surrounding them, he might still lose her love and respect when he was forced to kill.

He trudged back to the clearing he'd found earlier with Brody. Even though it was high on the mountainside, there was a small triangular-shaped area that was flat enough to make camp. Surrounded on two sides by a high ridge, it was protected from the cold winds. Three feet of snow sat on top of the ridge, and a steady stream of snowmelt had carved a small basin in a granite slab on the ground.

At the apex of the triangular clearing, a narrow cave had formed in the ridge. Inside the cave, more snowmelt had seeped through cracks in the roof to form another basin of water about waist-high.

Brigitta might be safe if she remained hidden in the cave. His nerves tensed once again. But it would be better if she left. He had to convince her to leave.

He stiffened as he heard them approaching. So Brody hadn't succeeded in chasing them off. Instead, he was leading them straight to the camp.

"Here we are," Brody announced as he led their horses into the clearing.

Rupert's heart twisted at the sight of Brigitta smiling at him. *Dammit.* He glared at Brody. "You were supposed to make sure they left."

Brody shrugged. "We didn't want to."

Rupert clenched his fists, and a wind whistled through the trees.

Stefan glanced up at the swaying branches. "Is that you being pissed?"

"Shouldn't I be?" Rupert gritted his teeth. "I gave you orders to leave!"

Stefan dismounted. "I've been watching your back for nineteen years. I'm not giving up now." He walked over to Brigitta's horse to help her down.

"Don't," Rupert growled. "Take her back now. You should be able to reach the border by sunset."

Brigitta slid off her horse. "I'm not leaving."

More rage seeped out and the trees thrashed overhead. "What kind of future wife refuses to obey her husband?"

Her eyes widened, then she marched up to him. "What kind of future husband thinks he can order his wife around?"

Rupert glowered at her as she glared back.

Stefan cleared his throat. "We'll just . . . uh, make camp over there." He led the horses into the clearing.

"You're not staying!" Rupert yelled at his old friend.

"We are," Brigitta answered. "And you should be grateful for our help."

"Do you expect me to be comforted by the fact you're endangering yourself?" Rupert asked through gritted teeth. "The terrain here is dangerous. And there are wild animals and dragons—"

"I know." She lifted her chin. "I've already encountered them."

"What?"

She smiled. "Don't worry. I'm perfectly fine."

He growled in frustration, then glared at Stefan and Brody, who were unloading saddlebags. "You're going to let her endanger herself?"

"We're staying out of this," Stefan mumbled.

Brigitta planted her hands on her hips. "I'm here to help. And if you weren't so busy being a grouchy ingrate, you would—"

"Grouchy?" He stepped closer. "Do you know what I've been through the last few days?"

"Yes! I was there. And it nearly killed me to see you risking your life over and over while I could only sit there, doing nothing!" Tears glimmered in her eyes. "You have proven yourself to be the brave and fearless hero. Now I need the chance to prove myself."

He swallowed hard. Did she really think he was fearless? Holy Light, he was terrified. If something happened to her . . . he pointed at the cave, ready to order her to go inside and stay put until it was safe. But even though he jabbed his finger at the cave, he couldn't make the words come out.

With a growl of frustration, he marched off. He headed

back up to the cliff where he could check on the captain and general.

Hunching behind a rock, he spotted them on the northern slope of the valley, slowly ascending to a ridged cliff that would take them to the end of the valley where it narrowed into a gorge. He'd already investigated the gorge. The north and south sides were close enough to shoot arrows across. If he hid behind some rocks on the south side, he might be able to pick one of them off.

With a groan, he sat on the ground and rested his back against a boulder.

"We have a fire going," Brody announced as he joined him on the cliff. "Dinner will be ready soon."

Rupert sighed. He doubted Brigitta even wanted to see him now. "Why did you bring her here?"

"She can be very insistent. And—" Brody sat beside him. "I caught the scent of the Chameleon at the camp."

"What? You mean he followed us?"

"I think he's masquerading as one of Gunther's soldiers, but I haven't located him. If I can smell him, he can probably smell me. So he's staying away from me."

Rupert frowned. "Do you think he plans to kill Gunther and take his place?"

"Perhaps. One thing is for sure. He's up to something bad. So I thought Brigitta might actually be safer with us." Brody peered around a boulder to look at the captain and general. "I don't think they know we're here, so we should be fine for the night."

Rupert sighed.

Brody gave him an amused look. "You're thoroughly smitten, aren't you?"

"Sod off."

Brody chuckled as he rested against a boulder.

With a groan, Rupert leaned forward, cradling his head

with his hands. After a while, he muttered, "I don't know what to do."

"If you don't want to kill a dragon, then don't," Brody said quietly. "One of them saved Brigitta earlier from a bear."

He lifted his head. "Really?"

Brody nodded.

Rupert frowned. "I don't want to be a king who has murdered his way to the throne. And I don't want to start a war with the Norveshki by attacking one of their dragons."

Brody was silent for a while, then said, "We might need Brigitta. She can speak Norveshki."

That would definitely come in handy if the Norveshki captured them. "Even if I solve the dragon problem, I still have the problem of the two bastards over there." Rupert motioned to the northern ridge. "At some point, they'll try to kill me."

"How about I fly over there and listen to their plans?"

"Good idea." Rupert peered around the boulder at the captain and general while Brody stripped and shifted into an eagle.

Soon Brody was circling high over the gorge, then easing down to the ground above the two officers, where they wouldn't see him.

As Rupert waited for Brody's return, the sun lowered in the sky. His stomach rumbled with hunger. He hadn't eaten since breakfast.

After a while, Brody landed nearby, then quickly shifted and dressed. "They don't know your location. The captain thinks you've run away like a coward, but the general thinks you're planning to ambush them. Meanwhile, they came up with a plan to kill a dragon tomorrow morning. They're going to lure one into flying close to them where the gorge narrows, and that's when they'll attack."

Rupert nodded. "Then I'll be at the gorge tomorrow, too."

"Good. Let's see if they have any food left. I'm starving." Brody headed toward the clearing.

"I'll be along soon." Rupert watched the sun as it set over the mountains, painting the snow-covered peaks pink and gold. Could he ambush the two officers and kill them?

You're an honorable man. Brigitta's words haunted him. There had to be another way. It would rip his heart to shreds if he lost her love and respect. But he had to eliminate all the threats if he wanted the throne, and that was the only way to keep Brigitta safe.

A soft bark woke Brigitta from a light slumber. It was Brody, she thought, back in dog form for the night.

Over a dinner of dried beef and boiled potatoes, Brody and Stefan had urged her to take the oilcloth and most of the blankets inside the cave to make herself a bed. They would sleep outside by the campfire, taking turns with guard duty for the night.

Inside the cave, she'd wedged a small torch between several rocks to provide some light, then she'd set to work. First, she'd piled up a layer of spongy dried leaves and needles, then she'd covered them with the oilcloth tarp, and topped that with a blanket. After washing with the icy snowmelt that gathered in a stone basin, she'd folded up her skirt and blouse to make a pillow. Then she'd huddled beneath the last remaining blanket, wondering where Rupert had gone.

Was he still angry? Had it been a mistake to come here? Would he really try to kill a dragon? Questions had swirled in her mind till she had finally dozed off.

With Brody's bark, she woke, but now it was too dark to see anything. The torch had burned out. She sat up and spotted a red glow in the distance through the narrow entrance to the cave. The campfire was still lit. She caught the sound of Rupert's deep voice.

He was back.

She sighed with relief. Hopefully he was helping himself to some food. She lay back down and closed her eyes.

A few minutes later, she heard the soft scrape of booted feet entering the cave, and a light flickered against her closed eyelids. Was that Rupert?

She cracked open one eye to find that he'd wedged a small torch into the same spot where the burned-out one was. He leaned against a boulder and pulled off his boots. Then his socks.

When he started to walk toward her, she quickly closed her eyes. All was quiet for a while, but she could feel him looking at her. Beneath the blanket, her breasts felt heavy and her thighs—oh, no! Was this a reaction to the tonic she'd been taking? Her hands curled into fists, clenching the fabric of her shift.

The sound of splashing water tempted her to take another peek. Rupert had removed his cloak and shirt. With his breeches low on his hips, he leaned over the basin to scrub his face. Then he cupped some water and doused his hair. When he straightened, rivulets of water meandered down his muscular back. He lifted his hands to smooth back his wet hair, and the movement caused his muscles to bunch and ripple along his back and broad shoulders.

She sighed. How could a man be so beautiful? Perhaps he was more than a sorcerer of the wind, for he had certainly cast a spell on her. The flickering flames of the torch sent light dancing along the contours of his muscles. And goddesses help her, she wanted to run her hands over him and relish each and every inch of his body. Her thighs squeezed together as she recalled how he'd made her squirm and scream when they were in the grotto.

Dear goddesses, she wanted that again.

He dropped his breeches to the ground, and for a few breathless moments she stared at his buttocks. When he leaned over the basin to gather more water, a whimper escaped her mouth. He immediately straightened, pivoting toward her.

She turned her head, biting her lip and tightly shutting her eyes. Oh dear goddesses, he'd nearly caught her ogling him. But what was he doing, stripping and washing in front of her? He could have washed up outside at the waterfall. Did he intend to sleep inside the cave with her?

Oh, yes, please.

At the sound of more splashing water, she turned her back to him and clutched the blanket with her fists. Was it the tonic that was making her heart pound and her skin itch to be touched? She thought back to Rupert's conversation with her in her bedroom at Lourdon Palace. It was only him that she wanted, no other man. So no, this wasn't the tonic. This was her.

She wanted him something fierce.

Behind her, Rupert settled on her makeshift bed. "Are you awake?" he whispered.

Her eyes opened. Her fists tightened. "Are you still angry?" She could barely hear her own whisper over the sound of her heart thundering in her ears.

"No." There was a pause. "I'm terrified. If anything were to happen to you, I don't know how I could bear it."

Her heart squeezed. The poor man. He'd lost everyone he'd ever loved. "You won't lose me."

"Brigitta." He stroked her hair, and she rolled onto her back. Their gazes met as he leaned toward her, his golden eyes glimmering in the torchlight. "I love you."

Her breath caught with a small gasp, then she reached for him. "Rup—"

Before she could finish his name, his mouth was on hers. A whirlwind of sensation shook her, and she clutched at his shoulders, holding on tight, willing the storm to engulf them both. The more desperately he kissed her, the more she reveled in it. The more frantic he became, the more she craved him.

When he invaded her mouth, she invaded his. When he nuzzled her neck, she shuddered and delved her fingers into his damp hair. His hands moved along her shift, giving her breasts a squeeze before desperately fumbling for the hem.

He tugged at the hem as he sat up. "Take this off before I tear it."

She sat up and for the first time, she saw his manhood. Good goddesses, had she really referred to that as sweet? It was more like a weapon. Well-tempered steel, indeed.

"Brigitta," he said softly. "You deserve better than a cave. You can always say no."

Oh, how she loved this man. She rested the palm of her hand against his cheek. "I want you now."

His eyes glinted with so much heat and desire, she wanted to dive straight into the fire with him. She grasped the hem of her shift and pulled it up and over her head.

Before the shift was completely off, he grabbed her waist and pulled her up onto her knees, his mouth latching onto a nipple. With a groan, she let the shift drop, then ran her fingers through his hair as he suckled hard.

He moved to the other breast, teasing and tugging at her nipple while his hands kneaded her sore buttocks.

She moaned, then kissed the top of his head. "I love you so."

He tumbled her back onto the blanket. "Do you?"

"Mmm." She squirmed when he tickled the hardened

tips of her nipples. "I want to be thoroughly ravished. Now."

His mouth curled up. "I can do that." He smoothed a hand down her belly, then cupped her.

She cried out as his fingers gently stroked her.

"You're already wet."

"Rupert, please."

He moved between her legs. "Holy Light," he whispered. As he looked her over, more moisture seeped from her. He hooked his hands beneath her knees and lifted her legs, spreading them wide. "I want to taste you."

"Huh?" Her thigh quivered as he kissed a trail toward her core. "Rupert?"

He glanced up at her, one side of his mouth tilted up with a smile. "I've never done this before, so let me know if I do something you don't like."

"What?" She jolted when his tongue slid right between her folds. Shock and sensation whirled around her, escalating into pure pleasure and greed. *More, more*, she thought as she squirmed beneath him.

She cried out when he flicked his tongue over an especially sensitive part. He took that as an invitation for a full assault, driving her quickly up a precipice.

For a few seconds she hovered in a cloud of pure ecstasy, then with a cry she shattered. She squeezed him with her thighs as wave after wave crashed through her. She was still shuddering when she felt his hard length ease just inside her.

With a gasp, she opened her eyes.

He was leaning over her, watching her with glittering eyes. "Do you know how beautiful you are when you climax?"

"Rupert," she whispered, cradling her face with her hands.

"I need to take you now. I can't wait any longer." He

nudged himself a little farther in. "Wrap your legs around me and squeeze me tight."

She snorted. "You've been saying that since we first met."

His mouth twitched. "And I finally have you where I always wanted you."

"Scoundrel." She wrapped her legs around his hips.

His smile faded. "I don't want to hurt you, but . . ."

"I'll be fi—Ow!" she cried out as he plunged into her.

"Are you all right?"

"No. You stabbed me with your . . . well-tempered steel."

He gritted his teeth. "Don't make me laugh now. I'm barely hanging on."

"I wasn't joking." She winced at the burning sensation deep inside her.

He pulled out a little. "Did that hurt?"

She shook her head, then gasped as he plunged back in. "Good goddesses, can't you be still?"

He gave her an incredulous look. "No."

"But—" Her breath caught when he slid out and back in once more. "Oh."

"Oh, what?" He gritted his teeth as if he were under some kind of strain.

She wrapped her arms around his neck. "I want more."

"Thank the Light." He quickened his pace, pounding into her faster and faster.

Rugged. Relentless. Powerful. This was even more magnificent than the grotto, for this time they were spiraling up together. With a hoarse shout, he pumped into her, and the desperation of his movement sent her over the edge.

She cried out as he collapsed beside her. "Rupert."

He pulled her into his arms and kissed her. Then he rolled onto his back, taking her with him.

She rested her head on his chest where she could feel the pounding of his heart. *Rupert.* How she loved this man.

"Brigitta." He stroked her hair. "Be careful tomorrow."

"You, too." No matter what happened to them in the future, they would always have this night to remember. "You were right. It was magnificent."

He snorted, then kissed the top of her head. "I'll do better in the future. You deserve more than a cave."

She smiled to herself. "I loved it." A setting like this would have been exactly what she'd have chosen for one of her *overly dramatic* stories.

"No matter what happens tomorrow," he whispered, "don't leave me."

Chapter Thirty

❧

The next morning, Brigitta woke up alone, and her heart sank with disappointment. How could Rupert beg her not to leave him, then turn around and leave her behind? As she dressed, she winced at the soreness between her legs and grew increasingly annoyed. Did Rupert expect her to hide like a frightened rabbit whenever danger was near?

When she strode into the clearing, she was surprised by the chill in the air. Goodness, it had been warmer in the cave. She pulled the hood of her cloak over her head.

Stefan was sitting by the campfire with a blanket wrapped around his shoulders. "Good morning." His breath vaporized in the icy air.

"Good morning." With a shudder, she hurried across the clearing to some bushes where she could relieve herself. Afterward, she rinsed her hands and washed her face in the small pool beneath the waterfall. Only a trickle was landing in the pool now, for most of the waterfall had frozen over, making the cliff wall glisten with icicles.

"Come and eat." Stefan motioned to a copper pot by the campfire. "I've been keeping the oatmeal warm for you."

"Thank you." She settled close to the fire and dipped

a wooden spoon into the pot. "Where is Rupert? And Brody?"

"Brody's an eagle for now." Stefan pointed up at the sky. "I need to collect more firewood. Do you mind being alone for a little while? You won't really be alone. Brody will be watching over you."

She glanced up to see the eagle circling above them. Far off, she heard the screech of a dragon. "I'll be fine." She ate some oatmeal. "Where is Rupert?"

"Up the trail by the gorge. It's so narrow there, he can see the captain and the general on the other side. They're trying to lure a dragon in close enough to attack."

Brigitta swallowed hard. "Is Rupert planning to kill a dragon? I suppose he could use his wind power . . ."

"Killing a dragon would only anger the Norveshki and prolong the war with them. Rupert would rather Tourin be at peace." Stefan sighed. "Unfortunately, taking over a country's throne is rarely a peaceful process."

Brigitta set down her spoon. She was losing her appetite.

"Stay here." Stefan rose to his feet and handed her the blanket. "I'll be back soon."

As she wrapped the blanket around her shoulders, she wondered how Rupert was faring. It had to be even colder up on the cliff with the wind whistling through the gorge.

A few flakes of snow floated down, melting into raindrops as they neared the campfire. Was it snowing on Rupert? He needed the oilcloth to stay warm and dry.

She rose to her feet. This was something she could do.

Her heart pounding with excitement, she readied her supplies—the oilcloth from the cave and a canteen filled with water. She wrapped a piece of dried beef in a handkerchief and slipped it into the pocket of her green woolen skirt.

As she headed up the path to the cliff, the air grew

colder and the wind stronger. A dragon screeched overhead, and she spotted it, circling above the gorge. An answering shriek came from another dragon she could barely see in the distance.

The one overhead swooped down suddenly. Its black scales gleamed an iridescent purple and green in the morning sun. Such a beautiful creature. Its wingspan was enormous, its eyes golden as they fastened on her.

She froze, frightened for a moment that it might unleash a torrent of fire at her. But maybe this was the dragon that had saved her yesterday. With a tentative smile, she waved a hand in greeting.

With a screech, it shot up into the sky.

She took a deep breath. Safe, for now. As she continued her climb up the steep, narrow path, she began to suspect that the dragon had checked her for weapons. She doubted she looked like much of a threat. But Rupert might, since he was probably armed.

The air grew more frigid, and flurries of snow swept around her. She draped the oilcloth around her shoulders, holding it tight in her fists as the wind snapped at it. The trees became more stunted and gnarled, a sure sign that it was hard for them to grow this high on the mountain. Even she was finding it difficult to get enough air.

She eased around a curve and stopped in amazement as the gorge finally came into view. The wind burst through the narrow opening with so much power, no trees had been able to survive. Between cracks in the rocks, a few scraggly bushes had emerged, most of their leaves blown away and the twigs outlined with white snow. Large boulders had fallen onto the path, and by peering between two of them she could see the cliff on the north side.

Captain Mador and General Tarvis were there, shouting and shooting arrows at the dragon overhead.

Keeping low, she maneuvered up the rocky path to the cliff on the south side of the gorge. There she spotted Rupert, hunched down behind some boulders. Snowflakes flurried around him, some sticking to the brown wool of his hooded cloak.

Her feet crunched on some gravel, and he turned toward her. His eyes flared with emotion. He looked angry that she had come, but there was also hunger in his gaze. Perhaps, like her, he was remembering what had occurred the night before. He put a finger to his mouth to signal silence, then gestured for her to keep low.

Crouching, she approached him.

He gave her an exasperated look. "Why are you here?"

"It's snowing." She handed him the oilcloth. "And I brought you some food and water." She retrieved the dried beef from her skirt pocket.

He tore it in half and handed her a piece. "Are you all right?"

She nodded, her cheeks growing warm.

A screech sounded overhead as the dragon flew by. Across the gorge, Mador and Tarvis yelled at it and let loose a volley of arrows.

"Here we go again," Rupert muttered, then with a flick of his hand, the arrows stopped in midair and plummeted into the canyon.

"You're protecting the dragon?" Brigitta whispered.

"Trying to. So far, the dragon has been staying out of range, but the bastards over there are using the wind to their advantage. I'm just taking the advantage away."

She sighed with relief. "That's good."

With a frown, he bit off a piece of dried beef. "I'm not sure if I'm helping. The dragon must think the men over there are lousy shots, because it keeps getting closer. I might actually be helping the bastards to lure it in."

"There's a second dragon coming." She pointed to the east. "I saw it as I was coming around the bend."

Rupert's eyes narrowed on the second dragon. "I keep getting the feeling that they're intelligent."

"Me, too. I think the one overhead checked me for weapons."

As Rupert's gaze shifted to the first dragon, Brigitta moved closer, draping the tarp around his shoulders. He squeezed her hand, and his grip was icy cold.

"You're freezing." She took his hand in hers, rubbing it to warm it up.

He lifted her hands to his mouth and kissed them. "I want you to go back."

She shook her head and handed him the canteen. "I brought you some water."

He frowned at her. "You need to go back. If the captain and general see you here, they'll know you're helping me. Once they report that to Gunther, you'll—"

"They won't see me."

He arched a brow. "Are you planning to never obey your husband?"

Husband? "I am obeying you. You told me to never leave you, so here I am. Besides, we're not married."

"We will be."

Her heart lurched. "Is that a proposal?"

He gave her a wry look. "I suppose I should propose before you do it for me."

Her mouth twitched. "That would be wise."

He pulled her close for a quick kiss. "Thank you for the tarp and the food and water. Now please—"

A screech rent the air above them, and they both glanced up. The second dragon had arrived. As the two dragons circled, Brigitta wondered if they were communicating.

Suddenly one zoomed toward them, headed for the gorge at an incredible speed. Across the way, Mador and Tarvis ran to the cliff edge and nocked their arrows.

"It's coming too low," Rupert whispered.

Mador and Tarvis shot at the approaching dragon, and Rupert quickly blew the arrows off target.

With shouted curses, the two men readied another volley.

The dragon kept coming, drawing in its wings as if it planned to career straight through the narrow gorge.

Mador and Tarvis gave a shout of excitement.

Brigitta tensed. With the dragon this close, they couldn't miss. And Rupert would be unable to stop the arrows since the dragon would be in the way.

With a wave of his arm, Rupert swept the dragon up high in the air. The dragon screeched as it flipped backward, head over tail, losing control of its own flight.

Meanwhile, the second dragon shot into the gorge, and flames erupted from its mouth, engulfing the northern ridge with a torrent of fire.

With a gasp, Brigitta ducked down, but she could feel the heat and hear the horrendous screams. She ventured a peek and spotted one of the officers, his body swallowed up in flames. He flailed about, then plummeted off the cliff. His screams continued, then came to an abrupt stop.

She pressed a hand to her mouth. Smoke stung her eyes, and the stench of burning flesh made her stomach roil.

"I think that was General Tarvis," Rupert whispered as he peered between two boulders. "I can't see the captain." He shook his head. "The men thought they were luring the dragons in. But it was the dragons that sprang the trap. They're definitely intelligent."

Brigitta swallowed hard at the bile in her throat, then glanced up. The two dragons were still circling. "They're not leaving. Do you think they're planning to attack the captain?"

Rupert's eyes widened. "Holy crap. If they realize I blew one of them away, they might think I was attacking them." He jumped to his feet. "We need to go now."

"Damn you, Seven!" A hoarse shout filtered toward them on the wind.

Brigitta peered through the two boulders and spotted Captain Mador on the north ridge. His uniform was singed, but somehow he'd managed to survive.

He nocked an arrow and sent it flying straight at Rupert. With a wave of his hand, Rupert sent the arrow off course.

"What the hell—" Mador stopped when a dragon shriek interrupted him. With a frantic look, he dashed behind a large boulder.

Brigitta froze in terror as both dragons zoomed toward the gorge. The first one shot a stream of fire at the northern ridge, and the second one was heading straight for her and Rupert! "Ca-can you blow it away?"

"I don't want to get into a fight we might lose." He grabbed the oilcloth tarp, then pulled her to her feet. "Wrap your legs around me and squeeze me tight."

"Now?"

"Trust me!" He lifted her up so she could latch on to him. "Whatever happens, don't let go!"

As the dragon grew closer, fire erupted from its mouth. Rupert clutched the corners of the tarp in his hands, then ran up the path.

Brigitta looked around frantically. There was nowhere to go. The path came to a dead end at the cliff.

The fire shot up the path, flames billowing toward them.

Rupert leaped off the cliff, taking her with him.

With a cry, she squeezed his neck and buried her head

in his shoulder. They plummeted a short way, then suddenly, with a snap, their descent slowed.

With a small shock, she realized Rupert was holding the tarp over them and blowing into it to fill it with air.

Above them, the dragon screeched. She tensed, worried it would breathe more fire at them. An eagle circled them. Brody. She kept her gaze focused on him and Rupert, for she didn't even want to look down.

They continued to descend, and soon she spotted hillsides covered with trees. Rupert managed to blow them toward a meadow in the valley. When his feet hit the ground, they tumbled over each other, then came to rest on the thick, green grass.

He propped himself up on an elbow and touched her face. "Sweetheart, are you all right?"

"I-I think so." She gazed up at the cliff far above them. "How did you do that?"

He smiled. "I've always thought it would be possible to control a fall that way, but I never had the chance to test it before."

She sat up. "That was a *test*?"

"We didn't have a lot of choice at the time." He jumped to his feet and gave her a hand to help her up.

As she stood, Brody gave a small shriek overhead. She waved at him. "We're fine!"

Rupert stiffened. "I think he was warning us."

"About what?" Brigitta gasped when Norveshki warriors dashed from the woods on either side of the valley.

Within seconds the warriors had surrounded her and Rupert and were pointing their spears straight at them.

Chapter Thirty-One

No wonder he hadn't noticed these buildings from the cliff, Rupert thought. Each of the log cabins had a roof entirely covered with grass. Looking down at them, they would be nearly impossible to spot.

At first, when the soldiers had surrounded Brigitta and him, he'd been tempted to blow them away. But the chances of escaping all the way to the border had seemed slim. Not when he could see more Norveshki warriors in the forest. And there were still two dragons overhead.

Besides, he didn't want war with the Norveshki. He couldn't prove himself peaceful if he attacked them. And their behavior was completely understandable, given the fact that he'd invaded their country fully armed.

Brigitta had immediately told them in Norveshki that they came in peace, but there had been no reply. Two soldiers had stepped closer, pointing at his weapons, then extending their hands. He'd easily handed over his spear, bow, and quiver of arrows. After all, his greatest weapon was something they couldn't take away.

Then they'd pointed their spears eastward. As he and Brigitta had walked with them, he'd carefully scanned the soldiers and the surroundings. Brody had flown away, probably to let Stefan know what had happened. There were more soldiers in the woods, watching their progress.

The soldiers were tall, dressed in brown leather breeches and green woolen shirts, covered with brown leather breastplates. Their heads were covered with green hoods so only their eyes showed. They hadn't said a word.

Something about the way a few of the soldiers walked caught his eye. They were as tall as men, but he suspected they were women. With their heads and bodies all covered the same way, it was hard to tell.

He estimated that they had traveled less than a mile when they arrived at a forested area. There were wooden platforms built high in the trees, but camouflaged with branches. Sentries peered down at them.

In the middle of the forest, there was a clearing with several dozen log cabins, each one boasting a roof covered with grass. Just like the lookout towers and the soldiers' uniforms, the cabins were designed to blend in with nature.

One of the soldiers opened a cabin door and motioned for them to enter. As they did, the soldier said something in Norveshki, then shut the door.

Brigitta whirled around, gazing at the door with a surprised look. "That was a woman."

"Several of the soldiers were female." Rupert glanced around the one-room cabin. It was simple. A bed. A table with four chairs. A stone hearth with no fire, but then it was much warmer here in the valley than it had been up high in the mountains. "What did the soldier say?"

"She said to wait here for General Dravenko. Have you ever heard of him?"

"No." Rupert wandered to a window to look outside. A guard glared at him.

Brigitta drew close. "What should I tell the general?"

"Stay as honest as possible."

"But how honest? Who should I say you are?"

The door opened and a soldier strode inside with a tray of food and drink. Her hood had been pushed back to reveal dark-red hair. She set the tray on the table, then marched out and closed the door.

"She reminds me of Sorcha," Brigitta murmured.

"Who is that?" Rupert picked up the pitcher and sniffed at the contents. It smelled like tart apples.

"One of my sisters from the convent. We always suspected Sorcha came from Norveshka. And Gwennore is an elf, so she obviously hails from Woodwyn." Brigitta frowned. "We were never sure where Maeve came from." She sighed. "I miss them."

He set the pitcher down. "They were the ones hugging you at the pier in Ebport?"

She nodded with a sad look.

"Don't worry." He pulled her into his arms. "You'll see them again."

The door opened, and Rupert stepped in front of her.

A man strode into the room, dressed the same as the other soldiers, except for the four brass stars embedded in his leather breastplate. He looked about the same age as Rupert, but even taller. He appeared unarmed except for a sheathed dagger strapped around the thigh of his brown leather breeches. His black hair was pulled back into a queue and tied with strip of leather. His eyes, a brilliant green, scanned Rupert and then Brigitta. He motioned for the guard behind him to leave.

The door closed, leaving them alone.

The man spoke, his voice deep and confident. Rupert didn't understand Norveshki, but he caught the word *Dravenko*. So this was the general.

Brigitta answered as she moved to stand beside Rupert. He heard her say her name, then the name *Umberto*

Vintello, and the word *Eberoni*. So she was sticking to his false identity as an Eberoni nobleman.

The general motioned to the table, then took a seat and filled three brass cups from the pitcher.

Rupert moved a chair close to Brigitta's and whispered to her in Tourinian as they sat down. "Don't eat or drink anything till he does it first." He watched the general's face for any sign that he had understood, but the Norveshki warrior's stoic expression remained the same.

The general asked a question, which Brigitta answered at length until he interrupted her with a few lines that made her stiffen with shock.

"What is it?" Rupert whispered.

"He already knows about the competition," Brigitta muttered. "He even knows that you're Seven. But he doubts you're who you say you are."

Rupert shot a wary glance at the general. There had to be a Norveshki spy at the Tourinian court. *Dammit.* He would put a stop to that once he took the throne.

General Dravenko took a sip from his cup, then sat back to watch them with an inquisitive look. He said something to Brigitta, and she quickly replied.

"What now?" Rupert whispered.

"He knows I'm the princess and Gunther's sister. I had to explain that I hardly know him and have no loyalty to him."

The general said something, and Brigitta blushed as she answered.

"What?" Rupert wrapped a protective arm around her. "Was he rude to you? Do I need to punch him?"

"He asked if I was in love with you," Brigitta whispered, her cheeks still pink.

Rupert stiffened. "What business is it of his?" He glowered at General Dravenko, then leaned close to Brigitta. "You said yes, right?"

"Of course."

As Rupert patted her shoulder, the general muttered something else.

Brigitta winced. "He just said Gunther is an ass."

"Well, that's true." Rupert snorted. "Apparently, it's an acknowledged fact over all of Aerthlan."

Dravenko's eyes glinted with humor before he took another drink.

Did the general understand Tourinian? Was the jackass playing with them? Rupert asked Brigitta a question in Eberoni. "Does he know why we're in his country?"

"You're here for the head of a dragon," the general answered in excellent Eberoni before setting his cup down with a clunk. When they stiffened in surprise, his mouth twitched. "Did you think the barbarians from the north are uneducated?"

"How much do you know?" Rupert asked in Tourinian.

"Not everything, or I wouldn't be talking to you," Dravenko replied in the same language. He motioned to the food and drink. "It is safe. I need you alive to answer my questions."

Rupert sat back. "I have questions, too. Why have you taken us prisoner?"

"You are our guests." The general's eyes hardened. "But that could change depending on how you answer." He leaned forward, propping his elbows on the table. "Did you blow away a dragon?"

Rupert tensed, not willing to admit he had such a power.

"It was very odd, what was happening at the gorge," Dravenko continued. "According to the reports I received, the two men shooting arrows were the captain of Gunther's personal guard and his general. Naturally, one would assume they were skilled archers. And yet all their arrows made an abrupt plunge into the gorge. Our dragon made multiple passes to verify the situation, and in each case, you made a hand movement as if you were manipulating the arrows."

Rupert winced inwardly.

Brigitta leaned close to him. "They must be able to communicate with the dragons."

Dravenko nodded. "Some of us can." He arched a brow at Rupert. "So I'll ask you once again. Did you blow away a dragon?"

Rupert took a deep breath. "Yes."

"Was it an attack?"

"No. I was trying to save it."

The general's eyes narrowed. "You expect us to believe that when you were ordered to bring back a dragon head? You invaded our country fully armed."

"I never intended harm to a dragon. That's why I jumped off a cliff rather than blow the dragon's fire back at it. I didn't want to burn it."

Dravenko's mouth curled up in amusement. "You can't burn a dragon. The scales are impervious to fire."

"I . . . didn't know that." Rupert took a sip of apple cider.

Dravenko picked up a piece of cheese and bit into it. "Are you Embraced?"

Rupert exchanged a look with Brigitta.

Dravenko waved a hand dismissively. "I won't kill you for it. I'm just curious if harnessing the wind is your special gift."

"I am Embraced," Rupert admitted.

"Ah." The general tilted his head, watching Rupert closely. "I've heard of only one person on all of Aerthlan who can control the wind. He's called a Wind Sorcerer. The Tourinian pirate called Rupert."

Brigitta inhaled sharply, and beneath the table, Rupert squeezed her knee. He cleared his throat. "I believe that pirate was captured and killed."

Dravenko smiled. "I heard the same thing, but apparently Gunther isn't convinced, because he asked the Eberoni king to send him the body. The dead pirate should be arriving in Lourdon in the next day or so."

Rupert shrugged as if he wasn't interested, but now he wondered if the Norveshki had a spy at the Eberoni court, too. This damned general knew far too much.

"It's very curious how you have the same gift as the sorcerer Rupert. Also curious that for years, Rupert has targeted only Gunther. He even kidnapped Gunther's sister." Dravenko motioned to Brigitta. "Yet here she is with you. The competition has gone on for only a week, but she is already in love with you. It makes me wonder if she knew you before the competition. Whoever you are."

Rupert's mind raced. If he admitted who he really was, would this Norveshki general be on his side?

"It would seem that this Rupert has a serious grudge against Gunther," Dravenko added.

Rupert shrugged. "Everyone hates Gunther."

"Not enough to become a pirate in order to steal from him. Or to join a competition where failure means death." Dravenko frowned at him. "I know you must be Rupert. What I don't know is why you've been risking your life to be a thorn in his side. Who are you really?"

Rupert swallowed hard. Then he took a sip of apple cider while he debated just how much to say. "I am Tourinian."

"And?" Dravenko prompted.

"I want Tourin to be at peace with the Norveshki."

The general gave him a pointed look. "You would have to be king to make that happen."

Rupert stared back. "Wouldn't the Norveshki be relieved if there was a new king of Tourin?"

"Who would accept a sorcerer pirate as king?" Dravenko leaned toward him. "You must have amassed a great deal of gold by now, but apparently it is not wealth you want. You desire the throne. Why?"

Rupert's hands clenched. "Because it is mine. It was my father's before me, and it has belonged to my family for four hundred years."

Dravenko's eyes widened. "You are King Manfrid's son? The lost prince?"

Rupert nodded. "Ulfrid Trepurin. The rightful king."

Dravenko stared at him a moment, then took a drink. "Do you have proof? Your father's crown? The royal seal?"

Rupert shook his head.

"He is the prince," Brigitta said, taking Rupert's hand. "I have seen it in his memories. That is my gift as one of the Embraced."

Dravenko glanced back and forth at them. "Didn't her father kill your father?"

Rupert squeezed her hand. "I trust her."

"He also has the support of King Leofric of Eberon and my sister, Queen Luciana," Brigitta added.

The general gave her a dubious look. "How is the Eberoni queen your sister?"

"Adopted sister," Brigitta explained. "We grew up as orphans on the Isle of Moon, along with Gwennore, Sorcha, and—"

"Sorcha?" Dravenko sat back.

Brigitta nodded. "We've always believed that she—"

Dravenko held up a hand to stop her. "If Trepurin here takes the throne, do you intend to be his queen?"

Brigitta's cheeks bloomed pink as she gave Rupert a shy look. "Yes."

He smiled at her. "Definitely, yes."

Dravenko scoffed. "So the House of Trepurin and House of Grian will be united."

Rupert nodded. "I want there to be peace in Tourin and with our neighboring countries."

"How do you plan to take the throne?" Dravenko asked.

"Once I win the competition, I'll be able to marry Brigitta. At the wedding ceremony I'll capture Gunther and announce my true identity."

Dravenko rose to his feet. "You can't win the competition without the head of a dragon. Wait here." He strode from the cabin.

"What?" Brigitta gave Rupert an incredulous look. "He's not going to kill a dragon, is he?"

"I don't know." Rupert dragged a hand through his hair. Had it been a mistake to reveal his true identity? But surely it was beneficial to the Norveshki to have Gunther removed from power.

Brigitta ate a piece of cheese. "Didn't it seem like he knew Sorcha's name?"

Rupert nodded. "The Norveshki know a lot more than I ever imagined."

Less than an hour later, General Dravenko opened the door and motioned for them to join him.

As Rupert stepped outside with Brigitta, he spotted an enormous woolen sack that was large enough to fit a person inside. Something bulky was inside. "What is it?"

The general loosened the drawstring to show him the contents. "A skull. It's several hundred years old, but it's still the head of a dragon."

"Thank you." Rupert bowed his head. "I am in your debt."

Dravenko nodded. "Just remember that when you take the throne. And if you need military assistance, send that eagle shifter of yours to let us know."

Rupert glanced up at Brody who was circling overhead. "You know about him, too?"

Dravenko snorted. "We also know that Captain Mador fled across the border over an hour ago. And your friend,

Stefan, has been escorted to the border with your horses. He's waiting for you just beyond the pass."

"Thank you," Rupert said. "I appreciate it." He was never going to underestimate the Norveshki again.

A dragon screeched overhead, and Dravenko's eyes glinted with humor. "The dragons are not happy to lose one of their ancestor's skulls to that bastard Gunther. If you send the word, they will be delighted to rain fire on him."

"I'll keep that in mind." Rupert offered his hand, and the Norveshki general shook it.

"Your Highness." Dravenko bowed over Brigitta's hand. "Your transportation is arriving."

Brigitta squealed as a dragon landed nearby, then lumbered toward them. "Heavenly goddesses." She eased closer to Rupert.

He stepped in front of her and watched as the dragon scooped up the large woolen sack in its forelegs. "So it's going to transport the skull for us?"

"Yes." Dravenko smiled. "And the two of you. It is the quickest way to return you to the border."

"We—we're going to fly?" Brigitta asked.

Rupert grinned. "Holy crap, this is awesome!"

The flight was over before it had barely begun. They soared over the gorge and the barren area of geysers, then the dragon swooped down to the promontory close to the mountain pass that led to Tourin.

The dragon settled onto the ground, folding its wings under so they could slide off its neck. Rupert landed on his feet, then turned to find Brigitta still clutching the dragon's neck, her eyes squeezed shut.

"We're here." He smiled as he pried her hands loose.

"Oh." She slid into Rupert's arms, then turned to face the dragon.

It set the wool-encased skull gently on the ground, then tilted its head, regarding them calmly with its golden eyes.

Brigitta touched its neck, patting it gently. "You're so pretty."

The dragon snorted puffs of smoke from its nostrils.

"It could be a male," Rupert reminded her.

"It's still pretty." She patted it again, then stepped back. "Thank you for the ride."

The dragon leaped off the promontory and flew away.

Rupert took one last look at Norveshka, then motioned to the narrow pass into Tourin. "Let's go." He dragged the cumbersome sack through the pass, followed by Brigitta.

On the other side, Stefan was waiting with the horses. He helped Rupert tie the large sack onto the back of Brigitta's horse. Then Rupert mounted his horse and pulled Brigitta up in front of him. After Stefan mounted his horse, they started the trek past the waterfall. Brody gave a squawk as he flew over.

Before reaching camp, Brody landed and shifted into dog form. Then he led Brigitta into camp as if he were her pet dog and had just found her wandering in the woods.

Stefan rode back to his camp nearby, and Rupert waited, hidden in the forest. He didn't want anyone suspecting that Brigitta had been with him.

After an hour, he rode into camp, leading the horse with the skull packed on top. The soldiers immediately surrounded him and escorted him to Gunther's tent. When he spotted Brigitta peering out her tent, he breathed a sigh of relief that she was all right.

The soldiers helped him drag the woolen bag inside Gunther's tent. The king was seated in his golden chair behind his desk.

"Leave." As the soldiers left, Gunther glared at Rupert. "You bastard. I didn't expect you to survive."

Rupert eyed the king carefully, remembering Brody's warning about the Chameleon. But Gunther was acting the same as always.

Captain Mador burst into the tent. "Your Majesty, I made it back first! I'm the winner of this round."

Gunther scoffed. "How can you be the winner when you didn't bring back the head of a dragon?"

"There was no way to do that!" Mador exclaimed. "The dragons were vicious! They kept attacking us with fire, and they burned Tarvis to death! I was lucky to get out of there alive."

Gunther's mouth twisted with disdain. "So you failed the quest."

"The quest was impossible!" Mador shouted.

Gunther glowered at his captain, then switched his glare to Rupert as he motioned to the enormous bag. "What do you have there?"

Rupert opened the sack. "The head of a dragon."

Mador gasped.

Gunther jumped to his feet and peered inside the bag. He straightened with a huff. "This dragon is long dead."

"It's still the head of a dragon." Rupert motioned to Mador. "He came back empty-handed. Since there are only two of us left, and I won the quest, I wish to marry the princess immediately." *And never be separated from her again.*

Gunther snorted. "You think I would have an Eberoni fathering the heir to my throne?"

"There was supposed to be one more quest," Mador said. "Allow me to prove myself. I will not let you down."

Gunther shot him an annoyed look. "Beg."

Mador's mouth thinned, and Rupert thought he saw a

glint of anger in the captain's eyes before he ducked his head and fell to his knees.

"Please, Your Majesty," Mador murmured.

"Louder," Gunther growled.

"Please!" Mador shouted.

With a smirk, Gunther circled around his desk and sat in his golden chair. "All right. One last quest. The one who brings me the lost royal seal will be married to the princess."

Chapter Thirty-Two

❦

"Are you all right?" Sister Fallyn asked. "I was so worried about you."

"I'm perfectly fine," Brigitta whispered in their tent. Even though she missed Rupert so much that it hurt. They'd confessed their love to each other and had become one, only to be separated once again.

She sighed. "Gunther yelled at me for wandering off during the storm, but he was relieved that I made it back."

Sister Fallyn lowered her voice. "Wasn't he suspicious that you were missing for so long?"

"Yes," Brigitta admitted. "He had soldiers combing the forest, searching for me, so he wondered why they didn't find me. I told him I stumbled upon another campsite, and they let me sleep there for the night. Brody overheard my excuse and left. I'm hoping he went to Stefan's camp to warn them, so their story will match mine."

Sister Fallyn nodded. "That would be good."

A bark sounded outside their tent.

"Oh, he's back." Brigitta let Brody in, then she and Sister Fallyn waited outside while he shifted.

"Is Stefan all right?" Sister Fallyn whispered.

"Aye. He asked about you." Brigitta looked over at

Gunther's tent. She'd spotted Rupert being escorted inside a few minutes ago. Had he delivered the dragon's head? Would he be declared the winner?

Brody called softly for them to enter, and they found him dressed in breeches and buttoning his shirt.

"I flew over to Stefan's camp," he whispered. "When Gunther's soldiers go there to ask about you, they'll confirm you were there."

"Thank you." Brigitta poured him a glass of wine. "Do you know what happened in Gunther's tent? Was Seven announced as the winner?"

"I lurked around the back of the tent, and luckily, they were yelling loud enough that I could hear." Brody took a sip of wine. "Gunther is too pissed to acknowledge Seven's win. He decided on one last quest to determine which of the final two will be marrying you."

Brigitta groaned. "What does he want now?"

"The royal seal." Brody winced. "Unfortunately, once he gets his hands on the royal seal, it will be even harder for the House of Trepurin to regain their power."

"The seal is missing?" Sister Fallyn asked.

Brody nodded. "When King Manfrid was assassinated, his queen took the seal and the young prince and fled north. From the stories I've heard, she hid the seal before they fell off a cliff. Since then, no one has been able to find it. The contestant who presents it to Gunther will be the final winner."

"And my husband," Brigitta added as an exciting idea struck her mind. No one could find hidden objects better than her. "I need to see Gunther."

"Why?" Sister Fallyn gave her a worried look. "What are you up to now?"

"I'm taking control of my own destiny." Brigitta strode from the tent. She would choose her own future and her own husband.

The guard at Gunther's tent announced her and let her inside. Rupert was no longer there. He was probably being held somewhere under heavy guard. The large sack containing the dragon head had been shoved into a corner.

Gunther was seated behind his desk, using his fingers to flick gold coins off the polished surface. Whenever a coin flew across the tent, Mador scurried after it as if he were a dog playing fetch.

"Hurry, Mador," Gunther growled as he flicked three in rapid succession. "You're falling behind."

"Yes, Your Majesty." Mador scrambled about the tent.

Gunther gave Brigitta a passing glance. "Go and pack your things. We leave at dawn to go north."

"Yes, Your Majesty." She bowed her head. "If you recall, I was given permission to participate in the competition."

"I'm letting you tag along. That's enough." With an annoyed look, Gunther flicked a coin and it hit one of his giant golden candlesticks with a *ping*. "Don't get in the way, Brigitta. And no more getting lost."

"Yes, brother dearest . . . I mean, Your Majesty." When he snorted, she continued, "I heard the last quest is a search for the lost royal seal."

Gunther jumped to his feet. "Where did you hear that? Who has a loose tongue around here?"

She winced inwardly. "I . . . overheard some soldiers . . ."

"Ha!" Gunther glared at Mador. "They should be better trained than that! Dock their pay for a week."

"Yes, Your Majesty." Mador bowed.

Brigitta edged closer to her brother. "If I could speak to you in private . . ."

Gunther scowled as he sat behind his desk. "Mador will be your husband. You can speak freely in front of him."

"Thank you, Your Majesty." Mador gave her a look that was both heated and possessive.

She repressed a shudder. He'd never looked at her like that before. "I'm not sure if you know this, Your Majesty, but as one of the Embraced, I have a special gift."

He waved a jeweled hand in the air. "I don't care as long as you can squeeze out an heir."

Mador's eyes narrowed. "You're Embraced?"

Gunther threw a tied-up scroll at Mador, hitting him in the head. "Sit!"

"Yes, Your Majesty." Mador sat on the rug.

Brigitta ignored the captain and turned to her brother. "My gift enables me to find lost items. I am your best hope at finding the lost seal."

Gunther's eyebrows rose. "You can find it?"

She nodded. "I would need to touch something that once belonged to the deceased queen. Then I should be able to envision the seal's whereabouts. So if you will allow me to find it—"

"Of course!" Gunther smiled. "By the Light, you may be worth the gold I've had to spend on you. So, once you help Mador find the seal, he will win the final quest."

Brigitta bowed her head. "As you wish." But it would be Rupert she would be handing the seal to, for he was the rightful owner.

Gunther's smile faded as his face turned sour once again. "I'm having some soldiers check to see if you really spent the night at the camp that Seven's servants set up. If I catch you anywhere near that Seven, you will be sorry. *Painfully* sorry. Do you understand?"

She swallowed hard. "Yes, Your Majesty."

Brigitta looked away as the heavy stone lid was pried off the top of a crypt. *Forgive me, Your Majesty.* She hadn't wanted to disturb the late queen's grave, but apparently, there was nothing left of the woman's belongings but a pair of shoes. After the queen's body had been burned, Garold's soldiers had dumped the bones in this crypt, along with the shoes that had slipped off her feet as she'd fallen to her death.

Brigitta had traveled for three days with Gunther's caravan. They had headed north, and as the terrain grew increasingly mountainous, their progress had slowed. The Highlands of northern Tourin were famous for their mines of gold, silver, and precious jewels, which had made the northern clans rich and powerful.

The most powerful clan had been the Trepurins, who had owned the gold mines. For four hundred years, they had been the reigning House of Tourin. But when Brigitta's father, Garold, had defeated King Manfrid, he'd taken over all the gold mines and palaces.

Last night they'd spent the night at the old palace from which the Trepurins had once ruled the country. It was nothing but an empty shell now, for everything of any value—all the gold, tapestries, furnishings, and dinnerware—had been looted and taken south to the palace at Lourdon.

Brigitta hadn't been able to see Rupert, but according to Brody, he had spent the night in the stables under guard. Her heart had ached, knowing how hard it must have been for him to see his childhood home this way. She'd wandered the empty hallways, imagining Rupert growing up as the young Prince Ulfrid, surrounded by a loving family he would lose before the age of seven. She'd sat in the overgrown garden, picturing Rupert there, playing with his younger brother, Bjornfrid.

And if that hadn't been hard enough on Rupert, now they were disturbing his mother's grave. He hadn't even been allowed into the chapel. He was under guard outside in the village square.

They had arrived at this village around noon. When the queen and young prince had fled north, this village was as far as they had reached before Garold's army had caught up with them. Looming over the village was the mountain where Garold's men had chased the queen to her death.

A loud grating noise echoed through the stone church, and Brigitta gritted her teeth. *Forgive me, Rupert.* The bell clanged overhead, and she wondered if a sudden gust of wind had swept through the bell tower, a gust of wind that might have been caused by Rupert's distress.

"Get on with it," Gunther ordered as Captain Mador held a torch over the gaping dark hole at the foot of the crypt.

Brigitta ventured a peek inside. Bones, and the faded red leather of a woman's slipper. With a grimace, she reached inside to touch the shoe.

A deluge of emotions struck her so hard, she withdrew her hand and stepped back. *Horror, fear, grief.* She steeled her nerves and this time when she touched the shoe, she concentrated on the royal seal.

She squeezed her eyes shut as anxiety and fear enveloped her. She saw the seal, the top portion made of blue lapis lazuli with an arched handle of gold in the shape of a dolphin. Blue and gold, the colors of Tourin, and the dolphin, a symbol of the coastal nation. A woman's hands were holding the seal, and they trembled as they wrapped it in brown wool.

"We must hide it," a woman's voice whispered. Rupert's mother. She set the seal in a golden bowl and stuffed lamb's wool all around it. "You must never tell anyone where it is."

"But Daddy will want it when he comes back," a young voice whined.

"He . . ." The woman's voice broke with a sob. "He can't come back anymore."

"What about Ulfie?" the young boy asked.

The woman sniffed. "I hope he can. I hope he's still . . ." She quickly stuffed another golden bowl with lamb's wool. "If Ulfrid comes for the seal, you can give it to him. Understand?"

There was a whimpering sound, then the boy cried, "I miss Ulfie."

"I know." With a muffled sob, the woman fit the two bowls together. With a twist, they fastened together, forming a golden orb. She wrapped the orb with more brown wool, then slipped it into a woolen bag. "If something happens to me, you must hold on to this. Remember, Bjornfrid. It is precious. Never let it go."

"I'll remember, Mama."

Brigitta withdrew her hand from the crypt as the vision faded. A golden orb. Her gaze shifted to the church's altar. Traditionally, all the churches of Enlightenment had a golden sphere or disk at the altar to symbolize the sun god, called the Light. Unfortunately, Gunther had long since confiscated all the golden orbs in Tourin. Churches had been forced to make their sun globes out of brass or yellow-painted wood.

This church was no different, for there on the altar was a yellow, wooden orb on a cushion of blue velvet. Could the seal be inside? Or had Gunther taken the golden orb to his treasury in Lourdon? If he had, he might actually have the seal in his possession without realizing it. Hopefully, the queen had managed to hide the orb containing the seal.

"Well?" Gunther peered at her closely. "Did you see the seal? Do you know where it is?"

"It was buried in a garden," Brigitta lied. "A castle garden."

"That's all you know?" Gunther scowled at her. "Every castle has a damned garden."

She shrugged. "I believe it would be a castle that belonged to the former royal family."

Captain Mador watched her carefully. "There are several castles nearby that were owned by the Trepurins."

"You could try Trepurin Palace," she suggested. It was a three-hour ride from here. That would give Rupert the chance to check out the local churches.

"I'll check the palace," Gunther said. "Mador, you take some soldiers to search the other castles."

"Yes, Your Majesty." Mador motioned for the soldiers to follow him out.

"Are you coming?" Gunther asked Brigitta. "Or shall I have some guards escort you back to camp?"

"If you don't mind, I'll go back to camp. I'm really tired of traveling."

"Suit yourself." Gunther strode out the church's door, followed by his personal guard.

Brigitta heard the sound of barking and rushed to the church door to peer outside. The dog Brody was circling the king's entourage and growling at them.

"Brody!" Brigitta ran toward him as Gunther aimed a kick at him.

"Control that mutt of yours," Gunther growled as he mounted his horse. "And behave yourself. Remember, I'm having you watched. Don't go near that damned Seven."

"Yes, Your Majesty." Brigitta curtsied as Gunther and his entourage took off. The sound of horse hooves clattered on the cobblestones of the village square.

She spotted Rupert across the square with his horse saddled and ready to go as he conducted his own search for the seal. There was only one guard assigned to him now. Apparently, Gunther didn't consider him much of a threat, since he believed he and Mador would find the seal. Nearby, there were two guards watching her.

Kneeling down by Brody, she patted him on the head.

Instantly her senses went on alert. Brody was also keeping a great number of secrets. "Now be a good dog, and don't get in the soldiers' way," she said loud enough for her guards to hear.

As she leaned close to hug him, she whispered in Brody's ear, "The seal was hidden in a golden orb like the ones used in churches. Tell Seven that I'll check this church, and he can check the others in the area."

Brody yipped in response, then trotted off down a narrow street.

Rupert strode down a parallel street, his guard trailing along behind. No doubt, Rupert intended to catch up with Brody soon.

As Brigitta headed back into the church, her guards started to follow. "Could you wait out here, please? I'd like some privacy while I pray."

With a nod, they took up positions on either side of the door.

Brigitta closed the church door, then hurried down the main aisle to the altar. There she examined the yellow, wooden orb until she was able to open it.

Nothing inside.

With a sigh, she fastened it back together. Hopefully, Rupert would have better luck.

Rupert dashed around a corner, then waited for his guard to appear. A quick punch to the jaw, and his guard crumbled to the ground.

Brody trotted up and shifted into human form.

"Did she see where the seal is?" Rupert asked.

"Inside a golden orb, like the ones used in churches," Brody replied as he yanked the breeches off the fallen guard. "She said she'd try the church here, and we could check the others nearby."

Rupert turned toward the village square. "I want to see her."

"You can't. She has two guards watching her."

Rupert glanced over his shoulder at Brody, who was quickly getting dressed in the fallen guard's clothes. "You could send them away. I need to see her."

Brody shot him an annoyed look. "Do we have time for this?"

"We'll make time." Rupert handed him the guard's boots.

Brody sat and tugged them on. "I caught the scent of the Chameleon. He hasn't taken Gunther's place yet. But he's definitely close to him, maybe one of his personal guards."

"Let's go." Rupert headed back to the village square, then waited, hidden around a corner.

Brody, now dressed as a guard, dashed toward Brigitta's guards in front of the church. "Hurry! Seven has escaped with some of the king's gold!" He pointed north. "He went that way!"

The two guards took off.

As soon as they were out of sight, Rupert led his horse across the village square. "Stand guard," he told Brody, then eased inside the church.

Golden light filtered through the long windows, illuminating the altar with its yellow orb. On the right, barely visible in the shadows, he saw Brigitta kneeling beside a crypt. His heart stuttered. *Mother.*

The door behind him swung shut with a *clunk* that echoed throughout the small church. Brigitta glanced toward him and rose to her feet.

He took a step forward, then stopped as memories seized him by the throat, choking the air from him. Once again, he was that young, frightened boy, sprawled over the crypt, crying for his mother. *Don't leave me.*

"Is it safe for you to be here?" Brigitta whispered as she moved to the main aisle.

It would never be safe. Not until he gained back his father's throne.

"Did my guards see you?" Brigitta asked.

He shook his head. "They're gone. Did you . . . see my mother?"

"Her shoes." Tears glistened in Brigitta's eyes. "I saw her hands in a vision. And I felt her fear and grief. I'm so sorry. I wish there had been another . . ." She paused when he strode toward her, his steps faster and faster.

She ran to him, and he swept her into his arms, holding her tight. "Brigitta."

"I'm here." She grasped his shoulders.

"Don't ever leave me." He cradled her face with his hands and kissed her. She returned his passion, her hands skimming up his neck and into his hair.

Brody cleared his throat at the door. "We need to go."

Rupert stepped back, slowly releasing Brigitta.

"The seal isn't here." She motioned toward the altar. "But I think it could be somewhere close."

Rupert nodded. "I'll find it."

She smiled, her eyes glimmering with tears. "And if I find it, I'll give it to you. Trust me."

"I do." As Rupert left the church, one of Brigitta's guards was returning and spotted him.

"Seven!" The guard ran toward the church.

Crap. Rupert quickly mounted his horse.

"I'll catch him," Brody yelled at the guard.

As Rupert rode away, Brody pretended to be chasing him. By the time Rupert had reached the outskirts of the village, Brody was soaring overhead as an eagle.

Chapter Thirty-Three

Brigitta's guards accompanied her as she wandered from the village to Gunther's encampment. The troops had set up camp in a wide, green valley where they would have access to the water of the nearby stream. She shuddered at the sight of the large mountain that loomed over them. That had to be where Rupert's mother had fallen to her death.

She motioned to a flat boulder alongside the stream. "I'd like to rest there for a while, if you don't mind. Please feel free to return without me."

"We're supposed to watch you," one of the guards protested.

"You can see me from the camp," she replied. "I won't go anywhere, I promise."

They bowed their heads and hurried off to the camp where, no doubt, the smell of roasting meat was calling to them.

Brigitta settled on the flat boulder. The shallow stream splashed over rocks as it started its long journey to the Great Western Ocean. Upstream, it flowed through the village, providing it with water. Here, it bisected a meadow, dotted with wildflowers. Across the stream, just beyond the meadow, a forest began and ascended into foothills and the high mountain.

Her gaze wandered up the mountainside and stopped when she spotted a cliff about one-third of the way up. Good goddesses, was that where Rupert's mother had fallen? It must have broken Rupert's heart to have to camp so close to the spot where his mother had died.

It was a shame, Brigitta thought, that her sister Luciana wasn't here. If the ghost of Rupert's mother still lingered about, Luciana would have been able to talk to her and find out the exact location of the royal seal. But all Brigitta had to go on was the vision she'd seen.

Closing her eyes, she replayed the vision in her mind, searching for any clues that she might have missed.

"Put the basket down by the stream, lad." A woman's voice interrupted Brigitta's thoughts.

She opened her eyes and saw an elderly woman emerging from the forest, accompanied by a young man carrying a basket full of laundry.

"Here, Grandma?" The young man set the basket down on a grassy bank halfway to the village.

"That will be fine, Freddy." The old woman patted him on the shoulder. "Now be a good boy and play while I work."

"Yes, Grandma." The young man took a woolen bag from the basket and hitched the drawstring over his shoulder.

Brigitta narrowed her eyes. This Freddy looked a year or two older than her, yet he was still being treated like a child.

He wandered along the grassy bank, headed in her direction, while the old woman crouched beside the stream and swished a man's shirt in the water. "Look at me, Grandma!" He picked his way across the stream, balancing on rocks.

The old woman glanced up. "Try not to fall in this time."

Freddy laughed. "I'll be careful." He reached the side where Brigitta sat and waved at her. "Hi! I'm Freddy."

"I'm Brigitta. How are you?"

"I'm good." Freddy smiled as he approached. "Do you want to be my friend? Do you like to play ball?" He swung the cloth bag off his shoulder.

"Freddy!" his grandmother called out. "How many times have I told you not to talk to strangers?"

"She's not a stranger," Freddy argued. "She's Brigitta. She wants to play ball with me."

The old woman lost her grip on the shirt, and it floated downstream. "Freddy, can you catch that?"

"I'll get it!" Freddy dropped his bag on the ground, then jumped into the stream to chase after the shirt.

"Come here, lass." The old woman motioned to Brigitta.

As Brigitta drew closer, she suspected the grandmother had released the shirt on purpose. Her suspicion was confirmed when the woman whispered in a low voice.

"You don't have to play with him if you don't want to. He means well, but he's . . . well . . ."

"A bit like a child?" Brigitta asked.

The old woman nodded with a wry smile. "That's a nice way to put it."

"I got it!" Freddy splashed around in the stream, waving the wet shirt in the air.

"That's a good lad!" his grandmother called to him, then lowered her voice. "Folk around here aren't usually that nice to poor Freddy."

"I'm sorry to hear that." Brigitta glanced at Freddy. He was a sweet and handsome young man with his golden-brown hair and brown eyes. She narrowed her eyes as an eagle swooped down and landed on a nearby boulder. Was that Brody? It didn't look quite like his usual style.

"Look, Grandma!" Freddy pointed at the eagle as he climbed up onto the bank. "Shoo!" He flapped the wet shirt in the air, and the eagle took off, then landed at the top of a nearby tree.

"You see the mountain?" his grandmother whispered as she motioned to it. "When he was six years old, he tried to climb it and fell. Hit his head really hard. We were afraid he was going to die, but he pulled through. Then after a few years, we realized he was stuck at the age of six."

"How old is he now?" Brigitta asked.

"Twenty-two." The grandmother sighed. "He's had a hard time of it, poor thing. When he was four, his mother died, falling off the cliff over there. I don't think he ever fully grasped that she was gone. He seemed to think she was still there, waiting for him. That's why he tried to climb the mountain."

A prickle ran down Brigitta's spine. How many four-year-old boys would have lost a mother on that mountain? Could this Freddy be Rupert's younger brother, Bjornfrid? He was the right age, and he even looked a bit like Rupert. But then, where did this grandmother come from? Had she adopted Freddy? If he was actually Bjornfrid, did she know?

"Are you from that camp over there?" the old woman asked. "Whose camp is it?"

"King Gunther," Brigitta replied.

The woman stiffened and a flicker of panic crossed her face before she shuttered her expression. "Freddy, come here. Quick!"

She does know. "The king isn't here," Brigitta reassured the woman. "I sent him south on a wild goose chase. He'll be gone for hours."

The old woman eyed her suspiciously. "Who are you?"

"A friend."

"I knew you would be my friend." Freddy smiled at Brigitta as he joined them. He handed the wet shirt to his grandmother.

"Hey, look!" a boy's voice yelled.

Brigitta spotted three boys running toward them from the village.

"It's Freddy!" one of them shouted. "The village idiot!"

The other boys laughed, and Freddy ducked his head, frowning.

Brigitta stiffened with anger. Just as she was about to yell at the young boys, she spotted the look on Freddy's face, and his pain seemed more urgent than the rudeness of bullies. "Don't let them hurt you," she whispered. "Their cruelty speaks badly of them, not you."

She touched his arm, and a wave of terror and grief struck her so hard, her knees gave out.

"Mama!" The young boy's scream felt like it had been wrenched from Brigitta's throat. She saw the world through his eyes and watched in horror as his mother plummeted off the cliff. She struggled along with the boy as he tried to run to his mother, but strong arms held him back.

A woman next to him sobbed. "Our poor queen."

"She led the soldiers up there on purpose, so they wouldn't find the boy here," a man said. He tightened his grip on Freddy's arms. "We have to hide the prince. If the soldiers find him, they'll kill him. And his mother will have died in vain."

"We can take him to our cabin in the woods," the woman suggested. *"We'll tell everyone he's our grandson."*

"Mama!" Brigitta twisted on the ground as she felt the young boy trying to escape the man's grasp.

"Quiet!" the man hissed. *"Come with us."* He dragged the boy away.

"My ball!" the boy cried, reaching for a woolen bag on the ground. *"Mama said it's precious. I can never let it go."*

The woman peeked inside. *"By the Light, it's an orb, made of gold."*

"We'll have to hide it," the man replied. *"Disguise it so no one will ever know."*

"Miss?" The old woman leaned over Brigitta. "What happened to you? Are you all right?"

Brigitta sat up and looked around her. She was back in the meadow with the old woman and Freddy. Her heart filled with joy as she realized what Freddy's hidden memory meant. He *was* Rupert's little brother! How thrilled Rupert would be once he learned that his little brother was still alive.

"Freddy." She smiled at the young man. "I'm so glad I found you."

He ducked his head, blushing.

"Oh, Freddy!" One of the three boys called as they approached his woolen bag. "We're going to get your ball."

Freddy spun around. "No!"

With a laugh, the boys snatched up his bag and darted across the meadow toward the forest. Freddy ran after them, yelling. Under the shade of a tall tree, one of them upended the bag and let the ball slip out onto the ground.

"No!" Freddy threw himself on the ball. "It's precious! I can never let it go."

"Precious!" The boys taunted him, dancing around him.

Brigitta sprinted toward them, her heart aching that poor Freddy was still repeating the words his mother had told him years ago.

"Come on, Half-Brain, let's play." One of them kicked Freddy in the ribs.

"Stop it!" Brigitta yelled.

"Who's going to make us?" the tallest one jeered.

"I am." Brigitta seized him by the ear and pulled him away. He looked to be about ten years old, so she was still taller and stronger than him.

"Ow! Ow!" The boy squirmed and tried to kick at Brigitta, but she knocked his feet out from under him, and he fell onto his back.

She smiled to herself. Rupert would be impressed by how well she'd learned self-defense from him on board the ship. She glared at the other two boys. "You want to play?"

"My lady!" Her guards dashed toward her from the camp. "Do you need any help?"

"Yes. Please take these boys back to the village and inform the constable that they have been behaving like cruel bullies."

The boys started to protest, but when they saw how well armed the soldiers were, they went along quietly.

"Are you all right?" Brigitta hunched down beside Freddy.

"I guess so." He slowly sat up, cradling a brown leather ball in his lap.

Brigitta sat beside him. "May I see your ball?" When Freddy passed it to her, a vision flitted across her mind. She saw his adopted grandmother carefully wrapping the golden orb with more wool, then sewing a layer of brown leather tightly around it.

She hefted it in her hands. "It's much heavier than it looks."

The grandmother joined them under the shade of the tall tree. As she settled on the ground, she gave Brigitta a wary look. "Who are you that the king's soldiers follow your orders?"

"I'm a friend." Brigitta passed the ball back to Freddy. "Have you heard of the pirate Rupert?"

The old woman snorted. "Everyone's heard of him."

Freddy nodded. "He steals gold from the bad king." He covered his mouth. "I'm not supposed to say he's bad."

Brigitta smiled. "You're right, though. Did you know Rupert is Embraced? He can control the wind."

Freddy looked confused. "I thought Ulfie could do that."

"He can." Brigitta lowered her voice. "Your brother, Ulfrid, is alive. He's been disguising himself as the pirate Rupert."

Freddy blinked. "Ulfie?"

The old woman leaned close. "Are you serious, lass?"

"Ulfie's alive?" Freddy shouted. "Where?"

"Not so loud," his grandmother hissed, casting a worried look at the camp and then at Brigitta. "If you're on Ulfrid's side, why are you traveling with Gunther?"

"I'm trying to help Ulfrid regain the throne. I want to set things right."

"So you're a spy?" the old woman asked.

Brigitta smiled. "I suppose you could call me that."

The woman continued to eye her suspiciously. "I'm not sure we should trust you."

"I would never do anything to harm Ulfrid. I love him." Brigitta's cheeks grew warm. "We . . . we plan to be married."

"I love him, too," Freddy boasted, then his bottom lip protruded. "Why did he stay away from me? I missed him."

"He doesn't know you're here." Brigitta slanted a grateful look at the old woman. "You did an excellent job of hiding Freddy. Thank you."

The old woman sighed. "My husband died two years ago. I've been so worried about what will happen to the boy if I . . ." Tears shimmered in her eyes.

Brigitta gave her a hug. Her senses didn't pick up any secrets, other than Bjornfrid's identity. "What is your name?"

"Dorina."

"Thank you for saving Freddy." Brigitta squeezed Dorina's hand. "Rupert is going to be so happy to know his brother is alive." Her eyes burned with tears as she smiled at Freddy. "Will you let me give the royal seal to your brother? It will help him reclaim the throne."

Freddy frowned at the ball. "Mama said he might come back for it someday." He offered it to Brigitta.

"Thank you." She set the ball in her lap. "I'm going to hide this in my tent until I can pass it on to Rupert." She glanced toward the camp. It was quiet. No one there seemed interested in the three people talking in the shade of a tree. Overhead, the eagle squawked as it left its perch and flew away.

Dorina gave Brigitta a stern look. "If anything bad happens with that seal, I will rain curses upon your head for all eternity."

"Don't worry. I'll hand it personally to Rupert." She smiled. "I guess I'll have to learn a new name for him. Can you wait here? I want to send a friend to help you take care of Freddy until Rupert is able to claim the throne. Then you won't have to worry about anything happening to you."

"Thank you, lass." The old woman struggled to stand up, so Freddy pulled her to her feet. "Come along, lad. We'll finish the laundry while we wait."

On the way back to the stream, Brigitta slipped the ball back into its woolen bag. Then she hugged Dorina and Freddy and headed back to the camp. There, in her tent, she explained everything to Sister Fallyn. She gave the nun the bag of gold she'd once stolen from Stefan.

"Please look after the prince," Brigitta told her. "I'll send Stefan to you as soon as I can."

Sister Fallyn nodded with tears in her eyes. "Can you imagine what it will be like to see the two princes reunited?"

"I know." Brigitta grinned. After she gave Rupert the seal, he would win the competition and marry her. Then he would announce his true identity and imprison Gunther. Then Rupert would become king and be reunited with Freddy. "It's going to happen now, and it will be even better than we had imagined."

Sister Fallyn quickly packed up her belongings, then gave Brigitta a hug.

"Good luck." Brigitta walked her outside and pointed out Dorina and Freddy in the distance.

She watched as Sister Fallyn joined them, then waved as the three set off into the forest.

"Brigitta," a voice whispered to her from behind her tent.

She turned. *Rupert*. She was tempted to tell him his brother was nearby, but she didn't want to be seen talking to him. She slipped inside her tent and grabbed the woolen bag containing the hidden seal. Outside, she glanced around to make sure no one was looking, then edged toward the back of her tent.

Rupert smiled at her.

"Where's your guard?" she asked.

He waved a dismissive hand. "I lost him. Couldn't find the seal, either."

With a grin, she handed him the bag. "I told you I was good at finding things. It's hidden inside the ball."

His eyes gleamed as he grabbed the bag. "Excellent."

"Now we can be married soon." She gave him a wry look. "By the way, I'm still waiting for an official proposal."

Rupert's eyes grew heated as his gaze swept over her. "You'll be mine soon, Princess." He strode away, carrying the seal.

A trickle of unease slithered down Brigitta's spine. Wasn't she already his? Why had Rupert seemed different?

That evening, Rupert's guard escorted him to Gunther's tent. Brigitta was there, standing next to her brother, and from the anxious look in her eyes he suspected something had happened. Had she found the seal?

When her gaze swept down to his empty hands, a flicker of panic crossed her face.

"So, Seven." Gunther eyed Rupert with his usual smirk. "Didn't find the seal, did you?"

Before Rupert could answer, Gunther raised his voice. "Mador, get in here."

Captain Mador strode inside the tent, carrying a woolen bag, and Brigitta gasped. She stepped back, clutching her hands together as her face grew pale.

Was she in trouble? Immediately, Rupert formulated a plan of escape. He would grab her and run for some horses while he obliterated the camp with a tornado.

"Did you find it?" Gunther asked.

"Yes, Your Majesty." Mador pulled a golden orb from the bag and set it on the king's desk. "It took a while to cut all the leather away, but the seal is inside, intact."

"Great! I want to see it." Gunther stepped behind his

desk and twisted the orb apart. He unwrapped the wool to uncover the seal.

Dammit to hell. Rupert's hands fisted as he watched Gunther handling the seal that had belonged to the Trepurins for four hundred years. Now it would be even harder to wrench the throne from the bastard. And if Mador had won the final quest, then Brigitta was in grave danger.

One look at the horror on her face and Rupert's anger flared, causing a wind to whistle through the tent.

"Excellent." Gunther smiled as he stroked the golden dolphin atop the seal. "You have won the final quest, Mador. And the competition. Congratulations."

The captain bowed his head. "Thank you, Your Majesty. I wish I could take all the credit, but I have to admit it wasn't me who found the seal." He aimed a smirk at Brigitta. "Thank you, Princess, for handing it to me personally."

Rupert flinched. She'd given the seal to Mador? His heart raced so fast, the room swirled around him. *No, no!* Brigitta was true to him. She loved him.

He trusted her.

She stumbled back, her face pale and stricken.

With a chuckle, Gunther caught her arm to steady her. "That's my girl. You pulled through for me. You're a Grian, after all."

A Grian. The words echoed in Rupert's head. *Gunther's sister. Garold's daughter. Dammit, no!* She couldn't have betrayed him. He'd trusted her.

"We'll head back to Lourdon Palace in the morning," Gunther announced. "And there, the wedding will take place. Oh, and the executions, too." He smiled at Brigitta. "Just like you wanted, my dear. I'll even throw in a little bonus. I know the top two contestants were supposed to survive, but I feel like changing the rules a bit."

"Guards!" Gunther yelled for the guards outside to enter, then he aimed a hateful look at Rupert. "You're going to die with the rest of the losers. Arrest him!"

Chapter Thirty-Four

❧

Rupert blew the guards back with enough force that they hit the poles supporting the tent. As the canvas overhead wavered, threatening to fall, he lunged for the tent entrance, then paused, glancing back at Brigitta.

While Gunther screamed about his tent, Brigitta gave him a frantic look and mouthed the word, *Go!*

Was she refusing to come with him?

In the second that he hesitated, Mador rushed toward him with a knife. Rupert leaped to the side, wrenched the knife from Mador's hand, then slammed a fist in his face. As Mador stumbled back, Rupert ran from the tent.

Had all been lost? Brigitta? The throne? Confusion and rage built up inside him as he raced for the pen of horses. Guards dashed toward him, intent on capturing him, but he blew them away. As more and more soldiers charged after him, his rage increased, along with his determination to survive.

They would not take him, dammit. His life would not end with an execution at the hands of his most hated enemy. He blasted the soldiers away, sending them flying through the air along with uprooted tents.

He wedged the knife under his belt, then jumped on a saddled horse. As he rode away, he ravaged the camp with hurricane-force winds. The campfires leaped from their pits, catching tents on fire. The sound of screams filled the valley. Soldiers struggled to escape the devastation, running for the shelter of the nearby forest.

Rupert reached the edge of the village, where people were gathering to gawk at the destruction of the king's encampment. He slowed to a stop, glancing back.

Brigitta. How could he leave her?

But he couldn't go back. Even she had told him to go. Was she trying to save him, or was she rejecting him?

She made her choice. She gave the seal to Mador.

No, dammit. She couldn't have rejected him. He'd given his heart to her. How could she have betrayed him?

With an angry shout, he spurred the horse onward, skirting the village to reach the road headed south. Stefan and the Eberoni soldiers loaned to him by King Leofric were camped about a mile away. A screech sounded overhead, and he spotted Brody in eagle form, zooming past him. *Good.* Brody could reach Stefan first and tell him to break camp.

It was a race now. Rupert had to reach Lourdon before any of Gunther's men. The other contestants, Four, Five, and Six, were imprisoned there, and with the competition over, Gunther intended to have them all killed. At Brigitta's wedding.

Dammit to hell. He couldn't let her marry Mador. *But she gave Mador the seal. And she'd asked her brother to hold the executions at her wedding.*

He shook his head. This was not the Brigitta he knew. Something was wrong. She couldn't have been fooling him all this time. Or could she?

Crap. He didn't know what to think. The only thing

he was certain of right now was that he had to rescue Four, Five, and Six. He'd given them his word.

He would not let them die.

When Brigitta emerged from Gunther's tent, she was shocked by the level of devastation around her. Smoke filled the air from tents and supplies that had burned. Other tents had been uprooted and now lay in jumbled heaps. Somehow, Rupert had destroyed the entire camp while leaving Gunther's tent bedraggled, but still standing. Had he done it on purpose to keep from harming her? She hoped so. Holy goddesses, she prayed he still believed in her.

But how had Mador ended up with the seal? She'd given it to Rupert, and yet somehow, it hadn't been Rupert. And now she feared he would believe the worst.

He would think that she had betrayed him. Pain ripped at her heart when she remembered how he had flinched. *Please, Rupert, please believe in me.*

"Guards!" Gunther yelled. "Go after Seven! I want him captured now!"

One of them inclined his head. "Your Majesty, all the horses have escaped the pen and run into the forest."

"Then get them, you fool!" Gunther smacked the guard on the head. "And bring that Seven back. I want to see the bastard hang."

"Yes, Your Majesty." The guard dashed off with a dozen more guards into the nearby forest.

"That's twice now my camp has been destroyed," Gunther growled. He turned to scan the village in the distance. "No harm came to them. Why does the wind keep striking us?"

"Seven is behind it," Mador declared.

"What?" Gunther gave him an incredulous look. "How can that bastard control the forces of nature?"

"I believe he is a Wind Sorcerer."

Gunther huffed. "I thought there was something evil about him. That damned foreigner."

Brigitta grew tense. She didn't want them figuring out that Seven was the infamous pirate Rupert.

"What are you doing standing around?" Gunther glared at Mador. "Capture Seven and get this mess cleaned up. We leave for Lourdon in the morning."

"Yes, Your Majesty." Mador strode away, yelling orders.

"And you." Gunther turned to Brigitta. "Pack your things. As soon as we arrive in Lourdon, we'll have the wedding." He stomped back into his tent.

With a heavy heart, Brigitta trudged toward the wreck that was once her tent. It seemed fitting, since everything in her life was now wrecked. Her future with Rupert. His takeover of the throne. Hopefully, he would make it back to Lourdon in time to rescue the imprisoned contestants.

But what would he do then? Would he abandon her, believing that she had betrayed him? Would she be forced to marry Captain Mador? She shuddered. How could she let Rupert know that she still loved him? How could she tell him that she'd found his little brother?

At least Bjornfrid was safe for now.

A few soldiers raised her tent so she was able to pack. Her heart ached with despair as she contemplated her bleak future. Her sisters were gone. Rupert was gone. So many times he'd told her *Don't leave me*, but it was he who had done the leaving.

She had to leave, too, she suddenly realized. The camp was a mess and soldiers were scurrying about paying her no mind, so this was the perfect time for her to steal away.

Marriage to Captain Mador? Never! She had to take charge of her own destiny.

With a deep breath, she filled herself with renewed

strength and determination. *You can do this!* She dressed in her warmest clothes and checked to make sure her knife was strapped to her thigh. It was a shame she didn't have any gold. She'd given it all to Sister Fallyn to help her take care of Bjornfrid. But if the horses were running loose, perhaps she could find one and ride south. It was a long way to Eberon, but if she could just reach Luciana, she would be safe. And from there, she could help Rupert win back the throne.

She slipped out of the tent and across the camp. The soldiers were so busy, none of them stopped her. Once she made it to the forest, she weaved through the trees, carefully avoiding the soldiers.

There! In a grassy clearing, a horse was munching on grass. It was even saddled. She sent a prayer of thanks to the moon goddesses as she slowly approached.

"Where are you going?" a voice spoke behind her.

She spun around. *Mador.* Why hadn't she recognized his voice? She eased back a step. She was closer to the horse than him. If she could just make it before—

"Did you think you could escape, Princess?" He snorted. "Does the idea of bedding me make you want to run away? Perhaps it would help if I looked like this." His features wavered, then solidified into another face.

Rupert.

She gasped. How could he . . . ? So this was how he had tricked her to get the seal. But how had he known that she had it?

He stepped closer. "Or perhaps I should look like this." His skin turned a leathery red, and horns jutted from his brow. His breath hissed through sharp and jagged teeth.

Terror slithered icy cold down her spine.

He changed back to Mador, then lunged forward to grab her before she could run away.

Her gift instantly ignited, detecting a hoard of secrets,

as many as Rupert had, but so deeply buried she could only see a dark mist surrounded by rage, hatred, and pain. "You're not Captain Mador." His voice was different, and there was an odd, silvery glint to his eyes.

"I can be anyone. If you cooperate, I'll give you the face you want. Defy me, and you will be plowed by a demon."

She cringed. "Who—what are you?"

"The future king of Tourin. And your future husband."

"I will never marry you."

"Would you rather die?" He slid a hand up to seize her by the neck. "I've killed so many, I've become quite good at it."

She swallowed hard. "You can't kill me. You need me to take the throne."

He smirked as his fingers stroked her neck. "You're a clever one. Beautiful, too. I've been watching you for over a week now. Can you guess what I discovered?" He leaned close till his breath feathered her cheek and sent a shudder down her spine. "An incredibly strong desire to fuck you."

She flinched.

His hand tightened around her neck. "You did this to me. I've never wanted a woman badly enough before to change my plans. I had intended to kill Gunther and take his place." His face shifted into a perfect replica of her brother's. "See how easy it would have been?

"But then I started wanting you, and that created a problem." He chuckled. "We can't have Gunther fucking his own sister now, can we? So I had to take Mador's place. He's a subservient idiot, but not for long. I'll become king, and you, my dear, will be my queen."

"Never." She struggled to break his hold on her. If only she could reach her knife! What else had Rupert taught her? She took a deep breath and quickly lifted her knee.

The false Mador jumped back, releasing her.

She ran for the horse, but was jerked back by her braided ponytail. She winced as he twisted her hair in his fist.

"Bitch." He pulled her back and whispered in her ear, "Go ahead and fight me. I'll enjoy winning and forcing myself on you."

She gritted her teeth against the pain. "Never."

"Oh, you will surrender. I know exactly how to make you behave." He raised his voice. "Guards!"

When two guards ran toward them, he handed her over.

"The princess attempted an escape," he said, his voice now sounding like Mador's. "Take her to her tent, and don't let her out."

"Yes, Captain." One of the guards seized her by an arm, and his companion took her by the other arm.

As they dragged her off, she glanced back and saw the false Mador jump on the saddled horse and ride away.

When the guards escorted her past Gunther's tent, she dug in her feet. "I need to see the king. Take me there."

"We have orders—"

"I'm still the princess, and I demand to see my brother!"

"Very well." The guards pushed her inside.

Gunther was seated at his desk, stamping a stack of papers with the royal seal, as if he were playing with a new toy. He glanced up at her. "Are you packed?"

"Yes." She approached the desk. As much as she hated appealing to her brother for help, he was the only one with enough power right now to stop the false Mador.

"So you used your special gift to find this seal?" He smiled as he stamped another paper. "I have to admit you come in handy. I might keep you around, even after you give me an heir."

"Thank you." She cleared her throat. "Brother dearest, I think there's something . . . wrong with Captain Mador."

Gunther snorted. "Just because you don't want to marry him—"

"He's dangerous. He can take the form of different people. He intends to kill you and take your—"

"Don't be ridiculous." Gunther waved a hand impatiently. "Mador has been by my side for nine years. There's no one I trust more than him."

"He's not Mador! He's a sorcerer who can shift into any human being."

Gunther rolled his eyes. "There's no such thing."

"I saw him shift. He even took on your form and admitted he intends to steal your throne. Please believe me, your life is in danger."

"Enough!" Gunther rose to his feet. "I don't care what you think of Mador. You're marrying him as soon as we arrive in Lourdon."

Her mind raced. If she couldn't get the wedding called off, perhaps she could postpone it long enough to escape. Or maybe, please, goddesses, maybe Rupert would come back for her. "I need some time to prepare for the wedding. I should have a new dress. And we should plan a ball—"

"No." Gunther glared at her with gritted teeth.

"I need at least two weeks."

"No, dammit!" He strode toward her. "You will do as I say."

Her heart pounded in her ears. She had one last card to play, and once she said it, there was no taking it back. "I'll need two weeks to make sure I'm not pregnant."

Gunther halted, his eyes wide with shock. Then he snorted. "You're lying."

She shook her head. "The night I was gone from camp, I took a man to my bed."

Gunther's face flushed a mottled red. "No, you couldn't have."

"I did. If I'm pregnant, you might already have an heir. But Mador would not be the father."

Gunther's eyes narrowed, and his breath came out with a hiss. "Who? Who took you?"

She lifted her chin. "Seven."

He pulled back a hand and slapped her hard.

She'd lost favor with the king, but she'd gained two weeks. Brigitta rubbed her cheek. The pain had been worth it, for her wedding was now officially delayed.

As she paced in her tent, she sent a prayer to the goddesses. Hopefully, two weeks would be enough. In that time, she would look for an opportunity to escape. And perhaps, in that time, Rupert would come for her.

So many times she'd asked him to trust her. *Please, Rupert, don't lose faith in me.*

After a while, food was delivered to her. Only bread and water. She wasn't sure if Gunther was punishing her, or if the camp was still too much in disarray to produce a better meal. She ate every bite to keep her strength up.

Without warning, the false Mador burst into her tent, grabbed her by the arm, and dragged her out. The guards outside couldn't object since Mador was their superior.

"Where are we going?" she demanded, since Mador was taking her across the camp, far away from her and Gunther's tent. "The wedding has been postponed. You can't—"

"You think I'm about to rape you?" He chuckled. "An appealing thought, but believe me, when the time comes, no force will be necessary." He stopped in front of a heavily guarded tent and lifted the flap. "Take a look."

She stepped inside and gasped. Sister Fallyn and Bjornfrid were seated on the tarp, their hands tied in front. Another rope tethered their ankles together.

Bjornfrid gave her a confused look. "Why did the

bad man take us? He hit Grandma and knocked her down."

Brigitta's heart sank as she knelt in front of them. "Is your grandmother all right? Were either of you hurt?"

"Dorina is fine," Sister Fallyn whispered. "We cooperated so Mador wouldn't hurt her. How are you? There's a bruise on your face."

"I'm fine." Tears gathered in Brigitta's eyes. "I'm so sorry. Nothing is happening the way we planned."

Sister Fallyn nodded, her eyes also glistening with moisture. "I'll pray for deliverance." She made the sign of the moons with her tied-up hands.

"What happened to my ball?" Bjornfrid asked.

Brigitta blinked away her tears. "The wrong person took it, but I'll set things right. Somehow. I promise."

"Filling them with false hope?" Mador asked as he pulled Brigitta from the tent.

She ripped her arm from his grasp and glared at him. "You're disgusting. You hit a defenseless old woman."

He snorted. "You should be grateful I didn't kill her. And speaking of killing . . ." He leaned close to whisper in her ear. "If I tell Gunther about the young prince in there, he'll have him executed on the spot. Shall I keep my mouth shut?" He stroked her cheek. "It's all up to you."

She turned her head away. "How did you know about him? How did you know I had the seal?"

"I know everything. And I won't hesitate to kill the prince and the nun if you don't cooperate. So give me the correct answer. Will you marry me?"

Her tears returned, burning her eyes. This was the wrong proposal from the wrong sorcerer. "The king has granted me a postponement of two weeks."

He grasped her chin and forced her to look at him. "Are you hoping that your precious Rupert will save you?"

She flinched. He knew about Rupert?

Mador smirked. "Did I surprise you? I already told you I know everything. I know who Rupert is. I also know that when he hears you're marrying me, he'll believe for certain that you have betrayed him."

She shook her head, but he gripped her face harder, his fingers digging into her bruised cheek.

"Face the facts," he growled. "You will be mine. Rupert will not come to save you."

Chapter Thirty-Five

❧

It took three days for Rupert to ride to Lourdon, but only three minutes to free the prisoners.

After arriving in Lourdon, Brody, Stefan and the Eberoni soldiers had spread out to learn where Four, Five, and Six were being held. To Rupert's surprise, they had never left the stadium. Apparently, Gunther had planned to stage the executions there in front of a large crowd, so he'd locked the three men up in a cell beneath the royal box.

It was just before dawn on the fourth day when Rupert approached the cell. The two guards on duty drew their swords, but he blew them hard, slamming them against a stone wall and knocking them out. Then he helped himself to the key ring, opened the door, and greeted the sleepy prisoners.

"Wake up!" He unlocked the shackles that kept them chained to the wall. "We need to go."

"Seven, is that you?" Five scrambled to his feet.

Six rubbed his eyes. "Am I dreaming?"

Four pulled the scholarly Six to his feet. "It's real. Seven kept his word. We're going to live!"

"Come on." Rupert motioned for them to follow. "We have a boat ready on the river."

"You mean we're leaving Tourin?" Five jogged to catch up with him. "You didn't win the competition?"

Rupert winced. He would not admit defeat. Brigitta was his. Tourin was his. "I'm not giving up."

They mounted the horses he'd left on the playing field, then rode to a nearby pier on the Loure River where Stefan and the others were waiting. The Eberoni soldiers had stocked the boat with food and drink, so as soon as the newly freed prisoners came on board they settled down at the makeshift table to eat.

Rupert remained on the pier. "Take the boat out to sea, so you can meet up with Ansel," he told Stefan. "I'm going back for Brigitta."

"No." Stefan quickly crossed the gangplank to join Rupert on the pier. "You can't go back. We have to move forward. Our first step should be defeating the Tourinian navy, and we can't do it without you."

Rupert dragged a hand through his hair. *Dammit.* How could he plan for a future if it didn't include Brigitta? Several days had passed, and he still couldn't figure out what the hell had happened. "What if she's in trouble? I can't leave her—"

"She left you!" Stefan insisted. "She gave the seal to Mador."

"It had to be a mistake!" Rupert yelled.

"She made her choice, dammit." Stefan gritted his teeth. "She's Gunther's sister."

Rupert's anger stirred the wind around them, causing the boat to rock and pull at the ropes that tethered it to the pier. He couldn't lose Brigitta. Dammit, he would not lose her.

"We need to get out of here before the soldiers come." Stefan grabbed Rupert's arm and dragged him on board.

With a groan, Rupert collapsed on a bench by the table. "It must have been a mistake." Brigitta would have never betrayed him.

"Raise the sails," Stefan ordered, then helped the Eberoni soldiers since they didn't know what they were doing.

Brody, who had been sitting on deck in eagle form, shifted into his human body.

"Holy Light!" Five jumped in his seat, while Four and Six choked on their food.

"Hi, guys." Brody walked over to the table. "What's for breakfast?"

With a snort, Stefan threw him a pair of breeches. "You'll make them lose their appetite."

"Then it'll be more food for me." Brody pulled on his breeches.

"Y-you're a bird?" Six asked.

"Sometimes," Brody replied as he poured himself a cup of wine. "While I was flying around, I did a lot of thinking, and it could be true that Brigitta made a mistake. Since the Chameleon is there, he might have tricked her."

Rupert sat up. "You think he impersonated me?"

"It's possible." Brody stuffed a hunk of ham into his mouth.

"Who is this Chameleon?" Five asked.

"He's a shape shifter who can take on any form," Brody explained as he buttered up a piece of bread. "I don't know what he actually looks like, but I can detect him by his smell."

"He's a murderer." Rupert rose to his feet. "Brigitta won't be safe around him. I should go back."

"No, you won't!" Stefan shouted. "You think I don't understand how upset you are? Fallyn is there, too! I'm worried sick. But we'll have a better chance at rescuing them once we have all the power. First we need to defeat the Tourinian navy and take over the country."

"What?" Five jumped to his feet, while Four and Six stared with dropped jaws.

"I think Stefan's right," Brody said with his mouth full. "We should take the throne first."

Five stepped closer. "You're taking over Tourin?"

Rupert glanced at the three former contestants. "I'll understand if you want no part of this. We can drop you ashore wherever you like."

"You saved our lives." Six stood, and Four joined him.

Five gave Rupert a speculative look. "What is the plan?"

"We join my fleet and defeat the navy. Then we attack from the west." Rupert turned to Brody. "I need you to fly over to King Leofric. Ask him to move his army to the border on the south. Then go to General Dravenko. He can send the Norveshki army to the eastern border and unleash the dragons."

"Got it." Brody dropped his breeches, shifted into an eagle, and flew away.

"Damn," Four whispered. "He's fast."

"A lot faster than us," Five muttered. "At this rate, it will take us all day to reach the sea."

"Not really." Rupert gathered up some air, then shoved it forward. The boat lurched, causing Four, Five, and Six to stumble.

"What the hell . . . ?" Five gazed around as the boat zoomed downriver, then he gave Rupert an incredulous look. "You're doing that? You're controlling the wind?"

Rupert nodded.

"You're a Wind Sorcerer?" Six asked.

Rupert shrugged. "Some call me that."

"How many ships do you have?" Five asked.

"Ten."

Five's eyes lit up. "Then you really can defeat the navy."

Rupert smiled. "I've been defeating them for years. Half of my fleet are former naval ships."

Four eyed him suspiciously. "You're not a farmer, are you? You're not even from Eberon."

Five crossed his arms over his chest. "You're Rupert, aren't you?"

Six gasped. "The infamous pirate?"

Five nodded. "He's the only one on Aerthlan who can control the wind."

Rupert moved his hands again to keep the wind filling the sails. "Yes, I'm a pirate. If you don't want to be associated with me, I can put you ashore."

Five snorted. "You've been harassing Gunther for years. Why?"

Rupert shrugged. "He's an ass."

"Everyone knows that." Five stepped closer. "Who are you really? Why do you want Gunther's throne?"

Rupert gritted his teeth. "Gunther's father killed my father. His family has taken what is mine."

Five drew in a sharp breath. "The lost prince."

"What?" Six stared at Rupert.

"I am Ulfrid Trepurin, the rightful—" Rupert paused when Five dropped to one knee. "You believe me? I have no proof."

Five smiled as he straightened. "My grandfather was chieftain of the Trevelyan clan, and he told me a secret before he died. Only a few of the king's closest friends knew that his oldest son was actually Embraced and gifted with a magical power. That would be your ability to harness the wind, right?"

Rupert nodded. "True."

"When my grandfather was dying," Five continued,

"King Manfrid came to see him. It was over twenty years ago, but it was my first time to see a king, so I have always remembered it. The proof is in your face, Ulfrid Trepurin. You have your father's eyes."

Rupert swallowed hard. "You saw my father?"

Five nodded. "Yes, Your Majesty." His eyes gleamed with excitement. "I'll take you up on your offer to be set ashore. If you can drop me off in the north, close to the Trey River, I will rally the clans. In four days, we'll have an army of three thousand marching south."

Rupert gripped Five by the shoulder. "You didn't forget? You remained loyal?"

"Yes, Your Majesty. We've been waiting for you."

With a laugh, Rupert clapped Five on the back. "I knew you were more than an inventor."

Five grinned. "I knew you were more than a farmer."

"What can I do to help?" Four asked.

"I have an idea," Six said and quickly explained.

"I like it." Rupert increased the wind as the boat reached the mouth of the Loure River. Soon, they would be meeting up with Ansel.

And soon the country of Tourin would be in chaos.

It took five long days for Brigitta to return to Lourdon Palace, for Gunther's caravan moved slowly with its fully packed carts. For the entire time, Brigitta was heavily guarded and isolated, either alone in the carriage or alone in her tent. Whenever she was transferred from one place to the other, she scanned the area, searching for Bjornfrid and Sister Fallyn.

There was a guarded carriage traveling at the end of the caravan, and she suspected that was where Mador was hiding them. She also suspected he had a number of guards who were more loyal to him than her brother, for they were clearly keeping Bjornfrid's existence a secret. But then, she figured it was possible that they didn't know the identity of the young man they were guarding.

While she was alone, she had too much time to think and worry. Would Rupert believe she had betrayed him? How could she convince her brother that a sorcerer was pretending to be Mador? Would she be forced to marry the sorcerer in order to keep Rupert's brother alive? She considered telling everything to Gunther, but she feared he would have Bjornfrid executed. No matter what, she had to keep Bjornfrid and Sister Fallyn safe. And pray that Rupert would come back for her.

When they arrived at Lourdon Palace, Gunther escorted her into the Great Hall.

"Your Majesty." Lord Argus bowed low. "Praise the Light that you have safely returned. Did the competition finish as you had hoped? Were Captain Mador and General Tarvis the winners?"

Gunther grimaced as he sat on his throne. "Mador won. Tarvis was burned to death by one of those damned dragons."

"Oh." Argus blanched. "Oh, dear. Then Seven came in second place?"

"No," Gunther growled. "He's a loser just like the others. Once we capture the bastard, he'll die with the rest of them."

Argus's eyes widened. "You mean Seven has escaped?"

"Mador and his men will catch him soon." Gunther gave Brigitta a wry look. "Then our princess will marry Mador and watch her precious Seven hang."

Never, Brigitta thought. She might be forced to marry against her will, but they would never be able to capture Rupert.

"Excellent, Your Majesty." Argus inclined his head. "Shall I begin preparations for the wedding?"

"Yes." Gunther glowered at Brigitta. "She has nine more days."

Argus nodded. "Yes, Your Majesty." He cleared his throat. "It is unfortunate that we have lost our head general and admiral. It could leave us vulnerable if the country is attacked—"

"Not a problem." Gunther waved a dismissive hand. "Mador will be my new general. Promote Lieutenant Helgar to admiral."

Brigitta recalled meeting the lieutenant who hated Rupert with a passion. If Rupert attacked the navy, he'd be fighting the lieutenant once again.

"An excellent choice, Your Majesty." Argus bowed low.

Gunther snorted. "You're fawning more than usual. Did something happen while we were gone?"

With a wince, Argus straightened. "Well, there are a few things."

"Out with it," Gunther growled.

"An envoy from the Eberoni king has delivered the body you requested. The infamous pirate Rupert."

Brigitta stiffened, and Gunther shot her a curious look. "Bring the body here, Argus, so my sister can confirm it is truly Rupert."

"Yes, Your Majesty." Argus motioned to some guards, and they hurried from the room.

Brigitta swallowed hard. What body had Leo and Luciana sent? Should she lie or not?

"Anything else?" Gunther asked.

Argus clenched his hands together. "It's about the prisoners, the three losers from the competition."

Gunther narrowed his eyes. "What about them?"

Argus stepped back, wincing. "They escaped."

"*What?*" Gunther jumped to his feet.

Yes! Brigitta bit her lip to keep from grinning.

Argus fell to his knees. "It was terrible, Your Majesty. The guards were knocked out by a powerful sorcerer. They had no defense against his magic."

"Ridiculous!" Gunther shouted. "Have those guards whipped! And find the prisoners!"

Argus cringed. "We've been searching for them, but they're nowhere to be found. We—we believe they may have escaped by boat."

"Dammit!" Gunther knocked over a nearby golden candlestick holder, then glared at Brigitta. "Seven was behind this, wasn't he?"

Brigitta lifted her chin. "You'll never capture him."

"Damn you!" Gunther raised a fist.

Guards marched in, carrying a stretcher with a body covered by a sheet. Brigitta looked away, covering her nose as the stench of death permeated the room.

"Shit." Gunther grabbed Brigitta by the arm and dragged her toward the stretcher. "Be quick about it. Is this the pirate who kidnapped you? Is it Rupert?"

"I wouldn't know." Brigitta kept her head turned away. "He always wore a mask."

"Look!" Gunther shouted, and she ventured a quick look as a soldier folded back the sheet.

Kennet! She gasped, then quickly looked away.

Gunther's eyes narrowed. "You recognized him."

She covered her mouth as bile rose in her throat. Kennet must have been captured by the Eberoni army after he'd gone ashore. Then he'd been executed with the other pirates.

"Take the body away and burn it," Gunther ordered, and the soldiers carried the stretcher away. He turned toward Brigitta. "Was that Rupert? Be honest with me, girl."

She wished she could be completely honest with her brother. If only he were an honorable man. "That man was a pirate. But he wasn't Rupert. You'll never be able to capture Rupert."

Gunther gritted his teeth. "Damn you."

"I'm being honest!" She touched her brother's shoulder. "Please, believe me. A sorcerer is pretending to be Mador. He's dangerous."

"Oh, really?" Mador said softly as he entered the room. "Such a sad way for my betrothed to talk about me."

Brigitta shuddered.

"Don't worry," Gunther muttered. "She's just trying to weasel out of the wedding."

Mador arched an eyebrow. "That's not really possible, is it, Princess? You know what will happen if you defy me."

She swallowed hard. If she didn't agree to the wedding, Mador would kill Sister Fallyn and Bjornfrid. If she confided in her brother, he would also kill Bjornfrid. There was only one way to save Rupert's brother.

Tears burned her eyes. "I'll marry you."

Five days later, Rupert scanned the Tourinian coastline with a great sense of satisfaction. He'd blown eleven naval ships onto the rocks, utterly destroying them. The last ship, the flagship, had finally surrendered. He'd sent Ansel and his entire crew over to claim victory in the name of the rightful king, Ulfrid Trepurin.

Most of the Tourinian navy had managed to get safely ashore. Rupert had shot multiple arrows onto the beach with messages tied to them. Any seamen who wanted to pledge loyalty to King Ulfrid's navy would be accepted and paid their wages in gold. Many had accepted. The others had run away, not willing to fight for either the new king or the old one.

Admiral Helgar had been released so he could take a message to Gunther in Lourdon. The lost prince, Ulfrid Trepurin, was coming for the throne.

The news should be spreading across all of Tourin now. Six had described his idea as a method designed to win the hearts of the people. Four days ago, Six had secretly returned to his father's estate in central Tourin, while Four had been dropped off on his estate in northern Eberon. There, the two men would gather everyone who could write, so they could produce hundreds of notices. Then their servants would travel about, posting the notices in villages and spreading around the gold that Rupert had given them for the project. Four's servants would target villages in southern Tourin, just across the border, while Six would blanket the central part of Tourin.

"You did it," Stefan said as he joined Rupert on the quarterdeck. "The Tourinian navy is ours."

Rupert nodded. "I'm going to name Ansel as my admiral. And you, old friend, how do you feel about returning to the army? As my general."

Stefan snorted. "I think I know who should be second in command."

Rupert smiled. "Five?"

Stefan nodded. "The northern clans remained loyal."

"Yes, thank the Light." Rupert would always be grateful, but he knew, for the future of Tourin, he couldn't be just a northern king. He needed to unite the entire country. "I think Six would make an excellent chief counsel. And even though Four is an Eberoni, I would like to implement his ideas for farming. I don't want any of my people to live in hunger."

Stefan chuckled. "It looks like the losers from the competition are actually the winners."

"They're good men." Rupert snorted. "I need to learn their actual names."

"Is it true, Admiral?" Jeffrey ran up to him, his eyes wide. "Are you really going to be king?"

Rupert tousled the boy's hair. "That's the plan."

"Whoa," the boy breathed. "You're going to wear a crown and sit on a throne?"

Rupert smiled. "I don't plan on doing a lot of sitting."

Jeffrey bit his lip. "What will happen to me?"

"What do you want to happen?" Stefan asked. "You can assist me with the army, or you can stay on board and help Ansel with the navy."

"Oh." Jeffrey scratched his head. "I still want to be a sea captain."

"Then you will work for Ansel," Stefan told him.

"All right." Jeffrey gave them both a sad look. "I'll miss you, though."

Rupert patted the boy on the shoulder. "I'll see you whenever I need to travel by sea."

Jeffrey smiled, then pointed up at the sky. "Look! The pelican is back."

Rupert headed down the stairs to the main deck just as the pelican landed. "Brody?"

With a squawk, the bird hopped through the door to go belowdecks. Rupert hurried down to his old cabin, and Brody joined him there in human form.

"You have news?" Rupert asked as he tossed him a pair of breeches.

"Hungry?" Stefan walked in with a tray of food.

"Oh, good." Brody stuffed a piece of roast beef in his mouth, then put on the breeches. "I've been flying for days. I'm starving."

"What's going on?" Rupert asked.

"Good news." Brody poured himself some wine. "The Trevelyan clan has rallied the north and they're marching south toward Lourdon. On the eastern border, the Norveshki warriors are raiding villages and their dragons are terrorizing the people. They haven't actually hurt anyone, but they've got everyone scared to death."

Rupert winced. "And to the south?"

Brody downed his cup, then continued, "King Leofric has amassed an army on the border. He's claiming kinship to Brigitta and says they will attack if she's not delivered to them in three days. Meanwhile, the notices are being spread across the land, claiming you as the new king."

Stefan smiled. "Excellent."

Brody nodded as he bit off a chunk of bread. "I see you took care of the navy."

"Yes." Rupert refilled Brody's cup. "Do you know what's happening in Lourdon?"

Brody winced. "Gunther's skulking in the palace. Mador has been named the new general, and he dispatched a few troops to the north and east."

"But he didn't go with them?" Rupert asked.

"Not yet." Brody shook his head. "I couldn't get close enough to catch the Chameleon's scent. He's somewhere in the palace, but I don't know who he's pretending to be."

Rupert grew tense. "And Brigitta?"

Brody looked away, frowning.

"What is it?" Rupert demanded.

Brody grimaced. "She's getting married to Mador four days from now."

Rupert flinched. "No. No, she would never agree—"

"I heard she did," Brody muttered.

"No!" Rupert shouted. "She's being forced." He fisted his hands. "I have to get there before the wedding."

"You can't march into Lourdon yet," Stefan protested. "Mador is there with most of the army."

"I will blow them all away!" Rupert gritted his teeth. "If Brigitta wants a wedding, she can have one. But her groom will be me."

Chapter Thirty-Six

❦

THREE DAYS LATER . . .

Tomorrow morning she would be wed.

To the wrong man. The words echoed in Brigitta's mind as the seamstresses made the final adjustments to her wedding dress.

"I can't do this," she whispered.

Norah looked up from where she was pinning the hem. "Don't worry, Your Highness. Every bride gets nervous before the wedding."

"Do they get nauseated?" Panic bubbled up inside Brigitta's chest. "Do they feel like throwing themselves off the balcony?"

Norah and Marthe exchanged worried glances.

"Captain Ma—I mean, General Mador is a fine catch," Marthe murmured.

"Is he even human?" Brigitta cried. Dear goddesses, she had thought she could do this. She loved Rupert so much, she'd thought she could sacrifice herself to save his innocent younger brother.

Wrong man. Wrong man. "I can't do it! I won't!" She picked up her skirt and ran for the door.

The guards moved to stop her, but she knocked them

aside. "I'm going to see the king! If you touch me, I'll tell my brother that you molested me."

The guards gulped and stepped back.

"Where is His Majesty?" she asked them.

"The Great Hall," one of the guards mumbled.

She ran down the hallway and into the grand foyer, then up the steps to the Great Hall. The afternoon sun gleamed through the long windows, making the numerous mirrors sparkle as they reflected the gilt-covered walls and ceiling. Gold everywhere, from the countless wall sconces to the golden throne on the dais.

This was where the wedding would take place. Five-foot-tall golden vases held huge arrangements of white roses and gold-plated ferns.

"More flowers!" Gunther demanded, and the servants scurried from the room. He spotted Brigitta in the doorway and motioned to her. "Come in. We can practice our grand entrance."

She rushed toward him. "I need to talk to you—"

"I like the gown." He lowered his voice. "Do you know if you're pregnant yet?"

"No." She shook her head. "Please, don't make me go through with the wedding tomorrow."

Anger flashed in his eyes. "You agreed."

"I was forced! Do you remember the nun who came with me? Sister Fallyn? Mador is holding her hostage. He threatened to kill her if I don't marry him."

Gunther gave her an annoyed look. "Then marry him."

"You would have me marry a man who could kill a nun?"

Gunther shrugged. "He knows how to get the results he wants. That's an admirable trait."

Brigitta groaned with frustration. "He's not even Mador. He's an imposter who—"

"Enough! I'm sick of hearing that ridiculous excuse."

"Your Majesty!" Lord Argus ran into the Great Hall, then stopped with a grimace. "I-I have bad—"

"Out with it!" Gunther yelled.

Lord Argus inclined his head. "The people of Lourdon are in the streets, demanding that you . . . abdicate."

"*What?*" Gunther stalked toward his chief counsel. "Where would they get such a stupid idea?"

"It's because of these notices, Your Majesty." Lord Argus lifted a sheet of paper. "They're being spread all over Lourdon and in every village across the coun—"

"Let me see." Gunther ripped the paper from Lord Argus's hand. His face grew pale as he read it. "Is—is this true?"

Lord Argus winced. "I don't know, Your Majesty."

Gunther's hand shook. "It can't be true!" He turned toward Brigitta, his face flushing a mottled red. "Did you know about this? Have you been conspiring with him?"

"I don't know what that is," she replied.

Gunther shoved the paper in her face and shouted, "*Did you know?*"

She quickly read the notice.

Seven is the true hero of the competition for the princess Brigitta.

Seven is Rupert, who stole Gunther's gold so he can return it to you, the people.

Seven is the lost Prince Ulfrid, who will rescue you from Gunther's tyranny and bring you peace and prosperity.

Gunther crumpled the paper in his fist and threw it across the room. "Is it true? Seven is Rupert and the lost prince?"

Brigitta nodded. "It's true."

Gunther raised his fists in the air with a growl of frustration. "You conspired with the enemy!"

"*We* are the enemy," Brigitta said. "Our family murdered his and stole the crown. It belongs to him."

"No!" Gunther grabbed her by the shoulders and shook her. "You fool! The crown belongs to the one with enough balls to take it."

"Your Majesty!" A soldier ran into the room. "Admiral Helgar has just arrived. Th-the royal navy has been destroyed and taken over by the pirate Rupert."

Gunther flinched.

"Then I guess the crown will be his," Brigitta whispered. "'Cause he certainly has the balls to take it."

"No!" Gunther shouted.

"Let me marry him," Brigitta insisted. "It will unite the north and south. The kings will come from the House of Trepurin and the House of Grian. Your bloodline will continue to rule."

"The Trepurins are the enemy!" Gunther stormed across the room toward the dais. "Get General Mador in here. Now!"

"Yes, Your Majesty." Lord Argus dispatched a guard to fetch the new general.

"The Trepurins ruled this country for four hundred years," Brigitta said.

"Stop it!" Gunther hissed at her. "You're a traitor."

"I simply want to return our country to the rightful king. Rupert will take good care of our people. You can't trust Mador to do that. We don't even know who he is!"

Another soldier arrived and whispered to Lord Argus. The chief counsel stumbled back, his hand trembling as he reached for a wall to steady himself.

"What is it?" Gunther demanded.

"Our troops that went north have been defeated by the rebels. The northern clans are marching toward Lourdon.

The Norveshki dragons have burned three villages to the east. And to the south, King Leofric and the Eberoni army have crossed the Norva River."

Gunther turned pale as he stumbled onto the dais. "Attacked from all sides." He collapsed onto the throne.

Brigitta's heart pounded with hope. Rupert was on his way. She wouldn't have to marry Mador, for he would be too busy fighting. And Rupert could finally take the throne. Then he could be reunited with his brother, and she . . . she would tell him how much she loved him.

Gunther lifted his hands to touch the golden crown on his head. "It's mine." His gaze drifted to other people in the room. "It's mine, dammit!"

"Yes, Your Majesty." Lord Argus bowed.

General Mador strode into the Great Hall.

Gunther jumped to his feet. "Call out the troops! Tourin is under attack!"

Mador arched a brow, then motioned to the guards. "Tell the troops we march within the hour. Argus, step outside." They all bowed and rushed from the room.

"You have to leave, too!" Gunther shouted. "You have to save my crown!"

Mador sauntered toward the king. "Why should I risk my life for a crown that belongs to you?"

Gunther blinked. "What?"

"The crown." Mador's eyes hardened. "Give it to me, and I'll save it."

"You—" Gunther's face turned red with rage as he stepped off the dais and strode toward Mador. "How dare you speak to me like that! I'll have you arrested!"

"By whom?" Mador smirked. "All the guards are gone."

"Get out there and fight!" Gunther yelled. "That's an order."

"What's the hurry?" Mador crossed his arms. "All I

have to do is wait for the lost prince to show up. Then I shift into one of his trusted friends and slit his throat."

Brigitta gasped.

Gunther stiffened. "*Shift?*"

With a chuckle, Mador motioned to Brigitta. "She's been trying to warn you, but you wouldn't listen. Anyway, once Prince Ulfrid is dead, all the armies and rebels will give up and go away. The crown will be safe once more."

Brigitta stepped close to her brother. "Don't trust him. He'll kill you."

Mador shot her an annoyed look. "Stop interfering. I'm making a deal here."

Gunther eyed him warily. "Y-you can kill the lost prince for me?"

Mador nodded. "Definitely. But I have two conditions. First, before Ulfrid can arrive, I will marry the princess."

"No," Brigitta objected.

Mador's eyes narrowed. "Time for you to surrender, Princess. You know what will happen if you defy me."

"You can have her," Gunther said. "What else?"

With a huff, she turned toward her brother. "Are you crazy? He's a monster. You can't trust him."

Mador chuckled. "You will name me as your heir."

Gunther hesitated.

"You think you can stop me?" Mador turned toward the doorway as his face shifted into Gunther's. "Argus!"

"Yes, Your Majesty?" Lord Argus peered inside.

Mador had moved in front of the king to block Argus's view. "Make it official. General Mador is my heir."

"Yes, Your Majesty." Lord Argus bowed.

"And Argus," Mador continued as he impersonated the king. "Send for the priest and some witnesses. We're going to have the wedding right away."

"Yes, Your Majesty." Lord Argus scurried away.

The false Mador chuckled, his face turning back to resemble the general. "See how easy it is?"

Brigitta's heart sank.

Gunther stepped back. "Who are you?"

"Your most trusted servant." The false Mador smiled. "Until I decide it's time to inherit the throne."

Gunther exchanged a look with Brigitta. She realized he finally understood the situation. The false Mador intended to kill him.

"What did you do with the real Mador?" Gunther asked.

The shifter shrugged. "I was waiting for him when he crossed the border from Norveshka. The fool was so distraught he told me everything that had happened. Then I killed him and threw his body into a ravine."

"Bastard," Gunther whispered.

The false Mador smirked. "Then I turned into an eagle to wait for Seven to cross the border. But to my surprise, he was with the princess."

An eagle? Brigitta thought back to when she'd found Bjornfrid and the royal seal. There had been an eagle in the tree. That's how the shifter had known.

The false Mador's mouth twisted as he studied Brigitta. "That's when I knew you were conspiring with Seven." His hands fisted. "And I knew I would kill him and take you for myself."

An elderly priest arrived with several courtiers. "Are we rehearsing for the wedding ceremony tomorrow?"

"No," Mador growled. "The real wedding is happening now."

Trumpets sounded outside, and Lord Argus ran into the Great Hall. "A huge number of boats are moving incredibly fast up the Loure River. They're almost here!"

Rupert was on his way. Brigitta's heart raced. She only had to stall until he could arrive.

Mador seized her by the arm. "Great timing. I'll marry you, then kill Seven." She pulled away, but he grabbed her again. "Priest! Get started."

"Very well." The elderly priest hobbled slowly toward the dais.

"Quickly!" Mador shouted.

Gunther grabbed hold of the priest's arm. "It's all right, Father Bran. Take your time."

"No, make it quick," Mador argued.

Father Bran looked from the king to the general, then slowly stepped onto the dais and turned to face them. "Blessed be the Light and all who worship him. May he shine upon you—"

"Get on with it," Mador ordered.

"As you wish." The priest gave him a sour look. "Marriage is the sacred joining of two souls, so they can love and nurture each other throughout the years—"

"I need her to legitimize my claim to the throne," Mador said, keeping his grip on Brigitta's arm. "And I want her in my bed. Tonight."

Father Bran cleared his throat. "There is that, too."

Trumpets blasted outside once again, and the courtiers whispered excitedly to one another.

A soldier ran into the Great Hall. "Seven is coming! The townspeople welcomed him and escorted him to the palace. He blew away all the guards—"

"Hurry!" Mador yelled at the priest.

"No!" Brigitta struggled to escape his grip. "I don't want to marry him."

Father Bran frowned. "There seems to be a slight problem with the bride."

"She'll get over it," Mador growled.

"I'll throw myself off a balcony before I marry you!" Brigitta cried.

The priest shook his head. "Suicide is frowned upon by the church, my dear."

"Is a forced marriage all right?" Brigitta asked, stalling for time.

Mador pulled a knife and pointed it at her neck. "Say we're married, priest, so I can hunt down her lover and kill him."

Father Bran blinked. "She has a lover?"

"Yes, she does," Rupert announced as he marched into the room. He flung his arms open, and a blast of wind shot through the Great Hall, knocking everyone over and shattering all the windows and mirrors with a deafening explosion.

The courtiers screamed and huddled on the floor.

Brigitta scrambled away from the shifter. Rupert ran toward her, but before he could reach her, Mador seized her from behind and pointed his knife at her throat.

Rupert skidded to a halt. Stefan and Brody were behind him with a troop of armed seamen.

"Let her go," Rupert warned Mador.

"He's the Chameleon," Brody said, drawing closer.

"You, again," Mador growled.

"You won't escape me this time." Brody tore off his shirt and shifted into a dog, kicking away his breeches.

The courtiers screeched.

Brigitta stomped hard on the Chameleon's foot while she grabbed his fingers and yanked them back. The Chameleon hissed in pain, loosening his grip enough that she could pull away.

"Dammit, I'll kill you." He made a grab for her.

"No!" Gunther jumped on the shifter, and the two men rolled about on the floor until the Chameleon reared up and stabbed Gunther in the chest. He stood, dropping the bloody knife onto the marble floor.

The courtiers screamed.

Rupert and his men ran toward the Chameleon.

"Damn you!" The Chameleon ripped off his shirt as he ran for a window. He shifted into an eagle and soared through the opening.

Brody shifted into an eagle and flew after him.

"Dammit!" Rupert yelled.

Brigitta fell to her knees beside her brother. He was trembling, his face pale and sweating. Blood seeped from his wound, coloring his golden tunic red.

"Gunther." Brigitta placed her hands over his wound to try to stop the blood.

He hissed in a breath. "You were right. I should have trusted you."

"Don't talk. Save your strength."

He grimaced. "I think I'm going to die."

"No, you won't! I won't let you." Brigitta's eyes filled with tears. "You saved me."

Gunther snorted. "Well, I had to, didn't I? You're my sister. And my heir." He looked around. "Argus, did you hear that? She's my heir!"

"Yes, Your Majesty." Lord Argus fell to his knees, sniffling.

"What are you doing, man?" Rupert said. "Get a physician here fast!"

"Oh." Argus scrambled to his feet. "Yes, of course." He scurried away, yelling orders.

Rupert removed his cape and folded it up. Then he knelt on the other side of Gunther. "Here, let me."

Brigitta removed her hands and let Rupert press the folded wool against Gunther's wound.

"Damn you, Seven," Gunther grumbled. "Why are you acting like you want to save me? You'll just have to kill me later when you take the throne."

"You were wounded saving Brigitta." He glanced at her and his eyes softened. "I can't kill my wife's brother."

A tear rolled down her cheek. "We're not married yet."

"We will be."

She smiled. "Is that a proposal?"

"No, this is. Will you marry me, Brigitta, and be my queen?"

She nodded as more tears flowed. "I love you, Rupert. I'm so sorry that I was fooled by the shifter. He looked just like you, and I—"

"I figured something like that happened." He leaned toward her. "Don't cry. I knew you could never betray me."

She sniffed. "You believed in me. You trusted me. Thank you."

"I think I'm going to puke," Gunther muttered.

"Oh." Brigitta wiped her bloody hands on her skirt. "Should I find a bowl for you?"

Gunther snorted, then coughed up some blood.

Brigitta used her skirt to wipe the blood from his mouth. "Stay with me, brother dearest."

He gave her pained smile. "I know I've been an ass. When Father sent me off as a hostage, I felt so helpless. That's when I decided I would do whatever it took to get all the power. I thought it was the only way to be safe. But it only left me all alone."

"Save your strength," Brigitta urged him.

He coughed again. "I know I'm going to die." He turned his head toward Rupert. "She's my dearest sister, you bastard. You had better be a good husband to her."

"I will, Your Majesty."

Gunther winced. "And you had better be a good king."

Brigitta gasped and glanced at Rupert's surprised expression.

Rupert bowed his head. "I will do my best, Your Majesty."

Gunther snorted, then reached a trembling hand to the crown on his head. "Take it, you bastard."

Rupert wiped the blood from his hands, then accepted the crown. "This was my father's."

"Hurry up. Put it on and get married," Gunther grumbled. "I want to see the future of my kingdom."

Rupert stood and placed the crown on his head.

Stefan and the seamen cheered.

Lord Argus knelt beside the king to put pressure on the wound. "Don't worry, Your Majesty. The physician is on his way."

Rupert led Brigitta toward the dais.

"My lady." Stefan approached her. "Where is Fallyn? She should be here."

"Oh." Sister Fallyn and Bjornfrid! "Mador was keeping her prisoner in order to force me to marry him. She should be somewhere close to his rooms."

Stefan nodded. "I'll find her." He took half the seamen, and they dashed from the room.

Brigitta smiled, knowing that soon Rupert would be reunited with his brother.

Rupert squeezed her hand. "Let's get married."

She nodded. She was getting married. To the right man. Her pirate and Wind Sorcerer.

Father Bran looked them over. "So you two want to get married?"

"Yes," they both replied, then smiled at each other.

"In the name of the Holy Light, I pronounce you husband and wife," Father Bran said.

Brigitta's smile faded. "That was it?"

The priest gave her a sad look. "We didn't have much time." He glanced over at Gunther.

Brigitta turned. One look at her brother's glassy eyes, and she knew he was gone.

"I'm sorry," Rupert said. "We'll give him a funeral befitting a king."

Lord Argus rose to his feet. "The king is dead. Long live the king!"

Brigitta exchanged a look with Rupert. He'd done it. He'd taken the throne, but he hadn't sought vengeance against her brother. Her husband was an honorable man.

The courtiers bowed and curtsied, while the remaining seamen cheered. Brigitta started a curtsy, but Rupert pulled her into his arms.

"Come here." He kissed her, then whispered in her ear. "I have some business to take care of, but I'll see you this evening in your bedchamber."

"Our bedchamber."

He smiled. "I'm going to like being married."

"Brigitta!" Sister Fallyn rushed into the Great Hall.

Brigitta met her halfway across the room and hugged her. Then she saw Stefan with tears in his eyes as he led Bjornfrid through the door.

Bjornfrid looked around curiously. "What happened to the windows?"

"Freddy." Brigitta extended a hand to him. "There's someone I want you to meet."

"Brigitta, are you crying, too? Why is everyone sad?"

"Freddy." She led him toward Rupert, who was watching with a wary look on his face. "This is your older brother."

Freddy blinked at him. "Ulfie? You're all grown up."

Rupert drew in a sharp breath. "Bjornie?"

Freddy grinned. "Ulfie!"

Rupert ran toward him and pulled him tight into his arms. "Bjornfrid, I thought you were dead."

"No, I'm fine." Freddy grinned at him. "Do you want to play?"

Rupert's eyes narrowed, and a pang struck Brigitta's heart. Poor Rupert was realizing that his brother had never grown up.

Brigitta touched Freddy's arm. "We'll send for your grandmother, so she can live with us here."

Freddy nodded with an excited grin. "That's good. I miss Grandma."

"You found my brother?" Rupert asked her.

She nodded. "I told you I'm good at finding things."

He pulled her into another embrace. "You found my heart, all shriveled up with hate and the need for revenge. And you filled it with love and joy."

She touched his cheek. "I found the tall and handsome stranger I've always dreamed about."

"Ew." Freddy frowned at them. "You're not going to kiss, are you?"

Rupert smiled at her and winked. "Later."

Later was four hours, but Rupert had wanted to make sure everything was settled and peaceful before seeking out his wife. Stefan had taken charge of the army, and every soldier in Lourdon had personally sworn allegiance to the new king.

Arrangements had been made for Gunther's funeral the next day. Lord Argus had agreed to retire once Six arrived to take over his duties. And Brody had returned an hour ago, angry that the Chameleon had managed to get away by flying into a forest and becoming some kind of animal. When Brody had followed, there had been no trace of him.

Rupert found his way to Brigitta's bedchamber, remembering how the last time he'd come there, he'd had to climb a drainpipe and leap across a few balconies. The huge bed was still there, but no Brigitta.

He found her in the dressing room, soaking in a large tub. "There you are."

"Oh." Brigitta blushed as she attempted to cover her breasts.

He smiled. She was doing a poor job of concealing herself. "Are you coming out? Or shall I join you?"

With a giggle, the maid ran from the room.

Brigitta motioned to a tray on a nearby table. "Have you eaten? I had some food brought up for you."

He leaned over to kiss her cheek, then nipped at her ear. "I'll have a nibble."

She gave him a wry look. "Please do."

With a smile, he unbuttoned his shirt. Through the soapy water he could see her long legs and more. He pulled off his shirt and dropped it on the floor. "Are you coming out?"

She lounged back, smiling at him. "I'm enjoying the view."

He unbuttoned his breeches. "I never want to be separated from you again. I missed you every minute we were apart. And every five minutes, I wanted to go back and grab you and never let you go."

Her eyes glimmered with tears. "I missed you, too. I kept hoping and praying that you would come."

He dropped his breeches and stepped into the tub. "Move over."

"Rupert!" She gasped as he settled in, pulling her on top of him and splashing water onto the floor. "What are you doing?" She swatted at his chest. "This tub isn't big enough for two."

"That will be my next invention. A bigger tub."

She snorted. "And a bigger mop for the mess."

He slipped his hand around her neck and leaned in for a long and leisurely kiss. Her hands smoothed around his shoulders, then up into his hair. Their legs entwined in the soapy water.

"Brigitta." He kissed a path down her neck as his hand caressed her breast. "I missed you."

"I missed you, too." She touched his face. "I suppose I should call you Ulfrid, but to me, you will always be Rupert. The Wind Sorcerer and infamous pirate who stole my heart."

He smiled as he played with her nipple, rubbing the hardened tip between his fingers. "I hope you're well rested. Because I intend to keep you up all night."

"Really?" She smoothed a hand down his belly, then circled her fingers around his swollen cock.

He hissed in a breath. "What are you doing?"

She smiled. "Sweetheart, don't you know when you're being ravished?"

Epilogue

❧

THREE MONTHS LATER . . .

"So ye married a sorcerer," Sorcha said in their island dialect, her eyes twinkling with humor.

"Rupert is Embraced, like us," Brigitta explained to her sisters as they all sat around a small table. "He can control the wind, that's all."

"That's all?" Gwennore gave her a wry look. "I would say that was plenty."

Luciana's mouth twitched. "Just be careful if he blows in your ear."

"Aye." Maeve nodded. "He might blow ye all the way to Norveshka!"

They all laughed.

"I missed you so much," Brigitta told them.

Her sisters had traveled by boat up the Loure River to see her and King Ulfrid's official coronation at Lourdon Palace. Now they were all resting in her sitting room while Luciana's twins took a nap in the adjoining bedchamber.

"Ye must stay for at least a week," Brigitta said. "Ye won't believe what's going to happen."

Sorcha leaned forward. "What?"

Brigitta grinned. "Sister Fallyn, or I should say Mistress Fallyn, is getting married to our general, Stefan."

They all squealed.

"And ye must come to the ball tonight," Brigitta added. "I don't care what Mother Ginessa says about being careful and hiding yerselves away. I had beautiful gowns made for ye all and I want to show ye off."

Maeve clapped her hands together. "I can't wait! Thank you!"

Brigitta nodded. She was worried about her youngest sister, but didn't want to say anything that would alarm her. For she really didn't know what to say.

The day before, Brody had given her a cryptic warning. Maeve's time was coming soon. Something to do with her scent. But when Brigitta had questioned him further, he'd refused to say anything other than Maeve would need their support.

Gwennore turned her head in the direction of Brigitta's bedchamber. "The babies are stirring. I'll go check on them." She hurried off.

"I didn't hear anything," Brigitta whispered. Gwennore's hearing had always been better than theirs.

Luciana sighed. "Poor Gwennore. She spends all her time at Ebton Palace, either hiding in the nursery or the library. I appreciate her help with the twins, but I want her to attend the parties and have fun."

Brigitta frowned. "She'd better come to the ball tonight."

"I'll drag her there me self," Sorcha declared, then lowered her voice. "She knows everyone looks at her strangely because she's an elf."

Luciana sighed. "When people see her, they don't know what to think of her."

"The babies went back to sleep," Gwennore said softly

as she entered the sitting room. She gave them a wry smile. "Don't worry. I'm used to the odd looks."

"They don't know you like we do." Brigitta grabbed Gwennore's hand and squeezed it.

Gwennore sat next to her. "That's why I love being with you all. Ye're my true family. Even if I went to Woodwyn, I wouldn't be comfortable there. I don't know any more about the elves than anyone else."

"Ye don't want to be a queen like Luciana or Brigitta?" Maeve asked.

Gwennore shook her head, smiling.

Sorcha pressed a hand to her chest. "I might be destined to become queen of Norveshka."

"What?" Maeve laughed.

"I'm serious." Sorcha sat back, crossing her arms. "Luciana went back to her home country and became queen. Then Brigitta did the same. So why shouldn't I?"

Gwennore gave her a dubious look. "Norveshka already has a queen."

Sorcha waved a dismissive hand. "It could still happen."

"Let's play the Game of Stones and see if ye're right," Maeve suggested.

"Excellent idea!" Sorcha dashed over to a travel chest to dig through the contents, while Maeve emptied the fruit bowl on the sideboard.

Brigitta exchanged a worried look with Luciana. Her older sister's predictions had an odd way of coming true.

"Here they are!" Sorcha brought a drawstring bag back to the small table.

Maeve set the brass bowl down.

"Wait!" Gwennore draped a shawl in the bowl. "We don't want a loud clatter that might frighten the babies."

"Oh, good idea." Sorcha emptied the stones into the

bowl, and they made a muffled noise. "All right, Luciana, show us what ye can do."

Luciana leaned forward. "Are you sure about this?"

"Aye." Sorcha nodded.

Brigitta winced, remembering how her prediction from the Telling Stones had haunted her for eight months.

Luciana stirred the stones with her hand, then suddenly Sorcha reached out to stop her. "No. I don't want to know." She glanced at Gwennore. "Gwennie is older than me. It should be her turn next."

Gwennore snorted. "What future could I have?"

"We all have a future," Maeve insisted, then turned to their oldest sister. "Go ahead."

Luciana closed her fist around some stones.

"O Great Seer," Maeve whispered. "Reveal to us the secrets of the Telling Stones."

Luciana opened her hand and set two of the stones on the table. Green and brown.

"Maybe she'll meet a tall and handsome stranger with brown hair and green eyes," Maeve suggested.

Gwennore's eyes twinkled with humor. "Or brown eyes and green hair."

Sorcha sat forward. "This is an easy one. The royal flag of Woodwyn is green and brown. A green tree on a brown background. Gwennie will be returning to the elves."

Brigitta glanced at Luciana's face to see if she was in agreement, but only saw a flicker of alarm before Luciana's face grew blank.

What else could be green and brown? Brigitta suddenly recalled the uniforms worn by the Norveshki warriors. Green and brown. Was Gwennore destined to go to the land of dragons?

Luciana set the final stone on the table. Three.

"What does it mean?" Maeve asked.

"'Tis simple," Sorcha said. "In three months, Gwennie will meet a tall and handsome stranger. And most probably, he'll be an elf."

Maeve turned toward Luciana. "Is that right?"

Luciana shrugged. "I must be tired, because I'm not seeing anything. I'm sorry."

Gwennore smiled. "That's all right. I've always believed we make our own destiny."

A sad look glinted in Luciana's eyes. "Aye. That you will."

The babies cried in the next room, and Gwennore jumped up.

"Don't worry." Luciana stood. "I'll take care of them."

"I'll help." Brigitta followed Luciana into the bedchamber. She noticed that Luciana's hands were trembling as she reached for Eviana.

"Let me." Brigitta picked up the baby girl and hugged her. "Ye saw something, didn't you?"

Luciana nodded, her eyes filling with tears. "Danger."

Brigitta took a deep breath. "Was it dragons?"

"Yes."

"We'll protect her," Brigitta said. "We're queens. We can keep all our sisters safe."

"Aye. That's what we'll do." Luciana picked up the baby boy and gave Brigitta a tremulous smile. "It's good to be queen."

Read on for an excerpt from the next book
by **Kerrelyn Sparks**

Eight Simple Rules for Dating a Dragon

Coming soon from St. Martin's Paperbacks

Dammit. She was so damned quick at figuring things out, Silas thought. Hearing Gwennore's thoughts over the last few seconds had been like witnessing a shipwreck. Before he could stop her, she'd crashed onto the rocky shore of his deception. And she was pissed.

But once again, she'd proven how clever and discerning she was. He strode toward her. "We need to talk."

Her lovely lavender-blue eyes flared hot with anger. "I have nothing to say to you."

"Then you will keep your end of the bargain?"

She gritted her teeth. "It was not a bargain. It was an act of coercion and deception. You should be ashamed."

Silas shot Aleksi an annoyed look for not keeping his mouth shut, then turned back to Gwennore. "We still need to talk."

"Mayhap you need to talk, but I have nothing to say." She crossed her arms and looked away.

Mayhap? Where had she learned Norveshki? "We're going to be stuck together on this barge for the next three hours. Are you planning to ignore me the entire time?"

She studied her fingernails without responding.

"I'll take that as a yes," he muttered. "But wouldn't you like to vent your anger? I do deserve it, after all."

She snorted.

At least she was listening. "So for the next two and a half hours, I will allow you to berate me."

"*Allow* me? As if I need your permission. I'll yell at you whenever I please. And for as long as I want."

His mouth twitched. This was more like it.

"Don't you dare smirk at me." She glowered at him. "I am not entertaining."

She was delightful. He bit his lip to keep from smiling. "How about I let you throw me overboard?"

"Can you swim?"

"Yes."

She shrugged. "Then it's hardly worth my trouble."

He stifled another grin. "I'll promise to be wet and miserable for the rest of the trip. If I dry out too much, I'll jump back in."

With a huff, she planted her hands on her hips. "This is all a jest to you, isn't it? You tricked me!"

"Come." He took her by the arm to lead her toward the side railing where they could be alone. When she jerked her arm free, he added, "I'm just trying to put some distance between us and the child, so you don't wake her up when you start screeching at me."

"*Screeching?*" Her voice rose, then she winced and gave him an annoyed look. "For your information, I don't screech. I am not the sort to lose control."

He gave her a wry look, since he could recall her losing it the day before. Her hair had been loose and wild, unlike today's neat and tidy braid. She'd looked magnificent, so much so that a wicked part of him wanted to push her until she lost control again.

"Come on." He stepped toward the railing while he

smiled at her. "Aren't you curious why I'm so desperate to have you return with me?"

She glanced away, her cheeks turning pink. *Blast him. I am curious, and the scoundrel knows it. I should slap the smile off his handsome face.*

Silas took a deep breath. Her reactions to him were affecting him too strongly, making his heart race and his groin tighten. If he didn't teach her soon to close off her mind, he might lose control of himself, and take her to bed. *Fool*, he berated himself. He would need to seduce her more slowly than that. First, he would kiss her. A gentle kiss, then a more passionate one. *Dammit, what are you thinking?*

Thank the Light she couldn't hear his thoughts. But hell, she was going to be livid once she learned that Aleksi, Dimitri, and he could hear her.

He bowed his head. "Please accept my apology. I am truly sorry."

She scoffed. "Am I supposed to believe that? You've spent the last few minutes joking about the situation."

"That was my attempt to be so charming that you would forget about being angry." When she gave him an incredulous look, he winced. "Apparently, you are immune to my charms."

I wish.

Just in case you missed the previous book by
Kerrelyn Sparks, read on for an excerpt from

How to Tame a Beast in Seven Days

Available from St. Martin's Paperbacks

By the goddesses, he looked so handsome. The light from the twin moons made the angles of his face seem sharper. His eyes appeared a darker green, and the stubble along his jaw more ruggedly masculine. The sea breeze had tousled his dark-red curls, making him look so adorable she longed to touch him.

But she couldn't. With a wince, she realized that was something she could never do.

"Dammit," he muttered. "I shocked you, didn't I?"

"No, I—" Goddesses help her, how long had she been silently gawking at him? With a twinge of embarrassment, she ducked her head. Oh, no, her nightgown! With another gasp, she quickly gathered her cloak around her.

He leaned toward her. "Are you sure you're all right?"

No, I'm mortified. "I'm perfectly fine. I should go back to my room now."

"You didn't feel anything at all when I touched you?"

Her cheeks flamed with heat.

"My lord." A voice spoke behind her, and she glanced back to see two guards.

"Leave us be," the Lord Protector ordered.

They bowed, then retreated to the tower. Clutching her cloak tightly around her, she started to follow them.

"Wait." The Lord Protector caught up with her. "We need to talk."

"I should go. I'm not properly dressed."

"I like the way you're dressed."

With a groan, she hunched her shoulders, huddling deeper into her cloak.

"Are you cold?" He removed his heavier black cape and draped it around her shoulders. Holding the edges, he tugged her closer to him. "Now answer my question."

He'd trapped her. How dare he retain her against her will? Irritation flared inside her, but the fluttering in her stomach also increased. She'd never been this close to him before.

His hands fisted in the cloak. "Is it true? You would rather hurl yourself over the wall than marry me?"

He thought she was suicidal? Her irritation grew. "Of course not! Like you said before, we have no choice in the matter. So I have mentally prepared myself to go through with the ordeal."

His mouth thinned. "How noble of you."

"And what about you? Are you tempted to fall on a sword?"

He snorted. "Unlike you, I'm looking forward to the *ordeal*." He leaned closer. "And I'll be praying for a drought."

Her heart lurched. He wanted to marry her? And what did a drought have to do with them?

"I have another question." He gave her a wry look. "Actually I have many questions. Why did you leave your room? Why were you running at the wall?"

By the goddesses, how could she explain that? "I . . . wanted some fresh air."

"Try again."

She glanced down at his gloved hands, which still clutched the edges of his cloak and kept her trapped. How could she get free? Could she use his fear against him? She reached her hand toward the white shirt that covered his broad chest.

"No!" He jumped back, releasing her. "Don't do that. It's too dangerous."

"Nothing happened before when you grabbed me."

"There were several layers of insulation. My gloves, your cloak and nightgown." His mouth twitched. "Although your nightgown hardly counts as a layer."

Her cheeks burned with heat.

"I can never be sure how a person will react," he continued. "Especially when my power is this high. Even with my gloves on, my touch has caused some people to faint." His eyes glinted with humor. "Apparently, you're rather insensitive."

The rascal, now he'd asked for it. She lunged toward him, pretending she was going to poke him.

"Dammit, woman!" He leaped back.

She smiled to herself as she folded her arms across her chest. He wouldn't dare come near her now.

With a snort, he leaned against the wall. "You're too damned clever."

"I thought you liked that about me."

His mouth curled into a lopsided smile. "I do. So why did you run at the wall?"

"Why are you here? Shouldn't you be hunting down the assassins?"

His smile widened. "Another counterattack. Are you sure you're not a warrior?" He folded his arms, mimicking her stance. "Your father gave me permission to move into the southern tower. So now we're neighbors. And I can keep an eye on you to make sure you're safe."

She glanced at the tower behind him. It was the tallest tower along the curtain wall with an added turret on top. From there, he would have an excellent view of the sea and the entire fortress.

"As for the assassins," he continued, "I'm working on it."

"How?"

"I have a plan." He paused as if he was considering how much to tell her. "And my best spies are at work."

She blinked. Did he have spies watching her? "Who are they?"

"You needn't worry yourself over that."

She narrowed her eyes, then turned to gaze over the crenellated wall at the sea. "No doubt my spies are better. They'll find the assassins first."

"What? *Your* spies?"

"Yes."

He scoffed. "I don't believe it." When she merely shrugged, he stepped closer. "Fine. Who are they?"

She gave him a pointed look. "You needn't worry yourself over that."

His mouth fell open, then he grinned. "You know how to wrestle. I like that."

Her heart did a little leap as a vision popped into her mind of the two of them physically wrestling. And once he had her pinned down . . . but he couldn't. He could never touch her. By the goddesses, it was enough to make her learn how to curse. "I should be going now." She started toward the tower.

"Did you wonder why I'm praying for a drought?"

She halted. He'd come back with a counterattack of his own. An excellent one. For she *had* wondered.

His booted feet crunched on the stone wall walk as he approached her from behind. "No rain means no lightning. That means my power would slowly disappear."

The back of her neck tingled. "Why would you want to lose your power?"

"So I can touch you. Kiss you." His voice lowered to a whisper. "Bed you."

The tingle on her neck skittered down her spine. Then he might be able to touch her someday? And she hadn't imagined the hunger in his eyes. It was real. "You . . . want me?"

"Yes."

Her heart thudded as she turned to face him. "You hardly know me." He didn't even know her real name.

"I know you're clever, brave, bold, and beautiful. I know you're kind to servants. Kind to animals. You're not above working in the garden. You stand up to me. You intrigue me. I feel more . . . alive when I'm with you." He stepped closer. "Yes. I want you."

A sharp pang shot through her chest. He wasn't describing Tatiana. He was describing her. It was she, Luciana, that he wanted. "My lord—"

"Call me Leo."

She swallowed hard. "Leo. C-could you call me Ana?"

His eyes widened with surprise. "Does your father call you that?"

She shook her head. "It would be just for us." So she could feel that he was marrying her, not Tatiana. Tears stung her eyes, and she blinked them away.

"Is something wrong?" He stepped closer. "Ana?"

The goddesses help her, this man was making her heart ache. "I should go now." She headed toward the tower.

"Dammit," he grumbled behind her. "You never answered my questions."

She stopped and gave him a hesitant glance. "You shouldn't spend the night out here. You need your rest before the duel."

His eyebrows lifted. "Are you worried about me?"

Tatiana's request! She'd almost forgotten. "Could you do me a favor and not kill the captain tomorrow?"

"What? You're worried about *him*?"

Caw, caw. A seagull called out, and he muttered a curse.

She winced. "There are others who care about the captain. So I would appreciate it if you didn't kill him."

He gave her an exasperated look. "What do you think I am? I never planned to kill the bastard."

"Oh, thank you!" She ran into the tower as he growled a few more curse words.

"I'm not a Beast!" His voice echoed down the wall walk.

No, he was a man. Her eyes burned with tears as she hurried up the stairs. He was an amazing man. And he would be far too easy to fall in love with.